SHEILA MUGHAL

THE LINES OF
TAMAR

LIVING IN THE 21ST CENTURY, YET CONTROLLED
BY AN ANCIENT PROPHECY

SHEILA MUGHAL

THE LINES OF
TAMAR

LIVING IN THE 21ST CENTURY, YET CONTROLLED
BY AN ANCIENT PROPHECY

MEREO
Cirencester

Mereo Books

1A The Wool Market Dyer Street Cirencester Gloucestershire GL7 2PR
An imprint of Memoirs Publishing www.mereobooks.com

The Lines of Tamar: 978-1-86151-322-9

First published in Great Britain in 2015
by Mereo Books, an imprint of Memoirs Publishing

The address for Memoirs Publishing Group Limited can be found at
www.memoirspublishing.com

The Memoirs Publishing Group Ltd Reg. No. 7834348

The Memoirs Publishing Group supports both The Forest Stewardship Council® (FSC®) and
the PEFC® leading international forest-certification organisations. Our books carrying both the
FSC label and the PEFC® and are printed on FSC®-certified paper. FSC® is the only
forest-certification scheme supported by the leading environmental organisations including
Greenpeace. Our paper procurement policy can be found at
www.memoirspublishing.com/environment

Typeset in 10/15pt Bembo
by Wiltshire Associates Publisher Services Ltd. Printed and bound in Great Britain by
Printondemand-Worldwide, Peterborough PE2 6XD

Dedicated to my beloved mother

Ivy Green (Norris)

1921 - 2008

Who never stopped believing in me and taught me

the value of determination

And also to

My wonderful grandmother

Florrie Gibbons (nee Lee & Thomason)

1899 - 1984

Who taught me to read, loved books and will

always remain in my heart

INTRODUCTION

An ancient and hidden prophecy from thousands of years ago with a secret cult following begins to play havoc with the lives of two modern-day women. Ruby and Eenayah are twins who were adopted at birth and in differing ways they each have busy 21st century lifestyles, juggling the commitments of money, careers, motherhood and marriage. Despite living on different continents, the twins remain close throughout their adult life, completely unaware of their shared connection to a sacred lineage.

Unexpectedly and by a series of apparent coincidences, the sisters find themselves thrown back into a history of which they knew nothing. A search for their birth mother uncovers a direct link to ancestors from biblical times, and leads to the discovery that one of them fatalistically appears to be reliving a former life.

In the background, the forces of good and evil battle to control the outcome of the prophecy, and as such both equally influence and disrupt the lives of the living descendants. The twins remain unaware that each and every occurrence which superficially appears to be a chance happening is more often than not part of a premeditated plan. In the lives of Ruby and Eenayah, there is no such thing as coincidence. As the pages are turned, they open up more than just the next page. They open up a vision of the future from a snapshot of the past.

Some parts of this fictional story are factual and based on alleged real historical and biblical scripts. In order to appeal to a modern-day audience the story has been updated to a present-day setting.

Facebook:
https://www.facebook.com/pages/The-Lines-of-Tamar/853784174684920

Website::
www.sheilamughal.com

ACKNOWLEDGMENTS

Despite being loosely based around certain facts, this book is a result of my imagination and an assumed poetic licence to create a fictional story by way of recreational entertainment. Any resemblance to any living persons or situations is unintentional.

With no desire to spark a heavy theological debate, 'The Lines of Tamar' has been written to provide thought-provoking theatre for the reader's entertainment. The book is a modern-day story about two young women rather than a bygone fairy tale. Indeed there are some threads of historical accuracy, but I have taken the novelist's liberty of adding to this tapestry to make it more interesting and to bring an old story to a modern audience. Readers can make up their own minds up as to where the line in the sand has been drawn, but just know that there are some grains of truth buried deep within the sand.

With gratitude and apologies to my ever-supportive husband Sohail, whom I have shut out of my life and my office in order to actually complete this book. Thank you for your patience.

Also with love to my children Martin, Liana and Zarah and grandchildren Esmée, Isaac, Elijah and a new-born little boy called Oliver.

For my dear friends Julie & Malcolm - any humour intentional or otherwise is dedicated to you.

Also, with love to all my family in Australia and America.

Finally, thank you to my 103rd great grandmother for providing the backdrop to the material. I hope I did your story justice, Granny Tamar, and that my artistic interpretations are acceptable.

CHAPTER 1

'Coincidence is God's way of remaining anonymous' Albert Einstein

Monday October 7ᵗʰ 2009

Sir William Zemel, a much adorned and respected retired chief constable, was the keynote speaker at the 2009 Criminology Symposium in London. A week before the event, he went out cycling on a beautiful crisp autumnal day. His bicycle wheel met with a puddle which was concealing a submerged brick. The wheel hit the brick at an odd angle, buckled sideways and threw Sir Zemel into the path of an overtaking car. Tossed like a pancake unceremoniously over the bonnet, he fractured his pelvis. For Sir Zemel, it was a simple case of being in the wrong place at the wrong time.

All of this happened just seven days in advance of an already oversubscribed event. With such short notice the organisers struggled to find a worthy replacement. Busy people with full diary commitments had limited availability at short notice. In this strained and stressful situation and from his hospital bed, Sir Zemel suggested his dear friend Professor Roland De Vede as a replacement. Initially the organisers rejected his proposal. They argued that surely substituting a notable and distinguished criminal expert with a history teacher wasn't the most appropriate exchange. However in the interim periods when he was not in enormous amounts of pain, Sir Zemel contacted the organisers to convince them that Professor De Vede was in fact a more than creditable replacement and indeed could give a fresh and unusual viewpoint to the subject matter. 'The Professor may not know much about the criminal mind', he argued, 'but he does know a lot about history, and as we all know history is littered with evil people and tyrannical leaders. He will have more than enough ammunition to entertain and bemuse the delegates. Besides this, he is a confident and eloquent speaker. Bottom line: do you have anyone else lined up?'

The organisers conceded that maybe it was possible that an eccentric historian could talk with some authority about the wicked and ruthless motivations of men notorious for their acts of evil from a bygone era. It was all very last minute, but this could possibly work. They mulled, pondered and debated; perhaps events from the past could teach us lessons for the future. The justification had been assessed and the invitation issued, though maybe more out of desperation on the organisers' part. With a degree of trepidation on the Professor's part, it was accepted.

So this was how Professor De Vede, a genealogist and lecturer in history, curiously found himself in London presenting the closing lecture at a criminology convention on a foggy pea soup of an October day several years back. As with the Charles Dickens Christmas Carol trilogy of visitations, the Professor would encounter three different people at this convention, people who years later would have a part to play in a profound fight between the forces of good and evil.

However, for the time being the Professor had a speech to deliver. He had given his presentation much thought. He was better accustomed to younger university students with designer rips in their jeans, as opposed to the mature well-dressed audience now expected. However he had devised an interesting twist for his presentation, which he was now looking forward to with much anticipation and eagerness.

Hindsight is a wonderful thing, and looking back now 2009 was the beginning of the start of a series of chance happenings which all seemed to evolve unintentionally, but then became entangled with each other, twisting and turning into happenings of a more bizarre and extraordinary nature with the passing of time. Three delegates - all of them as yet unknown to each other - attended this convention and each by little more than a fluke invitation. Not for the moment, but one day, their connection would be of immense significance. For now they were just people in the audience, all at the same place at the same time awaiting the final keynote speaker.

Ruby Kyfinn was a 35-year-old sales manager working for a large pharmaceutical company. With much reluctance she had been persuaded by her childhood friend Becky (who was taking a degree in Criminology) to take a rare skive away from the office and keep her friend company at the convention. It had been a tiresome challenge for Becky and took weeks of persuasion, pulling juvenile emotional strings that only an intimate friend could master and using only the infantile language a childhood pal could respond to: 'Come on, don't be a bore Ruby, you never bunk off work. It will be fun playing wag, and you never have fun these days. There will be free food and wine at the after dinner thingy, oh and lots of intelligent men I can peruse. Maybe we can hit the wine bars later, fancy making a night of it?'

Ruby was less than impressed by the argument presented, responding 'Fun….at a criminology convention….really?'

Ruby was a reluctant workaholic who was often sitting on the first train to London whilst normal humans would still be snoring away in dreamland. Watching the world fly past at 100mph, she would be logging onto her PC whilst many of her co-workers would just be entertaining the thought of breakfast. Becky was a good friend to Ruby, and often like a cyclone of fresh air. Ruby considered that maybe a change of scenery would do her good. 'Lots of desirable men, in a criminology convention - oh come on you can do better than that Becky', she laughed. Ruby considered that every married person living in an unwavering world of domestic normality should have at least one wacky single friend to challenge their idea of a fun night out, and Becky was most certainly it, and then some.

Ruby was very married and Becky was most certainly very single. Becky was a police officer in the Metropolitan police force and was taking a degree to advance her career and help her onto the mostly macho-sweat-stained ladder to promotion. She was as dedicated to her work as Ruby, but not with the same single-minded selfishness. Becky was a fun-loving, larger-than-life woman who had recently come out of a long-term relationship and was now in man-hunting mode. Lacking any single female friends to join in with her predatory search, Ruby would have to suffice to act the part of a semi-single friend, being alone in a London hotel room several days per week.

Back home in Wales, work was quickly forgotten as Ruby entwined herself into the cosy world of marriage and motherhood. Her adoring husband Owyn and their lively dimple-chinned toddler Harry were her entire existence. Living in a sprawling listed manor house (which in parts was a semi-ruin) amid the stunning scenery of Snowdonia, Ruby hated to be away from her family and the pure Welsh mountain air. However, in a swapping of the traditional gender roles, Ruby had become the main wage earner, and with a building renovation project which drank money like water, she had little choice in the matter but to work hard, long and tiresome hours. Meanwhile Owyn, with his occasional website work, stayed at home, either tapping away on his laptop or with his hammer. He was very much the stay-at-home parent to young Harry. When not parenting or immersed in software design, Owyn was either rewiring, plastering or knocking down walls. Ruby didn't like the gender swap, but she was the one with the ability to earn more money and Owyn was the one with multiple building and IT skills.

For some reason his wife failed to fully understand, Owyn had insisted they purchase a large rambling ruin built onto the side of a crumbling castle with more holes than roof. Having been swayed into the purchase because of the awesome mountain backdrop, Ruby now had to work to fund its repairs.

Finally conceding and giving in to her pushy assertive friend who wouldn't take no for an answer, Ruby found herself sitting in the audience awaiting a closing speech about crime throughout history. She noted it was to be made by some random Professor who hadn't been listed in the programme and seemed to be a last-minute addition. As he started his introduction, she watched the clock with a degree of restlessness. However, by the time he was five minutes into his delivery, Ruby had become both immersed and engaged by the Professor's captivating lecture.

Professor De Vede had put an unusual spin on the topic of 'evil throughout history' and unpredictably focused on female villains. He explained: 'acts of terrible crime and violence are always more shocking when a woman commits them. Society perceives its females as warm, nurturing and caring and so we are collectively flabbergasted when a woman gains notoriety for her cruelty and brutality.'

Ruby's attention perked up. She sat upright in her chair and became totally engrossed in the professor's words. 'Wow, this guy is good!' she murmured. Quite unexpectedly, she found herself enjoying this final speech more than those of any of the other previous presenters, and from the stillness of the audience, it seemed that the other delegates were equally enthralled. Starting with Countess Elizabeth Báthory de Ecsed (nicknamed the Blood Countess), he moved onto Ilse Koch (the Nazi Bitch of Buchenwald). Skiing off-piste for a moment to ponder the effects of power, domination and subduing one's subjects by fear, he then moved on to Bloody Mary, Queen Mary 1st of England and finally finished his lecture with Isabella the Catholic, queen of Castile and León. He argued that for a powerful woman to be a true tyrant, she probably needed to be more malicious and controlling than any man could ever be. The Professor also argued that the fairer sex possessed the more intelligent form of evil; manipulation, something he felt that men hadn't quite mastered as yet.

The audience stood to applaud, quite stunned how this unusual journey into the past had been so unexpectedly thought-provoking and engaging. The convention organisers were of course delighted that the replacement keynote speaker had not only saved the day, but done so with overwhelming success. The Professor was taking a question and answer session which went on for double the time allowed, such was the participation of the audience.

Unexpectedly and totally out of the blue, Ruby found herself wanting to ask a question. The microphone came in her direction and as per protocol she introduced herself with all the assurance of someone who was used to addressing an audience in a presentation situation.

'Good afternoon Professor. Can I just say how interesting your presentation was. My name is Ruby Kyfinn and I am a sales manager for a pharmaceutical company. I have nothing at all to do with the criminal world.'

'Neither do I', responded the Professor with a smile which extended across most of his face, 'but do go on dear. What is your question?'

'I just wondered,' began Ruby 'have you ever considered that evil or maybe any other personality characteristic could be inherited, as in your DNA? Can history ever show a familial pattern of crime?'

It was a great question, and Becky was impressed. She flashed her friend a look of astonishment. 'Hey, who is the one taking the degree here pal?' she muttered under her breath in the direction of Ruby's ear. The Professor was also impressed. He struggled to know quite how to compose his answer, which he needed to do with care so as not to offend.

'Fantastic question Ruby, and back to the nature versus nurture debate from an earlier session', replied the Professor. 'I don't really know for sure if behaviour is an inherited trait as such, but nature does show us patterns and as a statistician as well as an historian, obviously I quite like patterns.'

He took a sip of water and carefully considered what words to follow on with. Her question was really quite clever, and he didn't want to say the wrong thing. A criminology audience was not the norm, and he was slightly out of his comfort zone.

After some thought he continued: 'Being average applies to most people, but outside the majority who are average there are the outliers, the ones that fall on either side of the extreme. They are like the curtains at the end that window. For example, a close friend of mine has ten living female relatives, and I have met all of them, so I know this to be true. Seven of them are about 5ft 2 inches tall, give or take an inch. Two of them are over 6ft tall and he has one sweet aunt who is only around 4ft 11 inches. I could ask if their variance in height was due to their DNA, and in the most part the answer would be yes. It is as though Mother Nature knows it needs to create lots of averages, but in order to get an average it also needs to create extremes.'

He paused to think how to adapt this answer to the question. 'Statistically, when it comes to good versus bad, I do believe that the majority of us humans both now and in the past, were and are averagely moral. As a population we are mostly good, but not quite perfect. On either end of that norm, we find extremes. There are those who become saints, who dedicate their lives to charity and acts of great goodness. On the other extreme we have the villains of history, who debatably seem to have no conscience and commit crimes of great wickedness without thought or concern. As with the height example of my friend's female relatives, one could argue that for nature to create lots of average norms, it has to balance it with radical outliers. I am aware of the belief that criminals are mostly bad, mad or sad and of course what you are exposed to in life does mould who you are. However statistically it would appear that some people are born to be bad, and if that is something that arrives on a string of DNA then I guess maybe that is what happens. Sorry - went off at a tangent a bit. Did that answer your question?'

'He would make a great sales person or politician', thought Ruby.

Surrounded by many experts in criminology, the Professor circumnavigated the question with slick professionalism, not totally committing to either a yes or a no but settling on a probability. After all, this wasn't even his field.

Ruby responded, 'Yes thank you, that indeed is food for thought Professor.'

Becky looked puzzled and enquired, 'what made you ask that question Mrs Sales Manager?' Ruby just shrugged her shoulders; she didn't really know.

As the two women stood to leave, the audience gave their final applause in appreciation of the replacement speaker. The Professor had succeeded in fascinating and captivating the mostly austere audience throughout the final session of the day. Squeezing her way past knees, chairs and hidden handbags straps placed strategically to entangle themselves around her ankles, Ruby replied, 'You must surely remember, Becks, that I am a twin. When you get to grow up with someone who has similar DNA as you, you always keep an eye open for who they become, just in case you go the same way.'

Becky had almost forgotten Ruby had a twin, who she vaguely remembered from their schooldays. She asked, 'and is she still very similar to you now that you're both all grown up?'

'Nothing like me at all. We act differently, our lives are polar opposites and we don't even look that much alike any more', responded Ruby.

'Is she a nasty evil person then, is that why you asked your question?' responded Becky, pretending to be nervous. Ruby teased her amusing friend.

'Yes, she has been locked away for mass murder and I was just wondering when it was my turn to kill someone, especially if it is a genetic thing.'

Ruby laughed and pretended to strangle her friend. 'Now Becks, where is all this food and wine and men you promised me, huh?'

The two young women laughed and joked as they walked out of the great hall. Just prior to reaching the exit, Ruby turned to look over her shoulder, as she instinctively felt eyes watching her. As she turned, she spotted the Professor gathering up his papers on the podium. He just happened to glance in her direction as she just happened to glance back. By way of a reflex action he gave her a wave, the type of wave a child would give when nothing more than the fingers moved. By impulse she mirrored the gesture back at him.

That was the end of that. Two total strangers, neither of whom were supposed to be in that particular conference centre in London on the 7th October 2009. However, each persuaded by their own respective friends, they found themselves in a brief yet profound conversation. One day their paths would cross again, but for now they were just passing ships in the night. They would have to wait several years before fate would cause their universes to collide, in far more unusual circumstances.

'Goodbye, Professor' she mouthed.

'Goodbye for now' he whispered under his breath. Maybe it was *déjà vu*, but the Professor felt he had somehow met this young woman once before.

As he gathered his things together, stuffing a variety of hand-written notes hurriedly into a well-worn leather briefcase, the second fateful meeting of the day was about to occur. A portly man with vivid carrot-red hair and matching beard walked onto the stage to greet him. With arms outstretched in a gesture of brotherly affection, Frank hugged his long-lost friend from bygone college days. With his soft, lilting southern Irish accent, he patted his friend's shoulder.

'I cannot believe it, after all these years! Bloody Roland De Vede! You are the last person I ever expected to be delivering a speech at a criminology symposium. It is so very good to see you, my old friend. Your presentation was the best of the day.'

The Professor was slightly taken aback by the mixed emotions of nostalgia and joy at meeting up with a long-lost friend totally out of the blue. Flummoxed by the unusual circumstances of this random reunion, the bewildered professor caught his breath for a moment.

'Frank? Surely not Frank O'Byrne, after all these years? My God, how long has it been? What do I call you these days? Are you still a priest? Do I address you as Father Francis?' The Professor had noted that Frank was wearing a layman's suit.

Frank smiled. 'You should know better, Roland. One never moves on from the Church. But if you are asking me if I still do baptisms and weddings, the answer is no. I have a doctorate in theology and most of my time seems to be engaged in teaching the subject. I am known better by the name Dr O'Byrne rather than Father Francis these days.'

Professor De Vede smiled in recognition of the fact that despite going their separate ways many years ago, that they had both somehow ended up teaching. Frank picked up the Professor's heavy and over-stuffed briefcase for him.

'If you are not in a hurry Roland, I am a member of a terribly stuffy private gentlemen's club around the corner from here. They do have a great Irish whiskey, accessible to a privileged few, and I would love it if you could join me for a drink and a chat about times gone by'.

The Professor had been invited to the convention after-dinner event, but given the choice between a free meal with strangers and the option to catch up with an old friend, Frank and his whiskey supply would always win hands down.

The club was pretty much as the Professor expected; a typically aristocratic and pompous establishment, but none of that mattered. The friends had accumulated forty years' worth of news to share, and indeed just as Frank had promised, the double-distilled single malt and grain whiskey slipped down the throat like smooth velvet.

'What brought you to a criminology convention Frank? I am curious' asked the Professor.

As a former priest, the ex-Father Francis still possessed a devilish sense of humour. 'Always best to keep an eye on the opposition Roland,' he said. 'You can't preach goodness without understanding what makes the bad people tick. Anyway, I could ask you the same question but for the fact that you addressed all of that and more with the brilliantly-executed presentation you delivered today. You certainly made people think. Well done, my old pal.' Frank gave the Professor a complimentary pat on his back.

The Professor was quietly delighted by his friend's endorsement. 'Less of the old pal please, Frank,' he said. Frank was a smart cookie, who had always been intellectually superior to most of his peers, and as a child the Professor had traditionally had to put in double the effort just to attain the same grades as his former classmate.

'What did you make of the question the young lady asked about character traits, in particular evil characteristics being inherited?' asked the Professor. That question quite caught me on the hop. It isn't something I had ever considered before, and seeing as though I was a last-minute substitute for my dear friend William with his broken pelvis,

I didn't want to say anything too controversial. I am not a geneticist, so how am I supposed to know about DNA traits? Do you have any opinions about this Frank, you being a former priest and all that?'

Francis clasped his whiskey glass and rotated it so the golden liquid licked the sides of the crystal. He moved his nose close to the rim to inhale its fumes and take in the honey, citrus and oak cask aroma. He considered his answer carefully.

'You have me in a bit of quandary here, Roland. You see, going back to Genesis and the Tree of Knowledge and all that, we are supposed to be in control of our own destiny, having had a bite of a forbidden apple and been given free will. We have been equipped with a powerful brain to allow us to make our own decisions and choices. I have been taught that if we elect a good path then we go to heaven, but if we walk with evil, then of course hell is the ultimate destination. So basically, what we reap is what we sow. However that theory could fly in the face of any sort of fatalistic pre-destiny. Many religions would say that our future isn't a fated mythical passage and maybe even science concurs that personality traits don't necessarily come packaged up in a DNA barcode and perhaps are more to do with external influences. Who really knows? I'm not a scientist either. All I know for sure my friend is the theological argument that states that God gave us free will and control of our own lives.'

It was a confusing answer, maybe deliberately so. Frank paused for a sip of whiskey and sucked on his cigar. 'However, if it was true that we were programmed pre-birth to be either good or evil, then we have no blame, as without fault, there is no sin. With no blame, there can be no punishment and therefore no hell. If, according to your suggestion when answering the young lady's question Roland, that nature (and by that I mean God of course) actually assigns lots of averages and occasional extreme outliers, how can anyone be castigated for falling into the outlier sector, if you were just put there by a throw of a dice at birth?'

The professor became a bit defensive, not wanting to get into any mind-blowing religious debate after three very strong neat whiskeys.

'I don't think I actually said that, Frank. I just put the observation out there that in all matters of physics and maths, there is usually an up and a down and a bit in the middle. Or a black, a white and a shade of grey, or a left and a right and something in between. You must surely agree that averages do make up the greater proportion in all measurements, and to get an average you first need an extreme on either end. That's the law of numbers, surely? I didn't reach any conclusions. It was just a way to get the audience to think and get that darn awkward question off my back.'

The Professor continued, 'Okay Frank, let me ping this back to you. As an expert in this field, what does the bible say as regards inheritance?'

The Professor knew his limitations. He was an expert in history and quite adept at genealogy, but alas he knew nothing about theology. It had been a long day, he was tired, and he certainly did not wish to get into a deep debate about this subject with someone he knew to be an expert. He wondered how best to deflect this back, tap dance around a fairly profound theory and then maybe take the conversation to a more normal and mundane level.

Frank did not have to think long about the question, and with his soft Irish lilt, he answered with speed and clarity.

'You have raised an interesting point, my dear old friend. You see the Bible loves genealogy. It is full of long lists of who begat whom. It is like ye olde version of many family trees. Bloodlines were of immense importance, and by that indeed I guess we mean DNA, in modern speak.' He leaned closer. 'Between you and me, Roland, there are several religious sects or cults who still exist today, who indeed follow and hold sacred certain biblical bloodlines. However, I do get your point. This flies in the face of traditional belief, because if we are saying that a person is either more or less holy or evil because of the bloodline they are born into, then that takes away free will. And surely neither the award of heaven nor punishment of hell could be inflicted on anyone if in reality there is minimum choice in the matter. You have a point, my friend.'

By now the Professor, either through drinking too much whiskey or enduring way too much deep philosophical theory, had become exhausted by the conversation. Yawning, he concluded, 'Well anyway, the lady asked a good question and I just threw statistics at the answer as best I could.' He paused to look at his watch. 'However, sadly Frank, I need to make tracks back up to Oxford now. I have to get a tube to the station before I miss my connecting train home. Since you last met me I have had a daughter and trust me, she has more balls than any man I know. She keeps track of me all the time and if I am not somewhere I should be by the time I should be, I swear that girl gets an ex-SAS hit squad to retrieve me. You think I'm kidding Frank, but really, if only you knew.'

The two gents swapped cards, with a promise to keep in touch. The Professor had enjoyed the company of this friend from his youth, but the conversation had become heavier than he had intended and he was now looking forward to a bit of shuteye and peace on his homeward journey.

As he stumbled outside, the cold October air hit him like a bowl of cold water. The Professor was grateful to be awakened by the sobering chill. The night was starting to draw in and he was mindful of the need not to miss his connecting train back to Oxford. He had diligently procured an off-peak ticket, and his acrobatic mind was turning cartwheels trying to figure out what trains that meant he could catch and when.

As he passed by the convention hall, the third of his fateful meetings was about to occur. A young man stopped him in the street.

He was a handsome young chap, dressed in an exceedingly dapper fashion in a smart tweed suit which looked older than he did. He wore a single red rose in his buttonhole, which caught the Professor's attention; it seemed an unusual adornment for one so young. The man was leaning slightly on an antique walking cane, made from black Palmira wood and topped with an Indian silver pommel. The Professor gave the stranger a visual once-over. He considered the stick an uncommon fashion accessory for a fellow who was probably the same age as his denim-wearing students.

The young man went to shake the Professor's hand, which was still occupied in holding closed his undersized coat.

'Professor De Vede, it is lovely to meet you sir. I am Tobiah Zemel.'

The Professor looked puzzled. He had no idea who this well-spoken young man could be. Tobiah registered the bemused look on the Professor's face with some amusement.

'Don't you remember me? I am Tobiah, Sir William's son. My father wanted me to come here to thank you in person. He is so grateful that you substituted for him and he wanted me to pass along his gratitude. That really was a most noteworthy speech.'

The Professor was indeed aware that Sir William had a large family and probably at least five of them were boys, but he didn't recollect any of them having the name of Tobiah. In a very British way, he didn't want to admit that he didn't know who the young chap was and besides he could see no reason why he would lie, so he played along with the conversation.

'Thank you Tobiah. I am sorry if I looked puzzled but I don't think I have actually met you before. I hope you give a good report back to your father about my performance, and please tell him that I hope he gets better soon.'

'I surely will. Thank you, Professor De Vede.'

The young man went to shake his hand again, and the Professor noted a thin purple cord entwined with gold thread which encircled his right wrist. What made this cord remarkable was that it was clearly broken, and yet it had not actually fallen from his wrist. The wristlet appeared to defy gravity. The Professor wondered if the regal-looking trinket signified anything.

For reasons he was unable to fathom, the Professor felt uneasy in the presence of Tobiah. He was grateful that he had the excuse of a train to catch so he could cut the meeting short. As he walked away as quickly as his creaky knees would allow, he turned to say a hurried goodbye to him. However, the young man had vanished as quickly as he had appeared.

The Professor made a mental note to ask Sir William about this so-called son of his. He felt unsure that he was who he had claimed to be.

★★★

Almost four years on, the people he had met at this event would each have a part to play in a more sinister and mysterious story; one that was already in progress. One that had actually began to unfold many years earlier.

CHAPTER 2

Monday June 3rd 2013

Eenayah Baratolli stretched her long, slim olive arms above her head and sighed a deep, audible sigh which seemed to last forever and vibrate its way throughout her entire body. Someone somewhere had once told her that sighing was body language for saying 'what if' or 'if only'. However Eenayah had shut out any 'what ifs' that might have dared to plague her conscience, fully understanding that no alternative universe could possibly compete with her glittering and privileged life. How could she have regrets? Eenayah had married well, and to the outside world she was living the dream. Secretly she knew she had several hidden demons and occasional 'if only' moments, but nothing she dared to admit to and little that a life without financial concerns could not soothe. 'A spoon full of sugar' she thought, mentally singing a line from *Mary Poppins*. Forget sugar. It was money that made this shit easier to swallow.

She contemplated her blessed kismet with a self-satisfied inner shrug, and the kind of assured confidence that sometimes comes back to haunt you and kick you in the shins. Her mother's words 'don't tempt fate' often haunted her, but none the less she was pleased with her catch. At times, she had to work hard to convince herself that she was really as happy as she believed herself to be. It was possibly the only hard work she actually committed to these days.

The Miami skyline looked mischievous, with dirty white cloud formations curling around themselves, growing and merging into one another, devouring each other cannibalistically and with visible malice. It was growing darker by the minute, and the tell-tale tropical breeze predicted the start of a storm. Eenayah abandoned her poolside morning yoga and retired indoors, commanding Roserie, her maid, in loud Spanish, as Eenayah's perfectly pedicured feet picked their way along the palm lined decked pathway, '*Tráeme un Bloody Mary Roserie, lo convierten en uno grade.*'

Roserie anticipated the command, as indeed she always did, and the Bloody Mary on its iced rocky bed with a twist of lime was already awaiting Eenayah on the bar by the time she arrived. 'Yoga deserves rewards', she thought, justifying her early start into cocktail hour. It was Monday, and morning cocktails had recently become a ritual weekly treat. She lifted the glass and saluted all the many photos of loved ones, and several not-so-loved ones, that lined every wall of the huge games room. '*Salados amigos*, after all, somewhere in the world it's always five o'clock,' she said. Breaking the time/drink rule had become something of a ceremonial event.

She sighed yet again and watched as raindrops the size of golf balls started to plip-plop heavily onto the glass panes. A crack of thunder followed by a streak of lightning which illuminated the dark sky made her pay attention to the weather outside. She was hypnotically drawn towards thunderstorms. They entranced her. Perhaps they reminded her of her childhood back in the UK, although nothing back home could even remotely compete with the dramatic drama queen tempests of Florida. She loved the unpredictability of Miami's climate and how one moment it was hot and sultry and the next a fusion of wind, hail, rain and pure ion-regenerating electricity. She adored her beautiful waterside villa with its moorings and expensive Oceanco silver white yacht waiting patiently at the bottom of the long garden path. However Eenayah also missed her childhood home for many reasons, mostly to do with former emotional and family connections.

A forensic scientist had once told her, 'Everywhere you go you leave part of you behind and take some of where you have been with you.' Although it was a layman's explanation about the basics of forensic science, Eenayah had taken it as a personal description of her life and indeed, there was much she had left behind in the UK and her island home. Her past was a tapestry of many colours, some darker than others.

Looking back over to the snooker table, her eyes were drawn to the multiple photographs framed upon the deep maroon walls, along with rows of gold and platinum discs. Many memories and moments were captured on those nostalgic walls. She always smiled as she cast an eye towards the group ensemble 'DLV' with her husband pictured in the centre shot and standing out so much more than the other group members, who just seemed to fade into the background of his irradiating aura. It was nigh on impossible for her ever to look at that bizarre photo without breaking into stifled laughter. Wild, outrageous, carefree and charming, she often wondered what had happened to that young, crazy musician. How had he got so bloody boring? More to the point, how had she ever got so lucky as to marry him? Why her? It was a question that always puzzled her. When she had first met Reed he had enjoyed an average amount of musical success and fame. He was by no means the greatest or most prosperous of musicians, but compared to the neighbouring farmers' sons on the Isle of Man, he was way out of her league. She knew about the many other women hanging on to Reed's shadow who had far more curves, glitter and glamour than she could ever dream to possess, but somehow he had chosen her for his wife. She had brought him luck. His fortune became stratospheric from the second he put a wedding ring on her finger. Her total unconditional love and admiration for Reed was beyond question.

Even now, almost 50 and with silver streaks highlighting the once-famous luminous dyed hair, Reed was still a fine-looking man. With striking green eyes, an immense ambition and a well-maintained and toned body any man would be proud to own, Reed was still an attraction to other woman. Eenayah was well aware of this threat.

Reed Baratolli was indeed the brazen 18-year-old teenager in the photo, with his heavily-lacquered indigo spiked hair and the eye liner and make up which characterized the 80s glam rock era. Add to this the billowing pleated bell-bottomed pants and platform heels and Reed looked like a perfect advertisement for bygone 80s fashion.

Eenayah smiled yet again. 'Silly boy!' she murmured. She blew a kiss to his image. It was the closest she would get to intimacy with him any time soon. Reed was away on a global talent scouting tour and she had no idea when she would next see him. Weeks, months – she knew not.

Reed, born Anthony Mort, was a classically-trained musician who had been gifted with an obscene ability to play any instrument and compose just about any genre of music, to such a standard and excellence that it was a major irritation to less-talented musicians. A well-known music magazine had stated 'the pavements were littered with those who could sweat blood and tears for hours over something that to Reed Baratolli was an insultingly quick and simple process.' Beyond any doubt he was a genius and a recognised child prodigy, destined for a music scholarship at the prestigious New York Juilliard Music Conservatory. However, by a twist of fate, a chance talent contest propelled him into stardom, less for his musical ability and ironically more for his exquisite good looks. He had the boyish charm every mother loved and the innocent challenge every daughter relished. He was often teased that it wasn't so much his ability that delivered his success, but, as Eenayah put it, 'a cute butt, white teeth and killer abs.'

Reed was quietly philosophical about his career path. '*Faciam quodlibet quod necesse est*' was his reply to any bitchy accusations relating to his road to success. Eenayah never ceased to be blown over by the fact that her cultured boy-band glam rock husband could speak Latin, but she had come to understand that 'do whatever it takes' was his motto and MO for life. He always got what he wanted, and that was all that seemed to matter to Reed. She concluded that successful men often have to have a degree of selfishness and that maybe this single-minded focus went with the territory. Everything in life has a price, and being the wife of a rich, successful man possibly required the price of loneliness.

She glanced along the row of awards and shimmering disks mounted on the wall. De la Vie were one of several successful boy bands of the glam rock era. Not overtly illustrious, they were certainly never a group to challenge the mighty legends of the day. However they had had more than their five seconds of fame and with several number one hits, a handful of bestselling albums and a few surprise music awards, De la Vie (DLV) were YRF (young, rich and famous). They could easily afford to retire in their mid-twenties, and once the band split after seven years together in the late eighties, most of the band members did indeed retire. Globally cast in different directions, none of them ever had to be concerned about money again. They settled in the predictable mansions, castles and remote islands with their supermodel trophy wives. However Reed was addicted to music, and the thought of letting his plectrum gather dust was never going to be an option. He was still in his mid-twenties and with lots of money invested wisely, retirement was not even a vague consideration.

Eenayah sighed at the thought; not then and not now, maybe not ever. She often wished that her go-getting high-powered husband would settle down and become a slipper-wearing retiree, but she sadly had to admit this was highly unlikely any time soon.

Following his marriage to Eenayah, Reed had created the Great record label, and in fact it was Great Records Ltd rather than De La Vie which had delivered Reed his true fortune as well as his greatest pleasure. He often described DLV as treading water until the big wave caught him and took him to the place he was always meant to be.

It always amazed and amused Eenayah that Reed could walk anonymously and unrecognized through many city streets. Reed Baratolli was the ultimate icon of the music world, seldom recognised by those on the outside of the industry, yet revered as music royalty by those on the inside. It was the very best sort of fame, as it still gave Reed the freedom to live a normal life without being mobbed, yet those who needed to know him had his number on speed dial. He was very protective of his privacy. Reed loved fame but hated recognition.

Driving down the road and listening to the radio, Eenayah had calculated that approximately one out of every 18 records played over the air waves in the US somehow had a connection with her husband. Either he had written the song or produced it or signed the artist or discovered the artist or GREAT records had touched the music somewhere along its path and sprinkled it with some harmonious fairy dust in one way or another.

She was proud of Reed, and yet annoyed with him. Proud that he had evolved from being just another glam rock boy band member and progressed deservedly into a leading figure in his industry. However she was annoyed that his drive and ambition took him away from home, and mostly away from her. Eenayah often felt like a bird in a gilded cage, sitting alone in her diamond-encrusted ivory tower watching the thunderstorm outside and feeling totally alone. Even with the heightened decibels of a raging wind and the clap of thunder, in her heart she felt a deep uneasy silence. She contemplated how they could be both enjoying a serene retirement by now; travelling the world with freedom and wanton abandon. Yet she was here in Miami in the rain, bored, lonely, maybe slightly tipsy. She wasn't used to drinking alcohol any more. Years of medication had prohibited it in case of a reaction, and now, much as she enjoyed it, she struggled to handle it, especially so early in the day.

Reed was somewhere in the world, but she knew not where. She guessed that he would be in a studio, or in a meeting or writing more songs in a hotel room or whatever it was that he did in his life. She couldn't keep pace with his fast-moving agenda and diary commitments. His PA Arabella knew more about his whereabouts than she did.

With that thought she swigged back the last dregs of her Bloody Mary and sighed. If only. She envisaged the life she could be living and then reflected sadly on her reality and the silence of her loneliness. Maybe Mary Poppins was wrong about the sugar, she thought, reflecting back on a song from her childhood. Maybe sugar didn't help at all.

She needed to do something - anything. Eenayah was intelligent, an ex-journalist. She had a sharp, enquiring investigative mind. Reed had often told her that he had fallen in love with her not so much for her beauty (although with her dark, sultry features she did have an exotic Eastern look), but because she wasn't a typical bimbo trophy wife with all the meaningless accessories such as fake tan, false boobs and typically dumb conversation. He respected her drive, her energy, her kindness and her spirit, but mostly her brain. However, she now contemplated the killer thought that she had possibly become all of the things Reed once said he hated in a woman.

She looked down at the genuine tiny rubies which had been carefully drilled into each of her fingernails and realised that the cost of her cosmetic frivolity (a token gesture to remember her sister Ruby), could have fed a few families for several weeks in a third world country. She couldn't be bothered to calculate the finances involved, but suspected it to be true. Had she really become the materialistic and shallow WAG that she believed Reed deplored?

Sinking into a depressive mood, she coiled herself up into the foetal position. Maybe, just maybe, if her world revolved less around Reed and his empire and she considered more of her own life and desires, he would gain respect for her again. Maybe he would want to come home to her, if he knew she wasn't just sitting there waiting for him like some pathetic lap dog.

Could there be something, anything in life that she really wanted to do? She had been a journalist in her earlier years, but did she have anything to investigate now?

Her mind ran circles as she realised that indeed yes, she did have loose ends in her life. There were many unanswered questions from her past. She had boxes in need of ticks. There were people back home she needed to see, places she needed to be, conversations she needed to have.

Roserie tiptoed into the games room almost apologetically. The storm was raging and she hadn't seen her mistress for several hours. With almost maternal concern, she delivered a platter of sandwiches and hot cocoa.

Eenayah was grateful. She often considered that she didn't know how she would survive without her loyal maid.

'You are an angel. Thank you Roserie,' she said.

By the time the rain had subsided and the sun had started to create a layer of warm steam around the outside porch, her plan had been hatched. She had found a purpose. Deep down she partially suspected that the main impetus for her plans could possibly be more aligned to winning back the respect and attention of her husband. He had once taught her the power of the 'backward bye-bye.' 'Nothing quite like walking away to get someone to chase after you' he had often murmured, although mostly in connection with some music contract. Reed often used the legal language of contracts, as this seemed to be how he now thought about life. Ironically his recent long absence in Europe on some talent scouting tour had made Eenayah want to chase him, so perhaps he had a point. '*Faciam quodlibet quod necesse est,*' she murmured whilst finishing off her Bloody Mary. Time to make some phone calls and do whatever it takes. Uncovering the ghosts of her past might well be the most challenging battle she had had to face so far.

CHAPTER 3

Ruby sat hunched over her PC studying tedious sales forecasts, spreadsheets and emails. She took the occasional cursory gaze out of the window at the London skyline, mostly wishing the vista was more akin to the green Welsh mountains of home. This job sucked the life out of her. Her neck hurt, her shoulders were full of knots and her eyesight was worsening from the hours spent looking at a bright screen.

Just occasionally she noted the time, wondering why her twin sister hadn't rung her yet. Eenayah knew she hated the start of the week, and it had become a sort of sibling ritual that Eenayah called Ruby at 5pm GMT every Monday. More recently this involved Eenayah sipping on some cocktail by the pool, with the justification that it was 5pm somewhere in the world, and indeed in London it would be. Oh how Ruby envied her sister's lifestyle. Eenayah seemed to do so little for so much, whilst Ruby did so much for so little. Life was so unfair.

She gazed at Eenayah's photograph perched on her desk, deliberately placed to hide a mountain of expenses requiring her scrutiny and signature. Once upon a time they had been cute little twins, but just take a look at what nature versus nurture had created since.

She caught sight of her own reflection in the large office windows and mentally protested at the contrasting images. Of course Eenayah could be several dress sizes smaller, she had a chef who could cleverly remove all carbs and still make a meal taste delish. As for Ruby, she would get a petrol-station sandwich eaten at speed on her lap whilst driving around the M25. Why would Eenayah have cellulite? She didn't have to sit at a computer for 12 hours a day. Ruby sat while Eenayah swam. Still, no point being jealous. At least Ruby had a husband who loved her.

It was an unintentional mental Freudian slip, but Eenayah had often wondered if it was possible that maybe her sister had actually led a solitary and lonely life, despite all her good fortune. Forever the career woman, Ruby did understand her brother-in-law's work commitments. She also had to spend a lot of time away from her husband and young son, but in her case it was out of financial necessity and certainly not out of choice. Whenever it was humanly possible she would be back at home in the rural idyll of North Wales. Not one to interfere in her sister's relationship, it seemed to Ruby that this simply wasn't the case with Reed. On the surface, he appeared to enjoy being away from home more than being at home. Ruby often felt secretly sympathetic towards her wealthy, privileged sister.

An hour late, her mobile rang. She rushed to pick it up as Eenayah's red carpet pose with accessory bling smile flashed up on the screen to indicate caller ID. She had mastered that pose so well. Ruby smiled at the sight of her ever-confident thinner twin.

'Ruby, Ruby, Ruby!' sang Eenayah loudly into the phone as her sister picked up, reciting the song made famous by the Kaiser Chiefs. 'Sister, sorry I am late. Busy life, things to do, people to see, lots going on' she blurted out in a much overstated and exaggerated manner. Eenayah always over-compensated when she was covering up some truth. Ruby noted it was a trait of deceit to go into too much detail; call it a sales person's intuition. 'The lady doth protest too much', as Shakespeare once wrote.

She cut to the chase. 'Eenayah, you are too loud, too giddy and you sound like you have made an early start on the vodka. Plus you are an hour late in calling me, so cut the crap and tell me what the problem is. Do I sense trouble in Paradise?'

'Ouch! A bit too direct, sis,' Eenayah jested in a slurred response. She knew that the downside of being a twin was a total inability to get away with pretence. Eenayah had often told people, 'You don't get to share an amniotic sac with a sibling and not have some sort of telepathic connection'. Yet she still avoided the question.

'Ruby, I was just thinking that I was due a trip over to England,' she said. Ruby was pleased, but correspondingly disappointed. Coincidentally by the same thought process of escapism, Ruby was equally thinking that a family trip to Florida might be just what her own small family needed after months of dust, mopping up and enduring a freezing winter on a Welsh mountainside. The ancient house she lived in was indeed lovely, but the ongoing renovation was a painful exercise and no amount of showering could truly get the cement out of one's hair. She had needed a vacation so badly.

'Eenayah, when you refer to England do you also mean Wales?'

Eenayah laughed. 'Yeah you know, the whole UK thing. Isle of Man, England and yes of course that includes your beloved Wales. However Ruby, from what you tell me you seem to be in London more than you're at home these days. You need to watch how much you are working.'

There was an unusual silence, and Eenayah detected a note of disappointment in her sister's voice.

'Are you okay, Ruby? You have gone all quiet on me.'

Ruby hesitated slightly. 'You just beat me to the post, that's all. I was hoping we could all cross the Atlantic and take some time out in the Florida sun with you and maybe even Reed if he's around. Life has been tough here as well, and we could do with a break. Screw it, I need a break. I am totally exhausted.'

Eenayah wasn't quite sure what to say next, so she remained mute. After a few moments of thought and with the prolonged silence at risk of becoming embarrassing, she responded, 'Look sis, I would love to have you over and you're welcome in Miami at any time, but I would have preferred to be under the same roof as you when you got here. I would want to treat you and take you out to special places. I have a wonderful luxury boat at the end of the garden and we could all play pirates and go explore the Caribbean together and have the most amazing time. I bet Harry would love the whole Pirates of the Caribbean thing.' She paused for a moment. 'It's just that I'm having a sort of personal crisis right now and I need to get back to the UK. Can you handle a few weeks' delay?'

How cruel! Ruby was sitting in a tall office block constructed of bland concrete, looking out at a grey smoggy sky with only the raindrops on the windows occluding the view. The mere mention of the word 'Caribbean' had her drifting into some fluffy turquoise dream world. Ruby was pissed off that her sister had even said the 'C' word twice. Mentally Ruby was swimming in a warm translucent lagoon with dolphins, followed perhaps by some idle daydreaming in a hammock on a white sandy beach.

After a momentary lapse of concentration, she suddenly realised that her sister seemed to be having some sort of mini crisis. Ruby concluded that her own dreams of escapism would have to be put to the back of the queue in order to deal with whatever new predicament Eenayah had to work through – yet again.

Acting the part of emotional detective, she retorted, 'ah ha then. So it's true, there is trouble in Paradise. Tell all, and be honest.'

Eenayah was unusually cagey. 'I also need some time out on my own, Ruby. I'm not so much running away from something, more like running towards something. Who knows what? It may be something old or something new. I haven't worked that out yet. I just feel I am being called back home. Hey, maybe I just need to reinvent myself. I don't like who I have become, if I'm truthful Ruby. Plus, I have some lost ground to cover and there are people, friends and family, who I haven't seen in a long time. You understand, don't you?'

Ruby deliberated for a moment. Either her sister was being a spoilt little drama queen or she wasn't telling her everything. What was the other story, she wondered? She continued to listen with sisterly interest.

Eenayah jumped in before her sister had a chance to trash the moment. 'I've already booked my flight over and I also have an itinerary,' she said. Ruby nearly choked on her herbal green tea.

'When have you ever had an itinerary? What to choose, a massage with hot stones and ylang-ylang oil versus a stretching session with your hunky young personal fitness coach Miguel? Decisions, decisions!'

Eenayah fell silent. It was almost as though her twin sister had played back a tape of her own thoughts and concerns earlier in the day. Was this how people saw her? Some useless little rich wife who did lunch with the ladies at the tennis club and pampered herself for the rest of the day? Her resolve to find a mission and meaning in life suddenly took on a new energy. Her twin had confirmed her shallow existence in just one killer sentence.

'Bugger! I think I have become superficial,' she muttered.

Eenayah continued in a matter-of-fact way. She seemed to have found a new source of energy now that she had a plan for the summer.

She went on, 'Well, first things first Ruby, yes I do have a vague itinerary. In no particular order, I intend to visit the farm to see Mum and Dad and all our aunts and uncles and check out the pigs and sheep and horses, maybe even go riding in Naylor's Wood and then avail myself of some of Aunt Ginny's home-made damson wine. Been a long time, so lots of catching up.'

Eenayah paused for a reaction, but none was forthcoming. It was an outburst of sweet childhood reminiscences, and she realised herself that a trip down this lovely old cobbled memory lane was in fact long overdue. The mere thought of hitting reverse gear and realigning herself with who she had once been gave her a warm, comforting glow. She couldn't wait to be back at the farm on the small island where she had grown up.

Ruby made no comment; she seemed bewildered by her twin's sudden urge to reconnect with family after years of apparent minimal interest. She wasn't accustomed to having a conversation with her sister that went much beyond the colour of her nail varnish. She had long since given up trying to understand how a woman as intelligent as Eenayah had become so mind-numbingly dull post marriage. Disappointed as she was about being beaten to a vacation, she was also pleased that Eenayah was taking time out to reconnect with who she was. To a remote observer, it often seemed that Reed enjoyed keeping Eenayah medicated and enclosed behind 10ft security fences in her Miami gilded cage, and she wondered how he would react to his wife's plans for a new adventure.

Ruby asked, 'so what does Reed think about your travel plans?'

Eenayah giggled and responded in an exaggerated southern drawl. 'Reed doesn't know. I'm going to surprise him. Not sure exactly where and when, as he is all over the place at the moment. His PA tells me he will be in London soon after he has completed something in France with some new promising artists or whatever. We haven't seen each other in what – five or six weeks, and I think he will be so shocked and delighted when I just turn up. He will be at the Mayfair Hotel in London I think, so I plan to spend some time with him and who knows, maybe we can get some of that mojo back. I need to make an effort, sis. I am more than aware that we have both taken things for granted.'

Again Ruby responded with a politely English, 'hmmm, how nice; good idea' but said nothing further. Ruby was still very disappointed and slightly angry that her own plans for a tropical escape had been overturned by her mollycoddled sister's badly- timed midlife crisis. She was only 38 – she didn't deserve a bloody midlife crisis yet. She hadn't earned one.

Eenayah was obviously excited about her planned schedule, which had given her a new focus in her usual pampered, boring life. 'I also have a meeting arranged with someone in Oxford, but I can't tell you about that yet as I know you won't approve,' she said. She had thrown out the bait and awaited a response.

It was not forthcoming. Ruby hated it when her sister told her half a story in the name of dramatic suspense, dangling a carrot to leave her hanging on and begging for more detail. Ruby was not going to beg or salivate, so again she retained a dignified silence.

Eenayah sensed the inaudible protest, but knew Ruby wouldn't be able to stifle a comment about a certain item on the agenda. 'Ruby, while I am over here I thought I may as well call in on Jonathan. He still lives up in Newcastle.'

Eenayah was playing games. She paused and awaited some sort of reaction. Deep breath, count to five. She didn't need to wait long.

'Oh my god, Jon-a-thong!' Ruby always pronounced his name in three distinct syllables to caricature his identity, deliberately mispronouncing the last syllable as in a childish schoolgirl playground taunt. 'My oh my, Jonathan Cook!'

The beautiful and smart Layne twins had gone to different UK universities. Ruby Layne had studied Pharmacology at Lancaster and Eenayah had majored in English Literature at Newcastle, the party capital of north-east England. It was during her university days that Eenayah had met Jonathan. They dated for a few weeks, but being too young to commit to any sort of meaningful relationship, they became the best of buddies. Eenayah was going through a difficult phase in her life at the time; she was just getting over the tragic death of her teenage boyfriend James. She met Jonathan shortly afterwards, so understandably she wasn't in the mood for any serious commitment. So it was as it was; just casual mates at the time, but lifelong friends and drinking partners going forward. Jonathan was a kind and caring spirit, in a blonde hippy sort of way. He was the sort of guy who was unbelievably cute without knowing it, and with a lovable unknowing innocence which seemed to be hormonally appealing to many a maternal instinct. In many respects he was the polar opposite of Reed, who always seemed to know exactly what effect he had on women and was willing to use everything he had to his advantage.

Jonathan had a less-than-secret unrequited crush on Eenayah, which she didn't exactly shun, but so as not to offend him she had conveniently converted into a friendship. They both ended up married, to other people. Jonathan owned a garden centre and lived a happy normal life with his pots, plants and fertiliser. He had a lovely stay-at-home wife, Pam, and she bore him two adorable children, a boy and a girl, and by all means he appeared to have a normal and satisfactory life. Normal aside from his occasional obsession with Eenayah.

Once upon a time, Eenayah had been the ultimate teenage wild child. As a student she partied in the city of Newcastle, but later in life she became a serious journalist for a heavyweight paper in the US. After her first husband Greg died, she needed to get away from the UK. Eenayah always ran away from tears, not always understanding that she couldn't leave her emotions behind at an airport. Then somehow, in an unexpected 360-degree turn, she quit her high-flying position with a serious newspaper and took a job with a gossipy Hollywood tabloid. It seemed to those around her to be a downward career move. Jonathan always considered that maybe his good friend had suffered some mini nervous breakdown at the time, so he was hardly surprised when within a year of all these major life changes she met and married an older guy, a wealthy ex-musician whose wife had died a year or so earlier.

The unusual union was indeed show business news in the tabloids at the time, and for a while Eenayah appeared in every popular gossip magazine in circulation, including the one she herself worked for, much to her annoyance. So in protest she handed in her notice, and in truth she was no longer in need of the money anyway. Public interest in this most unlikely of marriages calmed over time, and eventually life became relatively normal.

However, throughout all the turbulence, Jonathan remained a good and loyal friend, and one who deep down was still totally in love with her. Indeed, it was complicated. This was a friend who adored her as though she was a Greek goddess. Eenayah had always been aware that with just a click of her fingers he could be hers at the sacrifice of all else, but that would never happen. Tempting as it often appeared, they were both now married, and it was a line that could not and would not be crossed. Both Eenayah and Jonathan had individually thought that they might have ended up together - had it not been for Reed B walking through the door.

Ruby repeated the words teasingly. 'Jon-a-thong! No way, you are reconnecting with him, really? Is that wise?' She was concerned, as she could tell by the tone of her sister's voice, no matter how heavily disguised with frivolity, that she was in a vulnerable state. Ruby had no reason to mistrust Jonathan, but after all, she thought, he was a guy.

Eenayah, sensing Ruby's disquiet, became a tad defensive.

'Come on sis, it's been a while since I last saw him in person and things change, people change. We're just meeting up, that's all. Don't make a big deal about it. It's just that after a year of letters and emails and tweets and Facebook messages, I just want to meet my mate Jonathan again. It's not anything to get either worried or excited about.'

Again, another unfamiliar silence from both twins. Eenayah spoke first.

'Ruby, I have a suggestion and trust me, I hear your silence. I have a real need to come back to the UK for a whole variety of reasons which are important to me and with an itinerary that you seem to find amusing, but to me this is probably the most serious thing I have done in years. Perhaps it is more of a pilgrimage than a vacation, but I am in a sort of crisis right now and this visit is essential for my sanity. I am so bored being locked away in Utopia. Reed is never at home, and I'm lonely. I think I've become little more than a useless accessory to him and I hate that feeling. I am like a trinket, and who really treasures a trinket?'

She paused for thought and then continued, 'Look, I know you have your own issues and pressures, so maybe a trip out to Florida is something you feel you and your lovely family really need. So here's my suggestion. Roserie has the keys to the villa and she lives there all the time anyway, so why don't you all take yourself off there and go grab some quality time to recover and relax? In return you swap the keys to your place with me, and as long as I am under no pressure to stay there and milk goats, perform exorcisms or maybe even stay there at all if there's a five-star hotel in the area, then it's a fair deal – don't you think?'

Ruby was slightly taken aback, both by the insult to her crumbling Welsh mansion house and the offer of a free holiday.

'Hey madam, that's my home you're downing and it's not bloody haunted, it's just very old and it creaks at night, as we old people do.'

Eenayah swallowed her words. 'Not meaning to insult where you live sis, and I don't want to offend you, but the idea of being isolated on a mountainside next to a castle ruin really spooks me out. I don't want to have to deal with anyone or anything that doesn't have a heartbeat. As long as you don't get insulted with me booking into a local hotel on a full moon, then I'm good for a swap. Hey, swap or no swap, the keys to my place are yours. Maybe you and Owyn can have a chat about it and get back to me with some dates.'

Ruby was delighted. Even though the conversation went on for about another 10 minutes, she didn't hear anything more beyond the words 'the keys to my place are yours.' She was mentally already packing her bags and swimming with the dolphins. She couldn't wait to share this with Owyn. He would be jumping over the moon at the thought.

CHAPTER 4

Thursday June 6th 2013

Thursday evenings were always a welcome part of Ruby's weekly calendar. In fact she lived for them. She rushed back up the familiar gravel path, this time in the right direction. As she pushed open the big heavy oak door of her ageing manor house, her nostrils were immediately suffused with the smell of lamb hotpot simmering in the slow cooker. There were maybe a few scented cinnamon candles in the background, but nothing that could drown out the comforting smell of home cooking.

Owyn was nowhere to be seen; not that it mattered, as she soon caught sight of the red and white chequered tablecloth laid out with immaculate precision. A warm crusty loaf straight from the oven had been placed in its centre and two very large glasses of deep red wine had already been poured and were waiting. A single red candle flickering away next to the crusty cob was obviously Owyn's attempt at romance. She beamed at the warm welcome her lovely, considerate husband had lovingly prepared for her, wherever he was, that is. Perfect. Every wife everywhere should walk home to this, she thought, especially when exhausted from a week in the London office.

Nights were still damp and cold in North Wales, even in the early summer. She noted Owyn had lit the log fire, placing a bottle of cognac plus two buxom brandy glasses next to the hearth for an after-dinner drink. 'Ah' she muttered, 'he's hoping to get lucky, I see the plan.'

She kicked off her high heels and rushed upstairs to see their little son Harry. She had no need to worry; she never had need to worry. He was clean and warm and smelled lovingly of baby talcum power. He was tucked up in bed with his teddy bear, Mr Moses. Trying not to wake him, she kissed his cute little forehead tenderly. Her love for this little boy quite overwhelmed her, and she missed him so much when working away from home. She often felt a weighty internal struggle between her need to earn money and the pull of motherhood. It was difficult.

Ruby changed into her PJs and big brown unsexy gorilla slippers, transforming immediately from career woman to the wife and mother who was indeed very content to be at home. Ecstatic to be within familiar walls after her long train journey, she was in unwind mode and glad that she no longer had to adorn herself with power clothes and layers of makeup. She was comfortable in the knowledge that Owyn would love her in her PJs, scrubbed face and stupid slippers.

Blissful and relaxed, she rushed down her centuries-old creaky staircase and flew into her husband's arms. It seemed he had just popped outside for more fire logs. Owyn's embrace almost crushed her ribs and took her breath away; his delight in seeing her after four days was more than apparent. Ten years of marriage had not dampened their total delight in just being together.

Owyn was an amazing and caring husband and father. Ruby could work away from home without any fear that either their renovation project or pipsqueak of a baby son would ever come to any harm. Thursday was indeed a great day. Friday she could work from home, and then this lovely little family would have the weekend all to themselves. Maybe they could go to the beach at Llandudno, or perhaps hike in the Snowdonia mountains sitting magnificently on their doorstep, or just sit outside a pub in Betws-y-Coed drinking beer and watching all the bikers and climbers go by. Happy, happy, happy!

Settling at the table and tucking into their lamb stew, Owyn was hardly able to contain his excitement. Ruby had merely mentioned the idea of a Miami vacation a few days earlier and from that tiny glimmer of hope he had already purchased a tourist book, a new suitcase, a map of Florida, and had spent several hours researching flights and 'things to do.' All that was really required now was for Ruby to agree the annual leave dates with her manager Robert, and let Eenayah know the dates. She had tried to push for four weeks' annual leave, but depending on who could cover for her it was likely to be less. Still, it was better than nothing and a much-needed break for the family.

She hadn't allowed herself to think about it much during the last few days. She had been in London for two days at the beginning of the week and then working with the sales reps in Bristol and Birmingham after that. There wasn't time to do personal thinking when managing a group of sales people and negotiating the logistics of working remotely. However, now she was home, and sensing Owyn's enthusiasm about the holiday, she was starting to get excited herself.

Owyn was hyped up and geared to talking Florida all night long. They hadn't had a holiday in years, and little Harry had never even been on a plane. Owyn was so animated that Ruby could see this was going to absorb his thoughts and energy until he had checked into the airport and set foot on the tarmac. However Ruby had a secret she wanted to keep tucked under her hat, so, confusing as this was to Owyn, she tried to divert the conversation away from their vacation in Miami in case she let the plot slip.

Ruby had always refused any financial help from her rich sister, because to her it was demeaning. She wasn't about to take hand-outs from her twin, even though Eenayah always offered. However on this occasion it was Owyn's 40th birthday and Eenayah wanted to treat them both, as well as lavish treats for her adorable only nephew. Indulging her sister and her family was high up on Eenayah's new bucket list of tick boxes, and she was determined that they would have the most wonderful time.

Planning their trip had been a welcome diversion to Eenayah's loneliness, and she had enjoyed the distraction. Following several phone calls between the sisters that week, the holiday had been arranged and paid for with the highest degree of sisterly secrecy. Eenayah had booked first-class plane tickets for Ruby and her family on the date of Owyn's 40th birthday (1st July), and it was a done deal. Champagne and birthday cake mid-flight had already been arranged. So had a private helicopter taking them from Miami to Orlando on the second week of their three-week vacation, with a hotel suite at Walt Disney's All-Star Movies resort. The plan hatched between the sisters was for a week initially in Eenayah's Miami sea front villa, followed with a week at the Disney resort and then back to Miami for the final week when Eenayah would fly back home to join them.

Ruby discussed the possibility of Owyn and little Harry staying on in the US a little while longer, in case Ruby had to come back sooner. Owyn worked via the internet and as long as he had wi-fi and a laptop, he could be at work anywhere in the world. There was no point making him fly home early if it was possible for him to extend his stay.

Ruby had long realised that in true love there was no jealousy. If you loved someone, you wanted them to have fun and enjoy themselves. If you wanted your partner to be miserable, you couldn't really love them. However this young couple were fortunate, as neither of them suffered from the evil green-eyed monster and each gave the other as much freedom as they needed or desired.

Owyn knew nothing about these clandestine arrangements and was still looking online at economy flights. Ruby played everything down and distracted the conversation away from Miami as best she could. She was naturally keen to divert the chit chat back to the unusual phone call with her twin and what Eenayah had referred to as her 'pilgrimage to the UK'. This wasn't easy, as Owyn was excessively excited about the vacation and bouncing from subject to subject; Busch Gardens, Universal, Sea World, the Space Centre, Epcot; he was like a child who had just found the keys to a candy shop.

After they had finished their stew, the couple curled up on the settee in front of a crackling wood fire. The house was so large and rambling that it echoed, so they chose to spend most of their time in the smallest room in the house, the snug. Their ginger cat Barnaby made it a cosy threesome, and they all wrapped themselves around each other in an almost sitting-up spooning embrace. Sipping cognac, Ruby totally let go and relaxed. Every pore in her body seemed to breathe out, each breath letting go of the stress of the week. This moment was picture perfect; this was what she worked for. Being with her husband at this very moment in time was all that mattered to Ruby.

It had been a childhood custom that when Ruby and her twin shared some special moment in life, they would tell each other that they were 'putting the moment in their pocket to keep for later.' She had taught Harry to do the same. 'When Mummy is away from home' she would say to her four-year-old son, 'just look in your pocket and you will find some love from Mummy to keep you going until I get home again, and then when I get home I will fill your pocket back up with some more love.' It was a simple, loving gesture between mother and son.

Ruby thought about more profound things as her mind wandered and she drifted into another consciousness. In those few minutes she realised that the special moments in life were more often than not nothing unusual, and probably not even that exciting. Special moments were just snapshots in time when everything, just for a few minutes, was simply perfect, and all in the universe was as it should be. Should anything happen between Ruby and her husband, she knew her better memories would not consist of them abseiling down a cliff together or parachuting out of a plane, but most likely simple moments like this, curling up together on a settee and drinking cognac in front of a fire. However she also understood that for Owyn in his Welsh laddish way, it would more likely consist of the rib-clenching G-forces of the Incredible Hulk ride at the Islands of Adventure.

Owyn interrupted her drift into deeper thoughts, pulling his wife back into the present moment.

'Hey, Darcy is really keen to hang out with Eenayah if she does actually get to stay in our house,' he said. 'She would be good company for her, but I believe she wants a whole level of detail and gossip I just don't have.'

Ruby shrugged. 'Tell your sister not to get too excited. Eenayah thinks a headless horseman may come jumping out of a turret, firing poisonous arrows. I doubt Princess Eenayah would want to stay here anyway, but I'll do my best to persuade her otherwise. I would prefer it if I didn't have to put my babies in the cattery and kennels.'

'Why doesn't she like it here? Why does she think the place is haunted?'

Ruby shrugged, as though not entirely sure herself. 'Well, I suspect it's partially due to a degree of agoraphobia. Ever since Eenayah had her so-called breakdown, she has preferred to be locked away in the safety of her Miami mansion. And let's face it Owyn, she gets totally spoiled by Roserie. She doesn't have to chip a fingernail doing the washing up or anything remotely domestic. She wouldn't have that luxury here, so I think Princess Eenayah is just a tad spoiled. Oh, and it didn't help matters that when she was last here that Mrs Lear down in the village post office told her that this entire area was haunted by the ghosts of Druids who walk around underground tunnels in the middle of the night chanting spells or something.'

Owyn's expression altered on hearing this. He didn't seem too happy with what he had just been told.

'I will have a word with Mrs Lear about that. I am not having her telling scary stories just to frighten our guests.'

'Aww, she is an old lady Owyn. Cut her some slack. Anyway, I believe there really are secret underground tunnels in the area.'

Owyn was keen to close this particular conversation down. He replied, 'only disused mine shafts. I grew up in this area and if there was anything other than just mining tunnels, then I would know. Sorry to put a damper on Mrs Lear's mysterious ghost story, but the old lady is exaggerating.'

Ruby knew her sister too well, and she also knew Owyn's sister well enough to quickly figure out that this was not a friendship match made in heaven. Darcy was a 'ladette' who could down beer, throw darts, shoot pool and curse better than many a man. She loved her sister-in-law, but knew she had an uncultured yet jovial side to her nature. Darcy would want to drag Eenayah around every bar and night club in North Wales, and this would be Eenayah's worst nightmare. Ruby and her husband hadn't often discussed her twin's past, for no other reason than it did not seem important. However, now that the wife of a well-known music star might be staying in the village, local folk were bound to be curious. This would be a big thing for the village. Darcy would not be able to resist coming to the house if Eenayah stayed over, and Owyn was keen that Darcy shouldn't put her foot into anything hot and sticky.

'You never did tell me the full story about how Reed and Eenayah met,' said Owyn. 'I understand there was some major tittle-tattle regarding his first wife. What was all this scandal our Darcy talks about? You never did give me the full details, Rube. You know Darcy is about as subtle as an elephant with ballet shoes on, so we need to tell her what subjects to avoid.'

Actually Ruby hadn't told Owyn anything because she had presumed the entire world had known the story about her sister Eenayah and the music god known as Reed B. However she now considered that maybe she had been mistaken and perhaps the news had bypassed Wales; after all it was just a small bit of land attached to England. She knew her Welsh-speaking husband would swing for her if he knew what she had just thought, and it brought a mischievous grin to her face. Sorry Wales, she murmured. However she felt vindicated, as she was from the Isle of Man, which was a much smaller plot of land and not even physically connected to England. She wasn't totally sure why she was mentally justifying the geography of Wales.

Ruby was sure she had already told Owyn about Reed's past at some point in the last ten years, but the chances were that he had paid no attention whatsoever and this new interest in the finer detail had probably been instigated by Darcy, who probably saw this as an opportunity to impress her friends with her show business family connections. Ruby adored Darcy, but recognised that she tended to be a bit of a chameleon who was prone to change her appearance, hobbies and even her taste in music, according to whichever boyfriend she happened to be seeing at the time. Whenever Darcy had a new favourite band, one simply knew she had swapped lovers. Darcy was quite a character. Loud and often drunk and well - loud. However, this change in conversation did play into her hands, as she was keen that they should stop talking about their Florida vacation as soon as possible. It would be too easy for Ruby to slip over her words and accidentally give the whole secret plan away.

'I'm going to keep this short and simple, because I can't believe you don't remember any of this anyway and I suspect Darcy has put you up this little inquisition,' said Ruby. She took a long, deep breath, flicking her eyes up to the ceiling in mock chastisement. The special moment had now passed, but it had been tucked away in her pocket for another time.

'Where do I begin?' pronounced Ruby.

'Well let's start with Reed. I am sure you know all about the boy band thing when he was a teenager and his moderate degree of success and him being a busker prior to that and this talent contest changing his life and all that. Am I right?'

'Erm yes, I do know about that', responded Owyn sharply.

'So then they split up and he started writing music.'

Owyn grunted, 'Yep, know all that, move on.'

'So then he met Eenayah at a party when she was a reporter for a sleazy gossip mag, and they got married - which was a shock to everyone as they hadn't known each other long. As for music, he moved on to being a producer and then owning a record label and then getting rich and all that.'

Ruby had repeated the story many times to colleagues, and she was getting bored with telling it.

'So what was the ground-breaking scandal in all of that? Darcy hinted at something far meatier than what you have just told me.'

Ruby yawned. The combination of a full stomach, the brandy and overheating by the fire after a long train journey home was finally taking its toll. However, she knew Owyn wouldn't let her rest until she finished the conversation.

'Okay Owyn, but I'm warning you that I need to get to bed soon. So, where did I get to? Right; so you know Reed was married before, don't you? It was to one of his backing dancers, an ex-Las Vegas show girl, all sparkles and no bra. I guess dating a dancer happens a fair amount to pop stars when they're young, rich and surrounded by lithe toned nubile bodies.'

Owyn grinned like a Cheshire cat. 'Well yep, I can certainly understand how that happened.'

Ruby gave him a poke in the ribs, sensing that some male sexual fantasy had just momentarily crept into his thoughts. 'God, I forget her name, I think it was Julia. They were married quite young and had a few kids. They were together a fair amount of time; about 10 or 12 years, something like that – maybe longer.'

Ruby mentally tried to count on her fingers, calculating that Eenayah had told her that Reed was about 25 when he got married, but then found she didn't know enough dates or detail. She would have to ask Eenayah about it.

'So what happened?' asked Owyn. 'Didn't she die?'

At that point Barnaby the ginger cat made a sudden loud squeal and jumped off his lap.

'Bloody hell! Crazy stupid cat, scared the shit out of me.' A spark of fire had just been spat from the flames and landed on Barnaby's tail. Ruby ignored Barnaby's antics and took a big swig of her cognac, as though what she was about to say next would be fairly dramatic. Her mood changed as she recalled the headlines at the time.

'Yes Owyn, Julia died in a car accident. It seems she lost control of the car on a bend and it drove off the cliff and into the sea. It was all very dramatic. The police couldn't find any reason why it had happened. She wasn't drunk or anything. She left three young children motherless, and it was an awful tragedy. It made all the newspapers at the time. As you can imagine, Reed Baratolli was famous in the music industry, so it was bound to make the news.'

Owyn looked appropriately saddened. 'But wasn't their some sort of twist to this awful story, I seemed to recall some scandal although I didn't pay much attention at the time? Too busy having fun with you I suspect… didn't it happen around the time we met?'

Ruby stood up to warm herself by the fire, as though the room had suddenly become chilled by a ghostly presence. 'Owyn, do you recall the name Bert Montana?'

'Heck, that's a name from long ago. He was an actor. As a kid I used to watch some comedy show every Wednesday night after school – what the heck was that called again?'

Ruby shivered, still feeling a chill in the room. 'Captain Bloom,' she replied.

'Yes, by heck that's the one. You have a good memory, Ruby. Bert Montana was Captain Bloom. I loved that show.'

'Well' responded Ruby, 'when Bert Montana wasn't at sea playing the part of Captain Bloom on a big sailing ship, he was messing about with Julia Baratolli's porthole and pulling in more than just a fishing net, if you get my drift'

Owyn looked visibly shocked. 'Bugger me. Reed's first wife and Captain Bloom! Who would have bloody believed it? Small world. God, that's ruined a childhood memory now.'

Ruby nodded her head in agreement. 'It gets worse. When Mrs Baratolli the first died in the car accident, Bert Montana was in the passenger seat. It seems they had been on their way to some hotel for a – I guess you Celts would call it a dirty weekend.'

Owyn was becoming more engrossed with the story, his eyes widening. 'So, when did Reed find out? I take it he did find out, since it was in all the papers?'

'Not until after the funeral. There was an inquest of course, and the truth was known well before, but the police kept it from Reed until he had gone through the whole burial thing.'

Owyn subsided into his Welsh boy-at-the-bar lingo. 'Wow, and did it all kick off then?'

Ruby smiled at her husband's inappropriate use of the phrase. 'Yes it kicked off bloody big time, Owyn. All the dirty laundry came out in the wash. Turned out Mrs Julia Baratolli and Bert had been seeing each other for donkey's years. It wasn't an on-off thing, it was a full-on relationship. They had both been living double lives. Remember that Bert was married as well, so two families were torn apart by this disclosure. Reed had all his children DNA tested and it turned out the youngest one (the boy) wasn't even his.'

Owyn looked shocked. 'Gee, Darcy is going to love all of this, unless of course she already knows it all, as I suspect she does. She has probably been on that Google interweb site looking it all up. So what happened next, what did Reed do?'

Ruby sighed, slightly perturbed that Owyn seemed to be enjoying the details of such a tragic story. 'Well, from what Eenayah has told me, and she hasn't gone into the finer details, Reed wrote lots of very sad negative songs about infidelity and cheating women and made tons of money from them all. I remember him telling me once that a happy songwriter often can't write. I quote his exact comment, 'the best songs are always written with a broken heart', or at least that is what he claimed.'

Owyn poured himself another shot of cognac and downed it in one. 'And so he made even more money out of grief - fancy that! But what about the kids? What about the one that wasn't his?'

Ruby pulled Barnaby back on her knee, and stroking him, she seemed to be in deep thought. She felt genuine sorrow for what Reed had had to go through.

'He had a nanny for the kids. He didn't turn against Konnor, who bless him was only about five or six at the time. I guess it wasn't the boy's fault that his biological father was Captain Bloom. Reed was still his dad. I guess Reed did the best he could for them all. I suspect he just worked long hours and the cook, cleaner and nanny became surrogate replacement mothers and the kids probably hardly ever saw their father. At least he was wealthy enough to make sure they were well cared for.'

Owyn continued to probe. 'So what about his love life? How did he meet Eenayah?'

Ruby shrugged, as she lacked some of the finer details. Eenayah had been quite coy about the whole dating thing.

'I only know what Eenayah has elected to tell me and what the gossip magazines wrote about at the time. I believe he spent the following year just jumping on everything and anything with two legs and a short skirt. I guess it was his way of dealing with anger. Reed got quite a bad reputation as a playboy, but I also think a lot of people understood the reasons for his behaviour and were sympathetic to him.'

Owyn gave his Welsh-laddish smile of approval. 'Sounds fair enough to me, there are worse ways of dealing with anger.'

Ruby gave him another poke in the ribs, not totally happy with yet another sexist comment.

'Soooo…' asked Owyn, obviously enjoying the subject matter, 'how and when did Eenayah come along to interrupt his shagathon recovery process?'

'Hmmm.' Ruby thought for a while before replying. 'This is only what Eenayah told me.' She sat back down on the settee, looking wistfully up at the ceiling in deep thought, and spending a bit too long focusing on a cobweb she had just noticed and which she was now determined to eradicate.

'Eenayah was always so much smarter than me. Ironically she started off as this shrewd, determined career woman, far more so than I ever was or even wanted to be. She landed this top job with a New York newspaper after her first husband Greg died. She couldn't handle his death. It nearly sent her off the rails. So off she ran to the US to escape from the memories. Then she was offered a much bigger salary to write tittle tattle for some gossip magazine, so you could say she went to the dark side. I guess her press pass got her into all the right press conferences and TV interviews, and of course VIP entrance to some celebrity parties.'

Owyn was suitably impressed, 'Wow, I never knew that. She must have some interesting photos on her walls.'

'Indeed she does. Just wait until we visit this Miami mansion of hers. I understand there are photos of hundreds of famous faces all over the wall in the games room.'

'Can't wait to see them' replied Owyn, temporarily taken back to the thoughts of his forthcoming vacation.

Ruby looked at her watch, it was getting late and her eyes were starting to become heavy.

'I can't keep awake much longer, Owyn' she yawned. 'If you want any action tonight, be warned that I'm nearly asleep, so your window of opportunity is closing fast.'

'Okay bedtime it is, but just finish off the story. You are nearly at the end.'

Owyn was keen to hurry Ruby along, yet curious about the outcome. How had Eenayah Layne made such a big catch? Reed must have been the most eligible bachelor in the US at the time, and although Eenayah was a pretty woman, she wasn't as stunning as some. She didn't come with a huge dowry of money in the bank, and neither did she come with an impressive network of connections. She was just an ordinary person, a journalist working for a woman's magazine and to boot, a widow with a broken heart. Many people simply didn't understand it, and poor Eenayah was the victim of a lot of jealousy and bitchy remarks. They had got married within a few months of meeting, and that in itself caused a few raised eyebrows.

'Nothing much else to say. When she had her serious job with the New York paper, she occasionally mixed in the same circles as world political leaders. All I really know is that she was at a celeb bash at San Francisco and it was there she met Reed, and the rest is history.' She paused. 'Except...'

Becoming more impatient and checking his watch now, Owyn sensed another line.

'Except what?'

'People said some really cruel and mean things about Eenayah. Personally I think Reed probably fell for her because she was different. She was smart and English and they had both experienced losing a partner, so maybe they had a common bond. Eenayah wasn't like those other wannabe Hollywood wives. Back in the day, she was sassy and a great conversationalist and above all else, very sweet, kind and loyal. She had, maybe still has, a theory that Reed wanted to stay clear of any other Las Vegas dancers like Julia, or for that matter surgery-enhanced plastic blow-up dolls and gold diggers. She thinks he wanted a mother for his children, and at the time Eenayah was a lovely fresh-faced innocent English girl. Eenayah believes she was probably good wife and mother material and Reed selected her because maybe he could trust her. Don't forget, trust was always going to be a big issue with Reed after what happened.'

Owyn was shocked into a few moments of silence, and he thought long and hard before replying.

'So Ruby, if I am hearing you right, Eenayah believes she was selected like a farmer selects a prize bull at a market? In all you've said, I haven't heard the word love being mentioned once.'

Ruby didn't want to agree with him - the words were brutal - but silently she concurred.

'God Owyn, that is so cruel. I didn't exactly word it like that, but... I guess you're right. You know the sad irony from all of this is that with all the money and time she now has at her disposal, Eenayah seems to have become exactly the type of woman Reed was trying to avoid. Reading between the lines, I think she wants to come to England to find herself again, maybe rediscover that English girl Reed once fell in love with. I'm not sure, but I know my twin well enough to believe that is what this UK self-discovery trip is all about.'

Owyn picked up on her words with lightning accuracy and sharply responded, 'You just said 'once fell in love with'. What do you mean? Is 'once in love with' the same as saying no longer in love with?'

Ruby put her finger across her husband's lips. 'Shush; I've told you far more than enough. I don't know for sure and I am only surmising, but I would take a wild guess that their marriage isn't in that good a place. However, for this moment I am exhausted Owyn, so can we now end this conversation please? Bed, NOW!'

As the tired couple ascended the stairs to their bedroom, Reed Baratolli songs kept coming into Owyn's mind. Maybe for the first time he realised how painful and depressing some of the lyrics were and now he understood why.

He began to hum. *'The complicated life you're trying to live, has woven a web around my heart. So tangled and tight you cannot breathe, so you cut it loose for a brand new start.'*

'Hell's bells, that is a bloody depressing song isn't it?'

Owyn just wouldn't shut up, and as more songs came into his head he continued to sing all the way into the bedroom. *'There's a golden ring on your finger, see it's shining like a neon light. It says you can be mine for this moment in time, but I know you can't stay the night.'* Did Dolly Dawson sing that one?'

Ruby grew annoyed and threw a pillow at him. 'STOP SINGING! Do you want to get me into bed or not?'

CHAPTER 5

Sunday June 9th 2013

Reed strolled casually through the streets of Paris towards the Saint Germain des Près area, eager to meet with his long-term dearest friend Fabien. He would have appreciated a longer snooze wrapped inside the hotel's best silk duvet, but waking up to have Sunday brunch with Fabien was an invitation he could never pass up.

The warm Parisian sunlight kissed his pale cheeks with welcome beams of heat. He held his face up to the sky as though trying to drink in even more sunlight. Too long a period in the subdued darkness of a recording studio and too many late nights had wiped the colour from his skin.

Reed beamed as he caught sight of the unmistakable tall bearded figure, and rushed to greet his good friend in typical male bonding bear-hug style. Reed held him tightly, patting his back and displaying a genuine affection for his mentor and confidant.

'Bonjour, comment vas-tu mon ami?', whispered Fabien, always slightly nervous of any potential paparazzi frequenting the area and ever mindful of this friend's fame. Reed disregarded any such intrusions, but Fabien was always conscious of the need for privacy and discretion.

The two friends took a seat outside in the fresh summer air, both relaxed and happy on this most beautiful of June mornings.

'Monsieur, apportez-nous votre liste de vin' commanded Fabien in the direction of the waiter. Reed couldn't speak French, but he figured out the request involved alcohol. 'Just water and coffee for me Fab, too much partying last night,' he said. 'I'm getting to be an old man now, just can't do this hair of the dog thing any more.'

Fabien sat back on his wicker chair, drawing deeply on his treasured meerschaum pipe, which he considered his one and only vice. Taking a long analytical look at his friend with a medically-trained mind, he noticed the dark shadows under his eyes and the pallor. Scanning him up and down, he could see he had lost a fair amount of weight.

'Not looking so good Reed, what's going on?' asked Fabien, seemingly concerned.

'Thanks a lot mate, but I guess you are the doctor' retorted Reed.

'Yes indeed' Fabien replied with a cheeky grin, 'but I'm an obstetrician, so unless you are having a baby I don't think I can be of much service.'

The two men laughed and chatted and then laughed yet more. Fabien had originally been Eenayah's friend going way back to their university student days. However, as Reed spent more time in Paris than Eenayah, he got to meet up with his wife's friend on a regular basis and eventually stole Fabien away from her.

The one thing Reed loved most about his acquaintance with Fabien was that he neither knew nor cared about the music industry. He had no involvement at all in any business that in any way touched Reed's life. In the name of polite conversation he would enquire about Reed's latest project or hot new discovery, but aside from having teenage daughters who would nag their father for free concert tickets, Fabien had little interest in Reed's mixed up world of notes. They lived in parallel universes, often drifting through life casually alongside each other. Universes touching, yet never colliding. He felt he could tell Fabien anything and whatever he said would never go anywhere else. This was an easy, uncomplicated friendship.

'Reed, I know you won't take offence by my admission of not being enamoured by the latest hot new band to hit the music scene, but I have two teenage daughters who are interested and Anais and Valentine will refuse to talk to me for a month if I don't ask you who they should be looking out for. Having said that, not having adolescent female chatter clutter up my eardrums for a month may not be such a bad thing. Still, I had better ask rather than face the wrath of the daughters. So Reed, who have you got tucked up your sleeve from this latest megalomaniac global venture of yours, and more to the point, are any backstage VIP passes able to wing their way over to two cute but demanding French girls?'

Reed shook his head in amusement and smiled in a smug self-contented way as he was dragged into the land of his favourite subject. He knew Fabien didn't have the faintest snippet of knowledge about any type of modern music beyond opera. However he recognised that Anais probably had posters of One Direction, Union J, the Vamps and 5 Seconds of Summer plastered all over her already-crowded bedroom wall. Anais was a typical teenager, while her sister was anything but. Reed admired his friend's eldest daughter for her divergent musical tastes. Valentine reminded Reed of himself in his own younger nonconformist wild-child adolescence. He recognised that she was more of an Indie Rock and anything goes type of a kid. Music as we know it, as long as the decibels were loud and the melody challenging. Reed adored Valentine. She was slightly off centre, in her own quirky way.

After some thought, he responded to Fabien's reluctant paternal enquiry.

'Tell Valentine to look out for this alternative Indie rock band I am negotiating a tour deal with at the moment. British group called The Procession, on Circular Records I think. Oh hang on – I believe that they have changed their name to Sonificade. I struggle to keep up with all these bands sometimes. Anyway, pass the message on that I will try to get her some freebies once tour dates have been agreed with their managers. We have a great line up of sixteen or so new bands trying to break into the industry, and I think they are right up Valentine's street.'

Reed flicked though his iPad and the index-finger-typed notes he had made on various up and coming artists from his talent spotting expedition. 'Ah okay, I think these guys will suit Valentine. From our Australian visit tell her to keep an ear out for the Rivalries and a Christian heavy rock band called Prepared like a Bride. I will see what I can do for her re backstage VIP passes and all that. As for Anais, I think most of the current cute boy bands have already been signed up with other labels, but I am sure she will love Océane, you know the young French girl I told you about. For one so young she has a big voice. I have great things planned for Océane.'

Reed was becoming tired. Music and the latest, newest unknowns to hit the scene had always been his favoured subject matter, but at the end of the day it was still work, and he hadn't spent the last few days growing excited about a reunion with Fabien to sit and talk shop. He closed down his iPad by way of a signal to close down the conversation.

'That's about all my hot tips for the day, my friend. I could go on and on with a big list of who, where and when, but I think I may risk boring you, dearest Fabien. Just tell your daughters that if I know of anyone playing at the Stade de France or Le Zénith they will get first refusal on the best tickets in the house.'

Fabien was busy scribbling the names down in his notepad. He knew he could not come away from a meeting with the famous Reed

B without at least a few promises of future band encounters in the bag. Anything to keep the women in his household happy.

They sat silently for a moment, having done what had to be done in terms of industry updates for Fabien's awaiting family. It was a delightful Parisian day and a moment to simply sit silently, listen to the birds and watch the world as it turned on its axis.

Reed's mood seem to suddenly change, and he looked at his friend intensely.

'I'm not getting any younger mate. I'll be 50 soon and just beginning to wonder why I am still running round like I'm in my twenties and getting more and more knackered day by day.'

'Well my friend, you always told me it was because music was in your blood, it was an obsession. Is that not true any more?'

For the first time in maybe ever, his friend looked quite despondent. Reed answered with slow deliberation.

'Most of what I do isn't music any more, Fab. My job is all about contracts and lawyers and finance and marketing and PR and what adds up to what number on the bottom line of a spreadsheet. That's why I have been doing this whole global talent scout tour. It was mainly to get me out of my office and away from lawyers and in front of real musicians again. I just got bored Fab, but I am not sure it was such a wise thing. Eenayah seems to be really missing me. Maybe it's an early menopause thing. She is going through a weird stage at the moment. Just seems very distant.'

Reed continued as though he was at a confessional. Somehow Fabien always brought out that side to him. The verbal stable door had opened, and now it could not be bolted.

Fabien was curious. 'You have been doing a lot of travelling my friend. Do you really need to work as hard as you are?'

Reed considered the answer before thoughtfully replying to his friend, 'the thing is Fab, my industry is so bloody fickle. One minute the world loves you and the next thing they can't remember your name. Yeah sure, GREAT records has signed up some of the top artists of the decade and things are going well for the moment, but the truth is that 80% of them won't be around in two years' time. It's like a conveyor belt and we need to keep replenishing the stock. So that's why I am here and touring around planet Earth. Just looking for new talent to sign up. I want to retire in about ten years and pay Eenayah and the kids some attention, but I just want to make sure the finances are stable first so we can carry on enjoying our lifestyle. Just putting money in the bank, bro.'

Fabien carried on with his questioning, perhaps sensing that he was only scratching the surface. 'You seemed to become very successful very quickly just after you married Eenayah. Why do you think that was, Reed?' He looked at his friend with a semi-suspicious frown.

'I don't know Fabs. Maybe I went off the rails after Julia died and Eenayah just calmed me down. Plus you have to admit that a broken heart does wonders for a songwriter.'

Fabien continued, trying hard not to sound like a TV interviewer and failing, 'so what are your plans now, Reed?'

Without realising it, Reed picked up Fabien's glass of Bollinger, rather than his own Evian water, and knocked it back in one. He replied, 'The plans are ambitious mate. It's been manic. We kicked off the European leg of the tour in Venice Italy on 3rd May, and after that's it's been like one country a week – Germany, Spain, Portugal and now France. I've been here longer than some of the other places, but as it happens there has been a lot going on here, some real talent. Then off to London soon. Expect to be there for a month at least; GREAT has studios there, so lots of stuff going on. Then home at last for some R&R on the boat and a recap. It's been a bloody lot to do in a short period.'

Fabien inhaled deeply on his pipe. 'Yes, wow that is a lot my friend.

You need to take care that you don't burn yourself out. When did you last see Eenayah, and how is she taking you being away on your global adventures?'

Reed picked up the empty glass of Bollinger and shook it at the waiter to indicate a top-up was required. He seemed to be avoiding the question, but when the silence was becoming embarrassing he gave a reluctant answer.

'Gee Fabien, it was in Venice when we were last together. How many weeks would that be?' He stopped to think, counting on his fingers. 'One two three… I'm guessing about six weeks. Not exactly good husband material, am I? Not a great father either, I haven't seen my kids in months. I bet they can hardly remember what I look like. And as for Eenayah, oh yes, I'm in big trouble there Pal. Went out last night to the Cravate Bleue club with the French production team by way of a farewell party and left my mobile back in the room. Then when I finally got back to the hotel I had at least 10 missed calls from her. I am going to be in big trouble when she next gets hold of me, believe me. I am in the doghouse.'

Being the sociable person Reed always was and realising he hadn't once asked Fabien about his life, he suddenly remembered to enquire, 'But anyway, how are you Fab? How's Louisa and the family? Life treating you well?'

Fabien realised this was a well-intentioned but insincere line of enquiry, and his friend had a much greater need to offload his troubles than he needed to listen to Fabien wax lyrically about his wonderful life in the Paris suburbs.

'Never mind me amigo, I'm fine,' he said. 'But are you?'

Ouch! He had unintentionally hit a sore point yet again. Reed sighed. 'Get the waiter to bring more Bollinger Fab, maybe I can get drunk and sleep for the rest of the day. Hey, it's my day off. In fact I have a few days off now we've wrapped up the French round of business, so this is a bit like a mini holiday for me mate. I can do what the hell I like.'

Fabien cut to the chase. He cared deeply for Eenayah. She had been his friend long before Reed.

'Is your marriage okay Reed, how is Eenayah coping?' he asked. Fabien kept on pushing the buttons, not willing to be diverted from the question and sensing there was an issue that Reed wasn't revealing.

Reed was getting annoyed with Fabien's persistence and was reluctant to answer, so he took his time in doing so. He could see that his nosey French doctor friend wasn't going to give in so easily.

'Eenayah is wonderful. Really, she is a sweet considerate lovely lady, but I'm a shit husband. I don't think I treat her well. I make no bloody effort with her. Too wrapped up in my own little personal space Fab, and that my friend is the miserable truth. I have no idea why she stays married to me.' Reed's voice was beginning to slur, and as it was midday Fabien decided it was better to fill his friend's stomach up with food rather than Bollinger.

'Monsieur, nous aimerions commander de la nourriture s'il vous plaît' commanded Fabien.

'Where is Eenayah now?' enquired Fabien, still pushing to know more about Reed's personal life. He felt he had a right to be worried. Eenayah meant a great deal to him, and he couldn't help but be concerned. Not that Fabien would ever say so in so many words, but he often felt his friend should be slowing down and taking life a little easier, maybe even spending more time at home. Fabien hadn't known Reed when his first wife Julia had died in the car crash, but he had read all about his meltdown in the papers. However he had known Eenayah when her husband Greg had died, and witnessed for himself the devastating breakdown she went through. Both his friends seemed susceptible to mental stress, so the last thing he wanted was for this marriage to crash and burn.

Reed couldn't remember anything about his last conversation with Eenayah, and he had to pick up his mobile phone to look at the most recent text she had sent him. Fabien was quite shocked that Reed wasn't even capable of recalling his last conversation with his wife. He put on his glasses and read out yesterday's unread text.

'She says she is planning to go over to the UK. Says she is going to visit her sister and her family and then Jonathan, but maybe not in that order. That's some male buddy of hers from her university days. Ex-boyfriend I think, never met him but heard lots. Eenayah just loves the bugger.'

Of course Fabien also knew Jonathan as he had been at the same university. He recalled how much Jonathan had adored Eenayah. If it had been his wife, he would have been worried. Either Reed didn't care about Eenayah, or he trusted her blindly.

Fabien simply never missed a trick. He was a medical doctor with a lifetime's experience of dealing with patients who wouldn't actually tell him what was wrong, and this had taught him to pick up on the smallest of symptoms and clues. He noticed that Reed didn't seem overly concerned that Eenayah was spending time with some guy from her past.

'Does that not worry you, I mean your wife with some other guy? She is still a hot looking woman bud, and a lot younger than you old man.' Fabien put an affectionate arm around his old friend and patted his back in jest.

Reed hiccupped and responded, 'No worries Fab, he looks like Shaggy from Scooby Doo.'

Fabien leaned back in his chair, inhaling long and deep on his pipe. That might be what she had told Reed, but what woman is ever going to say her best male friend is good looking?

Reed was becoming more serious with each glass of wine, and it occurred to Fabien that perhaps he should change the subject some time soon. It was a pleasant afternoon on a lovely summer day in Paris, and this was the engagement he had been looking forward to for some time while he had been stuck in the hospital clinic. Yet it was quickly becoming far more serious and depressing than probably either of them intended. That was the problem with alcohol. It could raise your spirits when the mood was good, but bring you down when the mood went bad.

However Reed insisted on answering his friend, and he was talking in a more and more depressive manner.

'Yes of course, I do worry about Eenayah and yes I do still love her, but… we have become disconnected, if you know what I mean. I know I went through all that dark stuff when Julia was cheating on me and then she died and all that crap, but if I'm truthful I wouldn't blame Eenayah if she did have some fling with this the Scooby Doo bloke. The probability is though, that she wouldn't, in fact I know she wouldn't. She is just way too good for me. Out of my league Fab.'

Fabien was concerned about his friend's downbeat mood, further exaggerated by his pale skin and exhaustion. He discovered that Reed had a couple of days left off work before having to catch a flight to London with the 'next best thing' on the French music scene, along with her dangerously attractive mother as a chaperone. Fabien wasn't keen to leave his friend alone in a Paris hotel room in this frame of mind. Maybe just an instinct or a tell-tale shiver down the spine, but he just didn't trust the situation. He had known a former colleague once who had hung himself in a similar scenario, and Fabien didn't want to take any chances with Reed.

He helped the drained and slightly drunk Reed to his feet. 'You are coming home with me tonight, my friend. I've ordered a taxi and Louisa has cooked some *pôtage aux légumes*. You need to get some sleep and then we can talk about some brighter things when you wake up. I'm a doctor as well as a friend, and these are my orders.'

Reed grunted 'huh okay doc', but he was half asleep before he could finish the sentence. Fabien continued, 'I promise I will get you back to your hotel in time to pack for your flight to London, and if you give me your hotel keys I'll get Jean Paul to come back and pick up some of your belongings. Spend a few days with me, dear friend. Valentine and Anais will be delighted with what I have just dragged home. However, don't forget that you need to give that worried wife of yours a call. That is an order, Reed.'

Fabien observed his friend as he drifted into a deep slumber in the back seat of the taxi. He looked not unlike the actor Richard Gere, but with emerald green eyes and perhaps a slighter build. He was a handsome man who looked good for his age, but tried overly hard to dress less like a middle-aged man and more like a rock star, much to Fabien's amusement, considering both men were a similar age. With skinny jeans, oversized pointed boots and a tatty loose black tee-shirt, Reed looked nothing like the multi-millionaire he actually was. However Fabien understood why his friend shunned attention and how important his private life was to him. Dressing down was part of the charade, he presumed.

Winding their way through the noisy tree-lined Parisian streets towards his family home in Versailles, Fabien heard Reed's mobile ring, and as it lay lightly in his hand he saw the image of Eenayah flash onto the screen, along with her red carpet pose and flashing smile. In that instant he felt he had been subjected to an ethical dilemma between his loyalties to two friends whom he both adored. He didn't quite know what to do.

Fabien didn't want to wake his sleeping friend, as Reed had looked so weary and fatigued. Fabien knew he was in need of rest. What to do? Should he pick up the call on Reed's behalf, if only to stop Eenayah from worrying? The poor girl was also a dear friend of Fabien and his midwife wife Louisa. In times past they had often enjoyed many merry moments together as couples. Eenayah must surely be concerned about being unable to contact Reed. Did that mean that Fabien was duty bound to answer the phone on behalf of his friend? What a quandary!

As a doctor he was frequently faced with the ethical dilemma of choosing between truth and lies. Fabien was a devout Catholic, and as someone who always tried to obey the Ten Commandments, 'thou shalt not lie' gave him some concerns. If a patient was terminally ill, was he duty bound to tell them the truth, or should he give them a flicker of hope with the chance they would live out their final days without fear of death? Honesty was often the lesser desirable choice, yet the one he was often made to choose. Fabien was a good man, and sometimes that made his resolve difficult to reason.

The phone continued to ring, and Fabien decided he should answer it. He couldn't really tell Eenayah that her husband was now drunk in the back of a taxi and hence couldn't engage in conversation. Nor that he had missed all her calls last night because he was out in a night club until 4 am with a group of musicians and their groupies, who were most probably half his age. Fabien had no idea what Reed did behind closed doors, nor did he want to know. He suspected that his friend lived in a fantasy party world very different to his own normality, and he had heard rumours to suggest as much. Reed was a close friend, but there were some things he preferred not to know. Alas, nothing that Reed did would really surprise him.

He kept the conversation short and sweet. He told Eenayah that Reed was worn out from overwork and he was taking him back to his home for a few days. Eenayah was relieved to hear that her husband was in safe, reliable hands. Eenayah knew that men had two types of friends; the ones their wives, girlfriends or significant others hated and the ones they approved of. Fabien and Louisa were most certainly on the approved friend list.

'Don't wake him' said Eenayah, 'and tell him I will send him an email and oh, thank you so much Fabien. I am so glad you are there with him. Please give Louisa my regards.'

At that point, the taxi turned into the long tree-lined driveway leading up to Fabien's white rendered house with typical French slatted windows. Louisa was waiting at the large green door, as loving and welcoming as ever. Fabien took a moment to reflect, and for an instant he felt immense gratitude for the serenity and stability of his own life compared to the manic pace of Reed's nomadic existence. It sometimes took a rendezvous with Reed to remind him just how much he appreciated the consistency of his own unchanging and secure existence. Louisa had once told her husband, 'never knock boring', and he had come to realise she had a good point. '*Ne sois pas ennuyeuse*', he whispered to Louisa as he kissed his wife, his friend hanging off his shoulder.

As Reed lay in bed sleeping off his hangover, Fabien and Louisa sat at their rectangular kitchen table, picking at scraps of bread and sharing a bottle of Malbec. Fabien seemed uneasy.

'Louisa, I am not sure about Reed. He worries me. He has changed. He seems to be quite detached from Eenayah. I just have a feeling. I am going upstairs to check on him, just to see how he is you understand.'

Louisa knew exactly what her husband was doing. As he came back into the kitchen, she asked him the question he was expecting. 'Did you see anything?'

'Yes', came the blunt response.

'A birthmark?'

'No, a tattoo. Well actually, many tattoos.' Fabien wasn't a fan of tattoos, and his facial expression showed as much.

'Quoi?'

'Louisa, this is a guy from the world of rock and roll and he has every weird symbol on his torso and arms that one would expect of a guy in his industry. Honestly, I wouldn't read much into a skull or pentacle on a guy like Reed. All these music guys are the same, and Reed likes to blend in and make out that he is younger and more contemporary than he actually is. I mean, he is pushing 50. I think all these so-called illuminati symbols are little more than cool fashion statements at the moment, and I would put money on his ink being nothing more than that.'

Louise could sense a 'BUT' coming up, and indeed it did.

'But he did have one tattoo I haven't seen before. I think it means something, but I need to ask a few questions first. It could be a something or a nothing. It's just a tattoo around his right wrist, a purple band which has been broken by a dagger. I don't know what that means, but I have a suspicion, so I'll check it out. Let us both be diligent. Reed is a good friend, but we also have a duty to Eenayah.'

There was little else to be done for the time being other than wait for Reed to emerge from his drunken siesta and enjoy a family meal. None the less, Louisa and Fabien were apprehensive, without knowing why; it was no more than a gut feeling.

CHAPTER 6

Monday June 10th 2013

52 Carrington Lock was a most unusual workplace. Hidden amongst the spires of Oxford's antiquated buildings, the office was an eclectic mix of old school and the latest cutting edge technology, a bit like Oxford itself in fact.

The reception of MeDeVe Private Investigations Ltd had been designed to calm and relax the often anxious clientele. The pale lilac on its walls had been well researched as the colour most likely to transmit an aura of tranquillity and composure. Crisp white roses adorned the reception desk, and the bright, modern room exuded a subtle floral aroma. Three permanently-closed doors were tucked into the three corners of the spacious reception area.

Behind the first heavy oak door could be heard the chimes of the Professor's treasured Elliott of London eight-bell grandfather clock, noisily ticking away the passing of time. Professor Roland De Vede's office was all that could be expected of a much-renowned former University Dean, traditional and yet understated. The bookshelves were crammed with well-fingered literature and the walls proudly displayed certificates, awards and diplomas. The lingering smell of old tobacco gave the room a musty yet comforting atmosphere which left anyone entering with the undeniable impression that this was the domain of an elderly gent.

Behind the next door was a large room which was in complete contrast to the Professor's study. It would shock and astound any customers entering, aside from the fact that this was the nerve centre of MeDeVe Ltd and as such was strictly off limits to anyone other than MDV employees. As the only room with fob card entry, the security of this high tech office was paramount. With large plasma screens on each wall and a variety of James Bond- type gizmos carefully locked away, this brightly-lit workplace bore a closer resemblance to NASA ground control than the headquarters of a quirky Oxford investigation bureau.

The final office was that of Mercy De Vede, ex-CID police detective and now the CEO of a very successful international company which was in growth mode. Her office was minimalistic, with no clues on the walls, shelves or desk as to who Mercy was, past or present. The starkness was not totally by design, because in essence she did not sit down at her desk long enough to create any remnants of personal clutter. However part of her psyche did not really want clients to know too much about her friends or family. Mercy was there to do a job and not to become personally engaged with customers. She didn't want the distraction of someone picking up a family photo she had propped up on her desk and asking questions about it. Mercy's job was to find out more about her clients and what they required from MeDeVe, and not the other way around.

The boss checked into her office once or twice a week to have a 'catch up meeting' with the team, mainly to brainstorm the latest projects. These meetings were referred to as 'case conferences' and were mandatory unless a team member happened to be overseas; even then they would be required to join by conference call or WebEx.

Aside from meetings, she was mostly in transit. Mercy was a high-energy feisty lady who always seemed to be in a rush. She was the client fronting part of the team and the saleswoman who sold their services. They were the 'backroom team', as she called them - they did all the real work, but they were mostly kept well out of sight of the clients.

Mercy was intensely smug and proud about her boys' and girls' capabilities; the backroom team back at base. They were an assorted mix of carefully-selected people who had been researched and handpicked by Mercy personally and considered to be a perfect fit for the job. Her professionalism and demands were high, as her team had to work with maximum operational effectiveness.

Zac was the youngest of her employees. He had spent several years at a youth correction institution, having been found guilty of hacking into the Ministry of Defence's computer main frame. His punishment recognised the fact that he was an adolescent schoolboy who meant no harm and did this for his own entertainment. However in many ways he did the MOD a great favour, as he exposed a major security loophole in their software code. As soon as he was released, Mercy hired him on the spot. She knew that many secrets were hidden within computer hard drives, and having a master hacker on her team would be an immense bonus. There was very little Zac didn't know about any sort of technology and even though he caricatured the typical heavy metal long-haired rock look, he was actually one of the most crucial members of her team.

Lilly was a fairly new hire and an ex-paparazza. She came to Mercy's attention when she gained publicity for stalking a famous politician and uncovering enough grime about his personal and professional life to light up the tabloids brighter than the Christmas illuminations on Oxford Street. It was Lilly's sheer grit and resolve to publicly highlight his disgrace in 'people trafficking' that brought his criminal activities to public attention and forced his redundancy from public office, along with his subsequent arrest. She was one of the best photographers of her type, but much more important than her skill with a lens was the fact that she would do anything to get her shot. If it meant hiding under a car for hours and later emerging covered in oil and aching from every limb, so be it. If it meant getting the shot, Lilly would do it.

Carmen was predictably one of the more controversial assets to her team, in that she was the honey trap. To complete the portfolio of services offered by way of an investigation bureau, Mercy needed to have an entrapment service on the menu. The rest of the team often didn't agree with this part of the MeDeVe portfolio and indeed Carmen only worked for them as and when needed. Aside from some occasional work with MDV, she was a high-class prostitute and still traded as such. Employed by Mercy part-time on a contractual basis and not overly well paid for her services either, Carmen simply did the job for voyeuristic entertainment. She loved the whole play-acting part of waiting at a bar and testing her womanly skills out on unsuspecting husbands. She prided herself on her sexual allure and was nicknamed 'the siren' jokingly by the rest of the team. Intensely gratified by her high catch rate, Carmen would do the job free of charge if she had to - not that she disclosed this to Mercy.

JD was ex-SAS, and there wasn't a wall he couldn't climb, a tunnel he couldn't crawl through or a building he couldn't break into. If drawers needed to be rifled, hard drives confiscated or letters opened, then JD was the man. His work was often 50/50 as regards legality, and Mercy had to be strict about staying on the right side of the law. As such JD's activities had to be carefully logged and monitored. However any damage was always repaired and anything removed always returned. Plus JD was occasionally requested to work for the police themselves, as he operated undercover without the need of a search warrant.

JD wasn't a thug. He was a total professional and a slick operator. He could enter a room, delicately search through its entire contents and then leave everything exactly as it had been and with nothing harmed, scratched or broken. The owners would never even had known JD had been there. He was a strong man, ultimately physically fit and both a martial arts and firearms expert. When not required for his ability to break into virtually any building, he came in useful when a bodyguard was required for any of Mercy's more upmarket clientele.

Don was the opposite end of the social and physical ladder to JD and was, remarkably, an ex-librarian. A slightly portly man in his mid-50s, he was Mercy's hired bookworm. Every investigation needed a degree of research, and someone had to have the boring task of looking through old newspapers, reading through mountains of documents or sifting through a search engine. Don was painstaking meticulous when it came to finding out facts and proudly owned the title of Chief Research Assistant.

Finally came her two leading PDs, (Private detectives). Steve like Mercy, was an ex-policeman; however his credentials of working with Interpol for many years meant that he had a rich network of overseas contacts. In the last five years, MeDeVe Ltd had become increasingly engaged with international clients, and Steve's overseas contacts were proving most beneficial. Steve was very much a beer-drinking, cigarette-smoking 'bloke's bloke', but one of the most experienced members of the team. He was the traditional sort of private detective in every sense.

Simon was younger and an apprentice to the company. He was actually Mercy's nephew and had shown his interest in joining MDV since being a child. He had no other skills other than his youth and energy, however two years into his training Simon was becoming quite a successful PD. Mercy often thought he was just a kid who liked to play spying games, but whatever his motivation, he worked long, hard hours and was becoming a true asset to her diverse family of employees.

Kerry acted as both receptionist and PA. Managing many people's diaries and daily activities, she needed to be ultra-organised and efficient. None of the team were truly office or desk bound, and Kerry was continually having to juggle flights, trains, hotels, meetings and clients' cases. Her mobile was never switched off (to the annoyance of her boyfriend), as some of the team could be as far away as New Zealand, not just within differing time zones but sometimes on different date zones. However, their work could also be mundane and mind-numbingly boring. Long stake-outs were far from pleasurable, and Kerry was the bright, cheerful voice at the end of the line who could dial out for pizza and keep everyone going with strong coffee.

Occasionally the work could be risky and highly dangerous. They were forever mindful that their line of work sometimes ventured into the underworld of felons and those who would not take kindly to being investigated. As such, the company had a strict 'emergency pick up' policy. If a member of the team needed a quick 'get out of jail and do not pass GO' card, Kerry needed to be on the other end of the phone to organise a rescue. It wasn't something that happened very often, but when least expected trouble could escalate quickly in their line of work.

***

Kerry was having an unusual panic attack. Bursting into the back room (as it was known), she shrieked to Zac, 'Where the hell is the Professor? He has one of his genealogy clients due here in ten minutes and he is nowhere to be seen. Can you do a track on his mobile?'

Zac tapped a few keys on his computer. 'Nah, you're out of luck Kerry. The Prof has gone and left his mobile in his office, yet again.'

Kerry was seething. 'Amazing, isn't it. We can locate a bigamist with 12 identities living on a boat off Malta and yet we can't find a 70-year-old man walking around Oxford with a straw trilby on and a brilliant orange tweed jacket. Bloody useless. What's the point?'

Zac shrugged. 'Sorry Kez, don't know what else to suggest. Want me to phone the university to see if he's stuck in a lecture? What's the big deal anyway?'

Kerry snapped back, 'He's got an important client on her way and she's just flown in from the States especially to see him. So the Prof not being here for his appointment is way out of order.' She thought for a moment. 'Maybe Mercy can cover. Can you see where she is Zac?'

Kerry knew exactly who Eenayah Baratolli was. She knew the name of every client who walked into what she considered to be her reception, and had often researched them on line in advance, looking at personal profiles on social networking sites and the like. It often impressed new clients that Kerry recognised them and could even converse with them about their pastimes and interests. It was a small thing to do, but Kerry understood that first impressions mattered.

The Professor's time-keeping abilities often irritated Kerry. She recognised that he was a forgetful elderly gent, but his lateness for meetings was becoming a frequent occurrence. Then of course it was Kerry who had the job of apologizing and entertaining his frustrated customers.

Even though Prof Ronald DeVede simply shared office space with MeDeVe Ltd employees and wasn't actually part of the investigations team, he still had a 50% share in the company, and as far as he was concerned that entitled him to use the PA services of Kerry whenever he liked. Not only that but he would lean on Don to assist him with research work, which Don loved as the professor always had much more interesting research than Mercy. The professor even occasionally took his grandson Simon away from his PD work and frequently sent him scurrying off to some graveyard to photograph headstones. Mercy was often frustrated and annoyed with her father for stealing her staff, but she also realised that without his investment MeDeVe Ltd Private Investigations wouldn't exist, so it was more a case of her tolerating his behaviour rather than condoning it. However Kerry was slightly less tolerant. 'I am busy enough managing everyone's diaries and schedules without having to worry about Roland and his blimmin' family trees' she sighed.

Zac shouted over to her, 'Hey Kez, I have some good news and bad news for you then.'

'What?'

Zac brought up the tracking screen on his PC. 'Mercy is walking down Carrington Lock and has an ETA of about… say 10 minutes away. You have backup to save the day, hey Kez.'

Kerry hated him shortening her name to Kez, but he was a young dude and he had a habit of shortening everyone's names. It was part of his cool rock IT aura. She responded tentatively, 'So what's the bad news then?'

Zac swivelled around on his chair and pointed to the CCTV screen in the office. 'That' was his simple response.

The CCTV screen showed the image of an attractive young woman dressed in what appeared at a distance to be an immaculate designer outfit. Even with a slightly pixelated screen, it was still obvious that the wealthy client of Professor Roland De Vede had arrived and was spot on time for her 2pm consultation.

Kerry sighed. 'This is embarrassing. Simon, call your Aunt Mercy and explain to her what's happening. Tell her she is going to have to cover for her father again. I will try and entertain his client until Mercy gets in the office. And someone please find where the Professor is!'

'Yes sure' responded Simon, as keen as ever. 'Do you want me to look up his email exchanges and case notes so I can debrief my aunt when she gets here?'

'Good lad, you are so efficient Simon, you learn fast.'

Kerry was impressed, and Simon beamed like a little schoolboy who had just been praised by his teacher.

Eenayah sat in the cool lilac office flicking through the MeDeVe corporate brochure with some interest, whilst Kerry made small talk and handed her a mocha.

'You must be exhausted Mrs Baratolli, have you just flown in?'

Eenayah was unusually apprehensive in her reply. 'I'm not too tired actually; I flew in yesterday. My husband has a rented apartment in Mayfair which he hardly uses. It made more sense to just drop all my bags off yesterday and travel around light. I have a lot of this country to cover in a short time. I managed to get a good night's sleep, so I'm fine, but thank you for asking.'

Kerry felt relief that Mrs Baratolli's journey to the UK was not just for the purpose of meeting with the Professor, since she indicated she would be travelling whilst she was over here. Still, an apartment in Mayfair seemed a fairly expensive storage facility just for excess baggage.

At that moment a woman flew into the room like a fireball of positive energy. Dressed in a pistachio green dress which clashed teasingly with her vibrant red hair and with killer 6 inch stilettos worn with the greatest of ease, she had an air of vibrancy and total confidence. She reached out her heavily-jewelled hand and shook Eenayah's leather-gloved hand with a firm assertive grip.

'Pleased to meet you. Mercy DeVede at your service and you must be Mrs Baratolli.'

Eenayah was slightly taken aback by this poised, self-assured female who had immediately assumed such control and authority. She was confused, as she had been expecting an elderly, bookish professor, who so far seemed to be absent. With managerial authority, Mercy commanded Kerry, 'please seat Mrs Baratolli in the professor's room and I will join Mrs Baratolli in a moment. And Kerry, bring some iced water with lemon for us both.'

Mercy took this opportunity to rush off into the back room and have a quick debrief with Simon. She was a total professional and it would be below standard to walk into a meeting unprepared, even though this wasn't her client. She had an urgent requirement to understand why the wife of the famous Reed Baratolli was sitting in their Oxford offices and what possible business she had with her absent father.

Within a few minutes Mercy joined Eenayah in her father's office, looking demure and unruffled. She sank down into her father's antique green leather chair with the poise and decorum of a catwalk supermodel. With polite sincerity and composure she apologised for the missing professor, but assured Mrs Baratolli that she could open up a case for her and begin whatever process it was that brought her into MDV's Oxford HQ.

Opening up the file in front of her (which contained little other than printed email conversations in the smallest of font size), she began to determine the nature of the case. However Eenayah was curious and diverted the conversation into the direction she wanted to take it.

'I have noted that you have the same surname as the Professor,' she said. 'Is he your father?'

'Indeed he is' replied Mercy.

'I read his book coming over on the plane. He seems to be extremely smart.'

'Yes, indeed he is' replied Mercy once again. 'He can speak six languages, and as well as being an historian and a genealogist, he is also a statistician and is unusually well versed in pure mathematics. I guess he is your typical eccentric genius. However he isn't part of the

MeDeVe Company. He simply shares our office space and unofficially, many of my employees.'

Eenayah nodded in approval. 'My husband can speak Latin' she said. 'Can your father speak Latin?'

Mercy was slightly taken aback. She had still been a child in primary school when she had watched Reed B and his boy band play live on *Top of the Pops*, but she remembered Reed Baratolli very well. He was every young girl's pin up dream boy in the mid 80s and at one stage even she had pinned a poster of him next to her bed. Mercy couldn't quite believe that Reed B could speak a language such as Latin; it didn't fit the image she had of the former glam rock star. Even less could she believe that his wife was now sitting on the other side of the table. For a short moment she found herself slightly starstruck, but then, being the pro she was, she composed herself and returned to the matter in hand.

'That is impressive Mrs Baratolli. Not many people can speak Latin, but yes indeed, it is one of my father's languages.'

'Oh please call me Eenayah. You make me sound very old and formal when you say Mrs Baratolli and I'm certainly none of the above – I hope not anyway. What subject does your father teach?'

'Ancient history', responded Mercy. 'He doesn't really do any teaching any more, but he does the occasional lecture at the university, and I do apologise, but that is where he has been this morning. The chances are he has become too involved with some debate and is over-running. This really is most unlike him and I am so very sorry.' She bit her lip at the obvious lie about his timekeeping, but she had to cover for him somehow.

Mercy sank back into her father's oversized chair and smiled, despite feeling a little like Alice in Wonderland finding herself the wrong size for surroundings which did not suit her personality. Her father had too much clutter, she reflected, looking around the room in mild disapproval. She returned to her professional persona.

'So what can we do for you, Eenayah?'

Eenayah drifted off for a moment, as though she was considering her answer with great care. 'I can tell you why I came here, if that helps?'

Of course it bloody helped, thought Mercy, but she kept the smile firmly on her face. Eenayah continued, 'Mercy, I have heard many great things about your father. He has helped some celebrities and friends of mine find their family roots and his book on genealogy has been very well received in the States. You must know how much Americans like the whole family history thing. He is very highly regarded back across the Atlantic. I know he is late for our meeting and yes I am disappointed, very disappointed. I have travelled a long way for this. I do hope I can meet him some time while I am over here. I will be in the UK a while longer, not sure quite how long though.'

The lady was more spirited than Mercy had given her credit for, but she still hadn't answered her question. Time to do an eyeball scan of those emails. She put on her reading glasses, something she hated to do, and looked at the file in front of her, speed reading as best she could considering the small font.

'So Eenayah' she continued, 'I see that its Reed's 50th birthday on the 31st December and it says here that for his birthday you wish to present him with a complete family tree in a book. Is this the reason you had a meeting with the Professor?'

Mercy could see that Eenayah was less than impressed with Mercy's lack of knowledge about her requirements. She replied, 'Yes indeed. What do you buy the man who has everything? I thought it seemed like an unusual but thoughtful present. I know the professor is the best in the business and he prepared something similar for a friend's husband that went down very well. I just thought that with only a few months to go before Reed's birthday, I only have time to employ the best. Don't you think this would be a most unusual birthday present?'

Mercy could see the disappointment on Eenayah's face and tried to rescue the situation by being totally frank. 'Yes, I believe it will be a highly-treasured present and I am sure my father will be able to help you put it together.' She was playing for time. She wasn't familiar with the process of dealing with the genealogy clients and was hoping that if she stalled, her father would return at any moment. 'Eenayah, whilst we are waiting for Professor De Vede, it may help if I explain a few things about how we operate.'

Eenayah sipped her iced water and nodded as though she had all the time in the world.

'I own a business called MeDeVe Ltd Private Investigations and I have a large team of multi-talented and quite unusual people who work for me. We do the usual cheating partner type of surveillance, as sadly they are the frequent bread and butter jobs that pay the wages. However our specialty is finding people; people who are hard to find. Maybe people who have simply gone missing, or complicated, even criminal, cases of people who deliberately hide, covering up all traces of who they are and where they have been. Identity fraud is becoming more popular, and that's one of our specialist areas. Plus, even normal everyday folks are getting much better at covering their tracks. It takes a lot of time and expertise to find those who don't want to be found, but we are very skilled at what we do. Even the police hire us from time to time.

'My father also finds missing people. However his people are usually long dead. That's what differentiates what my father does from what I do; my missing people normally still have a pulse. As I said, my father isn't part of my team. He just takes up a corner of the office space and clutters it with rubbish as best he can.'

Mercy smiled, testing the water. Eenayah smiled back. She was beginning to understand the nature of this quirky business relationship.

She continued with her explanation, also playing for time in the hope that her father would turn up some time soon.

'However, occasionally his knowhow does come in very useful. He can track down birth, marriage and death certificates in seconds. I'm sure you can appreciate that when people try to mask their identity, just being able to connect them with something like an official document is an important part of our work. I just need to stress to you that I personally am not a genealogist. That is my father's job.'

Mercy was trying her best to backpedal and escape from the problem of her missing father and his disillusioned client. Then, glancing up at the old grandfather clock and realising that her father was highly unlikely to turn up any time soon, she decided to deputise in his absence.

'What I can do, Eenayah, is give you some advice as to how we can get the ball rolling quickly. The minute my father walks back through that door, I promise you that he will take over the proceedings. Is that okay?'

Eenayah nodded in agreement. Her schedule for the day was fairly relaxed.

'So to begin, where were Reed's parents born?'

'England. Reed is an American from New York, but his parents were born in England.'

Mercy began to tap some notes into her iPad. 'His name doesn't sound very English.'

Eenayah giggled, for a moment sounding like an amused schoolgirl sharing some childish secret. 'Does the name Anthony Mort sound more English?'

Mercy sat upright and was visibly shocked. All those years before when she had actually had someone she thought was Reed B pinned up on her bedroom wall, it had actually been Anthony Mort. Who would have thought it?

Eenayah understood the shock behind the look and found it quite amusing.

'Anthony Reed Baratolli Mort is his full name, but hey that's not very show business now is it? So in the same way as Norma Jean Baker became Marilyn Monroe and Reginald Dwight became Elton John, so did Anthony Mort become Reed Baratolli. At least part of it was his middle name. I think his mum's family is Italian, if that helps with the research.'

Mercy had listened to her father enough times to be familiar with the drill, so she continued, 'What was it I was just saying about people changing their IDs before? Very Hollywood. However I suspect having an English name makes it easier for the Professor. So next question, are his parents still alive?'

'Yes, still alive and kicking', replied Eenayah.

'Then this is where we start. Can you call them and get more details? We just need their full names at birth, dates of birth and if you know their town or city of birth, so much the better. We can take it from there with just that basic simple information, but of course the more details you have the easier and quicker we can get a result for you.'

Mercy paused for a moment. 'You know my father has always said that the best source of all genealogical research is the living. To put it crudely, you can no longer ask questions of a corpse. My best advice to you is, before his parents are six feet under, just talk to them. Ask them about their parents and grandparents and cousins and so on. My father doesn't need all this detail, but with only a few months to go before you wrap this up as a birthday present, information from his family will just add more speed and accuracy. Sorry I am not Professor Roland De Vede and just his daughter the detective, but I know he would give you the same advice. Just email him some details and he will be right on the case. I can promise you that. Yes he is the best, and you won't be disappointed. I think it's a great idea to give as a present for the man who has everything.'

Eenayah seemed assured, but there was something puzzling Mercy about her reaction, or rather lack of it. Mercy was used to selling her company's services to prospective clients, and she could read body language the way some people could read a book. There was something more, something Eenayah wasn't telling her.

'Is this okay for you?', asked Mercy, trying to uncover what else was concerning her.

'Yes' came the blunt reply. Eenayah thought for a moment and sipped on her water as though her throat had been cut. Mercy knew this to be a sign of anxiety.

Eenayah continued, 'Well actually yes and no.' She paused again and her eyes became slightly tearful. 'I was reading your company brochure outside, and I understand you can find the parents of people who have been adopted?'

Mercy had not seen this one coming. She sat upright on the big leather chair before answering.

'Yes Eenayah, this is one of our many services. Is this of interest?'

Eenayah shrugged, 'if I had my lawyer here right now, he would be making you sign an NDA before this conversation continued any further. You must know the way things are. My husband is a famous man, and by default that makes me of interest to the tabloids as well. What I am about to tell you is, er… delicate, and I wouldn't want this information shared with anybody. I hope you understand.' Mercy nodded, for once lost for words. Eenayah continued, 'I am a twin, and I have no idea who my parents are. We were adopted at birth and raised on a farm with very loving, wonderful people who I call my parents and are and always will be Mum and Dad. In fact I will be going to visit them some time soon. They live in the Isle of Man. It's a lovely place and certainly on my list of things to do whilst I am over here.'

She paused for a moment, looking tearful and slightly shaken. 'My sister and I always knew we were adopted, but it was a taboo subject and no questions were ever asked. And we were so happy – it wasn't as though we missed out on anything anyway.'

She wiped the smallest of tears from her eyes and gulped down more water. She had never cried about this before or even thought about it that much, so this newly-discovered emotion and curiosity about the woman who had given birth to her both confused and perplexed her. She continued, 'I didn't come here to find this out, Mercy. I never even considered it. Maybe it was just a moment of serendipity when I read your brochure.' She smiled. 'How dumb am I? I once thought serendipity was a vodka-based cocktail, before my sister explained it meant something like a chance happening, a bit like karma or kismet. I don't know if I believe in such things, but I do know there is some reason why I needed to come to England and maybe this is what it is. Maybe it's just one of many reasons. Do you think you can help?'

The tables had turned, and Mercy the ice-cool professional was back in charge whilst the new client she now shared with her father was emotionally crumbling. She preferred the position of power and authority and hadn't liked it when Eenayah had seemed to have the upper hand.

Without a flicker of emotion, Mercy gave a professional, matter-of-fact response.

'The way the law works Eenayah, is that those adopted in England and Wales before 12 November 1975 are respectfully required to seek a nominated counsellor before they can be given access to their records. My company will be quite happy to act in the capacity of nominated counsellor should you wish to proceed, and we can bring someone in to work with you and help you through this process. However the information you uncover doesn't just involve you but your twin. I strongly suggest you need to talk to him or her about what you intend to do, as well as the parents who adopted you. This is a big step to take, so just have a good long think about the impact it may have.'

Eenayah looked as if she was still in shock, as though this request had taken her by surprise as much as it had Mercy. This had come at her out of the blue.

'What do I do now?' she asked.

Mercy handed her a form to complete. 'I will give you the same advice my father gives to people he helps with genealogy research – go seek out the living. You need to talk to your present family, the parents who adopted you. Tell them what you intend to do and ask them questions. Here is my card. Call me or email me back with more details, but please do involve your twin, as this affects them equally and you need sibling buy-in.'

Mercy picked up the phone and dialled Kerry in reception. 'Kerry, can you bring the adoption forms into the Professor's office please as well as an authorisation contract?' Within a few short moments Kerry entered the office, bringing Eenayah a cup of tea, as though she understood the dynamics of the conversation had changed and to the English a cup of tea was always offered in a possible crisis situation or to calm the nerves. Eenayah was of course English, and the meaning behind the gesture did not go unnoticed.

Eenayah looked as though she wasn't quite ready to terminate the conversation merely by completing some paper forms. Again, Mercy picked up on her body language. 'Is there something else I can help you with Eenayah?'

Eenayah felt quite coy and uncertain about broaching her next request, but Mercy had given her some confidence in the ability of MeDeVe to handle any situation, so she felt brave enough to proceed with what amounted to a mini-confessional.

'Mercy, I don't know how to ask this, so let me explain my situation first. Many years ago I suffered a personal crisis and it had a lasting effect on me. I became scared of going out, and well… I live in a huge mansion in Miami with security guards and I have people who do everything for me, so I don't even have a need to go out any more. I am not sure why, but I don't want to live this life any more. My twin often jokes that I am a prisoner in paradise, and honestly, this is how it is beginning to feel. I decided to come to the UK to reconnect with family and old friends. Of course I also wanted to meet the Professor to engage him for my husband's book and family tree research. However, it has taken a lot of bravery for me to even step on a plane and be here on my own. I know this must sound crazy to a confident person like you Mercy, but this is the reality I have to live with.'

Yet again, Mercy was surprised. Eenayah Baratolli was delivering shockwave after shockwave this morning.

'Does your husband Reed know you are in the UK?'

'I don't think so, not yet. I have been trying to call him over the weekend, but he hasn't picked up and he hardly bothers reading my texts. I don't think he would be happy about me being here though. He worries about my safety and he's always keen to keep me at home. He will be in London soon, so I intend to surprise him, but I'm not sure he will be happy to see me.' She took yet another sip of water. 'I feel very vulnerable on my own, Mercy. Reed keeps telling me that I am at risk of kidnap because he has so much money and people could snatch me and then demand a ransom.'

'We do offer protection services. Do you want us to provide a bodyguard?'

Eenayah floundered. 'I am really not sure. Part of me wanted to leave Miami so I could grow up, learn to take risks, become independent and find a way to cope with life on my own. If I have a bodyguard around me 24/7, it will be no different to being back in

Miami where I have people watching my every move. I want to break free from all of that.'

Mercy often had to deal with clients in heightened stages of emotion, and knew the exact time when it was right to be warm, personable and comforting.

'I think I may have the perfect solution for you. I will give you a tracker device. It just looks like a normal watch and you can deactivate it if you don't want us to know where you are. Zac can set it up for you and it can only be deactivated by your voice. If you need help and want us to send a bodyguard out to you, all you do is press a button or say a pre-programmed code word. Some of our people can parachute from helicopters to any remote location at a moment's notice. Likewise, you can always just pick the phone up to me if you are feeling nervous. Does this sound like a good half way solution?'

Eenayah was delighted. This sounded perfect.

'How do I pay you for this?'

'A minor detail. Kerry will sort you out with an account and you just get billed for the watch and any occasions you need assistance. If you never need assistance, there are no charges.'

'Yes please Mercy. Thank you for seeing me. I feel so much better now.'

'Eenayah, I do apologise but I have do have to leave for my next meeting now. Kerry will help you complete these forms and will guide you through the contract process and our various charges. Zac will also set you up with a watch. You can stay here as long as you like. If the Professor finds his way here in the meantime all well and good, but whatever… please don't feel you have to rush out.'

Mercy was indeed a total professional and her attention to customer service was something that cascaded down throughout the whole organisation. Eenayah shook her hand. This time Mercy's handshake grip was softer, as she had come to understand the vulnerability of her new client.

'I hope you are not driving far, you look tired.' Mercy smiled thoughtfully as she turned to leave.

Eenayah had quite taken to the woman with the fiery red hair. 'No, don't worry about me Mercy,' she said. 'I'm camping out at some local hotel called the Manora or whatever, and then off to the north east tomorrow. I have a busy few weeks. I have a chauffeur waiting for me anyway, but thank you for concern. I will be in touch. It has been lovely to meet you Mercy, and please tell your father I am sorry I didn't have the pleasure to meet him on this occasion.'

Mercy walked out of the office, leaving Eenayah in the reliable hands of Kerry, who she knew would do a wonderful job of supporting her new client and was totally qualified to help her through the tedious administration process. Forty minutes later, with the task completed, Eenayah also left the office. As she walked down the stairs, Professor DeVede walked out of the lift. They had missed each other by seconds.

Mercy glanced up at the CCTV screens in her office. CCTV cameras were sited everywhere in the building and displays had also been placed liberally around the various rooms and stairwell. She saw her father on the monitor as he passed by their jointly-owned new super-rich client.

Serendipity, thought Mercy. If her father been on time for his appointment, Eenayah would have never sat and read through their company brochure. Maybe her quest to find her mother would never have materialized, or hiring MDV's protection services would never have occurred to her. More business for MDV. Maybe some things were indeed destined.

Her next client had just walked in and Mercy had to do what Mercy always had to do, which was wipe her head clean from the last encounter and give her full attention to the person walking into her office. However, before doing so, she gave Eenayah one last thought.

She liked her; she seemed to be a thoroughly nice young lady. However there was also something about her aura which made Mercy think Eenayah was actually quite lost.

She sighed and hoped that she would find whatever it was she was looking for, although she suspected that maybe that missing jigsaw puzzle piece was Eenayah herself. MeDeVe could find lost people, but not lost souls. With that final reflection, Eenayah was wiped from her mind whilst Mercy focused on her next appointment.

CHAPTER 7

Tuesday 11ᵗʰ June 2013

After an exhausting transatlantic flight and the confusion of time zone changes, Eenayah was finally drifting off to sleep in the back of her chauffeur-driven limousine. Over the last few weeks she had been suffering from a nasty recurring nightmare which had disturbed her normal sleep pattern and left her in a permanent state of tiredness. As her eyes grew heavy, she felt secure with the assurance that her husband was safe in the company of good friends. Dearest Fabien and Louisa would be sure to make Reed feel very welcome, and more importantly would steer him away from any mischief.

Knowing that she was planning some wicked fun nights out with her former student friends, did make her feel a touch hypocritical. None the less, she justified her planned evenings of merriment as medicinal. Having once suffered from depression, she knew it to be a condition that was never far away and could come knocking on her door again at any given moment. Recognising that she had been going through some strange sentiments recently, she told herself that a reminder of former carefree days might be the panacea she needed to perk her up.

Insecurity was an acquaintance she knew well, yet despite this Eenayah wasn't naturally a possessive or jealous person. She understood that her husband's choice of career equated to a wanderlust lifestyle. She also knew he was an incorrigible flirt, and that women naturally found him attractive. However, without trust, she could not maintain her marriage and so she chose to trust him. She was feeling smug that this was now her moment to party and refused to give in to any feelings of guilt. The jet lag finally left its calling card and she was lulled into a deep sleep.

***

Less than an hour later Eenayah was suddenly awoken by the tell-tale ping of a recorded message. In her exhaustion she must have slept through Jonathan's attempts to contact her. Dialling her answering machine, she recognised the husky Geordie tones of her friend Jonathan.

'Hi Babe, trust you had a good flight and got here safe and sound' the message said. 'I hope I have managed to catch you before you leave Oxford. Are you okay with a last minute change of plan, En? Just remembered that Pam is away on a hen weekend in Dublin from next Friday so I thought it would be better if we could meet up on Saturday rather than tomorrow, so we can make a weekend of it, that's if your liver is up to a weekend out on the town with the lads. I just think we will have more fun with the battle-axe out of town. Only joking - you know Pam isn't a battle-axe, whatever that means. Let me know if the change of plan is okay with you. Love you loads Enakins, and see you soon. Call me back.'

'Bugger, bugger, bugger!' exclaimed Eenayah, perhaps unintentionally cursing out loud. She didn't know what to make of this proposed change of plan. It was no secret that Jonathan idolised her, and it was also no secret that Eenayah only ever saw Jonathan as a friend. Eenayah had few close friends in her minuscule inner circle and Jon was the one person she felt she could be completely open and natural around, even though he did live on a different continent and their meetings were infrequent.

Their friendship went back a long way, having met when they were both at University in Newcastle upon Tyne in the far north east of England. Jon the student mate was fun and uninhibited in a Geordie-lad-meets-hippie convergence. Eenayah had started her university degree shortly after her fiancé James Bucklow had died in a tragic motorcycle accident during the Isle of Man TT races and she was in a fairly bad state at the time. Jonathan was the emotional crutch who had held her together during many a long sleepless night of beer and tears.

As for the 38-year-old Eenayah, now married to the famous Reed B, little had changed. Jonathan didn't care about who she was, or what infamous celebrity she was married to, or indeed where she lived or what she had in her bank account. He was just a simple bloke and a wonderful friend.

His plans for the weekend included a trip to a night club boat moored out on the River Tyne, and rudimentary as it was, he knew they would have an amazing night knocking back shots and attempting to dance on a psychedelic revolving dance floor whilst drunk. Eenayah recalled that this was difficult to do when sober, let alone when locked into a kaleidoscopic alcohol-fuelled haze. Jonathan was however also married to the ever-tolerant Pam, and between them they had a handful of children. Sexually Jon was out of bounds to Eenayah, as indeed she was to him. It was a line that had never been crossed, although it had occasionally been teetered upon.

Reed had never had any concerns about his wife's relationship with Jonathan. In reality, how could he complain? He had more freedom than most married men could ever dream about and Reed always (with a degree of self-interest) laboured on the point that trust equalled freedom. Eenayah often suspected that Pam was not quite as liberal and maybe had her concerns. However Pam tolerated this friendship with confidence, mainly because she knew Eenayah would never risk her marriage to her handsome superstar music mogul for Pam's bohemian scruffy horticulturist husband. So each spouse for their own reasons turned a blind eye, and neither viewed Eenayah and Jonathan's friendship as a threat.

However, neither Pam nor Reed ever realised that it exasperated Eenayah that Jon just couldn't take the hint about them being 'just friends.' Ruby would always joke with her about the film *When Harry met Sally* when referring to Jonathan. It was frustrating to Eenayah that no matter how many times she tried to clip Jonathan's wings he always held out one last hope that maybe one day he could get her into his bed. He had promised not to do this again, and yet here he was. She was exasperated and annoyed. They were supposed to meet Thursday night and all go out on the town together, Eenayah, Jonathan and his wife Pam. A very safe conventional threesome. Then she would fly back to London to meet up with Reed whenever he had finished with the Paris final round of his talent scouting expedition.

Suddenly and at the last minute, Jon wanted to delay the night out until his wife was safely tucked away on a plane to Ireland and strolling with the hens down the Temple Bar. Eenayah was uneasy with this suggestion. She wanted to see Jonathan badly, but she didn't want to be put under any type of pressure and without Pam around, she couldn't be sure of this. With a bit too much to drink and all the fun of the fair, it could be too much of a temptation. Eenayah also recognised her own vulnerability, and with many weeks of separation from Reed, she was craving attention and affection. Maybe this was a dangerous cocktail and best avoided. Her mind was too confused at the moment.

Decisions decisions. What to do? Darn it and blast it; she had been so looking forward to a wild party night out in her old university town and just letting rip, hitting the cocktails at happy hour and knowing nobody recognised her and nobody cared. All she had really wanted was to revisit her youth, and not revisit the relationship of her youth. She sighed and whispered to herself, 'Ah well, shame. I needed this time out, but it feels dangerous.' She raised her voice. 'Driver, can you turn around please?'

Surprised and slightly taken aback, he responded, 'erm err... yes mam. Where to?'

'Back to London please driver, and my apartment in Mayfair probably. I will confirm in a moment.' It was a very matter-of-fact instruction, something rare for Eenayah, but she felt too distracted to be overly friendly.

Eenayah texted Jonathan back. She was too displeased to actually talk with him in person.

'Got your message. Very disappointed Jon, as was on my way over. Just turned car back to London and will let you know about the weekend. I am not sure can make it now - will see how things work out. Reed is due back in the UK soon so need to check his dates with Arabella. Let me think about it. Eenayah.'

Yes she was disappointed, but no matter. She could use the time to catch up with Ruby and Reed instead. Delaying this reunion might just be the better plan. Eenayah decided she should focus on the people who mattered the most: her sister and her husband. Jonathan was after all a toy for her to play with, and maybe one best avoided, given the circumstances.

She sent her sister Ruby a text message. 'Hey sis, are you free for a get together anytime this week?' Ruby called her right back. 'Eenayah!' she screeched down the phone. 'Are you in London? You are in London aren't you? When did you land?' She couldn't hide her excitement. She hadn't seen Eenayah in a long time, too long.

Eenayah lied. How could she tell her twin sister the truth and admit that she had actually landed on Sunday and has been in the UK for two days now? How would Ruby feel knowing that Eenayah was only getting in touch because all her plans had changed at the last minute and now she was at a loose end? There was no way she could be so honest and direct without also being highly insulting. And so just like her friend Fabien, who took a well-intentioned diversion from the truth when talking to her, Eenayah did the same thing when talking to her twin.

'Yes, just landed at Heathrow', she lied. Sometimes when the truth was ugly, a lie could be the kinder alternative.

The sisters continued to have a long, light-hearted and cheerful conversation. Eenayah had not felt this relaxed in a long time. Just the sound of her twin's voice rejuvenated her, and the recent disappointment around Jonathan's not-so-hidden agenda faded into a distant memory.

Eenayah larked around on the phone. 'So Ruby, Ruby, Ruby! Seems like you are working in London far from your Welsh mountains and I am to be a tourist in London far from my swimming pool. So when can I drag you away from that desk of yours and tempt you with the five Cs – champagne, calories, carbohydrates, conversation and of course my wonderful company?'

Ruby was exhilarated by the thought of her twin being in the same city as her for once, but she asked, 'What about Reed? When are you going to meet up with that delicious long-lost husband of yours?'

Eenayah considered the question for a moment, wondering quite how she was going to juggle seeing Ruby with reuniting with Reed, itinerary permitting. She had now taken on board the extra commitment of finding their birth parents, plus she couldn't leave without a visit to the family farm on the Isle of Man. On top of this was a potential party weekend with Jonathan which might or might not happen. She reflected on how bored she had been back in Miami, while now in England she felt weighed down with the stress of having too much to do, with too many people and in too many places. She had forgotten what it was like to multi-task between commitments, but part of her was enjoying this new-found stress.

At last she responded to her sister's question.

'I need to sort something out with Arabella. He will be in London soon, but I just need to find out exactly when. Right now I have no idea when I will see him next.'

Ruby detected a tone of indifference in her sister's voice. It shocked her, but she did not want to explore things any further over the phone. Face to face was always the conversation platform of choice for sibling interrogations and responding confessionals.

Eenayah continued, 'Reed has been in France with some promising young wannabee as part of this bloody global talent tour pile of crap. Thankfully I am told he has been with Fabien most of the time in France, so not too many late nights in Paris night clubs, I hope. However, I am informed that musicians work on a different time zone, Ruby, late to bed and late to wake. It's okay. don't worry, I am used to it. Reed never knows the date or time. It's just the way it is.'

But Ruby was worried. Eenayah seemed to be changing. Her tone of voice, although she was clearly elated and madly excited to be in England, was remote and detached. She recognised that she needed to have a long talk with Eenayah sometime soon. She had to get to the root of whatever it was that was going on inside her head.

Ruby made a considered proposal. 'Eenayah, there's a lovely place I often take my VIP clients to because it's quiet and secluded. It's called the Flower Room, in Knightsbridge. Your driver should be able to find it. It's posh but not stuck up and the food is great. The main thing is that it's very discreet and private and some celebs use it when they want seclusion. Folks passing by can't just walk off the street and get a table, you need to be a member. I guess it's like a private club. I am a member, so I don't go on a waiting list. Let me book us a table for tomorrow and I'll text you an address and time. That way you can feed me vodka through a straw and we can have a sisterly catch-up. Does that sound good?'

Eenayah didn't have to consider this for long. The response came back fairly rapidly. 'Sounds perfect, it will give me time to potter around and do some shopping later on today. Just text me the details and I'll be there. I really can't wait. Love you Ruby! I have so missed you.'

Eenayah was now happy that Jonathan had cancelled. Meeting up with Ruby was a much better plan.

CHAPTER 8

Wednesday 12th June 2013

Eenayah felt like an animated schoolgirl as she walked into the Flower Room, and was instantly pleased with her sister's choice of meeting place. The reception was ornate and overstated, with six-foot-high copper statues of sunflowers and, unusually, delicate sweet peas climbing up the walls, their pastel shades illuminated by discreet uplighting. She was shown into a Moroccan-style seating area, designed to make guests feel comfortable prior to being seated. Soft delicate oriental incense wafted through the air, and it reminded Eenayah of a shisha bar she had been to in Egypt a few years back. Discreetly placed hubbly bubbly pipes were casually available for anyone wishing to partake, and the smell of mandarin and peaches diffused from the large hookah placed next to her sofa. She nibbled on the rose-flavoured Turkish delights and sipped her Mor-Chilcano whilst anxiously awaiting her twin.

She didn't have too long a wait, as within minutes the ever-enthhusiastic Ruby came dashing into the waiting lounge as though she had been rushing around all day and was struggling to climb down from her high octane work mode.

'Wow, look at Mrs Businesswoman!' screamed Eenayah as the sisters fell into each other's arms. They clung on to each other for minutes that seemed like an eternity. Even when they let go, they couldn't stop staring directly at each other as though checking out the reality.

The waiter kept a discreet distance, and then when appropriate led the two raucous young ladies to their table. Eenayah looked around and gasped. 'I have been to some amazing and wonderful restaurants in my life Ruby, but never to anything as unusual and wonderful as this place' she said. 'You have great taste Mrs Sales Director.' She had recently found out about Ruby's promotion.

The eatery was designed to be like one giant conservatory, perhaps like a modern version of the old Victorian orangeries built on the estates of the aristocrats. However, as discretion was the name of the game here, all the huge floor-to-ceiling windows were made from one-way security glass so the diners could 'people watch' and spy on the street outside, while nobody on the street could peer into the restaurant to watch them. It all felt one-sided and quite voyeuristic and nosey.

At the centre of the dining area was a contemporary waterfall consisting of multiple small marble balls which cascaded lavender-tinted and scented water onto larger and larger marble mounds as it descended downwards. The entire piece perfectly matched the marble floors, so that at a distance the onlooker could not tell where the floor ended and the waterfall began.

However the most breath-taking aspect to all of this was the flowers. They were everywhere. On the sisters' table the centrepiece consisted of pure white Japanese anemone mixed with a couple of flushed Singapore orchids and just a few stalks of gomphrena to add a tease of yet more perfume to the simple display. Each of the twenty or so tables had a completely different arrangement. The collective combined scents from all the many flowers was exquisite and heavenly.

'Surreal' gasped Eenayah, failing to find any other words for the fantasy setting she now found herself in. She was indeed enthralled. It took a great deal to impress the wealthy and much travelled Eenayah, but this small and unexpected piece of paradise in the middle of Kensington London was hitting some long-hidden nerve.

She noted that jungle flora-like plants were strategically placed, with ferns, palm trees and tropical grasses positioned at such angles as to give most tables an element of welcome privacy. Yes indeed, this was a place you could go to eat, drink, flirt and remain quite literally undercover. Eenayah could understand the celebrity attraction of not being an attraction. For a moment she considered the irony of those who had devoted so much time to seeking fame, then an equal amount of time shunning it. Her own husband fell under that heading, she understood the paradox well.

The sisters had much catching up to do, both wanting to do the asking rather than the answering. Eenayah got in first, ordering Dom Perignon to toast her sister's new promotion to Sales Director. Chinking Ruby's glass, she said, 'I can't believe it. I got better grades at school than you did Rubes, and here you are all successful and here am I, an unemployed Miami airhead. I am so proud of you Ruby.' At that they raised their chilled glasses to toast Ruby's new position, and gulped the contents down in one like giddy teenagers.

The conversation moved on to Ruby's recently completed renovation project with her antiquated and listed Welsh manor house.

'That place drank up so much money, sis' reflected Ruby. 'Trust me, this career chase of mine has been less to do with ambition and more to do with affording a new slate roof and lead guttering. Still, it makes for an interesting life. You need to come and visit. Walking through Darwydden Castle Manor is like walking through history. Honestly, I exaggerate not. The front door is the entrance to a former 11th century castle gatehouse, the only bit of the castle that survived

SHEILA MUGHAL

when the English bombarded it. By the time you reach the lounge you get to be circa Middle Ages and then you finally end up in the Georgian kitchen. It's just been added onto through the ages with each family and each era leaving its mark. You really must come and stay. It really is very unusual and it's not haunted - honestly I promise.' She added with a grin, 'Well, maybe there is residual energy from the past, but all the ghosts have a head in situ so nothing too scary.'

The sisters continued to chatter as though there wasn't enough time left in the day to exchange information. Although they talked by phone once a week, somehow a face-to-face meeting was more intimate, and they constantly felt they had yet more to say.

Competing for talking space, neither of them paid much attention to eating their first course. Ruby asked, 'And how are Armani and Asher and Konnor?' These were Reed's children from his first marriage.

Eenayah was nothing at all like the wicked stepmother from the fairy tales. She adored her stepchildren and had been the most perfect of replacement mother figures, treating all of them as her own. She had convinced herself that she never needed or craved her own children, and as far as she was concerned she already had a ready-made family.

She replied, 'Hey you know, they are great. The older two have finished college now and Konnor is holidaying with Reed's parents in Colorado at the moment. They are amazing kids and they have very privileged lives, but after losing their mother it's only what they all deserve.'

Ruby was impressed that despite the tragic and scandalous death of Reed's first wife, Eenayah never bitched about it and was only ever compassionate and considerate. Ruby admired her sister for her dignity and compassion.

Ironically, they both ducked and dived around the more serious

100

subjects they each really wanted to talk about. Maybe in truth neither of them wanted to ruin the reunion. It was a special moment in a special place, and they were both enjoying that space in time. Neither wanted to pop this lovely bubble.

Not wanting to spoil the moment, Eenayah avoided telling Ruby that she had commissioned someone to trace their unknown birth mother, and Ruby avoided asking Eenayah about her strange marital situation with Reed, or what exactly were these deeply-hidden and secretive loose ends that she needed to tie up in the UK. Plus for the moment, Jonathan was very much off the menu of discussion. Eenayah didn't seem in a hurry to leave the UK any time soon and they were both sure there would be other 'catch up 'moments in store. As such any serious conversation was parked up for another day, and they stuck to superficial chatter.

Ruby was about to venture onto the subject of their up-and-coming Florida vacation when a business call interrupted their conversation. The planned vacation had been the prime subject for debate in the Kyfinn household ever since Owyn had found out a trip to Miami was on the cards. However Ruby's boss was on the line, the call was important and for now the conversation stalled.

She apologised to her sister. 'Sorry Eenayah, I need to take this call. I need to go somewhere quiet, but I won't be long I promise', and with that she went back into full-on commercial mode. Blowing her sister a kiss, she disappeared back into the Moroccan lounge for an important and all-consuming conversation with the new CEO.

Ruby rushed out mid-conversation, leaving Eenayah momentarily sitting alone among the luxuriant foliage. She hummed some silly old tune to herself as she scrolled through the emails on her phone. Although it was June in London, it was a rainy summer day with a strong hint of a breeze. Eenayah unsympathetically enjoyed the sight of passing strangers through the secrecy windows, each fighting the wind with their umbrellas. It was quite humorous entertainment, as some won and others lost the battle of the elements. It made her giggle. 'English people and umbrellas!' she jested.

It was then that a woman suddenly came into view on the street outside who stood out from the rest of the crowd. Everyone else seemed to be wearing mundane shades of brown, black and grey, but this woman was beaming like a neon light. She was dressed in a brilliant red suit, but not the sort of serious business suit Ruby would wear. This was a suit designed to seduce, with a skirt raised to upper thigh level and targeted to show maximum leg. Indeed she had legs worth showing, long and thin like a Barbie doll's. She had long straight white-blond hair which cascaded below her waist. She walked with confident long strides, with an air of self-importance. Neither the wind nor the rain could create a smear on this lady's perfect presentation. Indeed the raindrops appeared to be avoiding her.

Eenayah sensed that this woman in red was here for a reason, and that somehow that reason involved her. She did not know how she knew; some primeval instinct maybe. The woman in red was coming into this restaurant and would be passing by Eenayah very soon. All she had to do was wait. This was a woman with a purpose.

She didn't have to wait long. The lady in red swept past her, leaving a perfumed trail of Shalini in her wake, and was escorted to a nearby table by a waiter who seemed to know her. Eenayah didn't recognise her, but none the less she was curious. She had a confident assurance about her that she had rarely witnessed before, and Eenayah had met her fair share of divas in her time as the wife of a show business celeb.

Within minutes the woman was joined by a man. He kissed her on each cheek and then sat down opposite her.

Eenayah was for a moment frozen to her seat and could do nothing but stare. She was transfixed, paralyzed and confused. Time stood still. The man who had just passed within inches of her was

Reed; the man she had been married to for ten years. The man whose children referred to her as Mom. Yet, Reed hadn't even noticed her sitting there. It was as though she didn't exist. He had been totally focused on the woman in red, and had seen nothing but the blonde target immediately ahead of him, whom he had located with missile precision. Eenayah must have been just an invisible blot.

Eenayah composed herself; after all, she wasn't the jealous type. Her husband owned a record label and was a well-known and prolific song writer and musician. By default he mixed with many young talented attractive people and had dinner meetings with them all the time, and besides, she trusted him. Didn't she? However, his PA, Arabella, had informed her that he was going to stay with Fabien in Paris for a few days and fly into London at the weekend. Why had his plans changed? Why had he not told her? But why should that surprise her anyway? Reed didn't tell her much about anything these days.

Eenayah was perplexed. She knew she should be okay with this situation, but it just didn't feel right and the woman in red didn't look like a musician or manager or promoter. Trying to find some sort of logic in her brain, she told herself that maybe she was a PR agent. However she also knew that Reed had a whole lower level of hierarchy below him to perform menial tasks such as meetings with PR reps.

Having not been in the same country - let alone the same room - as Reed for many weeks, she found the fact that he was now in the same restaurant as herself an unbelievable coincidence. Should she read anything into this, or had Arabella given her the wrong information? She was totally confused. Maybe he had instructed his PA to lie, or maybe Arabella just got the dates wrong. Would a highly-paid PA such as Arabella do something so stupid? Her mind was turning circles, rationality being replaced by imagination.

She was aware that her relationship with Reed had been remote recently. They hadn't had any blow outs or major disputes, it was just that they lacked closeness and intimacy and had spent about six weeks on different continents. Just a blip due to work pressures and distance, she had presumed. She knew Reed's stance on fidelity and she never had reason to doubt him -until the woman in red had walked in, that is.

Eenayah had no concept of how long she had been sitting there mulling over scenarios in her mind, when the slightest of actions created a whirlwind in her thoughts. Reed made one simple gesture; he took the hand of the unidentified woman and he affectionately gently caressed her knuckles with his thumb in circular motions for just a few seconds. That was it! There was nothing more than that; but that was enough for Eenayah.

She mentally debated that should a touchy-feely person caress knuckles, this might well be normal behaviour. However Reed wasn't a demonstrative sort of person and the lady in red sure as hell wasn't a relative and so this fell out of any parameters of normal. That whole knuckle thing just wasn't right.

By the time Ruby had come back from her business call, Eenayah had more or less mentally convicted Reed of having an affair. She sat at the table stony faced and in shock. Ruby recognised the change in her look and demeanour instantly and started to interrogate her sister to find out what the heck had spun the earth off its axis in just her 20 minutes' absence. Eenayah simply pointed her long, manicured bejewelled finger in the direction of Reed's table and his striking blond companion.

The reunion bubble was lovely while it lasted. They had enjoyed sisterly affection and joy in this place of beautiful blossoms and perfume. However the lady in red popped that bubble the moment she entered the room. Sweet while it lasted, but now the moment had gone.

Eenayah pleaded, and this wasn't something she often did.

'Ruby, you are the sales person here and you have always told me how good sales people are at reading body language and how you have this superior instinct going on.' Ruby felt a request working its way up.

'Erm yes, I guess that's right,' she said.

Eenayah continued, 'I can't do this Ruby'. With her head bowed down and her eyes shut tight, she fell silent. There were no more words. She didn't need to speak. She didn't need to ask. They were twins, and sometimes words were not required.

Ruby opened up her handbag and handed Eenayah her debit card. 'This treat is on me babe, and it's my way of celebrating my promotion and welcoming my sister back home to England. You know my PIN code, it's the one I always use. Now go pay the bill and grab your coat and wait for me by the hubbly bubbly things. This won't take long.' Eenayah did exactly as she was told, much relieved that Ruby had assumed control.

Ruby walked over to their table. She noticed that they both had one hand on the table directed towards each other, almost indiscernibly touching from the tips of their fingers. Reed looked up at the tall figure looking down on him and immediately removed his hand from the table. As recognition hit home, he stood up.

'Oh my God, Ruby!' He looked her up and down with an astonished yet pleased expression. 'Wow, you look amazing! The last time I saw you, you were in shabby jeans milking goats on a farm and now look at you – all Dior and business woman.'

The lady in red looked less than pleased with this interruption. Ruby looked at her contemptuously, thinking *see how you like it having your bubble burst, bitch*. Maybe she was simply siding with her sister and assuming a protective role, but intuitively she didn't like the woman in red.

Reed was in a hurry to get introductions over and done with, maybe to legitimise his liaison, thought Ruby, who was also now suspicious of the situation. Reed continued, 'Erm Ruby, this is Emmanuelle. She is the mother of my little French superstar in the making, and Emmanuelle, this is my…. erm… and this is Ruby.'

Both women shook hands and exchanged cold, icy stares. It did not go unnoticed that Reed was about to say 'this is my sister in law' and then retracted quickly from the statement. Neither did it go unnoticed that he wasn't wearing his wedding ring.

Ruby was determined to find out more, so uninvited she pulled up a chair to join them, even though the waiter was now placing their steaming hot plates out in front of them and it was awfully rude of her to interrupt their dinner. She held out a hand to shake the frosty, thin hand of the woman in red. Sarcastically she responded, 'nice to meet you Emmanuelle, I do believe I have watched your film.'

Reed was confused. This sarcasm and slight aggressiveness was not something he associated with Ruby, whose love of nature had always made him see her as a rural country girl type. This new Ruby person in the power suit with an acidic humour was puzzling to him.

'So, what are you doing in here?' He asked it in such a way as to suggest that Ruby's status was too low for such a posh establishment. Ruby shrugged off the question and didn't respond. 'Please don't let your meals go cold on my behalf, honestly, please go ahead and eat', she said. She knew they expected her to get up and leave at that point, but she lingered, deliberately making them feel increasingly uncomfortable by her playing gooseberry.

'Apologies Emmanuelle, but my brother in law didn't introduce me properly' she said. 'I am his wife's twin sister.' She paused and awaited a reaction, but none was forthcoming other than a sort of 'two's company but three's a crowd' awkwardness.

'So - tell me about your daughter' Ruby asked, stretching out the words deliberately to stress that she was in no particular hurry to leave. Emmanuelle broke her silence to speak for the first time, and her French accent backed up Reed's story.

'Thank you for asking Ruby. She is a lovely singer and Reed thinks she has a good chance, but she is only 15, so I try and be with her whenever I can. She is still a child.'

Almost to Ruby's irritation, this story was starting to sound genuine. She gave a look of mock captivation. 'Aww that's so sweet. What is her name? I must look out for her. I am sure if Reed has anything to do with her career she will be a massive music sensation.'

Reed interrupted, 'Her daughter's name is Océane, and thank you for the compliment Ruby. I am giving her some of my songs for her first album release, and her lovely mother is helping me convert the lyrics into French. Emmanuelle is fluent in both languages, thank God.' He laughed a little, now feeling slightly more relaxed. He continued, 'Have you any idea how difficult it is converting something that rhymes in English into something that still makes sense in another language?' Emmanuelle was also starting to loosen up, and she beamed back at Reed in a triumphant manner, as though she had won the day.

Ruby thought, you are not there yet lady, and changed the subject. 'Reed, did you know that Eenayah… your wife that is… is in England?'

Reed was taking a sip of his spinach and stilton soup as Ruby made her announcement and nearly choking on it, had little choice but to cough and spit it out. The green projectile shot across the table, landing in the perfectly-groomed golden locks of the lady in red. Emmanuelle was horrified. She uttered some expletives in French and went rushing out to the bathroom to check on the damage, cursing every step of the way. Ruby had to contain herself, although she was laughing inside.

Reed was both embarrassed and angry with Ruby's timing. 'Did you have to say that just then?' he roared at her. Ruby noted that he was more concerned about adding a few green streaks to Emmanuelle's hair than he was about the news that his wife was in the same country. She continued, not wanting to give up on the conversation quite yet.

'Eenayah would have come to find you Reed, if she knew you

were here of course, but I understand she was told that you wouldn't be in the UK for a few more days. I guess your PA isn't very good at knowing where you are these days.' There was more than a hint of cynicism in her observation.

Reed retorted with equal sarcasm, 'Well you see dear, let me explain my world to you shall I? Unlike somebody such as yourself who may go online to book a chartered flight and stand in a queue at an airport and the whole thing has to be scheduled and planned out in advance, I can be totally spontaneous.' Mocking her further, he raised his mobile phone to hammer home the point, 'and see this this device here? I simply make a phone call on speed dial and walk to the bottom of the lawn, or maybe the helipad on a hotel roof top, and a pilot just appears out of nowhere. It works differently in my world than it does in yours. So indeed my PA doesn't know everything about me, because money buys me the privilege of impulsiveness and a private plane or chopper.' He finished with a clear warning. 'Don't read things into situations that don't exist Ruby. Have you any other questions or observations dear sister in law, or can I get on with my meal now?'

Ruby felt there was nothing more to say or see in this situation; she had witnessed enough. As she got up to leave she turned and in a bland, monotone voice said, 'I will tell Eenayah you are in the UK. Hopefully now that you are in the same time zones, you can do that whole man and wife thing.' As she turned, her voice softened. 'She misses you Reed and she feels neglected. Pay her some attention, she is my sister and I worry about her - please.' Bingo, she felt she had made her point.

Reed was seething about the uninvited relationship counselling and Ruby's ill-mannered treatment of his guest. Before she left, uncharacteristically he shouted after her, 'Oh and Ruby dear; for the record I do know my wife is in England, we do communicate daily you know. Don't start mixing a bottle for me, I don't need your interference.'

Eenayah was in the reception settling the bill when the woman in red shot past her and flew into the toilets to de-green her yellow locks. Her facial expression was venomous, and an icy blast blew from her as she wafted past. She hadn't registered Eenayah as she exited, as indeed she hadn't seen her as she entered. It was as though Eenayah didn't exist. Waiting for Ruby to return from her confrontation, she recalled some words someone once told her: 'For whatever reason and by an apparent twist of fate, you may find yourself in a place you didn't expect to be and then experience a chance occurrence that could have a life changing consequence.' Who had said that? She couldn't remember.

Ruby reappeared from the jungle undergrowth and the sisters walked out onto the London pavements, which were shining and steaming as the sun warmed the wet cobbles after the recent downpour. Eenayah anxiously awaited her sister's verdict. She would trust Ruby's opinion. Ruby related the full conversation to her. Eenayah was by no means possessive, but she felt an instant dislike of Emmanuelle.

'What do you think Ruby? Gut instinct and be honest with me.'

Ruby was always candid with people. She began, 'there are two sides to this situation, sis. On the one side, I do think that they are both telling the truth. The lady in red is French, she does have a teenage daughter and Reed has signed her up to his record label and is helping launch her career. If you had a daughter as young as 15 being exposed to the showbiz world, I would imagine you would be doing exactly the same as her mother and travelling around with her. Reed is giving her some of his songs and her mother is translating the lyrics into French so the album can be released in her own country as well as English-speaking countries. I believe all of that. The daughter has quite a usual name, Océane, and I do recall reading something about her quite recently. Reed's name wasn't mentioned in the article, but some of what he told me was, and so yes, I do believe this is a genuine business relationship.'

Eenayah listened most carefully and picked up the nuances within the reply. 'So you said you thought there were two sides to the story. What is the other side, and when you said you believed this was a genuine business relationship, what do you mean by using the past tense? Is it not now?'

Ruby sighed. Her twin had asked her for her truthful opinion and she felt duty bound to give it.

'Eenayah, I have met women like Emmanuelle before, and so have you. I don't know if she is single, divorced, married – I don't think for a woman like her it matters anyway, although I suspect she is single. She is ruthless. Her type will do anything to get her daughter where she needs her to be. She will use every flash of her long legs and every wink of her false eyelashes to get what she wants. You need to realise that your husband is quite a catch to a women like her. I know you trust Reed, but in my opinion you have given him too much slack. If I was you I would pull in the reins before the woman in red gets her teeth into him, because trust me, if she hasn't done it yet I can bet he is next on the menu. Don't like her, don't trust her.'

Eenayah was losing her patience. 'You haven't really answered my question, Ruby. Yes I know about women like her, and remember that Reed was once married to one, which is why he married a woman like me. I am not asking you about Emmanuelle, I am asking you about Reed. Do you think he is having an affair? And just give me a straight opinion.'

Ruby was struggling with this answer and couldn't dress it up in daisy chains and marshmallows any longer. 'I don't know Eenayah, but if he isn't having an affair with her now, then I am guessing he soon will be. If I was you, I would be spending more time with him.' She paused. 'I suppose if you want to find out for sure, there are probably people you can hire.'

'Mercy' she whispered out loud. A strange reply, thought Ruby.

'It's okay Ruby, I have this one covered. I know who to call.'

And with that, they both jumped into Eenayah's waiting limo to carry on with their reunion celebrations somewhere else in London, they knew not where. They still had a lot of catching up to do and a bubble to rebuild. Eenayah had no idea why she found it impossible to approach her husband, especially since being apart for so long; she only knew that with that woman sitting at the table, she simply couldn't remain in the same room, let alone strike up a conversation.

As the car drove off, Eenayah could swear she saw Emmanuelle staring from the window laughing even though she knew the windows were built from privacy glass. It sent a chill down her spine.

CHAPTER 9

Friday 14th June 2013

It was case conference time again at Carrington Lock and MeDeVe's Oxford offices. This was the day of the week when they looked back in unison wearing a 'lessons learned' head, and also planned for the following week's activities. The usual team were seated around a glass rectangular conference table, facing a large plasma screen mounted on a clinically stark white wall. Everyone was present except for Carman, who tended not to be invited to these sorts of meetings and in fact was seldom awake until mid-afternoon.

Item by item, they worked their way through each of their present projects. Not unlike a building programme or software implementation, each case had an assigned project manager who controlled the timelines of who worked on what, when and where. MeDeVe Ltd were exceedingly busy these days. Their books were full and staff booked out to capacity. Managing everyone's time was critical. Mercy had considered recruiting more staff, but for the time being they were just about keeping their heads above water, and besides, she had franchise ambitions which took a greater priority.

They had just finished talking about the MacDonald case and the

21-year-old boy who had gone missing whilst on holiday in Greece two years back. It had been a strange case. The boy had become involved with some extreme religious cult and had been held captive, more by brainwashing techniques than physical imprisonment. The police knew none of this, and following a fruitless investigation had more or less given up on finding him. The file had never been officially closed, but the search for Rori MacDonald had hit a brick wall and more or less come to a halt.

Mercy always had at least one charity job on her caseload as she believed in such things as karma, and she had an almost superstitious principle that every corporation should do at least one act of kindness without charging. For some irrational reason she argued that this would bring them fortune and blessings. The MacDonald family didn't have the money to hire anyone like MeDeVe and the police had reached a dead end, so Mercy offered their services to the family for free. Perhaps against all the odds, maybe due to a scattering of luck but mostly due to the tenacity and competence of her team, MeDeVe were on the verge of solving the case.

If there was any truth behind the karmic philosophy, then indeed it seemed to have brought MeDeVe good luck, as they had never been so busy. They were close to making a positive announcement to the MacDonald family soon, which in itself would be great publicity for MeDeVe once the outcome was made public. However there was more work to be done to finish off some final details, and for that Steve had to fly out to Greece. He was a key member of the team and it was a pity to lose his services abroad, but it was the only way they could close the case and bring Rori home.

Everybody at MeDeVe was elated about the positive outcome within arm's reach. However it had been complicated. The team engaged in some 'lessons learned' discussions about how to deal with religious cults should this be required elsewhere in the future. They recognised that such extreme sects were not like any other typical criminal outfit and required delicate handling. Mercy was delighted at their success. She felt it gave her company yet another specialist notch in the bedpost which could be added to the company's portfolio of skill sets.

Next on the list came the Baratolli case, or to be more accurate, cases. This was an unusual situation for MeDeVe, as Eenayah had contracted them for four differing services, something a client had never done before.

The first of these was the family history book for her husband's 50th birthday. This did not involve Mercy's team, as it was the Professor's domain. None the less, the team had been made aware of the Professor's genealogy project and given the short time frame to complete this work, they were requested to assist him, should this be required. It was also possible that Mrs Baratolli could phone or call into the offices at any time, so the team were reminded to report such conversations. Mercy considered it vital that all her staff had a heads-up on all live projects, whether it involved them or not.

The second assignment was that of tracing Eenayah's birth mother. Don had been allocated the title of project lead, because in essence research was what Don did best. He had recently submitted the application giving his own name as the nominated counsellor. It was too early to have received anything back as yet, but Don hoped there would be something to report back next week. It was recognised that part of this research might overlap with the Professor's undertaking, so Kerry shaded in dates on her project planner to indicate an overlay. The proficiency of the company was such that all possible time allocated was accounted for.

The third requirement of Mrs Baratolli was that of protection services. Mercy explained that Eenayah did not want a bodyguard as such, but as a woman on her own and far from home, she was vulnerable. Also, taking into account that she was the wife of a famous and wealthy man, there could be a kidnapping risk. Mercy explained that she had persuaded Eenayah to wear one of MeDeVe's tracking watches, so she could at least call for help if required.

Mercy asked Kerry to indicate where Eenayah was going to be in the coming week, should there be a need to move quickly. Kerry flicked proficiently through the papers in the Baratolli file and then answered, 'She did put down that she planned to be in Newcastle this weekend.'

Mercy seemed concerned. 'Lilly, Kerry, hopefully you have both had an opportunity to look at Mrs Baratolli's personal history in some depth. What is her connection with Newcastle?'

The ever-competitive Kerry hurried to beat Lilly to the answer, quite pleased with the speed of her own response.

'She went to university there Mercy.'

'Great. To me that means she is meeting former student friends, drinking lots of alcohol, having a night out in an infamous party town and the possibility of our client drowning in the River Tyne. JD, if need be, how quickly could you get from Oxford to Newcastle should Eenayah push the button?'

JD gave it some thought. 'Realistically, even if I flew out, given taxi time it would still be 45 minutes absolute minimum.'

'Did you have any plans for this evening JD?'

'Just a gym session and then watching football on the TV.'

'Any chance you could book a hotel in Newcastle with a gym and watch the football in the hotel lobby?'

JD was single. He had no personal attachments, and work came first. 'Yes of course Mercy,' he replied.

Zac was playing around with the tracking software on his PC and interrupted the conversation. 'Sorry to be a party pooper, but according to the tracker, Mrs Baratolli is in central London.'

Mercy rephrased her request. 'JD, Any chance you could book a hotel in central London with a gym and watch the football in the hotel lobby?'

'Yes of course Mercy.'

'That's settled then. Thanks JD. We have an open account with Mrs Baratolli and we invoice her for any work we feel is necessary. Although she wants her freedom and privacy and we must respect that, we also need to be able to respond quickly if she runs into trouble. JD, I am not asking you to tail her as she hasn't asked for that service, but just stay close, huh? Zac, well done on updating us on her location. Can you keep us all up to speed on her logistics on a daily basis? She sounds to me like a lady who says one thing and does another. She is on vacation and entitled to be impulsive, but we need to monitor her. Is that okay for everyone?' They all nodded in agreement.

The final project was unexpected and a shock to everyone. It was standard practice at these meetings that Kerry issued everyone with an agenda the day before, and if it was a new client she would also give them a summary brief which toplined the nature of the case. Of course all the team knew of Reed Baratolli, but there were a few dropped jaws and stunned silences when they heard that Eenayah was considering commissioning MeDeVe Ltd to spy on her husband. Allegedly she suspected him of cheating on her. They were all briefed that a non-disclosure had been requested by Eenayah's lawyer, and each had to sign up for a vow of silence.

The group were all experienced in this sort of work, and for them it was usually a standard typical PD surveillance job. Catching a cheating partner was normally quite simple and easy for a team so well qualified. However, they also realised that this simplicity changed when the target was an astute celebrity who treasured his privacy.

Eenayah had raised the benchmark by offering MeDeVe a considerable hike on their usual fee, plus bonuses for an outcome that could be proven, one way of the other. Mercy would normally have put her most experienced PD on the case, if Steve hadn't been needed in Greece. As such, Mercy assigned Lilly as the project manager should they accept the job. They hadn't agreed to Eenayah's request as yet and so a team decision would be reached this morning around the table. Mercy encouraged a democracy, until that is, she had the final say.

Although Lilly was fairly new to MeDeVe and hadn't worked as a PM before, she did understand the world of celebrity, more so than anybody else in the room. In her former days as a paparazzi photographer she had occasionally mingled in the same social circuits as Eenayah, who had once been a journalist for a gossipy tabloid paper. They hadn't been formally introduced, but occasionally applied lipstick at the same mirror in the same night club. Lilly had even met Reed a few times at showbiz parties. Mercy needed someone controlling this who knew the prominent and crazy world they both lived in. Lilly was delighted with the challenge and had done a great deal of background work to impress her boss for her first PM presentation.

Lilly attached her laptop to the projector screen and the first thing to flash up on slide 1 of her PowerPoint was the photographs of six different men numbered 1 to 6. She asked everyone around the table to raise their hands when she shouted out the number representing the image of Reed Baratolli. She began – 1, 2, 3, 4, 5, 6… Nobody in the room selected the right person, which was exactly what Lilly expected, and she was relieved that her experiment worked. Mercy was impressed.

She began, 'Interesting that most of you selected number 4, I guess because he has the deepest sun tan and the most expensive clothes and perhaps you expect Reed Baratolli to always be lying on a Caribbean beach like a multimillionaire.' She paused and awaited a reaction, but none was forthcoming so she continued, 'Reed Baratolli is actually man number 5; he who has the whitest skin of all these guys. He is a musician, a songwriter, a record producer and the owner of a record label, Great Music Ltd. He works long hours and most of that is inside, not outside, probably with low lighting and lots of strong coffee. He also still sees himself as a bit of a rock star. Music is the world he mingles in and he dresses to fit in with that world.

'So why did you guys all put him in a Savile Row Desmond Merrion suit? Reed wears torn skinny jeans with whatever top he can find from the night before, and he has tattoos on both arms and just about everywhere else. We all, and I include myself in this statement, need to drop expectations of what you think he is and just look at what he actually is. He is a middle-aged music icon still trying to act young, but having said that he is still fairly handsome and addicted to his art with a passion that is admirable yet egotistical. That my dearest colleagues is Reed Baratolli.

'Just to add to that' - she paused for a few moments as though casting her mind back to a distant memory - 'Mercy always stresses the fact that we gather evidence and not opinions. I once knew of Reed vaguely and to be fair my impression of him was that he was a total slimeball who chased anything with an XX chromosome, but that was long ago after his first wife died with her lover by her side and possibly before he married Eenayah. So I am keeping my personal prejudice to one side. Should any of the team ever have read anything derogatory about Reed which could distort this case, can you do likewise and park it for now? If we do accept this job, we need to do so with an open mind and without prejudice.'

Mercy smiled; she liked the way this was going. Lilly had put together an excellent outline of Reed B, ageing musician.

Lilly continued, flicking onto the second slide so everyone now had a close-up view of Reed's face.

'The other thing I wanted to highlight by showing you all these photos is that even though everyone in this room has heard of Reed

Baratolli, not one person here really knew what he looked like. For an ex-paparazza like myself, that is worrying, because it means that Reed is very clever in NOT being photographed. Yes, he does attend award ceremonies, but not via the red carpet, but via the back stage door. He has even been known to walk out and about in disguise. This guy is a slippery eel, and that would make this job challenging.'

The team were unusually quiet. They hung onto her every word, enthralled. This was unusual for the normally mundane Friday case conferences. However in this instance, they were discussing a superstar, and this added an extra twist of lime to the day.

Lilly continued, 'If Mercy was to ask me to photograph the man next door who was cheating on his wife, I would be back in her office the next day with enough visual ammunition for her to hang his balls from the ceiling. If I am asked to photograph a celebrity who is an expert in avoiding the paparazzi, well, I'm going to put my cards on the table and say this will not be easy. There are plenty of expert photographers who once mixed in the same circle as me who would have earned enough money from a provocative shot of Reed B to pay off their mortgage. So if they haven't managed it, either he isn't doing it or he is good at doing it in secret. I am just saying that from a zoom lens perspective - this is near impossible.'

Mercy frowned. 'I get where you are coming from Lilly, but what is the solution?'

Lilly moved onto the next slide, which showed a photograph of Emmanuelle Poulain with her daughter Océane. Zak gave an appreciate wolf whistle at the sight of Emmanuelle and muttered, 'wow, can I work with the milf?'

Lilly shot him a disapproving look which cut him into quarters, and then carried on regardless. 'This lady and her daughter are not famous and not multi-millionaires, not yet anyway. The mother, Emmanuelle, and please no rude comments about her name Zak, is a

33-year-old divorcee. She is French and she is the person Eenayah suspects may be having some sort of a fling with Reed. However the challenge for us is that she is legitimately entitled to be spending a lot of time with him, because her 15-year-old daughter, pictured with her here, has just been given a lucrative record contract with Reed's label. Having a photograph of them out and about together doesn't mean they are having an affair. They have a joint business interest and they will be with each other a fair amount, now and probably for the foreseeable future. However if we get a shot of them kissing on the lips, hey that gives it a whole new sordid perspective. Just be aware that Reed is a pro and would be wise enough to avoid doing this in public, whereas Emmanuelle would not. Bottom line is, Reed and Emmanuelle spend a lot of time together – so what?'

Mercy repeated the question in the cold business-like manner which she occasionally pulled out of the voice tone closet.

'So again Lilly, can I ask what your plan is?' She was growing impatient.

Lilly answered as best she could. 'Mercy, I believe we need two photographers on this case. I am the experienced stalker with the long range zoom lens, and I should have the more difficult target of the celeb who is expert at avoiding being caught on film. The second photographer needs to go after Emmanuelle. She is the weak link, because she isn't a celeb. We don't really know much about Emmanuelle and her daughter as they seemed to come out of nowhere. I believe she came from a poor family in Toulouse, so she won't have the advantage of Reed's thirty years of fame and experience in knowing how to deal with people like us. She will be the easier catch in my estimation.'

Lilly awaited Mercy's response, but her boss just sat at the table tapping her fingers as though deep in thought. Lilly continued, 'if anyone is going to drop a clanger and make a mistake, it will be the milf lady. Simon is young and good with a camera and I can teach him a few extra tricks. I am suggesting that we assign Simon to follow Emmanuelle around. She and her daughter came from out of nowhere, but I think Simon can dig a few interesting facts up. Are you happy with that, Mercy?'

Simon grinned; he certainly looked happy with that proposal. Mercy loosened up slightly,

'Sounds like a plan, but carry on. What else have you got?' Mercy could be blunt at times, but she was the boss woman, so she could be a brusque as she liked.

Lilly clicked onto the next slide, entitled quite plainly 'CHALLENGES'. She went on, 'if we were tracking Mr Normal here, we could follow him on foot, on a bike, in a car or even on public transport. But how on earth do we ever tail a celeb who can just step into a helicopter or a private plane? How do we pursue in mid-air? I am looking at Zak here because I can only think there must be a technological answer to this. I am doubting that old time detective methods will work on this guy. Over to you Zak?'

If the company were invoicing standard charges for this detective work, Mercy, wearing her accountancy head, would possibly be calling a halt on this now. The more people she assigned to a case the more expensive it got, and once you started to apply Zak's technology then the cost usually soared through the roof. However Eenayah was paying well over the odds and the profit would easily absorb the cost, so Mercy sat there, bit her tongue and waited to see what Zak had to say.

Zak was in the zone, and indeed he was delighted to be pulled into the discussion so early. He responded with his typical slang version of English.

'Yeh, mi grees wiv Lills on this. All the follow that taxi stuff is old school. You are right Lills, specially with this famous bloke. We need to have something on the guy that goes where he goes, and if he is a typical guy then that would be his mobile phone. I need to have a think about it, but from the top of my head I would say we need the wife to get access to his mobile and handball it to us, at the very least for 10 mins or more. If we can load some tracking software on it, then that's a simps way of us knowing where he is, and bingo. Hey if we can get his SIM card and we can clone it, ding dong bonus! Then we just set up a spare phone which is an exact copy of his and read all his SMS sext messages and so on. Highly illegal and his Mrs will need to sign off responsibility for us to break the law with her permission, but it's the only sure way to track someone who is impossible to follow. Either that or I scan air traffic control and the course of his private plane and you guys just teletransport yourself in advance to track him at the other side, bit like Star trek hey!' With that he chuckled at his own fertile imagination. Zak was the teenage wannabe 'Neo' from the matrix film, and aside from letting his creativity run away with him, he always found even the most serious case quite amusing. Catching Mercy's stern impression, he went suddenly quiet, as though his mother had just scolded him.

Mercy interjected, 'the concern I have with that plan Zak, is aside from it being illegal, it also means we need Eenayah to be an accomplice in all of this, and one of the strict instructions she gave me when commissioning our company for this work is that she requested minimal participation in our planned activities. She desires to be the recipient of our investigations but not a collaborator. I doubt she would agree to sneaking her husband's phone away from him while we hide in the corridor to clone it, and as it stands at the moment, she doesn't even spend enough time alone with him to get that opportunity, let alone know where he leaves his phone when he isn't using it.'

This last comment of Mercy's created a dialogue between JD and Zak as to how they could overcome 'Mrs B's' non-participation. It ranged from having Carmen dress up as a maid offering room service (which resulted in lots a sexual banter between the guys) to JD orchestrating a break in to his hotel suite and placing cameras around Reed's hotel suite to monitor where he put his phone and the like. The two guys were getting way beyond themselves and were discussing the mission as though they were planning a bank robbery. In the end Mercy felt she had to call time out.

Mercy was a shrewd CEO who ran an ethical yet profitable operation. She understood the concept of short-term win versus long-term gain. She tried to educate all of her employees to think about results and client satisfaction first and balancing the books last; after all, get the first right and the second will follow. Usually, she was right. Mercy was also a typical entrepreneur, in that she struggled to relinquish control, so although she had given this case to Lilly to project manage, she couldn't help but step in with her own views and opinions.

To Lilly's astonishment and equal disappointment, Mercy stood up and walked to centre stage, regaining control of the situation and relegating Lilly to backstage. Lilly could do little else but stand aside and let Mercy do what Mercy did best, which was to govern and control her empire with total and regal ownership.

Mercy cleared her throat, sipped on some iced water and with a note of authority began, 'Team, we are not a company who exist to destroy lives, we have a moral responsibility to the clients we represent. This is our mantra and part of the MeDeVe mission statement. It is standard practice in cases which could be emotionally testing that we should perform a mini client synopsis. At the moment all I can hear is how we execute this plan. I haven't heard anyone mention what the outcome would be should Reed B be found guilty of cheating. How would that affect Eenayah Baratolli?'

Mercy was a genius. The team were silent in what could only be described as awe, each individually recognising that the sway of a bonus had taken control of their motivation rather than care for their client.

'Mrs B has requested that we assist her to undertake two major life-changing revelations at the same time. One is to find her birth mother and maybe any family members associated with her mother and the other is to find out if her husband has been cheating on her using just a sliver of ambiguous evidence as her reasoning. This sets alarm bells ringing in my head. If we do the wrong thing here, we could tip an unstable woman over the edge. We have a moral responsibility towards all our clients, and we all need to remember that.

'My other concern is that IF Reed is innocent and we get caught spying on him, it could well put Eenayah in an uncomfortable position. I don't know about you guys, but if a partner of mine had a private detective snooping on me, I might question if I wanted to stay in that relationship. If Reed is the expert Lilly believes him to be, he may click onto what we are doing. With such vague evidence against him, this worries me.'

Lilly was concerned that Mercy was taking a U-turn. 'Mercy, does this mean we could reject taking this case?'

Mercy pondered. 'Let me think about it, I'm not sure yet. In the meantime I asked Kerry with her formidable Internet search skills to dig up more information on Mrs B and for Don to do the tedious microfiche job lot of searching through old newspapers to see if he could find relevant news or gossip. As such, Kerry please step forward and share with us what you and Don came up with, if indeed anything?'

Lilly was furious and felt totally ousted. However Queen Mercy ruled and so with Lilly's position overthrown, Princess Lilly skulked into exile. She so hated Kerry.

Kerry, full of pride and confidence, began her report.

'On a superficial level Eenayah Baratolli may seem to us mere normal people to be the typical trophy wife, someone who married well. However, looking into her history there is another story, and ironically this lady has suffered more than most. Considering the scope of these projects and the vulnerability of our client, there are historical incidents you need to be aware of. Eenayah and her twin sister were adopted, and we are all aware of that scenario and understand what Don is doing as regards locating her birth mother. However, here is the news. Eenayah was engaged to be married when she was just 17 years old. At the age of 19 and just one week before she was due to be married, her fiancé, James, crashed his motorcycle whilst taking part in the Isle of Man TT races. He died in intensive care a week later … ironically on the exact same date and time he had been due to marry Eenayah. So tragedy of tragedies, her first future husband was killed at a tragically young age.'

Kerry hadn't made a presentation like this before and paused for feedback, but with none forthcoming and with Lilly glaring at her, she carried on. 'It took her many years to find love again, but eventually she did and about 5 or 6 years later she married a teacher called Greg. By coincidence, Greg was James' brother. Eenayah was a journalist by this time. An important news story broke and in order to cover it she needed to spend time away from home. By chance, whilst she was working away Greg contracted meningitis. It seems that when she came home she found him collapsed and in a coma behind the front door; he had been there for several days. There is a possibility that had she been at home at the time or she had found him earlier, that he might not have deteriorated so fatally. By the time she got back the illness had progressed and anyway, he died.'

A silence fell over the room. Nobody knew what to say. Lilly chipped in, trying best to regain some ground. 'Oh my god! I never ever realised that about Eenayah. I guess maybe that explains why she had such an instant deep connection with Reed - they both had the death of a spouse in common. How tragic. At the time people couldn't understand why Reed married someone like Eenayah. I guess that explains it.' Lilly hadn't meant it to sound like a bitchy comment, but that was how it came across, and just a second too late she realised it.

Kerry finalised her synopsis. 'It is fairly common knowledge that Eenayah had a nervous breakdown after Greg's death. She jumped on a plane to New York and then later accepted a job for some Californian gossip magazine. She met Reed shortly afterwards and the rest is history. My sources tell me that she has been on anti-depressants for many years and has just recently weaned herself away from them. A doctor friend of mine informs me that this could have repercussions if the withdrawal hasn't been medically monitored. Basically, she could have a relapse.'

Mercy paced up and down the floor. She walked over to the window and reflected upon the skyscape of Oxford. It was a typically lovely English day with lots of fluffy white clouds peppering a deep blue sky. She considered the money this case would earn MeDeVe, and she earnestly needed to put more money on the books to help launch her franchise plan. However she also considered the probable chance of success this case would attract. She appreciated Lilly's realistic synopsis of the surveillance challenges. The company's reputation had been built on their past achievements, and she didn't want MeDeVe to get a reputation for taking money from a vulnerable person knowing in advance they would be unlikely to turn up any evidence of significance.

She turned around to face the team to make her summation.

'JD, I cannot risk you breaking into a well-known hotel which one would presume has significant security precautions for what is basically just a marital issue. I know that you and Zak are more than able to compose an entire James Bond operation around all of this, and if we were rescuing a kidnapped child I would be in there helping you personally. But for a guy whose only sin was to rub the knuckles of a woman in a public place, it's just too big a risk.' Mercy paused yet again, as though in turmoil about what she was to say. 'So here is the deal folks. I am going to put it to Eenayah that unless she is willing to co-operate and get Reed's phone from him for around 30 minutes so we can do the whole clone and track thing, we won't be proceeding. I am not prepared to have my employees put themselves at an unreasonable level of risk for this.'

The team, especially Lilly, looked slightly disappointed, but Mercy had delivered her reasoning with logic, ethics and eloquence.

'So', continued Mercy with a slightly regretful sigh, 'now that has been decided, we need to move on. Time is short and we have plenty more to discuss and several new bad debtors to locate for the bailiffs. What's up next for discussion?'

It was dismissed as quickly as that. It was the right decision. Mercy knew it. Everyone knew it. Lilly hated it, and Kerry felt triumphant.

CHAPTER 10

Saturday 15th June 2013

Arabella answered the hotel door looking every inch like the ultimate classy Goth rock PA. She was a plain girl, but with an aura of self-assurance and excessive amounts of makeup accentuated by her long black Morticia-style hair, she carried herself very well. She gasped an exaggerated and totally false, 'Ena darleeng, so lovely to see you again', followed by a mwah-mwah cheek-dusting pretend kiss. For a girl born and raised in North Carolina, she did a very good job of imitating the English upper class.

Arabella loved being part of the whole music scene and made sure everyone she met knew exactly who she was and recognised the fame and importance of her boss. Basking in Reed's shadow, she was a minor celebrity back home in Morrisville. She didn't like or approve of Eenayah as Reed's wife and it was obvious the two women had nothing in common other than a basic toleration of each other.

Eenayah walked tentatively into Reed's hotel room suite, which as she expected had become a chaotic temporary office, meeting place, interview room, studio and anything else that was required of a working space with the luxury of room service. One of the reasons she was staying in their rented apartment rather than stay with Reed was that she knew Reed's hotel room would be anything but a peaceful bedroom to retire to at night, rather more a crowded and noisy place of work. It was one of the reasons she had stayed away from the hotel so far; that and the fact that she still felt hurt about the Flower Room intimate table encounter. She still had her suspicions about the woman in red.

As she walked down the hall into the lounge area, a sweet musty smell met her nostrils, and she rather suspected it wasn't the aroma of a scented candle causing her to cough. However she had entered Reed's world now, and few things were off limits. Music was playing loudly in the background as always. She instantly recognised the Kings of Leon song *Sex on Fire* and grimaced at the satire of the lyrics, considering her recent enforced celibate existence. With the curtains closed to blot out the blinding white daylight, a smoky haze still lingering and with last night's beer cans strewn on the floor, this looked more like a student flat share than a multi-millionaire's hotel suite. However she knew that musicians often had little appreciation of minutes, hours, days and sometimes months.

Reed walked out to greet her, looking casual and more relaxed than usual. A smile beamed from ear to ear as he looked genuinely pleased to see her. He held her warmly and kissed her forehead in a soft, brotherly way. Arabella shot them both a distasteful look, which thankfully neither of them registered.

'I am so sorry Eenayah', he whispered in a muted and comforting way, 'it's been too long, I will make it up to you I promise. It's lovely to see you, thank you for coming honey.' He then kissed her on the lips. Not with passion, but certainly with deep affection. He was mindful of his confrontation with Ruby in the Flower Room and knew that she had been sure to report the scenario to her sister. He had a lot of making up to do, and was keen to heed Ruby's words and pay his wife some attention.

Arabella interrupted the couple. 'Sorry about this R, but we need to get ready for the press meeting with Acre. The TV crew should be here in less than 30 minutes and you requested a prep session first.'

Eenayah gasped. 'Do you mean *the* Acre, is he here? Now?' She wasn't a big music fan, but like most women she loved Acre and suddenly fell into teenage girl hero worship mode.

At that moment, Acre sauntered out, looking much taller in real life than he did on TV and as one would expect, his presence sparkled brighter than a rhinestone cowboy. Eenayah's knees buckled as she resisted the temptation to beg for an autograph. Amidst this frenzy, Eenayah realised that this wasn't the time or place for a romantic reunion with her husband. All around her it seemed that a multitude of unknown people were panicking. It was chaos; make-up girls powdering faces, lighting guys pushing furniture aside, the constant 'one two, one two' of sound checks. This wasn't a hotel suite; it was a factory.

Lonely in a crowd - she knew that feeling well. How many times had she been to showbiz parties with Reed, and spent the entire evening ignored and invisible whilst everyone pandered to her husband's every whim? In the end she just stopped going. It was easier to stay at home with Roserie.

Just for a moment Eenayah stood totally still and watched as though from afar. She was in the room, and yet not really. Nobody noticed her; everyone was too busy. It was as though her world was revolving in slow motion and everyone else's world had speeded up.

Observing Reed, she could study his working life in a way she had never done before. It felt like looking into a goldfish bowl. Reed was totally in the moment and loving every minute of his crazy, frenetic job. She could easily comprehend that to him this wasn't work, but a way of life. Eenayah realised he was well respected as no matter who was doing what and where, they all seemed to refer to Reed for instruction or permission.

Arabella circulated like a mother hen trying to bring order to the bedlam, and was overly protective of her boss. Eenayah could see she was actually an excellent PA and totally proficient at her job, irrespective of the rock image she worked hard to project.

Despite many years of marriage, Eenayah still felt achingly attracted to Reed. She noted his soft brown sweaty curls huddled into the nape of his neck and the little kiss curl on his forehead which always seemed to fall in the same place no matter how he combed his hair. Despite some streaks of grey, he still had boyish good looks and in a moment's rush of hormones, she hungered to be with him, curled up naked next to his warm skin, abandoned to the moment. However, in her quiet observance of him, it was clear that he had more important things to attend to today. Pinching herself to escape the fantasy world she usually preferred to reality, she suddenly noticed some famous faces walking into and out of several doors. Acre was in the room. It still amazed her to discover the number of immensely talented and famous people who worked with her husband.

For a moment the room started to spin and she felt faint, so she decided to slip quietly away and take a walk through the streets of London. She had an urgent need for fresh air to blow out the cobwebs, maybe clear that confused head of hers. It was a lovely day, not too hot, not too cold. She just kept on walking, navigating through the tourists, casually window shopping and thinking deeply along the way. She paid little attention to where she was walking. It wasn't the destination that concerned her.

It was good to take time out to think as she considered the recent conversation she had had with Mercy about the Flower Room incident and the options she had been given as to how to proceed. It surprised her that Mercy had pushed back; after all she had bumped the fees up for her to undertake this surveillance work on Reed. On most occasions she could buy people's time instantly if she offered a higher rate than anyone else. Not this time, it seemed. However, she had also gained a new respect for Mercy, and deeply appreciated the common-sense advice which was given freely, and it seemed with good intentions. Mercy had acted almost like a counsellor, but with a business-like directness she had made it crystal clear that Eenayah would be required to participate with any subterfuge, and it was that or nothing.

Eenayah confirmed that she would not play any part in stealing Reed's phone, even for just a few moments. The risk of being caught out just seemed too big a gamble. She made the decision to wait a little longer and judge Reed's attitude to her. 'Let's see how it goes' she thought. Someone long ago had taught her that if you can't make a decision, then don't. When the time is right the answer will come, and in most part she had lived her life by that mantra.

She walked a little further along the busy main road and ended up on Westminster Bridge. Peering down onto the River Thames with a faraway look, she thought more about Reed and his work and what this meant to him and to her and the future. She longed for him to retire and spend more time not just with her, but with his wonderful children. They were all grown up now and saddest of all, Reed had missed most of their precious childhood years. There was absolutely no financial need for him to continue working, but this wasn't about money.

Her mind spun back to his crowded hotel suite and the look she had caught on his face. His eyes glistened, his face was alive, and his aura exuded exhilaration. He never wore a watch, he probably never needed or even cared to know the time or the date. He had Arabella to do his thinking for him and tell him where to be and when. If Reed was having an affair, it was probable that his mistress was music.

The reality struck home like a knife in her back; this was his life. Nothing would ever change. Even when he was lying on his death bed he would probably be composing his own funeral music with the last bit of strength he had remaining. Should it be within her power to force him to walk away from music, the chances are he would most likely resent her forever in pushing that decision. It was a sad moment of stark comprehension. She had no choice in the matter. The choice had never really been hers anyway. Reed would have to pick between her and the gypsy lifestyle of a musician, and she knew which he would choose.

She began to consider her own future. She loved Miami and the boat and all the places she could sail to. She loved the freedom that wealth could bring her. However, what use was all of this, when she was unloved and alone? She began to realise that her stepchildren had preoccupied her so much for so long and had filled so many empty spaces that she hardly noticed the vacuum in her marriage. But now that Armani was working, Asher just finishing college and off to see the world and the youngest, Konnor, now moving away to start college, the nest was empty.

She concluded that it must always be a strange, sad, and poignant time in anyone's life when they begin to reach the decision that their marriage isn't worth continuing with. Eenayah was approaching that moment. It almost didn't matter if Reed had been having a fling with Emmanuel or not. That possibility was almost irrelevant now. What did matter was that Eenayah was being subjected to an isolation which was emotionally torturing her, and she couldn't see any way of finding contentment in the future if she stayed with Reed.

Still watching the boats bob up and down on the River Thames, her mind went back to another time long ago. She hadn't thought about her first husband Greg for a long time; she tried not to. He had died in 2000, and she gasped at the thought. She remembered how they had come to London for the Millennium celebrations and stood listening to Big Ben as the clock struck midnight and the fireworks littered the sky with colours and noise. Little did they know at the time that 2000 would be Greg's last year on earth. Ever since then, New Year had always taunted Eenayah with the thought, 'and what if this was your last?' A cloud of doom and depression was beginning to settle over her head.

She tried to shake Greg's image away from her mind, but his soft, kind face continued to haunt her. As a couple they had very little money, but they did have love, romance and happiness by the bucketful, a little like Ruby and Owyn, she thought. Eenayah had been working hard to establish herself as a journalist at the time and… then the thought hit her. Was this karmic revenge for what she had done to Greg?

She recognised mournfully that maybe she had done to Greg what Reed was now doing to her. If only she hadn't been working away when Greg became ill, maybe he would have survived. Maybe they would have a couple of children by now; children that never got to be born. A tear came to her eyes. She would have loved to have had children with Reed, but after what happened with his first wife that was an option he instantly rejected.

The poignancy of considering her future with Reed on the same bridge on which she had stood with Greg a few weeks before he died was an irony Eenayah instantly recognised. Overcome by that thought and a wave of nostalgia, she started to sob, and the more she sobbed the louder it became. Strangers passing by looked concerned, but in their Englishness walked on by.

At that very moment, as if telepathically sensing the urgency of the situation, Reed called her mobile. He had noticed her missing, be it two hours after she had left, and he wanted her to come back so he could treat her to a romantic meal, just the two of them. His voice sounded anxious and concerned as he heard the sadness in her voice when she answered the phone.

Eenayah glanced up as she heard Big Ben strike 2pm. She was

tired and emotionally drained. She replied, 'I'm just going to the apartment to get a lie down Reed, I'm not feeling too well. I'll call you when I wake up and we can decide then.'

He accepted this answer happily and with some relief. 'Um okay, you get a nice sleep sweetheart and we can talk later. Bye, love you.' He could have probed more, asked more questions, maybe even tried to change her mind - but he didn't. He accepted her explanation and that was the end of that. Brief and to the point. Yet again he had been let off the hook of making an effort he didn't really want to make.

Thirteen years ago, when Greg had called Eenayah to say he had a headache and he didn't feel well, she could have probed more, asked more questions, but she hadn't. She accepted his explanation that he most probably just had the flu; and that was the end of that. That was the end of Greg.

Unbeknown to Eenayah, she was being watched. JD had come to central London simply to be in the vicinity, as per Mercy's request. Finding himself bored and at a loose end, he decided to go to the hotel where Reed was staying to see if he could glean anything whilst in the lobby. He had been surprised to see Eenayah walking out so shortly after arriving. He decided to follow her, despite Mercy instructing him that they weren't being paid to tail her. He noted her walking haphazardly through the city in no particular direction. She looked as though she was a million miles away. As she walked, he could see her frequently dab her cheeks with a white linen handkerchief. He recollected what Kerry and Mercy had said about Eenayah yesterday and her emotional state of mind. He could now see it for himself. She was crumbling before his eyes, and at one point he almost thought she was going to throw herself into the River Thames. He shuddered at the thought of what a cold, wet and dangerous rescue that would have been for him, although he would have attempted it without a moment's hesitation.

However JD noted something else, something worrying. It concerned him, and he simply had to report this back to Mercy.

In JD's years of working in the SAS in dangerous undercover situations, he had acquired a highly adept skill in surveillance techniques. He prided himself on being hard to spot. Throughout the winding, illogical walk through London, JD had noted a man who was also following Eenayah. The man wasn't as skilled as JD and his ducking and diving was easy to observe. He tried to get a photo of the man, but his skills with an iPhone camera couldn't match Lilly's paparazzi abilities. None the less, someone else had an interest in Eenayah's movements, and this was a concern.

Eenayah hailed a taxi. She was not pleased with Reed's lack of concern. She drifted back to her past experience with Greg, who had taught her to treasure every moment with the ones you love, as they may not be around forever. She wasn't sure Reed actually loved her. She thought that perhaps Reed might have also learned that same lesson, had it not become detrimentally twisted by circumstance when he learned that his dead wife was found in the mangled car next to her lover. Perhaps Reed had shut his emotions down and locked himself inside the safe world of music. Music was a mistress that would never disappoint him.

And yet, faint heart never won fair lady. She knew that if he had really wanted to he could easily have come over to her apartment and spent some personal time close to her. She knew his work with Acre was finished now and his job done for the day. He hadn't seen her in six weeks and he could have made just a bit more of an effort. It was like a nail in his coffin. He had just made the wrong move, and he didn't even know it.

Eenayah decided to go back to her penthouse flat and try to catch up on all that sleep she need so badly. She also resolved to give Jonathan a call, knowing he was all alone in Newcastle whilst his wife Pam was with her hen party friends in Dublin. Via helicopter she could easily be in Newcastle within 45 minutes, and maybe lots of partying and cocktails out on the town would lift her mood. She was seething with anger towards Reed, and starting to draw up unfair comparisons between him, Greg and James, which made the situation seem worse than it probably was.

Her mind was not quite made up about Reed, but the jury was out and the clock ticking. No longer would she be his lapdog who would come running when he clicked his fingers. As she opened the door of her apartment she thought, 'Remember the backward bye bye, Reed', and with that she slammed the door shut with immense venom.

Eenayah jumped into a red-hot shower to wash off all the city grime and the tears she so longed to be purged of. She rinsed off the sickly, musty smell of marihuana and Reed's smoky hotel suite from her hair, so as not to be reminded of him. As the water bombarded her face, the shower felt like a ritual cleansing. Naked aside from a thick white towel, she felt completely clean and pure, internally as well as externally. She dried her hair quickly, not overly concerned with how well-groomed the outcome might be. She switched off her mobile, unplugged the landline and even disconnected the wi-fi. Pressing the switch to close all the blinds and completely black out the room, she was in pitch darkness and eerie silence. There was not a sound to be heard. She didn't care that is was mid-afternoon, she just wanted to escape from reality.

She cast her clean, naked body inside soft Egyptian cotton sheets which smelled of nothing more than fresh air, and then, emotionally exhausted, she fell into the deepest of sleeps.

In her slumber, she drifted away into a surreal state. Maybe a dream, maybe a memory, maybe a reality. To begin with all she could see was a red orange colour. She didn't know what this was, until she felt the heat and knew it to be fire. The hot flames sent a surge of heat to her toes. She looked down and screamed as she saw the flames grow quickly at her feet. She was aware of being restrained, her arms tied behind her. Her fingers touched a solid pole of wood and the string bind that fastened her to it. She pulled frantically at the rope but couldn't escape, yet the flames continued to grow beneath her with menacing ferocity. She was heavy with child and she begged for mercy, pleading for her life and that of her child. She was about to die. She looked directly into the cold hazel eyes of the man who was her assassin and shrieked out a jumble of words. It was a cry for clemency, but spoken with a foreign tongue Eenayah couldn't understand.

She screamed and sat bolt upright in bed, wet with perspiration and her pulse racing. She had experienced this nightmare before, but now it was visiting her more frequently. She didn't know what it meant. The last time this had happened, she had almost jumped into Reed's skin as he lay besides her, but then she had had the luxury of his strong, soothing arms to comfort her. This time, she was alone in the blackest darkness.

Lying alone, panting for breath, eyes open as wide as they would open, every one of her senses was on high alert. She became aware that she was not alone. She could feel a presence in the room. She knew she should be terrified, but she intuitively she felt that she wasn't in any danger. In fact she was being soothed. The cool, dark room began to feel warmer, and a tiny flicker of light made its way towards her. She could sense her hand being touched. It was a warm, caring caress. There was a lovely smell aromatising the room. It was familiar, but she couldn't recall where she had come across it before. She then remembered; it was the scent of a daffodil.

She saw his face. He was right beside her, the features unusually clear despite the darkness. He was holding a daffodil. Greg was Welsh, and that had always been his favourite flower.

He whispered to her lovingly, 'You have been thinking about me today Eenayah, you have been thinking about me too much. I am worried about you.'

'Greg, Greg - is it you? What, why, how are you here?'

'Yes it is me Eenayah. I want you to be careful. Do not trust anyone. I fear you are in danger. Promise me that you will take care. You will be with me one day, so do not fret about the past. Just be careful. I love you - always will.' He faded away.

'Greg, please come back. Come back! Greg!'

He was gone. Nothing could bring him back.

Eenayah immediately flicked on a night light, and for now the nightmares, the visions, disappeared into the night.

She reasoned that she had endured a difficult emotional day and this incident had simply been her overactive mind playing tricks. She was also aware that she was withdrawing from medication, and maybe hallucinations were part of the course. Drained, fatigued, and covered in perspiration, she tried to block out the recent nightmare and unbelievably realistic vision of her ex. She pondered on how credible the vision had been. Perhaps it was time to visit the Doctor to reconsider her withdrawal programme.

Now fully awake, her mid was focused on the trip up to Newcastle for an evening of being drunk and disorderly on the streets of the northern city with her forever student friend Jonathan and his madcap pals. She smiled at the thought of the weekend to come and being with the one person who could always drag her away from any deep dark places of her past. 'Screw Reed', she mumbled to herself, 'I have my own friends, I don't need to borrow any of his.'

Flinging back the sheets, she jumped out of bed to make an espresso and run a bath. She failed to see the daffodil on the floor as she trod over it, trampling its orange pollen into the carpet. Had she done so, maybe she would have realised that Greg hadn't been a hallucination after all, and maybe she would have heeded his words.

CHAPTER 11

W/C Monday 17ᵗʰ June 2013

Looking down from a great height, she recognised the many familiar places of childhood: the school she went to, the lane she used to ride her bike down, the lake she skated on in winter and the hill she often camped out on during the endless summer holidays with Ruby and their friends from times long gone. The godlike panoramic view of the green fields, small roads and cloudy mountain peaks brought on a rush of nostalgia. At long last she was home.

Eenayah took a long, deep breath of pure contentment and fulfilment as she drank in the familiar vista. Why had she stayed away for so many years? It was a question she didn't need to answer because right now, it really didn't matter. None of the missing years counted for anything, because now she was home and back in the place she belonged.

The Isle of Man had been her little island home until she had left to go to university in the big cosmopolitan party capital of Newcastle on the English mainland. At the time she had needed to get away. There weren't enough square miles on an island to amuse the expanding social world of a teenager. It was an escape that she and her teenage lover James had planned to take together. They were too young to be married, and everyone had told them so. However with the exuberance of young love, they had both secured places at the same university at the same time and had planned to start a life there together, as man and wife. It was young love, full of adventure and ambition.

Catastrophically, their plans were destroyed by a patch of oil. James was motorbike mad. He was taking part in the island's TT races, but failed to make a turn. He came off his bike at an awkward angle and broke his back. Everything that day that could go wrong went wrong. The oil on the floor was wrong, he took the corner wrong, he fell off his bike wrong. It was as though the heavens had conspired against him. Motorbikes were his life, and motorbikes were his death.

Eenayah was heartbroken. Her family pulled together and encouraged her to carry on living. 'James would want you to carry on', her mother Ella told her. Eenayah made the journey to Newcastle alone, started university alone and met new friends on her own. Dear sweet James!

For a moment the sadness and shock came back into focus as though it was yesterday, but then she pulled herself away from the sombre thoughts of a former life and jolted her memories back into the fun-filled reality of recent times.

The sudden remembrance of her student days put a wide smile on her face, as it evoked recollections of the past weekend's activities. Newcastle was everything, if not more than, she remembered it to be. The friendly hospitality of the indigenous Geordie population was overwhelming. Jonathan pulled magical rabbits out of a hat and she was entertained for two wild, fun-filled, amazing days. She couldn't remember the last time she had laughed or drunk or danced as much. She was home and she felt young, and she wanted to scream in excitement. Eenayah was happy, and that was not often the case.

As the helicopter approached her parents' field, carefully marked out as per her instructions, she looked around among the ant-sized figures for her parents. As she caught their tiny forms from on high, she started to wave, even though she knew they couldn't yet see her. She couldn't help herself. Emotion overwhelmed her. As soon as the helicopter touched down, with the wind from the blades still creating its own mini-hurricane, she dashed across the field, throwing her designer stilettoes in the air with total disregard and running barefoot into the arms of her parents.

Her father's Range Rover bounced over the many bumps and boggy hoof holes that the cattle had left in the field, often sending her luggage flying all over the place; but that was okay. Mum was trying to talk as fast as she could, as though her voice was on steroids. She managed to condense a year's worth of questions into twenty minutes. They didn't bother with the Internet and by default any social media sites, so aside from a monthly phone call or more unusually a letter, Eenayah's parents hadn't been updated with her life. Not that there was much to update. Each year was much the same as the one before. Her stepchildren had grown bigger, she had grown older and she never saw Reed; that was about it.

Her mother had cleaned up her old bedroom in preparation, not that much needed doing aside from dusting away the cobwebs. She always kept the girls' bedrooms ready for them, just in case. Eenayah collapsed into her old bed, fun fatigue finally hitting home after a solid two days of merriment in Newcastle. The familiar smell and noises of her home acted like a lullaby, and before long she was curled up in a foetal position and deeply asleep.

Eenayah figured that she needed time out and motherly attention, so she planned to spend at least a week there. Eenayah always carried several mobile phones so she could filter callers, and aside from one they were all switched off. The 'do not disturb' sign had been activated inside her head. Eenayah is unavailable!

Her mother acted like any mother with a grown-up daughter who had left home many years previously and was now lying upstairs asleep. The apron string had been cut, but for now it was reconnected and her mother was delighted. She had spent an entire week cleaning the farmhouse spotless, and had even gone to the unusual level of having a manicure and her hair professionally styled. Ellie looked incredibly good for her age. She had been a hippy flower-power child of the sixties and ever since then had been into an ecologically-approved homeopathic existence. She had probably never consumed anything with an e-number in it, or used a frozen ready meal in a microwave. She did not even own a microwave. With hens and ducks running around the farmyard, she collected her own new-laid eggs. She had a herb garden and a vegetable patch, both of which were her pride and joy. Ellie seemed to know every herbal cure for almost any symptom, aside from a broken heart. As one would expect of an earth mother, all bread was home cooked and all beer and wine home brewed. It was Ellie who had influenced Eenayah to take up yoga, and even now her mother was remarkably trim and nimble for her age. With her rosy pink cheeks and recently-styled short grey hair, Ellie was the picture of health, in a way that perhaps only a balanced, happy life could bring.

Her father, Chris, was just a few years older than Mum, but arthritis had lessened his ability to be an active working farmer and several of his acres had been hired out to neighbouring farmers. He collected rent for allowing them to graze their cows and sheep and grow barley, maize and yellow rape. The rents were relatively small, but Eenayah had long been subsidizing her parents by sending them a monthly payment. She would have done the same for her sister, but Ruby was stubborn and refused any offers of financial help, so she broke her back working ridiculous hours to fund a massive mortgage on a dilapidated manor house.

Eenayah was awoken an hour or so later by the sound of the hire car being delivered as it made its way up the noisy shingle driveway. Time to get up from the warm fluffy bed that had just consumed her. Her mother called her from downstairs, something that hadn't happened in a long time. It was so lovely to be woken up by her mother's voice.

She had to sign the hire company's papers and show her driving licence. She hadn't actually driven herself in ages, and was quite animated by the prospect. She refused to drive on the wrong side of the road in the States and was too lazy to drive in the UK, but now, on home soil, she intended to explore the island and visit many friends and relatives. It felt liberating to be able to drive again. She was tired of being ferried around by chauffeur-driven limos. She considered this to be yet another restriction in her climate-controlled, CCTV-monitored, security-guarded life. She saw herself as a posh prisoner. To anyone else, this was just signing for a hire car. To Eenayah, it was signing up to freedom.

Her mother called her into the kitchen, where a hot bowl of bubble and squeak, leftovers from yesterday's Sunday dinner, was awaiting her with a mug of hot chocolate. Eenayah protested, 'mother, you are going to make me fat with all this food.' Her mother ignored the protest.

'You are too thin my girl, and you could do with a bit more padding, so eat up.'

Actually Eenayah was starving and with all its carbohydrates, fats and salt this was comfort food at its best. It was heaven, and she cleared her plate. As soon as she had eaten, she rushed out of the door with the keys to her hire car. Ellie knew exactly where she was going. It wasn't far from the farm, maybe five miles at most and on the more isolated west side of the island, close to the town of Peel.

As she drove around the corner of the sandy coast road, she saw the white church, old and worn but still striking against the backdrop of a brilliant cornflower-blue sky. She parked her car just off the road and walked up the well-worn pathway and through the gate into the churchyard. She hadn't been here in a long time, but she remembered exactly where to go. On the perimeter of the churchyard, with its headstones of mariners and fallen soldiers, was a granite wall. It was comfortably close to the cliff edge and not far beyond the grassy verge, but with a hazardous, sharp drop down to a cold, tempestuous sea. She could hear the waves lashing on the rocks and knew she was coming near to the spot.

One of the stones had been altered and was facing the wrong way round. It was a deliberate signal to those who knew its significance. The vestiges of forget-me-nots that had bloomed in May left only bare leafy stalks, but they still marked the ground beneath the stone.

Eenayah sat down and placed 12 deep claret roses on the grass beneath the stone. For a while she closed her eyes, listening only to the seagulls and the pounding sound of the waves. Tasting the salt on her lips, she tenderly caressed the grass besides her as though stroking a new-born baby.

She lay down next to the spot where James ashes' had been scattered some nineteen years earlier. His age had also been nineteen; a lifetime all over again. She closed her eyes and let the warm sun kiss her face.

At that moment, soft female hands stroked her forehead and she opened her eyes to see her mother Ellie sitting beside her. 'I knew you would be here child' she said. Her words were sympathetic and compassionate. 'Do you still think about him?'

'Not really Mum' she replied. 'I try not to.'

Ellie looked around at the beautiful backdrop, the white church and the seascape. She had not been to this spot herself in almost two decades, not since the day James' ashes had been scattered by his father so his spirit could always look out to the sea.

'I sometimes see James's mother around town', continued Ellie. 'I always stop to say hello, but she avoids me if she can. I think it must be too painful for her, too many memories I guess. Do you know his stepfather passed away recently?'

Eenayah seemed shocked. 'No, you never told me Mum. I feel very sorry for Mary, losing her son and now her husband, but I'm not surprised she won't talk to you. I guess life goes on. Bit by bit we forget and when we do we heal. James and I were far too young to commit to each other, if I'm honest. It was just a teenage infatuation and I suspect if he was still alive and we had got married, we could well be divorced by now. Maybe I would be hating him and fighting over who gets custody of the dog and who had what share of some little bungalow in Peel. As it is, I will always remember him as a boy I loved and in my thoughts he will be forever young and handsome. Perhaps it's better that way.'

Ellie was slightly taken aback by her daughter's matter-of-fact dismissal of James' untimely death. 'So what of Greg?' she asked. 'Was that also for the best?'

Eenayah grew angry, realising her mother was missing the point. 'Don't you understand mother, that sometimes as far as men are concerned I feel cursed? It was just the week before the wedding. If I had stopped him from entering that bloody race, James would be alive now. If it wasn't for me being away working when Greg collapsed in our living room, he would most certainly be alive now. I tell you, if I was a man I would be avoiding me.'

There were some truths only the closest of family knew, and the fact that Greg was James' half-brother was seldom discussed in the Layne household. The two men had different mothers, but the same father and the same surname. Even though Greg grew up in Wales and James on the island, some local people had put two and two together and made the connection. Gossip was difficult to contain within a tiny island community. It had created a minor scandal back in the day. Perhaps it was one of the reasons Eenayah seldom returned here. Even though now she was older and probably not recognised, she feared anyone pointing fingers and saying, 'Look, there's that harlot who married two brothers and killed them both.' Of course their deaths had been total accidents, but she knew local people wouldn't see it like that.

'Will you also be visiting Greg's grave?' asked her mother, almost guessing Eenayah's thoughts. Greg had been estranged from some of his family from the moment he had started dating Eenayah, who they still saw as his deceased brother's fiancée. Greg had followed her over to London when she had got her first job as a journalist. He had also secured a job in London as a teacher, just to be close to her. They had tried not to get involved with one another, but love had intervened.

At the time the rift between the families had caused quite a difficult situation. Eenayah failed to see why her marrying half-brothers had created so much of a problem. Mary was divorced from Greg's father Paul and had reinvented her life with her new husband, Gary. Eenayah couldn't understand why Mary still carried around so much resentment and bitterness for something that had happened so long ago.

Paul lived back on the mainland, by coincidence in North Wales and not far from Ruby's partially-restored manor house. When Greg died, his body came home to where his father and mother Katherine lived. He was buried in the grounds of a crystal white marble church in St Asaph's, Bodelwyddan, the church where Greg had married Eenayah. It seemed right and appropriate that his final resting place was in the grounds of the same white marble church.

As Eenayah drifted in her thoughts she realised she hadn't answered her mother's question.

'I don't plan to spend a lot of time hanging around my exs' graves and scatter places, mother' she said. 'Having said that, Ruby has forced me to go and stay in her gothic mansion in Wales while I am over here, and seeing that it's not too far from St Asaph's, I should go and put some flowers on his grave I guess. Maybe I will even call in and see his parents, if they will see me that is. The boy's father Paul was a nice guy and didn't seem to have the whole grudge thing that Mary had going on.'

Ellie interrupted her daughter. 'I am sorry to tell you this, but Paul and Katherine are divorced now. I thought you would have known.'

'I live in a prison in Miami, mother. How would I ever know about Paul Bucklow's private life? Having said that, I am not shocked. The guy was a professional footballer. He wasn't faithful to Mary. I doubt he was faithful to Katherine. None of this bewilders me. The man couldn't keep it in his pants. None the less, I liked Paul. He was always kind to me.'

'What about Reed?' enquired Ellie. 'You have been married for how many years now - eight, nine, ten? He is still very much alive.'

Eenayah hung her head down low, taking a sideward glance to the red roses on the grass and sighing.

'You know what I said about avoiding me if I was a man - well, that's exactly what Reed does. Maybe he is only alive because he is mostly on a different continent. Perhaps that's the secret, keep away from me and stay breathing.'

Ellie was stunned into silence, less by the sarcasm of the comment and more by what she was reading between the lines. She hadn't known marital problems were afoot in the Baratolli household, but sensed this wasn't the right time to enquire any further. Eenayah would tell her when she was ready. She got up to leave to leave her daughter alone with her reminiscences.

Eenayah got up to follow her. 'Mum, there's something I need to tell you.'

Ellie stood to face her daughter, taking note of the dark circles under Eenayah's eyes and sensing her unhappiness. Eenayah took a deep breath and braced herself for what she was about to say, words that she would find difficult to get out.

'Mum, over the last few months I haven't felt myself. I am not sure what it is, maybe it's my age or a phase I am going through, but I just feel I have lost my identity. I don't know who I am any more. I look in the mirror and the reflection seems like a stranger. I just needed to come over to the UK to connect with my old self and find out who I am. I know this all sounds crazy, but somehow I am lost.'

Ellie was speechless; she had always thought of Eenayah as being highly successful. She had done well in both school and university, had been a journalist and had finally married well, netting herself a wealthy husband. Yes, she had succumbed to moments of depression, but nothing that a mansion in Miami wouldn't cure, surely?

Eenayah continued, 'Part of that self-discovery is finding out who gave birth to me. I am sorry. I love you and Dad more than anything and you will always be my parents, but I just have this deep urge to know more about this unknown person who gave me away. I don't mean to hurt you but - will you be okay with this? If it wasn't important, I wouldn't be...' her voice trailed off.

Ellie had always known this day would come. She had often wondered why her twin girls had not asked the question before. She had been unable to have children and when her daughters had come into her life as new-born babies and given her an instant family, it had made life complete. She loved the twins so much. She had expected this to happen a lot sooner.

'Does Ruby know about this?' asked Ellie.

'Not yet', replied Eenayah. 'I have a feeling she may not approve somehow. With little Harry also being adopted, it could just hit a nerve. I am not sure quite what to say to her.'

Ellie had almost forgotten that her grandson Harry was also

adopted. It was something she had never thought about, but taking this into consideration she could understand why Ruby might not support the idea.

'Have you put the wheels in motion Eenayah?' asked Ellie.

'Well actually yes, I have hired an international search agency with a very good reputation and I expect to hear something any day now. Were you ever told anything about my biological parents, Mum? You never told us anything more other than we were adopted.'

Ellie didn't know what to say. Perhaps she should have said something sooner. Conceivably she had left it too late in the day. How could she now tell Eenayah the truth and admit that she had known all along and kept it from her? If Eenayah had instigated a search for her mother, she would find out soon enough that her mother had died shortly after her twins were born. Maybe this was one of those occasions when it was best to lie and let Eenayah find out for herself.

Ellie responded as best she could. 'Sorry Eenayah, the adoption agency didn't tell us anything about your birth mother, so I can't help you. I am sure you will have all your answers very soon anyway, but I do think you need to tell Ruby about this.'

Ellie felt uncomfortable. This was not the reunion with her daughter she had expected.

'I need to get back now sweetheart. I will leave you alone with your thoughts. Don't stay here too long, you father wants to take you somewhere. Don't ask me what he has planned because he hasn't told me. See you soon love.'

With that Ellie turned around, walking down the long, straight sandy pathway though the church gate. She got into the car and drove away. Eenayah stood there watching her mother go, feeling totally and utterly dreadful. She hadn't seen her mother in a year, the last time being when she had flown her parents over to Miami for a holiday. She had hardly been back on the island for half a day, and here she was breaking her mother's heart. She felt so cruel. Her timing was not the best. Her mother had been concerned about her and had come out here to the white church to find her and offer her comfort, and she had responded by doing this. She was sick to the stomach. She felt like phoning Mercy and calling the search off. However she knew she couldn't stop what had already been started. The wheels were in motion.

As Eenayah started to walk away, she cast her eyes over her shoulder to the rearranged stone in the wall which marked the spot where James's ashes had been scattered long ago. She drank in the exquisite sea view one last time, 'putting it in her pocket for later', as Ruby would say to her young son. She knew she wouldn't be coming back here ever again. James was gone, and she needed to move on. She blew a kiss in the direction of the twisted stone and walked away. Some strange destiny was beginning to unfold. She didn't know what awaited her and she was helpless to stop it. It had begun.

CHAPTER 12

Monday 24th June 2013

Ruby rushed down the old creaking stairs with her heavy suitcase banging against each step with a thud. She hated Monday mornings with a passion. The taxi headlights lit up the winding county lane where she lived, casting eerie shadows from the trees. She tried desperately to make her way out silently without waking her slumbering family, but at this hour of the morning in the quietness of where she lived, every sound was amplified. It was 4.45 am, and not a time most people would be awake.

There was a full moon, and as Ruby picked her way down the footpath, wheeling her suitcase loudly over the tiny stones, each piece of grit reflected the moonlight, turning her route into a glimmering starscape. The nearby mountains looked dark and menacing against the blue-black sky and one could almost imagine them as monsters with big yellow eyes, watching on with interest. A tawny owl hooted, and in the middle of rural Wales at dawn, the bird's noise added to the already spooky landscape.

Taken away by her waiting taxi, all she needed to endure now was two train journeys, a fair amount of waiting time, a tube ride through London and a short walk. None the less, it would still add up to a five-hour journey before she had even officially started work. From Sunday afternoon onwards she had begun to dread Monday mornings, and wondered if her new promotion would lessen the need for this painful weekly dawn start.

Finally on her way to London Euston and able to relax in her first-class carriage, she caught her own reflection in the window against the darkness. She frequently studied her own face and thought about the mother who had given birth to her and wondered who she was and what she looked like. However, as soon as the sun rose on the horizon, the window became less of a mirror and more of a portal to another world; the real world outside.

She watched as lights came on in the houses visible from the train track, and realised that there were people in these houses just waking up, making breakfast and doing all of this so much later than she had done. As the night became day, she saw dog walkers making their way along their pastoral pathways in the sunshine. She so envied them and vowed that one day, she too would become a dog walker. She would throw a stick and then watch the passing train go by with all its commuters rushing around on their little hamster wheels scurrying to make a living, whilst she would casually wait for her dog to fetch its stick as though that was all that concerned her. She so looked forward to that day.

However, for now, and with all these busy thoughts in her head draining her, she grew tired. She closed her eyes, and with the lullaby noise of the train in her ears, she dozed off.

Once in her familiar office, Ruby was catching up with weekend emails. There seemed to be an inner competition as to who could win the most Brownie points by writing emails on a Sunday. Ruby never joined in with these political rivalries and now that she had just been offered the position of Sales Director, she felt she had won the race without even entering it. Maybe that was the secret, not trying too hard.

Ruby was excited about what this new position would mean to her and her family. The wage rise would certainly be a massive bonus, but secretly she hoped it wouldn't mean yet more time away from home. She reasoned that a plane was probably about as quick as a train and it shouldn't impact on life too much.

As she was halfway through the email trails, Pippa ran excitedly into Ruby's office, barely knocking before throwing open the door. Slightly out of breath, she panted, 'You will never guess, but Reed B is here to see you. I think it really is him as well!'

'How do you know it is him, Pippa? The guy is rarely photographed.'

'Because he told me his name… duh!'

Ruby was shocked, as Reed had never come to visit her before and she didn't even know how he knew where she worked. However she was amused by Pippa's reaction. None of her colleagues knew that the famous Reed Baratolli was her brother in law. She suspected that had they known she would have been pestered to get autographs or discount concert tickets and the like. Ruby did not have the closest of relationships with Reed and didn't want to start begging him for freebies any time soon.

Reed marched into her office in a worryingly assertive and businesslike way. This didn't have any of the flavours of a friendly meeting. Before Ruby could say a word he yelled at her, 'where is she?'

Ruby was taken aback and wasn't quite sure what to say.

'You mean Eenayah?'

'Yes of course, my wife Eenayah, who else do you think I have come here to ask you about?'

Ruby was confused. 'The last time I spoke to Eenayah was when she was on her way over to meet you in your hotel suite. Gee Reed, that was over a week ago. I just sort of presumed you guys were having some fun time catching up and I didn't want to interrupt the marital blissathon.'

Reed sat down opposite Ruby, looking slightly calmer yet still quite worried. 'How did you know where to find me?' asked Ruby.

'Eenayah doesn't bloody share anybody's phone numbers with me. All I could remember vaguely was the name of the company you worked for, and even then I had to get Arabella to do some detective work to trace you to this building. I'm guessing you have the numbers of her friends and other significant people she hangs out with when she's in this country, so can you call them please? I'm worried about her. We were supposed to meet up nine days ago, and that's a long time without as much as a phone call or explanation.'

'Did you call the police?'

'Not yet, but it was my next step if you were unable to help. You know, Eenayah is on some ridiculous mission of self-discovery right now. She was perfectly content when she was on the prescription medication, but now she is weaning herself off the stuff, she is – what can I say? She is fucked up in the head. She wants all this freedom crap.'

Reed was continuing to surprise and shock Ruby. Prior to this, he had never come across as the over-protective husband. She also found this whole charade of him caring about Eenayah's longitude and latitude a tad two-faced. As for him feeding her sister a daily supply of therapeutic prescription tranquilisers so she would be a good girl, it seemed to smell a bit like the *Stepford Wives*. Her sister – his wife – often didn't know where the hell he was, but for his faithful PA Arabella being privy to his diary. Ruby shuddered as she thought about Arabella, a grossly cosmetically-enhanced woman. Ruby and Owyn thought she looked like someone who had just stepped out of the Michael Jackson *Thriller* video.

'But what happened when she came to see you?' asked Ruby. 'She was really looking forward to being with you.'

Reed sighed and threw the palms of his hands up to the skies to signal that he had maybe lost the plot.

'Well yes, she got to my hotel suite and it was mad busy. Acre was there and TV crews were all over the place and other hangers-on were doing the usual hanging-on thing, and it was this big interview and I got distracted by what was going on, as usual. When I stopped to look around, she had vanished. Then I called her and she said she was tired and going to lie down in the rented apartment. She promised we would meet up for a night out later and she would call me, but she never called. I went to the apartment and her bags were there, but she wasn't.'

'So what happened after this?'

'That was it', replied Reed. 'Her mobile has been dead ever since and it's been over a week. I don't know who to call. I didn't even have your number. So, here I am. Can you help?'

What was it about his humble desperation that made Ruby suspicious? She was in sales and had a gut instinct. Something wasn't right. He sounded overly concerned and yet… she mentally calculated it had been nine days since he had last seen her. Wouldn't a normal person have contacted the police by now? Especially considering his wife was coming off major mind-altering medication. It just didn't sound right.

She was trying very hard not to show any facial expression. She had known Reed ever since he had married her sister and in all that time she had never known this egotistical, arrogant man to beg anyone for anything. Throughout his marriage to her sister, he had always called the shots. He had enjoyed all the comforts of a marriage without any of the harsh and uncomfortable realities of normal domestic life and all its challenges. He had found this lovely kind English woman to act as a surrogate mother to his three children, and yet under the guise of his career he could travel the world and party around the globe and whatever else. At long last, Eenayah has grown some balls and bitten back. Now Reed would know what it felt like not to know where his partner was or who she was with. Ruby liked this. She sent a mental high five to her sis.

With all the newly-found confidence that came with her promotion, she stood up to close the deal. 'Reed, send me your mobile number and I will make some calls. I honestly don't think you should worry so much. Eenayah is a big girl with hundreds of friends and I am sure with a few calls I can locate her.' Okay, so she knew Eenayah didn't actually have hundreds of friends, but she was as sure as hell enjoying milking this for all it was worth and if she needed to exaggerate just to watch Reed squirm, so be it. About time the tables were turned, she thought as he stood to leave. Nice one, sis.

Reed became unusually humble. 'Thanks Ruby, keep in touch. You will let me know as soon as you find out, won't you?'

As he meekly left the office, the first call went out to Eenayah, whose mobile promptly diverted to voicemail. Eenayah never diverted calls from Ruby, so she knew by this that she was in avoidance mode. Ever since she had been a child, Eenayah had dealt with situations she couldn't deal with by running away. This was typical Eenayah evasion tactics.

The next call was to Jonathan. He picked up in his usual laid-back bohemian horticultural way and confirmed that Eenayah had spent the weekend up in Newcastle with him, but had flown out on the morning of Monday 17th to the Isle of Man. Ruby pondered. So she had gone to spend time with Jonathan rather than Reed - interesting. The next call was to her mother, who confirmed that Eenayah was with them, and was now out riding a horse along the beach. She had been having a great time back home on the island and it had been lovely to see her again. Ruby guessed their mother was exaggerating slightly, to accentuate the fact that Ruby and her grandson Harry hadn't been over to visit them in many months. A maternal guilt trip arrow aimed purposefully at the heart.

Excellent. She knew this game. As far as Ruby was concerned, her sister was safe and Reed was getting a taste of his own medicine. For once he knew how it felt not to be in control. Of course she would tell him where his wife was – when she felt the time was right.

CHAPTER 13

Tuesday 25th June 2013

Mercy looked impatiently around the small crowd gathered at the arrivals gate, searching for a familiar face. Within moments an enthusiastic young lady came running towards her, shouting her name. Wearing pink Bermuda shorts, a plain white oversized tee-shirt with the words '1D' printed on her chest, white ankle socks and pink Converse ankle boots, she didn't look like anyone Mercy would know or associate herself with. It took her a minute or two to recognise that this was actually her client - Eenayah.

The last time they had met in the MeDeVe Oxford office, Eenayah's dark hair had been swept harshly off her face and pulled back into a severe ponytail. Her lips seemed to have been spray painted with multi layers of brilliant red lipstick and her eyes had been heavily made up with sepia coloured eyeshadow and intense eyeliner. The female waving frantically at Mercy in the arrivals lounge had hair hanging loosely to her waist which was either deliberately or accidentally un-brushed or scrunched. She had gained some much-needed weight, and this had plumped up her make-up free rosy cheeks and even given her dimples.

Mercy scanned her client up and down. Although she did not approve of the casual teenage attire, she had to concede that Eenayah looked at least ten years younger. Eenayah registered the astonishment on Mercy's face and hurried to introduce herself.

'You do recognise me don't you?'

'Only just', responded Mercy. 'What on earth have you done to yourself darling?'

Eenayah laughed. 'I've just been enjoying myself with my family and relaxing, plus my mother has been feeding me way too much of her home cooking.'

Mercy remained unimpressed. 'You were so stressed out the last time we met. It's lovely to see what a week living on a farm has done for your serotonin levels, but dearie, do you have to dress like a One Direction fan?' Both women sniggered as they casually made their way over to the airport short stay car park.

Eenayah drove Mercy to her parent's farm, making small talk along the way. Mercy didn't normally visit clients personally to deliver the outcome of an investigation unless the news was too delicate to convey over the phone. Having made the journey to the Isle of Man, she was equally determined not to share her news during a car drive either, so she kept the conversation trivial until they were in a more formal setting.

They made their way up the heavily-potholed dirt track until the ivy-covered, cream-rendered farmhouse came into view. Mercy was quite taken aback by how humble it looked, realising it had seen better days. Her opinion of Eenayah was starting to evolve.

When she had initially met her in Oxford, Eenayah had come across as a shy, aloof celebrity wife, groomed to chisel-sharp perfection. To see this ramshackle old farmhouse where Eenayah had grown up, with its many cats, dogs, geese, hens and ducks, made her realise that this was the real Eenayah, not the WAG who lived in Miami.

Ellie gave them a warm welcome and immediately put on the kettle, placing a large plate of home-made ginger biscuits on the table.

'Ellie, it's lovely to meet you, but I can see how easy it would be to put weight on living with you,' said Mercy. If Ellie could have had her way, she would have ambushed Mercy for the rest of the day. They had few visitors at the farm and Ellie was reluctant to release this smart, elegant stranger to her daughter. However, nice as Eenayah's mother was, Mercy had a return flight to Gatwick booked in a few hours' time and she didn't have the luxury to spend precious moments in idle conversation.

In an attempt to engage Eenayah in private she cut to the chase. 'Is there somewhere we can go which is slightly more secluded Eenayah, or do you want your mother to join us?'

Eenayah was shocked at the suggestion. However she knew that Mercy hadn't taken all the time and trouble to come and see her for something trivial, so much as she loved her mother, she wanted to hear what Mercy had to say in private.

'No, can we keep this private, just us for the time being? Sorry Mum, don't mean to be rude. Mercy, can you follow me?'

Eenayah led Mercy into the drawing room. This room had always been kept neat and tidy for guests. It was a dark room and still furnished in 1950s décor. It was almost as though time had stood still in this room. It contained an unlit fire, a piano and an old oak sideboard displaying multiple porcelain figures.

The two women sat facing each other on a maroon three-piece settee covered with hand-embroidered throws. Mercy put on her professional head. Mindful of her flight home, she was eager to make a start. She placed a large file on the coffee table in front of her.

'Okay, so let's begin. You approached MeDeVe with several assignments and I have news about the progress of two of these, so it's your call. Where would you like me to start?'

Eenayah didn't have to think twice and jumped in quickly. 'Have you found my mother?' She felt both anxious and excited, so could hardly contain the question.

Mercy opened one of the files in front of her, although she already knew the answer to her query. 'I am pleased to say that we have found who your birth mother was. She was called Daisy Green.'

Eenayah sat silently for a moment pondering the name, repeating it several times inside her mind before responding. 'Daisy Green, Daisy Green... what a lovely name. Sounds like a place in an English village where you could play cricket on a Sunday morning. You said *was*, what do you mean by was?'

This was in fact the reason why Mercy had travelled to see Eenayah in the Isle of Man rather than deliver this news impersonally by phone or email. She confirmed, 'yes I am sorry Eenayah, but your birth mother is no longer alive.'

Eenayah looked down to the floor, focusing on a twirl pattern in the Worcester carpet. She heaved a huge sigh and then remained silent for a short while. A single tear escaped from her left eye. She wondered if perhaps she should have instigated this search much sooner. Now she had left it too late. She had never known her birth mother, and now she never would. This Daisy person was a stranger, yet she had shed a tear for a woman she had never known, a woman who, for whatever reason, had given her twin daughters away.

However she sensed there was more to this story. She requested additional detail. Mercy read the file and continued, 'Daisy was born in a village just outside a town called Bolton in Lancashire, England. Date of birth 1st February 1960. It says here that she was born and died in a place called Daisy Hill. Maybe that's why she had been given that name.'

'Seems like a coincidence,' remarked Eenayah. 'Hang on a second, I was born in 1975 so I am trying to compute this... Daisy was only

15 when she had twins. How awful for her. She was just a kid. When did she die?'

Mercy referred back to the file, already aware of the answer and how hard this revelation would be to her client.

'She died on the 27th August 1975.'

Eenayah was shocked for the second time and struggled to compute what this actually meant.

'Poor little Daisy! Ruby and I were born on the 26th August 1975 so that must mean that she died the day after we were born. I am beginning to understand now why we were adopted. This is tragic. What else have you uncovered?'

At that moment Ellie walked in with a pot of tea, the English (and Manx) therapeutic drink at times like this. Of course she had guessed why Mercy was visiting her daughter. At the time of adoption she had been informed that Ellie's birth mother was just a very young girl who had died shortly after giving birth. Rightly or wrongly she had elected not to share this information with her growing daughters.

'Do you mind if I join you?' asked Ellie.

Eenayah hung her head low and just nodded to indicate yes. Mercy understood that this was painful for both Eenayah and her adoptive mother.

'We have been in touch with her family, Eenayah, and sadly there are not many of them left. This is not a big family unit. We have spoken with your grandfather's sister. She understands the background to your adoption and she would love to meet you. She says there are things she wants to tell you. Your Great Aunt is called Elspeth. Your grandmother, your mother's mother, is a lady called Harriet Green. She is still alive, but she is getting on in years. I have been told that she has Alzheimer's and lives in a nursing home.'

Mercy leaned over and touched Eenayah's hand in a spontaneous act of compassion. 'I am not speaking to you as someone you hired from MeDeVe right now, but as one woman to another. In my experience I would strongly recommend that you do go and meet them. I don't know how progressive your grandmother's dementia is or how much she can remember, but it seems she may be your only living biological relative. My father, the Professor, has always said that it's best to try and talk with family whilst they are still alive and not wait until they are cold in the grave, when it can only ever be a one-way conversation. He has a good point. Don't leave it until it's too late. Salvage what you can, Eenayah.'

Eenayah was almost speechless and could barely manage to ask her last question. 'So did you manage to find out who my father was, or is?'

Mercy didn't speak; she just shrugged her shoulders and nodded her head to indicate that the answer was no.

'What next?' Eenayah asked despondently. Yet again Mercy reached out to touch her hand compassionately. 'Leave it with me. We will organise an introduction and you can ask as many questions of your great aunt as you need to. It may be good to include Ruby.'

At that point Mercy looked across to Ellie, making a discreet signal that she now needed to be alone with her daughter. Ellie flashed back a look of sympathy in her daughter's direction, having always known that some time in the future this day would come.

As Ellie left, Mercy waited until she had closed the door and then turned back to Eenayah to ask, 'I am sorry to raise this right now, but we do have other business to discuss. Is it okay with you if I move on?'

Eenayah was still in shock, but she realised that Mercy was a busy woman with a schedule that wouldn't allow her to sit and drink tea in her mother's drawing room all day.

Mercy continued, 'Delicate question, but what do you want us to do about the surveillance of Mr Baratolli? Have you had time to think about it?'

Eenayah seemed agitated and disturbed. She responded, 'I don't think I am in the right state of mind to answer your question right now. Would it be okay if I parked this for a moment and maybe get back to you when I know where I am going with this? I am not sure what is happening with my marriage at the moment.'

Mercy totally understood and thought this to be the more sensible approach. She had always been concerned that Eenayah was taking on too many life-changing challenges at the same time. She consistently counselled clients against the 'too much, too quickly' method of attack. Many years of experience had taught her that people usually had a limit on how many life-changing issues they could deal with at any one time.

Mercy felt awkward in having to press on with the agenda, but she had other business with Eenayah which was still in need of discussion.

'Eenayah, I understand that this may not be the right moment, but my father has made great progress with Reed's genealogy and he wanted me to discuss the book with you, in brief of course.' She paused and awaited a reaction, but suspected that Eenayah was still focusing on the news of her newly-found mother. She seemed to be in some faraway place. Mercy was a total professional when it came to optimising the moment, but she also knew when taking a step back was the more appropriate move. She resolved to keep this as short and as sweet as possible.

'My father has produced a draft version of a manuscript for you. It includes your husband's family tree with photographs and illustrations. It's not the finished product yet, but he would have liked to talk this through with you. When you get a moment, is there any possibility that we could arrange a call or meeting with him? Please understand that this is just a rough draft for you to read, but with your approval he will add some finishing touches and get this published into an impressive book which will be all about your husband's childhood and his family history. My father has been quite excited about what he has uncovered. Your husband's Mort ancestors are quite interesting I am told that there is a fair scattering of knights of the realm. This really is an incredible present for Reed's 50th birthday. It was quite imaginative of you to think about something as personal as this.'

Even for Mercy, this was a hard sell. Here she was trying to market a gift, when only a few moments prior to this she had been asking if they should be spying on the recipient. It felt terribly awkward, and it didn't sit well.

Mercy composed herself to raise one final subject with Eenayah.

'When you came into my office we also discussed your personal security and the possible threat that someone such as yourself, could be open to kidnap attempts. At the time you felt you wanted your freedom and dismissed the idea of a bodyguard. Is this still the case?'

Eenayah had so cherished the last week she had spent on her parent's farm. She had visited old friends, had a picnic under an oak tree, rode her horse along an isolated beach and played Blackjack in the casino. Freedom was high up on her list of priorities right now. The thought of losing her liberty and being shadowed by a bodyguard was unacceptable to her. She told Mercy as much. Mercy understood; of course she did. This wasn't the first time she had dealt with a celebrity family, and walking the tightrope between freedom and safety was always a tense walk for the rich and famous. Mercy told it as it was and didn't hold back.

'Here is the deal Eenayah. You have rejected our offer of protection and I can fully understand the reasons why, even though I may not agree with you. So by way of a halfway house, we have offered you a security watch that will not only monitor your temperature, pulse rate and oxygen saturation as well as pinpoint your location by satellite, it will also allow you to activate a distress call should you be in any danger.'

Eenayah showed Mercy her wrist. 'Look, I am wearing it. It's an ideal solution. Non-intrusive and helps me feel secure whilst I go about my business. I am delighted with the watch. It answers all my health and security concerns. Thanks for this Mercy, but with the watch I don't need a bodyguard.'

Mercy didn't quite know what to say next. JD had broken client instructions by tailing Eenayah whilst she had been in London. She felt unable to confess to Eenayah that her directive had been breached and her civil liberty violated. However perhaps if her client knew that some other man had also been following her whilst she walked around the city, she might reconsider the offer of a bodyguard.

Mercy mentally summed up the situation. Eenayah had met her at the airport in a mood of wanton abandon. Now this same woman looked stressed and tense, and for good reason. Mercy knew that delivery was all about timing. Perhaps now was not the best time to own up to JD's breach of orders and the sighting of a stranger also tagging her movements. She would attempt another tactic.

'Yes the security watch is a great invention. Last year we found a chap trapped in 10ft of snow after an avalanche just by using the watch alone, so it does work. The down side with it however, is our ability to rescue you quickly once you activate the distress signal. If you can at least tell us where in the United Kingdom you are, we can at least ensure that we have someone within a thirty mile radius who can get to you quickly. With all due respect, you gave Kerry an itinerary of your proposed locations and we almost sent an agent up to Newcastle, only then to find you were still in London.'

Eenayah was sulking like a school child being told off by teacher. Having to report in weekly or even daily with her planned movements did not sound much like freedom. She considered any threat to her safety to be negligible in any case and couldn't see what all the fuss was about.

Mercy detected the look of rebellion in her client's dark hazel eyes. 'Look, Eenayah, I get it. I understand that you are over here on vacation and you want to travel to a lot of places and visit a lot of people. I understand the whole footloose and fancy free thing. However, please, you must remember who you are. Right now you are dressed in pink shorts and seem to have reverted back to Eenayah Layne from the Isle of Man, aged 17. The reality is that you are Eenayah Baratolli from Miami aged 38 and the wife of a very wealthy celebrity and as such a possible target for the criminal fraternity. The watch is little more than a high tech trinket unless you allow my team the luxury of being able to get to you quickly if you are in trouble.'

Eenayah was still not happy. She looked down at the carpet again, this time as though she hoped a big hole would appear in it so it could swallow Mercy up, leaving her free to go out and play.

Mercy tried a different angle in the hope of knocking some sense into her clients thick and irresponsible skull. 'My company has been built up from scratch and it has been a labour of love. I employ a lot of people who need to pay a mortgage and rely on the continued success of MeDeVe to do so. We trade on our reputation. We have just solved a kidnap case in Greece which has been ongoing for two years, and once that goes public we expect to get a lot more work on the back of it. However, if for whatever reason something happens to you, and it becomes known that you were a client of ours and had approached us about your personal security and then we lost you, how would that look? What damage would that do to MeDeVe? The answer is, that with a couple as high profile as you and your husband, it could be commercially devastating. I must insist that you return the watch to us and go elsewhere as regards to your security issues, unless you can abide by the rules and call Kerry every morning to let her know your intentions for the following day. Have I made myself clear?'

'Crystal.'

'Do you want to hand me the watch back?'

'No, I will keep it.'

'You will be updating us with your location on a regular basis then.' 'Agreed.'

Ouch! Mercy did not hold back. During the last decade of her closeted and pampered little life, Eenayah hadn't been used to anyone challenging her in such a direct manner before.

Neither woman felt comfortable. Mercy was as keen to leave as Eenayah was keen to see her go. It wasn't personal, but the content of the conversation had become too heavy and oppressive. They were both equally relieved when Eenayah's father entered the room, offering Mercy a ride back to the airport. The two women shook hands with a promise to speak soon and to keep in touch. Mercy never enjoyed this type of meeting, but she understood that some projects did require that extra personal touch. None the less, Mercy was thankful to be on a flight back to Gatwick soon. Still clutching onto the draft copy of the Mort genealogy, Eenayah watched Mercy leave, peeping through the net curtains as Mercy was driven away.

She secretly felt quite envious of Mercy. Here was an independent single woman who was the CEO of a very successful company. She always dressed immaculately as though she was going to a wedding, christening, funeral or a day out at the races. Adorned in bright turquoise with matching pillbox hat and Sunday school white gloves, Eenayah concluded Mercy was wearing the christening look today. Her gut instinct was to trust her. Mercy was an expert in her field, but she was also compassionate. Her attention to customer service had not gone unnoticed or unappreciated. Eenayah was grateful that she had taken the time out to come and see her to deliver the news that her biological mother was dead. Dead; that was a big word to deal with.

She chewed the thought up in her head once again: 'my mother is dead!'

Eenayah felt a strong compulsion to run away from the situation. It was a trait of hers to flee from circumstances she felt unable to cope with. As soon as her father's car had left the courtyard, she headed off towards nowhere in particular to gather her thoughts.

She mumbled something to her mother about going out and then as if on autopilot she just walked and walked. It was late June and the fields coloured the landscape with their brilliant sunshine yellow, illuminated more so against a clear blue summer sky. She felt mentally exhausted and traumatised. The thought of some poor young child of 15 giving birth to twins and then dying herself just a day later had saddened her deeply, even though she didn't know Daisy or had any emotional connection with her. Eenayah rarely cried, but as she walked she started to sob quietly. The revelation about her teenage mother had affected her more than she had realised. She was beginning to wish that she had never instigated the search.

She lay down under her big oak tree. It was her tree; nobody else's. It was on top of a hill with the most wonderful panoramic views of the surrounding countryside and sea. This had always been her private childhood place of retreat, a special place. A place to gather her thoughts. With the heat of the sun on her face, she closed her eyes and fell into a peaceful deep slumber. She lay there for quite some time in a deep, restful sleep, but then was gently awoken by singing. A familiar voice recited a melody from many years past: *'I never made promises lightly and there have been some that I've broken, but I swear in the days still left we will walk in fields of gold, we will walk in fields of gold.'*

When she opened her eyes, Reed was looking down on her with the biggest smile on his face. Stroking her forehead he said, 'Your mother said I would find you here. I am told that this big old oak tree was your best friend when you were a little girl and whenever you needed to get away this is where you would come to.' He stood up to pat the tree as though it was another man rather than a tree. 'Well hey, this is a serious tree friend you have here. I feel a bit jealous. He is bigger, older, stronger and possibly closer to you than I am, so I think I may have some significant competition for your affections. However I bet this big wooden chap can't play a guitar or sing to you, so that has to win me some points surely.'

To her astonishment, Reed actually had a guitar with him, and continued to play the entire song. They were indeed in a field of gold on a lovely summer day, and it was nothing less than perfect. It was a memory for the pocket.

Eenayah was impressed. It wasn't every day a girl got her own personal recital from a famous musician in a picture-perfect location. 'You sure know how to serenade a lady' said Eenayah. 'You still got your mojo old man.'

'Thanks for the compliment, but where is the lady?' grinned Reed.

Eenayah sprang up to her feet up and mockingly pushed Reed over. He pushed her back and they both lay there in the grass laughing. It had been many years since they had both laughed together, certainly with that hysterical, stomach-hurting hysteria where you laugh until you cry. It was welcome light relief after what had otherwise been an oppressive day.

Changing the mood slightly, Reed became more sombre.

'Your mother has told me everything about what happened today. She tells me you have found out about your biological mother. Is this what's been bothering you lately? I've been worried about you. You haven't seemed yourself recently.'

Eenayah remained silent. Finally he was noticing.

Hearing the silence, Reed continued, 'Look, I can see how much better you are just being here at your parents' home. I mean seriously, have you seen what you are wearing? I would have never believed that low-cost adolescent high street fashion would look better on you than your usual designer couture, but you know, I've never seen you look as beautiful.'

Eenayah didn't know whether to thank him or punch him. Was that an insult or a compliment?

Reed put his arm around her protectively. 'I need to be at the studio in London to finish some work off, but by helicopter it's not too far away. Arabella has found a house we can hire here on the island and that way I can be home every night, just like a normal husband. Would that make things better between us? I'm sorry Eenayah, I know I haven't been around as much as I should have been.'

Eenayah was both confused and impressed. Could it be that the backward bye-bye trick had really worked? Walk away and be chased?

He continued, 'I was thinking about bringing all the kids over here, especially Konnor as he'll be starting college soon and that's the last we'll hear or see of him for years, until he runs out of money that is. Your parents haven't seen their grandchildren in an eternity and I'm sure they would all love to go horse riding with you. What do you think?'

So Reed was trying to back pedal and finally make an attempt to play happy families after years of acting like the single rock star playboy. She was totally bamboozled as to why the U turn in his attitude towards her, and she was suspicious. This was too big a change, but who knows? Maybe this was a genuine attempt to relight the fire?

Quite spontaneously she turned to face him. Assertively grasping at his neck and pulling his head towards her, she gave him a long lingering kiss. He had no choice but to reciprocate. Finally she relaxed her grip and ended the kiss as quickly as she had initiated it. Reed was surprised.

'Wow Mrs Baratolli what are you doing? I am a married man you know.' He gave her a mischievous wink.

Eenayah knew that her kiss had been nothing to do with love or lust. This was her making it perfectly clear to Reed that she was in control. From now on she would call the shots. If she wanted him she would take him, and if she didn't she would walk. Like a butterfly emerging from its chrysalis, the old, sad, pathetic Eenayah was beginning to turn into a strong, self-assured woman.

'Reed, thank you for the gesture of renting a house out here and commuting back and forth to London. I guess with a helicopter parked in the field it's not too big a commute. To be honest, I think it's a good idea for you to get out of that hotel suite of yours every now and then. That whole situation at the Mayfair is just too loud and crazy. I saw it for myself. Your bedroom suite is a place of work and not a place of rest. It would do you good to just go somewhere away from the city and just switch off at the end of the day. It doesn't necessarily have to be here on the island though. There are lots of nice places just outside London, the Cotswolds are lovely I believe.'

Reed was a little puzzled by his wife's response. 'But I thought with you being here on the island that this plan made sense? Just living on the farm, with all this smelly fresh air and ducks and horses and whatever other creatures all live here appears to have worked wonders for you. Look at you, you look so lovely and so young! I am sure your parents would love to spend time with Konnor, and if Asher and Armani can make it over here as well, they would be in their element. It would be nice for them, for all of them.'

Reed was pleading his case, and Eenayah had to concede that he was making sense. She would consider it, but in all truth she hadn't planned to spend much longer on the island. She now had another agenda which would take her over to Manchester. She had a new family to find.

'Come on, let's make our way back to the house. It's getting late and my mother probably has something tasty and abnormally high in calories cooking away in the kitchen.'

They walked back through the fields hand in hand, Reed with his guitar thrown over his shoulder, hanging casually off his back. He was wearing his Led Zeppelin tour shirt, which was many years old and his favoured NYC baseball hat. Casually strolling through the fields, he looked very much like a teenager himself.

After some thought he realised that Eenayah hadn't yet agreed to his plan. 'So, what do think about my idea of renting a house and bringing the kids over?'

Eenayah smiled to herself. She thought, 'so this is what control feels like. When someone older and richer than me has to ask my permission to do something. Hmm – me likes.' She replied, 'I think it's a wonderful idea Reed and will be good for all of you and maybe even all of us, if I was here that is, but at this stage don't rely too much on me being around.'

Reed seemed slightly shaken by her unexpected response. He had assumed she would embrace his suggestion.

She continued, 'Reed, I need to go over to the mainland and visit some place called Daisy Hill to meet with my great aunt and grandmother sometime soon. That's going to be quite a big thing for me and I don't know how long it will take or how long I will be there. And don't forget that Ruby and Owyn will be flying out to Miami next week for his 40th birthday and they will be gone for about three weeks, I understand. Ruby has asked that I look after the house while she is away and feed her pets. It's a bit remote and I am not overly excited about it, but I will be in North Wales for at least two weeks on and off.'

Reed wasn't used to Eenayah having a timetable. Back in Miami she mostly did nothing and was always there when he got back from the studios. She was as reliable and as constant as his Rolex. He was slightly dazed by this new Eenayah, a woman who seemed to have a diary packed with actions and people to see.

She sensed his bemusement. 'Oh but Reed, it is a wonderful idea and my parents would be delighted. There is enough room at the farmhouse, so why don't you all stay there? No need to go to the trouble of hiring a house. My parents would totally spoil you and once I've finished doing all I need to do, maybe we can plan some time to be together. It would be such a treat.'

Reed had been spoiled by many years of five-star hotels and privileged living, and so the thought of living in an ageing farm house didn't appeal, as indeed Eenayah knew it wouldn't. She had engineered it that way, knowing he would be unlikely to jump at the suggestion.

'Okay, I see what you are saying. Let's just have a think about it, huh? In the meantime, how much longer will you be on the island? I have a few days off now and I would like to spend some quality time with my wife, if that's okay with you?'

Eenayah liked this. Reed was asking her permission yet again. Now she was seen as the one with the schedule that he had to dance around. The tail was wagging the dog. The strategy was working.

★★★

Once back at the farm, Reed made an excuse to walk to the barn to make a private phone call. It was to his PA, Arabella. Hardly bothering with the niceties of saying hello, she launched straight in.

'Did you find her?'

'Yes, she is with her parents in the Isle of Man, just as her sister had said. That idea of yours about going to see Ruby paid dividends. Well done Arabella.'

'Any chance we can get her back to Miami any time soon so we can sedate her again?'

'I don't think so Arabella, she is going over to Manchester to track down her biological family. We didn't see that one coming. I had no idea that she was even remotely interested in these things.'

Arabella groaned. 'That's a disappointment. We need her back here before her birthday. Leave it with me and maybe I can come up with something to entice her home.'

Reed responded, 'If you can do that it would be great. She didn't fall for the idea of me living with her on the island so she could stay close to her parents. That would have been ideal. At least I would be able to keep an eye on her here, but she just didn't buy it for some weird reason.'

Arabella sounded concerned. 'You can't lose her again Reed. We could control her back in Miami. We have no restraints on her now that she is wandering around the UK trying to find herself. You should have done a better job in keeping her happy and content, Mr Baratolli.'

Reed knew that Arabella spoke the truth and he had to agree. 'I know, I know. It's all my fault. Let's just make sure that we have her followed so we don't lose her again, but make sure Tobiah doesn't lose her next time around. Only a few weeks to go and then it will be happy days! In the meantime, get me off this island. How quickly can you get a plane here?'

'Tomorrow too soon?'

'Tomorrow is good. Bye Bell.'

CHAPTER 14

Monday 1ˢᵗ July 2013

Eenayah had booked the 6am dawn flight over to the mainland. She planned to leave early and travel with haste from Liverpool to North Wales before her sister Ruby awoke. She knew it was an ambitious plan timing wise, but she had so wanted to make the effort to be with her sister whilst back home in the UK.

Her parents had got up with her to see her off, preparing a packed lunch whilst she was struggling downstairs with an oversized suitcase. It was such a sweet loving parental gesture. Much as she wanted to remind them that she was almost 39 years old, in their eyes she was still a little girl setting out on a school trip. It brought back some nice, wistful memories.

It was the most exquisite of sunrises. At 5am the sky was a misty burnt orange and the birds were still singing their ambitious dawn chorus. Her father helped her stuff her suitcase into the limited boot space of the hire car and with a forced shut of the trunk, she was all ready to leave. Her parents both hugged her at the same time, in a threesome embrace which almost squeezed the breath from her lungs. Her mother tried hard not to cry, but was obviously choking on her own emotion. Eenayah tried to reassure them.

'Hey guys, we will all be together in Florida soon. My house – my party – my booze – remember!' She cheekily winked at them both as she shut the car door and drove off down the driveway.

Looking back in her mirror, she could see her parents chuckling riotously as her mother chased Henrietta the hen around the farm courtyard. Her father caught hold of his wife, spun her around and planted a kiss on her cheeks. They were frolicking like teenagers. Rarely had she seen them so happy. Eenayah simply had to stop the car.

Her parents didn't notice her stopping in the lane as they were too engaged in their own private moment of hilarity. Eenayah sat there for a whole ten minutes watching them through her rear mirror.

The thought occurred to her that she might never see them like this ever again. Right here and right now; happy, together and for the moment still relatively young. She wanted to hold onto that vision of her parents for just a few minutes longer; a memory to put in her pocket for much later on in life.

She looked at her watch. She had a plane to catch and a future that wouldn't let her sit still for long. Life was pushing her to move on. One last glance in her mirror and she was reluctantly forced to leave the moment behind, surrendering it to a place called the past. A place that could never be revisited, only remembered.

***

Ruby was stirred by the familiar smell of bacon being fried. The bouquet of wild mushrooms, slightly burnt toast, fresh eggs and crispy bacon had drifted up the stairs, into her nostrils and pervaded her sleep. Still semi-conscious but beginning to rouse, she then had that momentary panic of not knowing where she was. Which hotel room, which city? Was she at home?

Drifting into a degree of alertness, she was comforted by the knowledge that she was at home in her own bed and her husband was in the kitchen making her breakfast. Then came the momentary realisation that it was Monday morning, and with a stream of light making its way through the curtains, she should already have been sitting on a train into London. Panic shook her into wakefulness, until she remembered with total relief that she was on annual leave and was flying out to Miami later today. Sinking back into her pillow, she indulged herself with the thought that for a glorious three whole weeks there would be no more early mornings, emails, taxis, trains or phone calls.

Turning on her side to enjoy a few more moments' rest, she put her arms around her slumbering husband Owyn, who was lying beside her.

So he couldn't possibly be in the kitchen. She shot bolt upright out of bed. 'Who the hell is cooking breakfast in my kitchen?'

Ruby pelted down the grandiose curved staircase as fast as her legs could take her. Dashing down the long corridor, past the giant baroque painting and following the smoke into the kitchen, she was fired up with adrenalin to confront a gastronomic burglar. Instead she found Eenayah, standing at the cooker wearing the shortest of denim shorts and a set of girly pigtails. She was humming one of her husband's songs from his eighties glam rock boy band days and casually pushing bacon and sausages around the frying pan.

Eenayah beamed with amusement as she saw her sister's confusion.

'Ruby, Ruby, Ruby', she sang, 'you still leave your front door keys under the plant pot, now how else do you think I got in here?'

Still slightly out of breath, Ruby ran to give her sister a big warm hug, 'but what are you doing cooking? You don't cook!'

'After a week on Mum and Dad's farm, yes I do. It's the first of July and Owyn's 40th birthday today….yeee!' She squealed like an over-excited child.

She had caught the first scheduled plane over from the Isle of Man into Liverpool Airport and driven to North Wales in an attempt to surprise them. She had intended to bring them both breakfast in bed by way of an unexpected gesture, but now of course Ruby had ruined this by waking up and catching her in preparation.

'Can you go back to bed Ruby?' asked her sister after lovingly setting out a tray to bring upstairs.

Ruby was flabbergasted. How long was it since Princess Eenayah had last set foot on a routine commercial plane, as opposed to a private jet or helicopter? She couldn't recall when Eenayah had last driven a car for herself either. And the kitchen was completely clean and tidy.

'Have you done this?'

Eenayah just nodded. Ruby was impressed.

'But you have servants, you don't do cleaning.'

'You mean Roserie. I don't class her as a servant. She is more of a surrogate mother than a maid, but I get what you mean. The thing is, I have enjoyed being normal over the last few weeks. It feels good to actually do normal things like normal people. I simply became fed up of having medication dampen my spirit and zap me of all my energy. I guess I felt like a lioness in a zoo, constantly having my next meal thrown at me without having to go out and hunt it down. Yes, the meal is nice, but I miss the thrill of the kill.' She made a clawing gesture with her fingers and mimicked a roar. At that moment little Harry walked in from the TV room, already bathed, dressed and fed. Ruby was astonished and impressed yet again.

'And you have done this for my little boy as well? My god, the lioness really is out of the cage. Welcome to Wales.'

Owyn rushed down the stairs, paranoid that they would be late for their flight. On seeing Eenayah there he called out, 'Oh mother of Jesus, it's Eenayah, what the hell!'

'Hey, bro in law, happy birthday big boy.' Eenayah handed him a huge birthday card. As Owyn opened it, several e-tickets and various printouts, admission permits and receipts fell out onto the floor. 'Everything you need for fun in the sun. I so hope you all enjoy it.'

Owyn glanced at the first folder that caught his attention. 'First class - seriously? We are travelling first class - no way!'

Eenayah shrugged it off as though it was nothing. 'Well, you guys deserve it. You haven't had a vacation in ages. Now once you've had this lovely breakfast I have made you, go get ready for Miami and go and be pampered.'

A little more than an hour later the taxi turned up on the doorstep. Eenayah had almost forgotten what it felt like to be excited about a long-haul flight, but she was reliving the moment through the eyes of her sister, brother-in-law and nephew. She thought back to the first time her parents had taken her on a plane to Jersey and how overwhelmed she had been just sitting at the window and watching the tarmac speed past her until the wheels had left the ground. Revisiting this moment through the Kyfinn family brought all the memories back. Saddened and yet happy for them, she waved the perfect little family goodbye as they made tracks on their adventure. True love was being happy on behalf of somebody else.

★★★

Eenayah soon recognised that a busy house that becomes quiet is much quieter than a house that is always quiet. In the stillness, she looked around and wondered what to do next. Maybe she should go and explore. She wished her sister had left her a map of the house; so rambling was this strange, expansive gothic mansion, which seemed to envelop so many differing centuries.

She was already familiar with the utility room, boot room, pantry, larder, snug, TV room, scullery, orangery and servants' hall, all of which led off directly from a tiny corridor from the main kitchen. This seemed to be the working part of the house. A cold stone staircase wound its way up from the servants hall to what she presumed would have been the servants' living and sleeping quarters. She had been up there once before and noted that the tiny bedrooms were sparse; plaster peeling from the walls and windows in need of repair. Ruby had explained that this area was unused and a lesser priority, so it had been abandoned in a much neglected state. Eenayah wasn't about to take another walk up the austere back stairs while she was in the house alone. She hadn't liked it the last time she had been up there and could see no reason why that would have changed. Ruby had once told her that on many an evening when sitting in the heated snug they could hear footsteps from above, even though that area was empty and unused.

Aside from the east wing, Eenayah didn't know much about the house. Ruby and the family had seemed to contain themselves in this portion of the building (which also seemed to be the warmest part of the manor), so on the rare occasions Eenayah had visited, the kitchen area was mostly the place where everybody hung out.

Ruby had explained that because the rest of the house had been going through a renovation process over the years, they had simply got into the habit of living in a small corner of the east wing. So aside from the much frequented ground floor wing and her allocated bedroom, Eenayah hadn't really seen any of the other rooms. She decided to set off to investigate.

She walked down the long, straight corridor which led from the kitchen and connected the east wing with the rest of the house. Opening each of the tall oak doors in the hallway to see what lay undiscovered behind them, she first encountered the library. It was an impressive rectangular room and its shelves were packed with old books. Taking the time to peruse them, she noticed that most of them were not actually that old; mainly recipe and travel books. The rest looked as though they had been amassed via many visits to a variety of car boot and jumble sales. The room was handsomely decorated with enriched panelled ceilings and boasted a grand mantelpiece of oak, cedar, and walnut, inlaid with other ornate woods.

As she opened the door opposite she found a formal dining room, with the table all laid out as though Ruby had been expecting to host a dinner party. The walls were lined with a varnished wood frame of pitch pine and contained many portraits of long dead strangers. Eenayah seemed to recall Ruby telling her that she often frequented auctions and sought to buy old paintings, just to give her house the authentic look of some National Trust building. 'Acquired ancestors' was how her sister often referred to her 17th century line up.

The door next to the dining room opened up to what had once been a schoolroom (it said as much on the door), but it had now been converted to a modern office complete with phone/fax and a Wi-Fi modem/router. Despite the more up to date décor, Eenayah noted that the decorative cornices and alabaster ceiling art has been feathered with a touch of shimmering gilt.

Opposite the study was the formal lounge (previously referred to as a parlour), which was occasionally used by the family, especially during parties such as Christmas gatherings. She had been in this room before. She recognised the unusual embossed tin ceiling which she recalled had cost Ruby an arm and a leg to restore. It housed the expected illustrious marble fireplace and the long sashed windows, the frames of which seemed to run almost the full length from ceiling to floor. A window seat must have been the origin of many a wistful thought by those gazing out to the surreal mountain backdrop.

Reaching the end of the east wing corridor, she found herself in the familiar grand entrance hallway, with its rectangular voids of space and subliminal statement of Victorian opulence. This was the beating heart of Ruby's vast home. The principal entrance to the house was on the south-facing side of the manor, and was entered via an enclosed porch, paved with a marble mosaic. It linked directly to the only standing remains of the castle.

This was the area of the house which confused Eenayah, as the Victorian and Edwardian east wing suddenly found itself embracing the medieval era. The original castle gatehouse or *logis-porche* boasted an oversized arch with twin turrets on either side leading up to a lookout balcony by way of steep spiral steps. Ruby grew herbs on top of the turrets, which Eenayah thought to be an inventive use of space. The former owners had converted the Victorian entrance porch so it diverted over to the gatehouse, making this the ultimate grand welcoming statement. Sadly it was rarely used, as most of the family entered via the rear, traditionally the tradesman's access with the key hidden under the plant pot. None the less the castle entrance was impressive, and when cloaked with purple wisteria in the early summer, it looked like something out of a film set rather than a real front door. It gleamed of old world charm.

Near the castle gate entrance a small 4ft side door led down to the casemate, which was the original vaulted chamber constructed underneath the rampart. Ruby and Owyn used this as a wine cellar, so reluctant as she might be, Eenayah knew she would be frequenting this part of the house before long. From the casemate a door led through to the undercroft, which was a vaulted storage room and a complete mess of 21st century clutter. Ruby and Owyn used this as most people used a garage; Christmas decorations, suitcases, pots of paint and of the like. Eenayah had no desire to explore deep into the bowels of this part of the house.

The castle's relationship to the main house was a curiosity. The rest of the castle was in ruins and was now little more than strewn stones on the hillside. However the gatehouse had been sympathetically restored and still displayed the remnants of a former drawbridge, along with a selection of portcullises, machicolations, arrow loops and sinister sounding murder-holes. It brought visions to mind of former battles and sieges. Not a mental picture one would like to associate with a family dwelling.

Eenayah had quizzed Owyn about the history of the castle, seeing as he was born and raised in the area and knew far more about Darwydden Castle Manor than Ruby, or probably anyone else for that matter. It was Owyn who had insisted that they buy the place, despite Ruby's objections; she felt they were 'biting off more than they could chew'. Ambitious and costly was an understatement. She recalled Owyn telling her that the castle had been built by Edward I circa 1280 as part of his efforts to subdue the Welsh. Eenayah had heard rumours about the castle dungeons being accessible by the undercroft, but it would be a cold day in hell before she would ever attempt to go to such a place.

Back to the main entrance hall was the imposing staircase. It was indeed a big old oak staircase of three flights, protected by balustrades of pierced strapwork, with large newels at the landings and dressed with heraldic animals and hellish-looking gargoyles. The staircase windows were filled with grisailled glass and displayed a varied display of coats of arms and other diverse symbolism.

Opposite the corridor to the east wing was a similar corridor to the facing west wing. This was the part of the house which had so far been mostly untouched. Aside from the oak beamed great hall, which was occasionally used during functions and large parties, most of this side of the house remained an unused idle waste. One room simply led into the other and both Ruby and Owyn struggled to dream up a good purpose for the east wing. Eenayah could see quite clearly that lack of money was an issue and despite her sister's refusal of help, she was thinking that maybe a contribution would at least lessen the financial burden of restoration.

Venturing upstairs, up on the first floor and following the same east/west divide, were ten bedrooms in total. All came with dressing rooms, some with en suites, and along the corridors were four shared bathrooms. Opening them door by door, Eenayah had established that only five of the rooms were actually liveable in. They were Owyn and Ruby's master bedroom, Harry's nursery and then three additional guest suites. Eenayah couldn't help but think that this was a heck of a lot of house going to waste. She also lived in a large residence, but with Reed's constant stream of guests, at least her house was occasionally used to capacity. On the other hand, her sister's house seemed to her to be mostly redundant. She failed to see why her brother-in-law had insisted in purchasing such a folly.

Back down to the main entrance hall, and the one door behind the stairs she had not yet explored. Ruby had explained that the house had two sets of cellars. One belonged to the gory old castle and the other to the more recent Victorian construction. The house had been 'added onto' over the years, and with piecemeal assembly which varied according to the era. The Victorian basement housed the boiler, the coal cellars and the former ice house. She had no burning desire to explore this dark grim area, unless a fault with the boiler forced her to descend the steep cellar steps. She knew she would just call out a plumber should this be the case, so the cellar was off limits.

Wondering where to spend an evening in the house alone, she opted for the more congenial east wing. She dismissed the snug, not wanting to hear ghostly footsteps pitter-patter above her, and instead opted for the TV room - ironically the smallest room in the mansion. She concluded that humans preferred small caves, especially when alone.

Eenayah then considered what she should do to occupy herself the following day. Ruby had left contact details for a local riding school where she could go trekking along the mountain bridle paths of Snowdonia, and of course Owyn's sister Darcy had invited herself over so she could acquaint herself to what was probably the nearest she would come to the world of the rich and famous. Listening to the slow ticking of the clock forever counting away the time by way of a constant reminder not to waste it, Eenayah resolved that she needed to stay busy and keep her mind active. She didn't want to sink into the sub-zero world of depression and was mindful that she had to manage herself with care. She knew that depression was a hole one could climb out of, but it always had its claws around its victim's ankles, just waiting for an opportune moment to drag you back down to its grim depths.

Wandering back into the old schoolroom, she connected her PC to the internet and looked at her location on a search engine. She noted she was less than 45 minutes' drive to St Asaph's. Unaccustomed as she was to visiting graves and cremation sprinkle places as well as placing flowers on such places (especially those of ex-boyfriends and husbands), it did seem to have become something of a habit on this UK vacation and so with time to kill, a visit to Greg's grave seemed appropriate.

The church at St Asaph was visible long before one reached it. The white marble reflected the sun and the church stood proud and prominent to any driver negotiating the A55 dual carriageway. Walking in through the gate, Eenayah was not oblivious to that fact this was the second white church she had visited recently. On this occasion, it was also the church where she was married. Her mind drifted back to 1997 when she had been just 22 years old. In her mind she could see the ghost of herself walking down the pathway in the traditional silk dress her parents had saved up to buy her. In her hands, white lilies, orange roses and lily of the valley with ivy cascading down in a long trail.

The Eenayah Bucklow, née Layne, of sixteen years ago had been a very different person. Maybe financially challenged, but with other riches to compensate, she had been determined, ambitious and yet always considerate. Life with Greg had been tough in a practical way, but it had also been fun. She had loved him dearly. On finding his tombstone, she laid on his grave the same mixture of flowers that had been in her wedding bouquet; it seemed appropriate.

More so than with James, she had cast her mind away from Greg after his passing and closed him down as quickly as she could. It wasn't that she hadn't loved him; she had, and missed him dreadfully. However with Greg came the searing pain of guilt. He had complained of feeling nauseous and having headaches, but she had ignored his pleas to return. She tormented herself with the certain knowledge that if only she had come home that night rather than staying away to work for a few more days, she would have made sure he received some medical treatment. As it happened she had convinced him that he was just being a hypochondriac, and so trusting of her was he that he believed her. She could not even allow herself the thought that he had lapsed into a coma alone in their house, lying on the cold hard floor for days. No comfort, no kind words, just alone on a hard tile floor while he died in isolation.

Eenayah had taken many hard blows in her life, but she could not bear the grief that came with Greg's tragic and needless death. She didn't linger long at the grave. Guilt wasn't a friend she needed by her side. She said a silent prayer and moved swiftly away. This was a much greater sorrow and one that she had not yet learned to deal with. She hadn't been to this grave for a very long time and wouldn't come back here again for a long time to come. She could not even cry a single tear, the remorse was too deep for even that most basic of human reactions.

Driving away from the church, she thought about his father Paul. She had always liked Paul, but recognised that he was a bit of a womaniser. He had two sons by different women and Eenayah had married or been engaged to them both. She still shuddered at the jolt of that realisation. Marrying both brothers had been a sword in her side and a source of gossip for those who chose to judge her, for far too many years.

As she recalled, Paul was the only person in that entire family with whom she had actually clicked. He always had a bizarre sense of humour and was totally supportive and non-judgmental about the situation of both his son's demise, unlike others, who openly blamed Eenayah.

She tried to recall where he lived and could only remember it was around and about a small Welsh place called Llanfairtalogogohom - a complex name that you either remembered or totally blanked and probably always miss-spelled. Thank God for sat navs. She figured that Paul lived about half way between St Asaph's and her sister's house in Snowdonia. She contemplated the bizarre thought of calling in to see Paul on her way back to Ruby's gothic residence. She was spooked by Ruby's place and any detour that entailed spending less time there than was required seemed most welcome. She set the navigation system for Llanfairtalogogohom as a half-way point and then would just take it from there. She considered that it would be interesting to see how good her memory was. How unusual was this situation? The pampered Eenayah from Miami of a month ago would never have dared be this adventurous, and even the new Eenayah was wary of casually calling in on a former father-in-law. But what the hell, she thought as she followed the automated robotic voice instructions.

The road seemed familiar, but it had all been so very long ago. Sheep, mountains, river, sheep, mountains, river. Everything looked the same. She needed to look out for a steep dirt track by the side of a pub car park, but on which road and by which pub?

She spotted a Christmas tree on the corner of a dirt track by such a pub. She remembered a tiny tree that Greg planted long ago on the corner of his father's driveway. What she now saw was a huge tree which looked out of place against the indigenous plantation. Could this be the same small tree that Greg had planted all those years ago? She was going to take a chance. What the hell, she turned into the steep winding dirt track and let providence or foolishness lead her where it may. Perhaps not for the first or last time.

At the top of the hill was a large L-shaped rendered Welsh cottage. Smoke was piping out of the chimney, so she concluded that someone must be at home. Outside on the shale driveway was parked a shiny black Porsche. She recognised the house, but did Paul still live there? The Porsche told her that maybe he did. The personalised number plate told her he most certainly did. She calculated that he was probably 60 by now, but if ever a man of that age was going to drive a supremely fast sports car, then Paul would be that man and a Porsche would be that car.

It took several deep breaths, much internal confidence boosting and a splash of bravado, but eventually she had the nerve to use the large metal dragon knocker on the door. Sooner than she anticipated a man answered the door. He was dressed in jogging shorts and general sports attire. With a towel around his shoulders and the odd pearl of sweat, he looked as if he had been doing some sort of physical exercise. He had a relaxed, friendly face and just asked simply, 'hello can I help you?'

It was indeed Paul. The years might have taken their toll, but the handsome, chiselled features were still apparent.

Paul was much slower in reaching his conclusion and genuinely seemed confused as to why a beautiful young lady had suddenly appeared on his doorstep. Forever the charmer and with a faint hint of recognition he asked, 'do I know you, you look familiar?' He had a mischievous glint in his clear blue eyes. Paul hadn't seen Eenayah in many years, and she was a lot thinner than the woman he had last known.

'It's Eenayah', she replied simply and sweetly.

Paul looked visibly stunned and shaken. 'Oh my God, Eenayah! I never thought I would see you again. I read all about you when you got married to that rich American music mogul. I can't believe it. What are you doing in Wales? What are you doing on my doorstep? Please come in, my darling girl.'

They had a lot of catching up to do – years of it. Eenayah was feeling slightly intrusive just turning up unannounced, but she was there now and there was no going back, so in she stepped. Whichever way, it delayed the time she would have to spend in Ruby's house of horrors.

Paul had been a footballer in his younger days. His father had been a consultant anaesthetist and his son was well educated and well spoken. He had wanted Paul to follow in his footsteps, and indeed for a while Paul had gone to medical school in Yorkshire. However he also had an undisputed talent with his feet. He had played for local clubs since childhood, but it wasn't long before a scout picked him up and persuaded him to play soccer professionally. It had been a major decision to quit medical school for sport and the decision caused all sorts of family tensions and rifts, but Paul did what he wanted to do, as always.

He was soon playing for a premier league club and made more than a decent amount of money, far more than his father ever had as a doctor. He had married Mary and she gave birth to James within five months of them marrying. At the same time he was also dating Katherine back in Wales, and she became pregnant with Greg around the same time as he married Mary. It was a major scandal, complicated and all very messy. As a footballer, Paul was known to the media and so this odd arrangement had hardly been a closeted secret. As far as Eenayah could recall, he later divorced Mary, who returned to the Isle of Man with James, married Katherine and raised Greg in North Wales. The two brothers didn't have a close relationship, each being brought up by a different families in a different country.

For Eenayah to meet and then become engaged to both brothers was nothing more than coincidence. She had never understood the fluke of fate by which her path crossed theirs. She often felt embarrassed and humiliated by how local people referred to her, especially after both boys had died. However the past was the past and she had escaped to America, where nobody knew her or was aware of her scandalous history.

Paul Bucklow had been a fine-looking, well-dressed man back in the day, and an unashamed and unapologetic womaniser. As a footballer and living the life that came with the profession, girls would throw themselves at Paul, and he rarely refused a free offer. He was a cad in the old-fashioned sense of the word, but as Eenayah looked at him now, she felt she was looking into Greg's eyes rather than those of his father's. His strong, square jawline was the mirror image of Greg's, whilst his smile was identical to that of James. She dared not even admit this to herself, but because he shared so many features with the men (his sons) that she had loved and lost, she found herself strangely attracted to Paul. This sudden sentiment and rush of hormonally charged blood was strange and unnerving.

Paul had always been a hospitable chap; it was in his nature. He made Eenayah feel perfectly at ease and at home, and before long they were playing catch up with the past. Moving the conversation forward into the present, Eenayah updated him on her time on the Isle of Man and shared with him the discovery that Mary's second husband had passed away and that Mary always avoided talking to her mum. They then discussed Ruby's career and Reed's non-compromising workload and of course she told him all about her new life in Miami.

By way of mutual exchange, Paul updated her about his retirement from the premier league. He now owned a gym and was a personal trainer, plus he had a portfolio of properties he managed. He also surprised her with his passion for Shire horses – not at all what she would have expected from someone like Paul – but then again he never did fit any sort of expected parameter. All in all it seemed that he only worked a few hours a day and for the rest of the time it appeared he worked out. For a man of his age it was obvious he was in great physical shape and was proud of his well-maintained six-pack.

Eenayah scanned the surroundings to look for signs of a Mrs Bucklow, and it was confusing. She couldn't make her mind up. She had heard rumours that he had divorced Katherine and wondered if a replacement had been on the horizon. The cottage was spotless, but then again she remembered Paul had ODC and was a cleanliness freak. The kitchen was full of cookbooks, but then she also recollected what an excellent cook he was, as indeed were both his sons. What she couldn't see was a vase of flowers, and most women she knew would treat themselves to fresh flowers if they could afford to. She jumped to her conclusions.

'Not wanting to be rude Paul, but I am presuming you are not married or with girlfriend?'

Paul was amused by her delicate fishing. 'You are one observant lady Eenayah. Some guys are just meant to be single and I think I fall into that category. I have an income or two, lots of friends, more hobbies than I can fit into a day and I am a bloody awesome chef, so aside from the obvious why would a guy like me need to be married? Been there, done that, had two wives, worn the T-shirt and moved on, and as for the other stuff – hey I have the internet, if you get my drift.'

At least he was honest, and she respected that. She was also more than aware that she had been there longer than intended and had probably outstayed her welcome. She stood to leave, only then realising that she was still wearing the shortest of bottom-hugging denim shorts and looked more like a cheerleader than a lady of her wealth and social standing.

'Bloody hell, I feel so embarrassed Paul. I only came here out of curiosity and I've only just realised that I am not exactly dressed for the occasion. I had better make tracks. Dog and cat to feed, TV to watch, ghosts to exorcize and so on.'

Paul surveyed her attire admiringly, but protested 'no need for you to leave Eenayah. I get fed up of cooking for one. You are home alone and I am home alone. Hey, why can't we keep each other company for a little while longer?'

The offer was very tempting and to be honest, she wasn't looking forward to the seclusion of her twin's big old house; plus her own cooking was by her own admission at best average and at worst unpalatable.

Having persuaded Eenayah to stay for a meal, he then persuaded her to stay over so she could relax, kick her shoes off and drink champagne, or maybe some ridiculously expensive wine from a collection that was really an investment purchase rather than an intended drink. It was an investment he would be willing to sacrifice.

Eenayah knew what was happening. She was in dangerous territory, but she was drawn in. Feeling like a fly which had found itself in a spider's web and was unable to escape, she felt helpless. Much as she was loath to admit it, she wasn't making too much of an effort to untangle herself from this particular web.

She told herself that Reed had spent most of his marriage to her being in the company of young nubile females, and who knows if what happens in Vegas stays in Vegas? Perhaps what happens in Wales could stay in Wales.

This was her time now. Her time to take control and call the shots. After all, she was only staying for a meal and a few drinks and she could always call for a taxi if she didn't want to drive… couldn't she? What the hell! She reasoned that his companionship was worth a taxi fare.

They still had a lot of ground to catch up on and Paul was a charismatic and entertaining conversationalist. Yes indeed, he was good; very good. Little by little and nothing too obvious. This was Paul Bucklow's seduction technique, and most times it worked.

CHAPTER 15

Tuesday 2nd July 2013

Her feet had started to blister as the flames licked up beneath her. Fear petrified her body as she mentally tried to break free and yet physically was unable to move. She tried to scream and her mouth opened, but no noise emerged. All around her men in long dark cloaks with hoods partially covering their faces watched impartially. Their coldness was in complete contrast with the heat reaching up her legs. With the last strand of energy she could muster, she finally managed to scream.

At that point Eenayah woke up with a jolt, her entire body covered in a strange iodine-smelling sweat. Breathing heavily and with eyes wide open, she quickly realised that this was just a nightmare. It was the same recurring night fright which had haunted her many times over the years, but was now harassing her with an ever more intense and terrifying frequency.

The early morning light hit her eyes and made her squint. She must have fallen asleep with the curtains open. The view out of Ruby's window was spectacular. The mountain peaks were embroiled in the early morning summer mist and the pink tinted orange of the sunrise projected unusual patterns against the slopes. However the strong smell of alcohol in the room was overwhelming. Surely she couldn't have drunk so much that she was sweating it out of her pores?

Eenayah's head hurt, her throat was dry and her body was dehydrated. How much had she drunk last night? She couldn't remember. She staggered out of bed in need of an urgent pee. Looking out of the window she spotted her hire car and was horrified to realise she must have driven home rather than taken a taxi.

'Stupid irresponsible bugger,' she uttered to herself in disgust. Looking down at what she was wearing, she noticed she was naked aside from a huge blue tee-shirt which quite obviously was not hers. She assumed she must have taken Owyn's shirt. She really couldn't handle alcohol since coming off her anti-depressant medication. She made a mental note to try and control her intake in future.

Eenayah had endured many years as a teetotaller; basically the meds and booze didn't mix. She now enjoyed having an occasional alcoholic drink and especially looked forward to her ritual Monday midday cocktail whilst on the phone gossiping with Ruby, but her body simply couldn't handle large amounts. Her detoxified liver just wasn't used to it. She guessed this was no bad thing, and her friend Jonathan always joked that she was a cheap date. Still there was a big difference between getting tipsy with trusted friends and totally blacking out in the company of a guy who after all these years was as good as a stranger.

She got dressed in the remnants of yesterday's clothes, as all her other clothes were still in a suitcase in the hallway. Unpacking was the order of the day. A strong coffee, lots of water and an aspirin would help. As she gingerly walked down the old creaky stairs she felt slightly confused by her surroundings. After yesterday's exploration she had become slightly more at ease with the configuration of the wings, but to Eenayah it was still a bewildering higgledy-piggledy place and she hadn't even got as far as the third floor.

She tried to gather her bearings. She knew that after the main entrance hall every other part of the building just spilled out in quirky directions, each reflecting its own century and individual character. She often considered that for young Harry growing up it would be a fantastic place to play hide and seek, but for a grown woman with a hangover, it was just a maze. Where the heck was she?

The main thought on Eenayah's mind was to find the kitchen. Where did Ruby keep her coffee? Fortunately she soon located it, at the bottom of the stairs. Easy! With half-closed eyes she failed to notice that the staircase was just a quarter of the size it had been the day before. All she knew was that if she put one foot in front of the other and held on to the banister rail, she would proceed in a downwards direction. This wasn't where she vaguely remembered the kitchen to be, but then again she would not be at all surprised if Ruby's eccentric old house had more than one kitchen, or maybe even one for each wing. Perhaps she had somehow found the servants' back stairs and had spent the night up in the haunted bedrooms above the snug?

As she scanned the kitchen for caffeine, a dash of red caught her attention; a single red rose on the kitchen table. It looked as though it had just been plucked from the garden, as it still had droplets of fresh dew on the leaves and felt cold to the touch. Who could have broken in? Had she not been home alone? It sent immediate alarm bells ringing.

As she carefully looked around at her surroundings an uncomfortable dawn of realisation struck her. A note had been left under the rose. It read: 'just out for my early morning run up in the hills, see you when you wake up sleepy head. Paul xx.'

The reality hit her like a bullet in the stomach. She looked outside the front door and the parked black Porsche confirmed all. Why was she still here? What the hell had she done?

She spotted her car keys on the same table. Time to vacate Paul's house with lightning speed, coffee or no coffee. But panic reigned and her mind spun. What if she passed him driving down the road? She would just have to press the pedal to the metal and drive on past as fast as she could. She had to get out, now.

She planned her departure in bite-sized steps. She would dash to the car, in the hope that Paul wasn't just approaching the courtyard after his run. She then would lock the doors and start the ignition with haste before completing the short journey down the driveway, in the hope that Paul wasn't running up it. She would drive around to the back of the pub car park to set her destination for Ruby's house, all along hoping that the car park wasn't along Paul's running route. That was the plan, no note, no goodbye - just go. Eenayah was doing what she always did - running away from any situation she couldn't handle.

With her heart pumping almost audibly, she turned left onto the main road, accelerating as fast as she could. She hoped that Paul wouldn't be running across the road in front of her car any time soon. It was only when she had driven 15 miles that she felt safe enough to pull over in a garage and get that strong coffee she so needed. She was shaking with the fix of adrenalin that had been propelling itself through her blood stream.

Finally arriving back at Ruby's, she felt an overwhelming sense of relief. Made to feel guilty of the sin of abandoning a hungry cat called Barnaby and an equally ravenous dog called Bertie, she could relax and reflect. What had just happened exactly? She had remembered eating some Italian pasta dish that Paul had made her, and she recalled drinking a tad too much red wine. They had seemed to talk and talk forever, and with years of catching up time had just evaporated. She laughed and he flirted. She did feel attracted to him, although he was a million years older than her, mainly because he had the look of two men she had once loved - his sons! The thought hit her like a steam roller, and on reflection felt quite vile. Paul was her stepfather. Revolting!

She admitted to herself that she had enjoyed his company, but she recalled nothing more than that. A ludicrous thought entered her head; had he laced her drink with Rohypnol? She dismissed the thought as fast as she had contemplated it. The thought was too uncomfortable to even consider, so she was determined to remove all references to this incident from her consciousness. Eenayah did escapism very well. Years of avoiding reality had taught her how to remove a memory with the click of a finger.

She decided that Paul had probably been the perfect gentleman, guiding her towards the spare room, allowing her to borrow a tee-shirt and then walking off to his own bedroom. Thinking rationally and now feeling a tad remorseful at running away with such haste, she conceded that this was the more logical of possibilities. She would not talk about this to anyone or make any further efforts to contact Paul. She hoped dearly that she hadn't given him her mobile number or Ruby's address, but in any case she would dump the mobile, put the pets in the vets and move out of her sister's mansion. There was always a solution.

With that final thought, she was going to unpack her suitcase, sit out in the garden and do what English people in Wales do best; drink tea, admire the views of Snowdonia and psychologically move on from unusual family reunions which would never be spoken of again. Skeleton tucked away in the cupboard!

Having spent a solid hour hanging clothes out in the wardrobe and now feeling exhausted, she had only just positioned herself in the rose-covered pagoda with what appeared to be a jolly good book when one of her several mobiles rang. She hoped against hope that it wasn't Paul and was delighted to hear it was Ruby.

'Ruby, oh my God I am so pleased that you have finally rung me! I was getting a bit concerned. How are you, how was the flight, did Owyn enjoy it? And is Harry okay, did you find my house easily or did you get lost? It's easy to get lost in Miami. Was Roserie there to meet you?'

Ruby was a bit overwhelmed by the machine-gun fire of questions. 'Hey Eenayah, slow down. Yes the flight was wonderful and thank you so much for the first class tickets. Owyn did not expect the birthday cake and champagne. The other passengers sang happy birthday to him, including the cabin crew. He was totally speechless. He has asked me to thank you. It was a lovely present for his 40th.'

Eenayah was delighted to be able to finally treat Ruby and her family. She had often offered them financial support, but Ruby had always been too proud to accept anything. This was the first time she had actually accepted a gift of this proportion, but only because it was for Owyn.

She was curious to know what they thought of the villa. Reed had only purchased it two years back, so it was relatively new.

'Did you find my house okay, have you settled in now?' she asked.

'Oh Eenayah, it is wonderful - pure luxury. Yes we got here just fine. Had a few problems with the intercom as we didn't know what button to press and Owyn forgot the gate code, but Roserie was at home and was expecting us, so she let us through. It is magnificent. We feel like we have arrived in paradise.'

Eenayah was excited on their behalf. 'Have you had time to look around yet? What time is it where you are?'

Ruby looked down at her watch, which she had reset to local time.

'Er – it's just 8 am sis. We haven't been here long enough to look around, but I guess the beauty of first class and a night flight is that you get to sleep on the plane in comfort and readjust between time zones fairly fast. I may try to catch a bit of sleep later this afternoon. Harry and Owyn have just jumped into your fantastic pool. As soon as they got here they had changed into their swimming gear. They are in their element. I doubt I will be able to pull them out of the water anytime soon. I may try out the infinity pool and a taste of Roserie's notorious Bloody Marys once I've done a bit of unpacking.'

Eenayah was pleased that they had arrived safely and seemed to be enjoying themselves so soon into their vacation. She had known that the last few years hadn't been easy for all of them and renovating their home had been physically and financially tough.

'How are you Eenayah, did you get up to anything last night?' she asked.

Thank God Ruby couldn't see her blushing. What was she supposed to say?

'Oh me? Nothing much. I got drunk and may or may not have slept with a man who is circa 25 years older than me, and did I mention that he used to be my father in law?' This was one of those situations where one lies by omission of the truth. She recalled a quote from Tad Williams: 'We tell lies when we are afraid... afraid of what we don't know, afraid of what others will think, afraid of what will be found out about us. But every time we tell a lie, the thing we fear grows stronger.'

Eenayah had hesitated in her response long enough for Ruby to sense a situation. She repeated the question with some concern. 'Eenayah, are you okay? Have you settled in all right? I know you are spooked by my big old house but I promise you it isn't haunted.'

Eenayah had to think on her feet. This was her twin sister on the end of the line and she struggled to keep a secret from someone with whom she had once shared a womb. She hadn't even told Ruby that she had found out who their biological mother was yet, let alone the fact she had instigated a search. Eenayah didn't want anything to ruin her sister's much-needed Florida vacation. She would tell her when she got back.

Eventually she responded. 'Yes I'm fine thanks Ruby, but it is rather remote where you live and I'm not too sure I do isolation all that well. If I needed to get some time out in London with Reed, would you mind if I put Barnaby and Bertie in the kennels up the road for a few days? I won't be gone long, I promise.'

Eenayah was proud of the way she had skirted around that particular awkward moment. She had played the ace loneliness card and considering her former depression, she knew Ruby wouldn't want to risk triggering any new episodes.

However it was not that easy to push Ruby off the scent. 'Why don't you get Reed to come over and spend some time with you in Wales?' she asked.

Darn it, Ruby hadn't taken the bait. Eenayah was horrified at the idea of Reed joining her in Wales and then Paul finding out where she was living and knocking on the door whilst she was there with him. She couldn't carry on with this conversation any longer without digging herself into a hole she wouldn't be able to get out of. She could do nothing else but tell an out-and-out fib. With a lump in her throat she responded, 'Wow yes, I hadn't thought of that. What a brilliant idea. I'll ask Reed to come over and join me. Thanks for that suggestion Ruby.'

Now keen to cut the conversation short before she dug herself into an even bigger hole, she terminated the call with a curt 'anyway got to go now as Mum's ringing on the other phone. Have a great time and don't worry about me. You kids go play in Florida. Have fun, byeeeee!'

Of course her mother wasn't ringing on the other phone at all. Paul only lived forty minutes' drive away and that seemed too close for comfort. He was a smart guy and she was sure it wouldn't take long for him to find out her sister's surname and then connect it to this house via a phone directory or online search. Ruby had also inadvertently alerted her to the fact that Reed might well be tempted to come and join her in North Wales, since he now seemed to be in damage limitation mode as far as their marriage was concerned. Bloody hell, she thought. Reed could land his helicopter at the bottom of Ruby's garden any minute now.

She would need to hit this nail on the head, and soon. She decided to call Reed and encourage him to rent a house over in the Isle of Man so at least she could put the Irish Sea between him and Paul. Whether Ruby liked it or not, the pets were going to be put in the kennels. Aside from that, she also had the task of calling Mercy and arranging a date when she could visit her great aunt and biological grandmother over in Manchester. She would need to book some accommodation locally. All that mattered to her right now was finding out about her mother, Daisy Green. This was her number one priority, and not lagging too far behind that was the urgency to get out of Wales.

Eenayah had believed that her problems had been settled simply by driving out of Paul's driveway, but she now realised that she needed to vacate the country. She planned to leave most of her clothes in the wardrobe to make it seem that she had stayed at Ruby's house to look after Barnaby and Bertie, and then perhaps return just before her sister got back from Florida. Her mind started to spin yarns, and she was immediately astounded by how deceptive she had suddenly become. The Eenayah of a year ago would never have been capable of such deception, but then again the Eenayah of a year ago had had nothing much to hide.

No time to read a book in the garden and relax in the sun. She could do that back in Miami. She had several phone calls to make.

CHAPTER 16

Thursday 4ᵗʰ July 2013

Eenayah had not always been a PPP (precious pampered princess). Growing up on a farm had its challenges, and like everyone else in the family she had been expected to muck in and get her hands dirty. Of course she had appreciated the life of a rich man's wife, but wealth also had many challenges of a different kind. She had welcomed the opportunity to simply drive herself around, cook her own meals and iron her own clothes. However, just for once room service and indulgence were most welcome. She had arrived at the sky-high luxury Hilton hotel in Manchester only yesterday, and had already fully availed herself of spa treatments and the luxury that reminded her of her charmed Miami lifestyle.

Today was an important day; she had waited for this day for a lifetime and she wanted to look her absolute best. Not that appearance's should matter, but this was a bit like wearing ones Sunday best; she simply wanted to show she had made an effort. It was hugely important for her to pay homage to the magnitude of the day. It seemed fitting that coincidentally it was also Independence Day, not that she knew if this was of any significance.

Wrapped in her fluffy white hotel dressing gown and eating eggs Benedict on her bed, she took the first of many phone calls, from Mercy.

'How are you feeling about today hon?' asked Mercy, forever the professional and consistently delivering customer service to perfection.

'Nervous but excited', came the reply.

'I am sure you are' sympathised Mercy, 'but don't forget to take notes and if your great aunt doesn't object, record what she is saying. You will be surprised at all the things you don't hear because you are on edge. Also take photographs, they will be forever precious. Don't forget that your great aunt may be feeling anxious as well, so be sympathetic to her needs.'

'Thank you Mercy, as always your advice is spot on' replied Eenayah in gratitude.

'One other thing Eenayah', continued Mercy, 'with regard to your grandmother, remember that she does have Alzheimer's. Don't raise your hopes too high. Hopefully her memories from the past may be good, even though she may not know what happened to her yesterday.'

Eenayah began to get slightly emotional and simply thanked Mercy for her call and recommendations.

'One last thing Eenayah, my father would like you to read the draft book on your husband's genealogy and get back to him about it as soon as you can.' With everything that had been happening recently Eenayah had totally forgotten about the book, but promised she would do as requested.

Within moments she received her second phone call, from her mother. Eenayah had made her mother aware of today's events and of course her adoptive parents were as anxious about the meeting as she was.

'I hope it all goes well today my love and please call us as soon as you get back to the hotel', said her mother, with a slight emotional wobble in her voice. Eenayah told her about the possibility of Reed and the stepchildren coming over to the Isle of Man to visit them. This news made Ellie spin with excitement, although Eenayah did warn her it was only a possibility at this stage.

Her mother suddenly adopted the voice she often used when sharing gossip, a slightly hushed tone in case someone over a fence could hear her.

'Hey, guess who I saw walking out of the Palace Hotel in Douglas yesterday?' As Eenayah had lived on the island from babyhood to university, this could have been one of many people. Impatiently she responded, 'who did you see coming out of the hotel mother?'

'Paul Bucklow. You do remember Paul, don't you? Greg and James's father.'

Eenayah's jaw could have hit the floor. She was frozen in shock. Maybe she should have considered the pitch of her voice before responding, but she was so shaken by this news that she hit back with a fiery, 'what the hell is that man doing on the bloody island?'

Ellie was taken aback by the passion of her daughter's response. She replied, 'Oh, is there a problem with him being over on the Island? I always thought you and Paul got along so well. You always told me how much you adored your ex-father-in-law.' Eenayah remained silent, so Ellie continued. 'I did tell you that Mary's second husband Gary died didn't I? Well Mary had some sort of memorial service for him – not that I was invited. Paul told me he was over on the Island to attend the service. I had no idea Paul and Mary were still friends. If I remember rightly it was quite a nasty and bitter break-up when they went through the whole divorce process. I mean, he did leave Mary for another woman when Greg was only a wee baby. Excuse my language love, but Paul was a bit of a shit to Mary. I honestly thought she detested the man, so I was a bit blown away when he said Mary had invited him over for the service. That didn't sound quite right to me. I think he was lying, but then, why should he lie about it?'

Eenayah felt butterflies rise up from the pit of her stomach. She cast her mind back to the night over at Paul's house and tried to figure out dates in her head. The realisation hit her that if Paul had been in the Isle of Man the previous day, Wednesday, he must have flown over either on the day she had run away from his house or the next day. Gary had only died a month or so ago. Would Mary really be having a memorial service for him so soon after his death, and would she invite Paul to it even if this was the case?

His reason for being on the Island sounded like a weak excuse, and the bastard was using Mary like an alibi. She concluded that Paul would probably be well versed in using alibis, since he seemed to have deceived most of the women he had ever had relationships with.

Ellie was confused by Eenayah's silence. 'Are you okay Eenayah? You have gone quiet.'

'Erm, yep I'm fine Mum. Just a bit distracted. Did Paul ask about me at all?'

Ellie answered in a confused tone, 'well actually yes as it happened, he did ask me how you were doing and if you were back on the island.' Eenayah's heart skipped several beats. She couldn't help but wonder if Paul had come over to the Island to find her. She had believed that getting out of Wales was her escape, but maybe it wasn't as simple as she had anticipated. She felt deeply ashamed and never wanted to see Paul Bucklow ever again.

'Did you tell him where I was, mother?'

'No love. Only that you had spent some time on the Island with us and you had now gone to look after Ruby's house in North Wales while she was away on holiday. I didn't tell him about your search for your birth mother and all that. None of his business really. That's personal to you, Eenayah. I wouldn't share this with anyone honestly. I promise I wouldn't.'

It was good that her mother believed her concern was more associated with her breaking a confidence rather than some unexplained reaction which would make her mother delve and ask yet more questions. Eenayah was happy to leave it as it was. She quickly bid her mother farewell, with a promise to call back later.

Eenayah was far from happy with what her mother had just told her. She still had good friends on the Island and it wouldn't be difficult to find out if the story about a memorial service was true or an out-and-out lie. She called room service for a fresh pot of coffee and then lay flat out on her bed pondering all she had just been told. If Paul really had gone to the Island in search of her, this was worrying; very worrying. Why would he go to so much trouble?

Thanks to her loose-mouthed mother, he now also knew she had been at her sister Ruby's house and with her unusual surname of Kyfinn, the house would be easy to trace. Much as she liked to run away from her problems, she considered that this was one situation she shouldn't run away from. At some point she might need to face Paul head on and tell him straight that she has no idea if anything had or hadn't happened a few days back when she had stayed over at his cottage, but whatever the reality of the situation, she didn't want any further dealings with him. The very thought made her sick.

With that on her mind, the ring tone on her mobile made her almost jump vertically out of bed. Thankfully it was Reed. The wholesome American accent on the other side of the phone gave her a nice warm glow which distracted from the seriousness of the last conversation.

'Hey, happy Independence Day sweetie!'

Eenayah joked back, 'Hey Reed, what's so happy about today when it marks the anniversary of us Brits losing part of our empire? You should be commiserating with us.'

Reed was in a light-hearted mood.

'Sorry – do you want it back? Joking aside honey, I know it's a big day for you today, so I'm just calling to wish you luck and hope it all goes well.'

They chatted informally for a while and it was good to hear Reed sounding so upbeat, instead of his more usual persona; tired, overworked and irritable. Reed told her he was flying over to LA for the weekend and asked if she wanted to join him.

'If you're just going to be working in a studio the whole time, I think I'll give it a miss' said Eenayah. 'As you know, I have some personal things to close down over here first.'

She also made sure to inform Reed that she had now gone off the idea of renting a house in the Isle of Man and bringing the stepchildren over. She had been a bit up and down about the whole idea, but she knew her husband would buy into the whole bipolar changeability aspect.

'I think it may be a better idea to fly my parents to Miami for a vacation' she went on. 'If we can arrange it quickly they may even be able to meet up with Ruby, Owyn and Harry while they are still over at our place. Perhaps we could get Armani, Konnor and Asher over for the weekend as well and have a big family reunion event. How does that sound? Have you any free time in your diary?'

Reed knew he had to be careful about how he handled this. He should appear to be not too keen but not too dismissive either. He had been plotting with Arabella to try and find a way to get Eenayah back to Miami, and this idea of a reunion could just play right into their hands. He made an attempt to sound puzzled.

'Yes it's a great idea and don't worry about my schedule. I am the boss after all and of course I can always find time for a party. But I thought you were enjoying your time in the UK and touching base with family and old friends. How come you want to go back home so soon?'

Eenayah could hardly tell him it was because she feared she was being stalked by her ex-father-in-law with whom she might have inadvertently slept with. She replied, 'Well, you know I have been here for almost a month now and it's been great and I've ticked off a lot of boxes on my bucket list, but I think I'll have done all I really needed to do quite soon and it may be time to make tracks. Honestly, I don't envy you your lifestyle, Reed. I feel worn out.'

Reed understood and knew today would be especially challenging for her. 'Do you want me to come over and hold your hand?' he asked with a rare show of spontaneous consideration.

Eenayah was quite shocked by his offer but politely declined. 'There are some things I have to do alone' she informed him. With that they said their goodbyes. Looking at her watch and realising it was getting late, Eenayah went off for a shower. It was time to get ready. She could hardly contain her excitement.

With foreboding as to the outcome, she drove her car slowly down the main street of the small village, trying to take in her surroundings as well as listening out for the directions from the satnav. She could envisage that maybe a hundred or so years ago Daisy Hill had been a poor working class Lancashire hamlet in the midst of the industrial revolution, with little more than a church, a shop and a couple of weavers' cottages. From the brief research she had done online, it seemed that the men had probably worked down the coal mines and perhaps the women worked in the cotton and silk mills. She imagined there would have been a workhouse in the locality and that little more than a century ago poverty had been rife. However in present times, Eenayah found it to be quite a pleasant leafy suburb of Bolton, surrounded by agricultural land and lots of green fields and paddocks. With many new housing developments the area had grown considerably in population, and she concluded it was probably now far more affluent than former times.

As old met new, it was hard to imagine the Daisy Hill her mother had been born into back in the sixties. All she knew for sure was that it was small place and so must have been a tightly-knit community where everyone knew everyone else. This must have made life difficult for a teenage pregnant girl in an era when such young illegitimate pregnancies were still taboo.

She had no idea what to expect from her Great Aunt Elspeth. She knew nothing about this secret family. She was sorry that Ruby could not be with her but had made the decision that Ruby had really needed a vacation and she didn't want to trouble her whilst she was away having much needed time out. There were some things she needed to do alone, and even though she was a twin, she felt that this was a private moment that belonged to her alone.

Eenayah pulled up outside her aunt's house and deliberated for a while before plucking up the courage to walk up the garden path. It was a tiny little garden, so this wasn't a big walk. She stopped part way to touch the stone wall and wondered if her mother had ever touched this same wall. Closing her eyes, she almost hoped she would pick up some vibrations from the past from the cold granite.

She knocked apprehensively at the door of a traditional two up/two down terraced house, and a warm, smiling grey-haired lady answered the door, leaning heavily on her walking stick. She gasped as she saw Eenayah, her eyes transfixed on her features. She clearly knew instantly who she was. She gasped in excitement, 'Eenayah, oh my darling girl! You are so like your mother. It is lovely to have you back.' She gave her a tender loving hug which seemed to come from the heart. 'Please do come inside,' she went on. 'Lovely to have you back.'

Eenayah hadn't expected to feel so emotional so early on in this process, but her great aunt seemed to have made a claim on her and simply calling her 'my girl' seemed to bring out all sorts of buried sentiments. Her great aunt's words made Eenayah aware that she was indeed back. This had once been her home. Maybe not this exact house or street, but it was possible she could have been born in this district or spent the first part of her life here. That thought had never occurred to her before.

Great Aunt Elspeth was a wise old lady. She knew this would be a difficult meeting, so she allowed Eenayah to drive it at her own pace. As was the norm, a pot of tea was presented centre table with posh biscuits which Elspeth had gone out to buy especially. She had made a great deal of effort in advance of her niece's visit.

Elspeth set the tone of the conversation, guessing that her young guest might be feeling overwhelmed.

'It is lovely to have you here with me Eenayah. The people you hired to find your mother got in touch and I guess I could have given them more information to pass onto you, but I wanted to see you again as a grown woman and I hoped you would want to come and visit me so I could tell you more in person. I hope you don't mind me dragging you over here, but I so wanted to meet you, my sweet darling. I last held you and your sister as new-born babies. It's a shame your sister couldn't be with you.'

Eenayah was dumbfounded that her aunt might have even considered that she wouldn't have wanted to come to see her, but then how was she to know how she felt about the adoption? It was delicate. She could tell that Aunty Elspeth was dying to know all about her life, as well as a full update about her twin. Eenayah was of course happy to share all of the details, but right now she was hungry for information about her own mother and wanted to keep the conversation on track.

'Aunty' began Eenayah, feeling like a little girl, 'can you tell me all you know about my mother Daisy and her pregnancy? I know nothing at all.'

Elspeth sat back in her chair in preparation for a long and difficult conversation, but none the less a conversation long overdue and much awaited. She had suspected that at some point in her life there would be a knock on the door and one or the other of Daisy's twin girls would be standing on the pathway wanting answers. Now this moment had arrived.

'My brother William was married to Harriet. That's the name of Daisy's mother, your grandmother. If you like we can both go and visit Harriet tomorrow in the nursing home, but I must warn you that she isn't very well Eenya, so be prepared for that.' Her great aunt insisted pronouncing Eenayah's name incorrectly and her thick Lancashire accent wasn't the easiest to comprehend, but none the less Eenayah was drinking in the moment of being with this dear old lady and long lost relative. It didn't feel real being in this tiny house with a total stranger and yet having such an intimate connection with her and everything that was around her.

Her great aunt continued with her account, which she narrated with the singsong tone of an experienced storyteller, pausing and exaggerating to labour or suppress a point.

'Anyway, William and Harriet had twin girls, Daisy and April. They were twins just like you and your sister.'

Eenayah was already dumbfounded. She wondered what other revelations would follow. 'My mother was also a twin? That is totally amazing.'

Elspeth sensed this conversation would take longer than Eenayah had anticipated. 'Yes, and her mother Harriet, your grandmother, was a twin, as well as her mother before her. I do believe twins run in your family, very strongly. Do you have any children?'

Eenayah replied with a hint of regret, 'only stepchildren Aunty. None of my own.' She couldn't process all that she was being told, but knew it was best she remained quiet and needed to listen intently. As Mercy had recommended, she was recording the conversation and she was grateful for Mercy's professional advice.

'Daisy was a lovely young girl', continued Elspeth. 'I will bring out some photographs of her later. She was a clever young lady. She went to church and sang in the choir. She was never rude. She studied hard and wanted so much to be a nurse. We never even knew she had a boyfriend. She never went out anywhere to even meet anyone.'

'What happened?' asked Eenayah, puzzled.

Elspeth sighed. 'I guess we will never know for sure. She became pregnant but she never told anyone. She was having twins, and it must have been hard for her to hide her swelling bump, but somehow she did. She wore big clothes and just kept out of people's way. We all just thought she had put weight on. Nobody paid much attention or asked too many questions back in those days, my love.'

Eenayah felt deeply compassionate for the young Daisy Green, the teenage mother she never knew. 'Pregnant with twins at such a young age, she must have been terrified.'

Elspeth agreed. 'She would have been very afraid. Poor child, she must have been in turmoil. Her father, that's my brother William, was a hard man. He would have whipped her black and blue with a trouser belt had he known, and maybe even thrown her out into the street. Men were hard like that in those days. Back then there were none of these namby-pamby rules about not hitting kids. He would have leathered her, that's for sure. We didn't have child benefit and all this other social support stuff in those days. She would have been on her own and she would have had to deal with the consequences. She must have felt very frightened and not known what to do or who to turn to. She did a good job of hiding it, none of us guessed.'

Eenayah sighed, not knowing quite how to feel but understanding what an awful situation Daisy had found herself to be in and maybe also in denial of what was biologically happening to her. This was a far sadder story than she had ever expected to hear. Since discovering she had been adopted she had expected that maybe one day she would find a mother who was a career woman driven by her own greed for success and with no time for children to clutter her social diary. Or perhaps a young actress or model who had been involved in an affair with a married man who had then abandoned her in favour of his wife and family. She had imagined all sorts of colourful scenarios, but never had she predicted the grim reality of a 15-year-old child trapped in such an impossible situation. It was sad beyond sad.

Elspeth went off to make yet more tea to wet her vocal cords, then sat down on the rickety old chair to continue with her story.

'We think she must have gone into labour early. You and your twin were little mites when you were born and you both nearly died. You had to go into a special unit for premature babies and you were there for many weeks. The doctors said they thought you might have been born about seven weeks too soon, which may not seem much now but was very bad back in those days. Your granny, Harriet, and I visited you both several times a week. We didn't know if you would survive. We would take the bus up to Bolton Hospital, but your grandfather, William, refused to look at you. He was too overcome with grief about Daisy.'

Eenayah was mesmerised. She was hearing a first-hand account of her own birth for the very first time and wanted to know more. It was as though she had once been a totally different person who had belonged to an unknown family, and she was hungry for more information.

'Where did she go into labour, Aunty and where were we born? What happened?'

A tear came to her aunt's eye. 'Daisy lived just three doors away from here. That's where she grew up. Poor girl, I believe she just sat alone in her room not making a sound. No cries for help, no screams. She must have been so terrified and confused, but she remained silent throughout. Can you imagine going through labour and not making a single noise of any sort? She delivered one baby by herself in her bedroom alone. Bless her, she was only a child herself.'

Her aunt started to weep at the memory and Eenayah also had tears in her eyes by now.

'What of the second twin? I have no idea if that would have been me or my sister Ruby. We have known nothing about our birth up until now, so we have never known who the eldest was. What happened next?'

Elspeth took a slurp of tea and a bite of a biscuit before she felt able to go on. 'Oh my dear Eenya, the second twin was a breech and there were complications. I was in Harriet's house at the time and my God, I heard it for myself. I guess Daisy could no longer keep silent, and the scream was like something I have never heard before or since. It was truly horrible. I heard it, all the neighbours heard it. Oh God, it was like the scream of death.' Eenayah sat in stunned silence. Elspeth went on, 'We called the doctor to the house, but he said she had to go to hospital because it was an emergency and an ambulance came. Oh bless that poor child! They managed to get the second twin out, but poor Daisy had lost so much blood. They gave her a blood transfusion, but I believe her organs shut down because of the amount of blood she had already lost.'

Elspeth began to sob; real heavy teardrops of tears, with just a gasp for air between each breath. It was a cry from the heart. She grasped Eenayah's hand and squeezed it tightly as the memories of that night from long ago overwhelmed her. Eenayah realised that maybe no matter how rushed she felt in her quest for the immediate truth, she had to respect the fact that this elderly lady had actually lived through this trauma. She might need to take this slowly.

She held her aunt's hand. 'I'm so sorry Aunty. I honestly didn't mean to put you through this pain, but if you could please tell me what happened next I would be so grateful, and then let's call it a day, huh? I think I have already put you through too much and I am sorry for that.'

Elspeth wiped her tears away. 'I am so sorry my darling. Your poor sweet mother was only a child really. Her body just couldn't take it. They tried all they could to save her, but within twelve or so hours of the second twin being born, poor Daisy passed away. It devastated all of us and her mother never really recovered. William was a changed man. His own health went downhill after that. We all felt it. We were never the same again. She just lost too much blood. I am so sorry, my dear child.'

Eenayah did consider pausing the conversation there and then as Great Aunt Elspeth seemed quite distressed, but she still had a vital question plaguing her thoughts.

'I apologise for having to ask you this Aunty, but can you tell me why the family didn't keep Ruby and me?'

Elspeth put her arms around Eenayah and gave her a warm, motherly cuddle. Even before hearing the reasons, she knew the decision was both difficult and valid.

'It broke our hearts Eenya, as we grew to love you both so very much, but Daisy's mum had another daughter to look after. April was Daisy's twin. She had suffered from cerebral palsy since birth and was in a wheelchair. She needed a lot of looking after. April was like a child in a woman's body. You didn't get the same support then as you do now and it was tough on the family. Harriet worked part time and all our family helped with April, but my brother wasn't in the best of health either. He had worked down the mines since being a young lad and he had lung problems. He was also in a wheelchair and he struggled to breathe. A lot of the miners had inhaled coal dust and became ill in later life. Back in the sixties life was a lot harder. Your grandparents didn't have the energy or money to look after two new-born babies. We didn't even know if either of you would survive anyway, but whichever way, it was impossible to keep you.'

Elspeth put her head down in shame, almost apologetically, and wiped her eyes with an antique-looking lace handkerchief. Clasping Eenayah's hands with a firm tight grip, despite knobbly arthritic fingers she looked Eenayah directly in the eyes. 'We never forgot you both and you were both always in our prayers. I am sorry.'

Elspeth got up and slowly shuffled out to the kitchen with her walking stick for support. Then she shut the door. Maybe she felt she had to just walk away to find some solace. The guilt in her voice was still quite raw.

Eenayah felt far sorrier for her elderly relative than she did for herself. She still had so many questions, and as yet Elspeth had not had a chance to ask about the lives of her and her sister. The conversation had been totally one-sided so far. Emotionally exhausted, Eenayah was also keen to call it a day soon. She had wanted to ask her if her mother's twin April was still alive, but didn't have the heart to put her aunt through anything more.

Eenayah looked around the room. Everything looked so old and worn, and Eenayah wondered if her aunt would be insulted if she offered her some financial help. She noticed fungus growing up the wall and the tell-tale signs of rising damp. Despite her present life in a Florida paradise, she had once been a young girl growing up on a rundown farm and she knew all the signs of a building that had been neglected.

Her aunt had been gone for quite a while, so concerned, she knocked on the kitchen door. Elspeth was leaning against the sink, slightly out of breath. She looked pale and weary. Eenayah put a comforting hand on her great aunt's shoulder.

'Aunty, let us continue this tomorrow as I think I have put you through too much for now. I will pick you up around 2pm and we can go and visit my grandmother and maybe afterwards we can go somewhere nice for dinner and I can tell you all about me and Ruby. I am sure you would like to hear all about our lives.'

Elspeth pulled a large brown envelope out of the kitchen drawer and Eenayah then realised that this had been what her aunty had gone into the kitchen to search for. Eenayah took the worn envelope; it was full of photographs. She couldn't wait to get back to the hotel to study them in private.

'I'll go now Aunty, but I will be back tomorrow,' she said.

Elspeth walked Eenayah to the front door and pointed to the orange brick church over the road. 'Your mother lies over there, Eenayah,' she said. Eenayah hugged her aunt and kissed her forehead affectionately. Elspeth did not come from a touchy-feely family and had rarely had anyone kiss her on the forehead before; it was a sweet gesture, one she found to be a bit peculiar, but nice none the less. Not a Lancashire habit!

As she walked out to her car, Eenayah's dark, glistening eyes wandered over to the church. 'Mother, I know where you are now, but we can wait until tomorrow.'

CHAPTER 17

Friday July 5th 2013, morning

Sitting at a typical hotel room table, clasping a cup of hot chocolate and glancing out of the window towards the Manchester skyline, Eenayah had woken in a strangely pensive mood. She had become reflective of yesterday's events and looking down at the unopened envelope of photographs, she felt a strange mix of excitement tinged with sadness. Today would have an even greater significance, as she would finally meet her biological grandmother and visit her mother's grave for the first time. She mused over the theory that everything seemed to be coming in threes: three weeks, three graves, three loves lost, three bunches of flowers. What flowers should she choose for her mother? Grave flowers were becoming an habitual purchase.

As someone who had struggled to cope with bipolar disorder for most of her adult life, Eenayah knew more than most about how the good days could suddenly flip into the bad days and how one's mood could change with the wind. As a sufferer from the highs and lows of depressive illness, she had somehow associated boredom with feeling fine, as though nothingness was an achievement and possibly even a preferred escape on the path to normality. She had always been unable to deal with the emotional roller coaster, as though it was an easy cliff to tumble from. Had she done the right thing by choosing the safer life option, thus avoiding the cliff edge? So far she had done just that back in Miami with her thirty pieces of silver, but then found that safety in a life of emptiness also had its mental monsters. She had fallen into a reflective mood, and deep inside her own melancholy wondered if, in her own loneliness and desire to be with somebody, she had settled with somebody who turned out to be nobody.

She put the kettle on to make her second cup of hot chocolate. Chocolate cured everything, and it was time to forget about her marriage woes and think about the immensity of today.

She had been feeling wildly optimistic about finally tracing her mother's family, yet she had now lapsed into a depressive mood regarding the tragedy of her young mother's death. It was the sort of resigned sorrow that hits you in the stomach and lingers to torment you even in your sleep. This was a grief she had not expected to find; a black hellish wretchedness that woke her early in the morning and no matter how tired she was, would not allow her the privilege of rest.

Sitting at her simple table and still looking out of the window, she finally mustered the nerve to open the well-worn brown envelope. She looked through each of the black and white and sepia photos with microscopic attention.

'April and Daisy Green from Daisy Hill.' How sweet and innocent was that sentence, and indeed what twee simplicity it conjured up. These were not the names of old women, but the fresh innocent names of childhood which shaped a vision of a garden in springtime. Daisies in April! Daisy Green and April Green would be forever young. Well-chosen names for twin girls who had been born in more innocent times and would never know old age.

The reality was not as sweet as the words deceptively promised. Poor little April's body was twisted from muscles that could not be used and had been contracted into distortion. Slumped in her wheelchair, she had the biggest of smiles, yet the father's firm hand placed on his daughter's shoulder seemed to be a protective yet despairing gesture. Eenayah could tell by the photographs that this small working-class family had been placed in a fairly hopeless situation.

Daisy, although physically perfect, must surely have felt the heavy weight of her sister's disability, and Eenayah could see sadness in the blackness of her mother's young eyes.

However, what struck Eenayah the most was how alike both her mother Daisy and Granny Harriet were to herself. Taking into consideration the difference in ages, variance of clothes, hairstyles, fashions of the era and reflections of the differing soul behind the eyes, Daisy was more or less Eenayah, and vice versa. Daisy was more or less Harriet, and vice versa.

Ruby was also a close match to her mother Daisy, but for the fact that Ruby was much heavier than Eenayah, and this had made her face rounder than her sister's. It had been presumed that Ruby and Eenayah were not identical twins. It had never been scientifically tested, but their features differed slightly. Daisy and Eenayah, however, did look to be identical in every way. It felt odd for her to look back at her own reflection in Daisy, as a younger and more old-fashioned version of herself.

She pondered a worn photograph of her grandmother, who on this occasion was an even older version of herself. She conceded that it must be every woman's worst nightmare to see what you are going to look like when you grow old. No female needs these images, and she considered that maybe that was why nature had been kind enough to mix the DNA between two parental sources.

★★★

At roughly the same time on the same day, Paul Bucklow sat at his

SHEILA MUGHAL

breakfast table at an Isle of Man beachfront hotel, glancing wistfully out at the seascape from the large restaurant windows. Mentally miles away, he twirled his spoon around a tea cup. He was sorry that Eenayah had fled from his cottage with such haste and with not even a note to explain her speedy exit. He had hoped he would find her on the Island, but now he knew that this hope was in vain.

Paul had been diagnosed with bowel cancer some years earlier, and although the diseased part of him had been removed, the cancer cells had a cruel habit of corrupting other tissues and organs. He looked the picture of health and fitness even into his early sixties. As a former athlete he still boasted a toned body and constantly enhanced sun tan, but internally he had been invaded by distorted cells which were slowly killing him.

Paul had not led the most righteous or purest of lives. He had treated many people very badly, especially the women in his life. He was now at a stage in his survival where he wanted to right his many wrongs. He had betrayed many of those who had loved him in his life, and now he was a man with the weight of repentance pressing down on his shoulders. Regret was a heavy emotion to carry to the grave and he so wished he could find Eenayah, if only to apologise.

Paul Bucklow was a dying man. He had never had any religious faith to speak of. All he had ever believed in throughout his life was living for the moment. The loss of his boys, his only children, seemed to bring confirmation that today was all he had for sure and tomorrow was a promise that might never happen.

One particular night, when he was feeling sorry for himself and drowning in whisky mixed with the tears of lament, he prayed to God for forgiveness. Karma was rapping at his door like the angel of doom, and religious or not, he could feel the beating heart of divine retribution.

He wasn't quite sure what happened next. At the time he put it down to a drunken hallucination, but as the seconds ticked by he became aware that what was floating in front of his eyes was not so much an alcoholic fog as a vision. It was an illuminous mist that had a reality and a presence. It spoke to him in an assertive and commanding way, to the degree that it could not be disobeyed. He was being given clear and direct instructions, and it was made clear to him that this was his final chance to make amends. He had been told that his former daughter-in-law Eenayah would be guided towards him. Powers that were beyond man's understanding would whisper directions to her and she would be delivered to his door. He was told what he then needed to do.

Paul had objected to the force that would not take no for an answer. His resistance had not been a wise decision. He felt as though a heavy weight was lying across his chest. The presence was unhappy with his lack of co-operation and refused to budge until he agreed to comply. The pressure increased with each second. A dull pain then descended from his left shoulder, slowly at first and then gaining speed until it met his heart. The dull ache became a pain, stabbing away at him like a million razor-sharp knives. He grew pale and he was covered in cold beads of sweat.

With what strength he could muster, he dialled for the emergency services.

The next thing he could remember was floating several feet above his body, watching the paramedics as they tried to shock his failing heart into action. The presence whispered to him, 'Paul Bucklow, do you want to die like this – here and now? Or would you like the chance to make amends for a life of sinful living? It is your choice, but you need to make your decision soon.'

Paul Bucklow made his decision. And how he was sitting at a breakfast table on a beautiful sunny morning on the Isle of Man. As he listened to the sound of the seagulls, the waves lashing up on the shore and the laughter of tiny children, he knew he was glad to be alive. He had made the right decision, but it was one that came at a cost. He needed to find Eenayah!

***

Reed Baratolli sat in the office of his LA studio. He had arrived at work around 6 am. He had a tired and weary body, but still living on UK time his mind was too active to sleep. For a moment he stopped what he was doing to look out of the windows and consider his manic life, which at present was being lived out in various hotel suites globally.

The street light caught the silhouettes of palm trees waving slightly in the mild Californian breeze. Pictured against an emerging orange sunrise, they looked quite surreal in the dawn light.

As he drank his third espresso of the morning, his thoughts turned to his wife Eenayah back in the UK. He understood she was unhappy and he understood why. He remembered his mental promise to organise a family reunion in Miami by way of both a gift and an apology. He scribbled on a piece of paper, 'get Arabella to sort it', and then having conceptually passed the job onto his PA to process, all thoughts of Eenayah vanished as quickly as they had emerged. Any sentimentality he had associated with the reunion plan dispersed when he recalled Arabella's words: 'we have to get Eenayah back to Miami.' He knew that the longer she was back in the UK, wandering around on her own, the more at risk she was. He needed to monitor the situation carefully. His part of the deal was to keep his wife under tight control, and right now the reins had slipped from his fingers.

Mentally moving on to his next task of the day, he was once again consumed with music, money and his own egotistic self-satisfaction in a job he no longer actually needed to do. Maybe he would call

Eenayah later to find out how she had gone on in her quest for self-discovery - if he could remember to do so. He added it to his 'to do list' before it slipped from his mind, as he knew it inevitably would.

Three people, looking through three different windows and in three different places, yet all connected.

CHAPTER 18

Friday July 5ᵗʰ 2013, afternoon

Back in Manchester, England, it was the day when Eenayah would be going to visit her Granny Harriet, who aside from her twin seemed to be the only other living biological relative she knew of so far. The florist knocked on the door of her hotel room, and she was elated to take delivery of two huge garlands of flowers. Both were bouquets of several varieties of daisies, as per instruction to the florist, from the simple traditional ox-eye daisy with its white flower and yellow heart to the multi-coloured and vivid painted daisy, which splashed the vibrancy of a rainbow onto the ornate sprays. The arrangement was quite exquisite, and Eenayah was pleased with the florist's creativity at such short notice.

'Have money, will get' she concluded. What other flowers could she have possibly placed on the grave of her mother Daisy but daisies?

The moment of pleasure did not last long before her alarm reminded her that she had a long overdue conversation booked with Professor De Vede at midday. She scurried around to find the draft book of Reed's family history with its variety of hand-written notes. She was by now feeling quite guilty that she had neither read the book nor returned the Professor's call. Although she was not in the mood for a lecture on genealogy, she felt she had no choice but to at least listen to what he had to say.

Professor De Vede was the epitome of an academic silver surfer, happily tapping away at his laptop when Eenayah's call came through. He knew who she was in an instant, and bullied into an apology by his vehement daughter Mercy, his first words were a reluctant and unconvincing 'sorry'. Eenayah had long since forgotten that he had failed to turn up to his meeting with her back in Oxford, whenever that was. It seemed so long ago now. So many other things had happened in the meantime that she was way beyond caring about his missed appointment with her, but she gracefully accepted his apology anyway.

Professor De Vede was keen to proceed with the overview of his findings. He explained, 'Your husband's family are really quite interesting, so I wanted to check with you that you were happy to just take this back to just to his great-great grandparents of which of course he has sixteen, just like the rest of us. It's almost impossible to get all the surnames of all sixteen, and sadly it is the women we struggle with the most as often we get little more than a Christian name. However with your husband we have 15 out of the possible 16 surnames, so this really is an excellent result.'

Remarkably, Eenayah found herself to be quite interested in what the Professor had to say, and looking at the diagram of his family tree and names she had never seen before, she was beginning to find this ancestral quest fairly thought-provoking.

The Professor continued, 'With little time to put this together Eenayah, I wanted to focus on his original birth name of Mort. I can take it back further on the other lines if you need me to, but his own original birth name of Anthony Reed Baratolli Mort gives such an interesting family background that I am sure he will be delighted to know what we have uncovered. This is why I wanted to talk with you first. I need to make sure that this is the direction you want to take. So far we have taken a deep dive into the Mort name and left the rest to 5th generation. Is that okay? It's your money, your present and your call.'

Eenayah had no idea how to respond. She knew nothing about the world of genealogy, so how could she know what was possible, plausible or just passable?

She scanned the words and illustrations in the book, and paid attention when she saw that Reed's great grandfather however many times removed was called Adam and he had married Jennet (also a Mort) on May 16th 1586. Eenayah had little prior perception that ancestors from almost 500 years ago could be identified. She kept repeating the year.

'1586 – are you sure Professor? That is ancient.'

Professor De Vede was slightly amused by her ignorance. He went on to explain, 'I can go centuries back if the connections are Royal. In my world 1586 is actually quite recent, but then I am an historian.' She suspected from his statement that historians might have a different concept of what equated to ancient. To Eenayah, last season's fashion was ancient. With that thought she could feel the old superficial Eenayah from Miami making a return, so she quickly blanked this temporary faux pas from her mind.

Looking through the book, she could immediately recognize the amount of effort which had been put into it. She asked about the illustrations and the Professor continued with his animated explanation.

'Adam Mort was a very interesting character. He was Lord of the Manor in Astley, known as Dam House. Mercy tells me that you are in Manchester at the moment and Astley Manor isn't too far away from there. I am told there is an inscription above the front door of the house and if you could possibly go there and take a photo of it for me, I will add it to the book'.

Eenayah told the Professor she would be delighted. She had played with the idea of going back up to the north east and visiting Jonathan in Newcastle for yet another party weekend, but now she considered the thought of connecting back to both her and Reed's ancestors more appealing. She had nothing much else to do that weekend, why not go and look around yet more cemeteries and ancient houses? How many other superficial spoilt wives from Miami would be willing to go on a history tour just for their husband's birthday present?

'Can you tell me more about Adam Mort please Professor?' she asked, and this time with a genuine interest. The Professor replied, 'It's all in the book Eenayah, so it's there for you to read for yourself. However if you can do a bit more research to add to it, that would be fantastic and also it would add a more personal touch if you could contribute. I believe there is a stained glass window which depicts one of the Morts in Leigh Town Hall. Leigh is near Manchester and not far away from where your mother grew up in Daisy Hill. If you could go there and send me a photograph of the stained glass window I will add it to the book and your name will be registered as the photographer. He will be more than aware of your input.'

Eenayah liked the idea of playing detective antiquarian and was keen to become involved. It would be good to make this present just that tiny bit more personal and it wasn't as if she didn't have the time. She agreed that this would be an excellent idea.

The brief meeting was concluded, and Eenayah was left with some homework to do. She could clearly see that Prof De Vede was a lecturer and was used to handing out assignments and course work to his students. By contrast, she was a client and was paying good money for the Professor's research. She could easily have been offended by his suggestion that she should explore the Manchester area with a notebook and camera at the ready, but actually she found herself keen to go on this mission into the past.

It was now time for her to get ready for her next adventure, but not before she quickly found out who the heck Adam Mort was. She opened the book and went to the section headlining his name.

'Adam Mort was a well-respected man who held high ranking positions within his local community. He was High Constable of the West Derby Hundred in 1612 and twice church warden (1615 & 1620). Adam built St Stephens Church in Astley, which was consecrated in August 1631 by the Bishop of Chester. Next to the Church Adam built Mort's Grammar School. This was the first school in Astley and was built because of Adam's desire that the children of poor families were to be taught free of any charges. Adam Mort was a generous man who believed that education should be available to all irrespective of social class. Adam died in March 1630 and in his will he left a sum of money for the relief of the poor in Astley and Bolton.'

Adam Mort sounded like a well-regarded, giving and caring man and Eenayah was keen to find out more about her husband's ancestor. Turning to the next page, she was then consumed with the story of the Mort side of the family who had emigrated to Australia and how Thomas Sutcliffe Mort had contributed towards the invention of refrigeration. As she turned page after page she became more engrossed in the book, but then she abruptly remembered that for now she had her own family connections to uncover. By the time she had concluded her call with the much respected Professor Roland De Vede, it was early afternoon and time for her to leave the hotel and collect her newly-discovered great aunt. However, clutching two huge and impressive bunches of daisies, she had a detour to take first.

Eenayah found herself walking along lines of headstones, scanning names, dates and various tributes. As she approached the edge of the cemetery, nestled under an old oak tree, she eventually found what she had travelled half way around the world to find. By unusual timing, the dark grey thunderclouds parted just for a moment and in that same second a ray of sunlight broke through and illuminated the white marble headstone. She looked up and smiled, almost as though thanking God for shining a torch in the right direction. In comparison with the surrounding tombstones, this headstone was minimalist, and aside from the engraving of two tiny angels, it stated very little, yet said enough.

Pacing around the headstone, which was still floodlit by a funnel of sunrays, she noticed some incongruous squiggly signs at the rear. The random scrawls made no sense, so she presumed them to be the mark of the stonemason. She took a photograph of them – just for the records. Aside from these small decorations, the inscription read:

At Peace
Daisy Green passed away 27th August 1975 aged 15
April Green passed away July 6th 1976 aged 16
William Green passed away September 1st 1978 aged 44
A loving father with his beloved daughters, reunited in heaven

Eenayah stood at the foot of the grave for a moment, and then knelt to the ground to touch the earth. Placing one of the floral garlands in the empty pitch vase, which hadn't been used in years, she whispered a prayer under her breath. Not normally a religious person, she wasn't sure what else to do. She looked carefully at the dates and realised that April had died less than a year after her twin sister. Eenayah was touched by the inscription. What an awful thing for any parent to have to do, to bury two of their children in such quick succession.

She then noted that their father William hadn't lived much longer either, dying just two years after April. Her great aunt had mentioned that his health wasn't too good and this was a contributory factor leading towards Daisy's family opting for adoption. She took another photo of the grave, still feeling nervous about how Ruby would react to this lone mission she had taken upon herself. She then touched the headstone, almost willing some kind of story to permeate out of the marble and whisper past secrets, but the stone was silent and cold to the touch. It had nothing to tell.

Studying the dates more closely, she then noted the date of April's death. She would have died 37 years ago tomorrow. What a coincidence. She calculated that had both girls survived, they would be around 53 years old right now, and had they been alive they would have been a lot closer to her husband's age than she was.

She thought about the aunty she had never known; April Green. From what her aunt had told her about April and from the photographs she had seen, which had clearly conveyed her medical condition, she doubted that April would ever have managed to survive until middle age anyway. However that wasn't the case with her mother, Daisy. If only she hadn't got pregnant or maybe even received timely medical intervention, she would still be here today. She could even have been with her right now, both of them together placing flowers on April's grave. It was an awful thought that her own conception had resulted in her mother's untimely and premature death. Looking back at the inscriptions and remembering that her mother was born in May, she then calculated that Daisy had been just fourteen when she became pregnant.

Somehow this comprehension of her own conception and what that must have done to such a young adolescent girl made her feel sick to the stomach. Pregnant at fourteen, dead by fifteen; poor, poor Daisy Green.

Being in the churchyard was becoming too emotionally charged for Eenayah, and she felt it best to leave. Standing back to admire the beautiful bouquet of daisies standing proud in a solo pot with a handful scattered on the grass, Eenayah knew that this was a place she would most likely not visit too often. She had said that about all her recent grave visits. With her former history of depression, she had to protect her mental state, and this trip back to her homeland had taken her to too many churchyards already. It was time to go. Time to say her goodbyes, or at least that's how it felt.

At that point the wind picked up and blew some leaves into the air, almost covering the grave. 'How odd', murmured Eenayah, 'it was awakened by the sun when I arrived and now put to sleep by a blanket of leaves as I leave.' She needed to watch her thoughts; they could be too deep for her own sanity sometimes.

***

Great Aunt Elspeth really was a sweet old lady with a jovial disposition and chubby red cheeks, but linking her arm as they walked down the corridors of the nursing home, Eenayah could appreciate how much old age and arthritis had affected her. Eenayah was in a hurry to get to her grandmother's room, but out of respect for her aunt she had been forced to shuffle at a snail's pace. Old age and the ravages of time could be cruel.

Opening the door and clasping the second bunch of daisies in her hand, Eenayah couldn't help but gasp as she saw her grandmother's face for the first time. The family resemblance was immediately obvious. Her aunt understood.

'Yes Eenayah, the apple hasn't fallen far from the tree, has it?' she said.

Granny Harriet was half asleep and was wearing a nasal oxygen tube. Eenayah felt almost too frightened to awaken her. She didn't want to shock her, and she was aware that she was a big enough shock to deliver anyway.

She needn't have worried. Aunt Elspeth, with little thought or care, brazenly shook Harriet awake. 'Harriet, wake up, come on wake up Harriet, you've got a visitor!' she shouted in a stout Lancashire accent. Her eyes almost seemed too heavy for Harriet to open, but slowly her grandmother stirred. Clearing her throat and recognizing Elspeth, she slowly reached out to grab her sister-in-law's hand with a deep affection. Harriet's skin was wrinkled and delicate and her hand was covered in liver spots. She managed a soft smile.

On catching sight of the huge bunch of daisies her face lit up, and she tried to shuffle up the bed to get a better view. She had never in her life seen a display of flowers so perfectly constructed.

'Where have these come from?' she asked, then, catching sight of Eenayah, 'and who is this lovely-looking lady?'

Elspeth had warned Eenayah that her grandmother's lucidity was quite random. She would have good days when she would speak quite rationally and other days when she wouldn't recognize anyone and make bizarre off-the-wall statements. So far, today seemed to be a good day.

'Do I know you?' she asked. 'My memory isn't very good these days, but you look familiar. Do I know you, sweetheart?'

Eenayah didn't know how to respond. She could clearly see how infirm and delicate her grandmother was and she didn't want to unsettle her. However Elspeth did not intend to be quite so tactful or diplomatic.

'Harriet, this is Eenayah. She is Daisy's baby girl. She is one of the twins. She has come to visit you'.

As Eenayah had expected, her grandmother became instantly confused. It took her a moment to compute what Elspeth had just told her. She then repeated the statement as if to reconfirm.

'Daisy's baby! One of the twins? Really, is this Daisy's baby?'

Eenayah came closer to the bed and touched her hand.

'Yes, my name is Eenayah and I have a twin sister called Ruby. We are the twins Daisy gave birth to and you are my grandmother. I am so happy to meet you'.

'Oh that is lovely. That is so lovely. What an exotic name you have. You look just like my mother. I can see her eyes in your eyes. Where is Daisy? I haven't seen my Daisy for a while. Has she come with you? Where is my mother? Is she here?'

Eenayah looked over at Elspeth and Elspeth simply shrugged. 'It comes and goes love, one minute she's fine and the next…' With that her voice petered out.

Granny Harriet was clearly getting exhausted, and possibly with the oxygen her throat was dry. Eenayah offered her some water, which she gulped down as though dehydrated. The room was clean and certainly didn't have the stale urine smell of some old folks' facilities, but Eenayah could buy much better care than this. Mentally she started to draw up plans as to how she could financially help these two old ladies who had played a significant part in her unknown past. She resolved that before leaving the UK she would put finance in place to ensure they were both well looked after. She made a mental note to call her bank manager.

Then, almost as though the water had revived her, Harriet opened her eyes again and stared deeply into the dusky hazel eyes of Eenayah, striking, unusual exotic eyes which were a perfect match for her own.

'You are my Daisy's child?' asked Harriet.

'Yes I am' Eenayah dutifully replied.

A solitary tear fell from Harriet's eye, as though at that moment she had a flash of realisation as to whom Eenayah really was. With what little strength she had, Harriet raised a warm hand from under her bed sheets and stroked Eenayah's face as a mother would stroke a baby.

'I can see the light in your eyes and I can see your mother in your face,' she said. It was a touching moment.

But the mood soon turned. Harriet turned her thin neck, which seemed to be made out of tissue paper, and looked directly at Elspeth, who was sitting on the other side of her bed. She made direct eye contact with her and with a look of total determination and slightly raised voice she commanded, 'You need to tell these girls what fate awaits them. They need to know about the curse'.

Eenayah had not been expecting such an enigmatic yet forceful statement as this, and almost fell off her chair in shock. She had presumed that Harriet had lapsed into one of the crazy moments her great aunt had warned her about. Looking over at Elspeth, she could see that the colour had drained out of her. She had clearly understood the message that had been given to her.

Harriet once again raised her head to catch Elspeth's attention. 'Promise me Elspeth, it's not fair for them not to know,' she said.

Harriet had now used up all her energy, and relaxed back into the considerable stack of pillows with a sleepy, satisfied smile on her face. Eenayah hoped she would remember her visit when she awoke, but couldn't be too sure. Maybe the vase of daisies would serve as a reminder.

Totally bewildered, Eenayah shot her Great Aunt Elspeth a look of confusion.

'What the heck was all that about?' she asked.

Her aunt looked concerned. 'Not here, not now. You drive me home and come in for a drink and I will tell you as much as I know.'

***

Elspeth was delighted when Eenayah pulled a bunch of yellow roses out of the boot of the car. She had almost forgotten to bring flowers for her aunt, and by the look of total elation on Elspeth's face, she could tell that she had never been given a bunch of roses before. She had no vase, but requisitioned the tall metal jug in which she brewed her obnoxious-smelling wormwood herbal remedy. Eenayah made a mental note to buy her a crystal vase and have flowers delivered weekly. Just seeing the old lady's delight was a joy.

Outside the weather had changed, and a summer storm was beginning to brew. The faint crack of thunder could be heard in the distance. Elspeth lit a fire and put the kettle on to boil, opening all the windows at the same time. It was a curious thing to do, but her aunt explained that if lightning struck it would simply pass through the house and the open windows. As a woman who lived in Florida storm central, Eenayah knew this old wives' tale was ridiculous, yet charming.

Eenayah had never drunk as much tea in her life as she had during the month she had been back in the UK, but as always it was most welcome. Her great aunt also poured them both a Sandeman's sherry, something Eenayah suspected she didn't do too often. Eenayah guessed there must be a reason to ply her with this old-fashioned drink, most likely reserved for visitors. She presumed sherry indicated a serious conversation.

'So what's this curse then?' she began.

'It's not exactly a curse,' replied Elspeth, trying to play down the situation, 'more a case of something that seems to happen a lot and so suspicious folks presume it's a sort of curse.'

Eenayah sipped her sherry, mindful that she was driving but in need of just a little something to prepare her for whatever strange story was about to follow on. She sensed it was going to be a slightly oddball conversation.

Elspeth seemed to be considering her words carefully, something Eenayah suspected she didn't do very often. Her great aunt appeared to be Lancashire old school, a 'cards on the table' woman, but on this occasion she was searching for diplomacy, and diplomacy wasn't going to arrive from her lips easily.

Elspeth took a sip of sherry and began. 'You must know how some tales just get passed down from generation to generation and over time the story changes?'

'Like Chinese Whispers?'

'Yes indeed', replied Elspeth 'just like Chinese Whispers. So read into this as you like, but I can only tell you what Harriet has told me.'

'Okay Aunty,' replied Eenayah, 'just go for it and try me out.'

Elspeth removed her glasses from her face and looked down at the table as though she expected it to help her find the right words. This conversation would prove difficult.

'Well, from what I have been told and as far back as can be known, twins run in your family. There hasn't been a generation yet that hasn't spawned a set of twins'.

Eenayah smiled, considering that maybe this was some familial ignorance of biology.

'But Aunty Elspeth, it's a well-known fact that twins do run in families. That isn't any sort of curse; that's just a natural fact'.

Elspeth shot her one of her looks to suggest that she was far from stupid and not to treat her as such. She carried on, 'Yes, we know that darling, but this is quite different. You see, the twins are only ever female'.

'I am sure Aunty that there will be some biological reason for the twins only being female. I have a friend called Fabien who is an obstetrician in Paris and I'm sure that if I asked him he would tell me it was something to do with an X chromosome or whatever. I can ask him if it helps dispel this as some sort of a magical myth.'

Elspeth was not be put off her stride and was becoming irritated by Eenayah's constant interruption and presumed knowledge of biology. Elspeth liked to tell a good story, and this was indeed a very good story, and she intended to deliver it as she intended.

'I think you should just listen to what I say first, Eenayah. There is far more to this than just twin girls being born into each generation. There is something unusual about the twins. To begin with, they only go from daughter to daughter, they run down the female line. So if the past repeats itself, then Ruby's little boy Harry cannot have twin girls because this cannot be passed on from a son. Only if Ruby has twin girls herself can this line of twins continue, unless of course you become pregnant my dear.'

Eenayah couldn't help but respond, despite the instruction that she should just shut up and listen. 'Well I doubt that would ever happen, Aunty. After Reed's first wife betrayed him he had the snip and he can't father any children as far as I am aware. Plus we are hardly on the same continent to actually do the whole procreation thing. I don't know too much about genetics, but this still sounds like some X chromosome thing to me and probably has a medical explanation'.

Elspeth was growing tired of Eenayah's theorising, but none the less she continued to weave intrigue into her tale. 'There is a so-called curse attached to this as well Eenayah, so make of this what you will. For some reason, only one twin can produce the next set of twins and in fact more often than not I am told that either one twin will die before she can have children or be unable to reproduce. It is complicated to explain, but you must agree that there is something very peculiar about only one twin being able to give birth to twins who can only be girl babies. Don't you find that odd in some way?'

Eenayah did not accept this was a curse and was quite adamant that it was coincidence. 'I suspect this is Granny Harriet's theory of events, because of course Daisy had the twin girls and April had cerebral palsy and died young, and to someone who is a bit superstitious and heartbroken and desperate to find a reason or something to blame, then maybe a curse seems a viable option. I'm sure my French doctor friend would tell me that not too far back in history twin births were considered very dangerous and maybe more often than not, one twin would either be born stillborn or damaged by the birth process, as with April. From what you told me on the way to visit Granny Harriet, April was a breech who got stuck and her brain was starved of oxygen and the result was cerebral palsy. That must have been so common with twin births in times gone by. These are just medical facts that can be explained, Aunt, not a crazy curse'.

Undeterred, Elspeth added, 'well the same thing happened to Harriet's mum and her grandmother, and that seems a bit of an odd coincidence don't you think?'

Eenayah despaired. She looked up to the paint peeling on her aunt's ceiling and sighed with frustration. 'Yes indeed Aunty, it is indeed sad and tragic, but Mother Nature can sometimes be a bad midwife and with regards to twin births I suspect that the second twin to be born was indeed vulnerable and may have been subjected to damage which equated to a shorter life span. Heck, as recently as 100 years ago, working-class people in this part of Lancashire had short lifespans just from poverty alone, twin or no twin. Infant mortality was probably horrendous. Your own brother William didn't exactly live a long life, did he?' Eenayah bit her tongue the moment she made the statement, but could not undo what had been said.

Elspeth was beginning to feel that no matter what she told Eenayah, she would find some historical, environmental or medical reason to logically explain away what Granny Harriet had regarded as some dark curse. She was about to throw the increasingly stubborn Eenayah the last and final shot and this time diplomacy left the room.

'I understand what you are trying to tell me Eenayah, twins run in families and there could be a rational reason as to why one twin would be childless or die young, but there is a final part to this story which Harriet would want me to tell you.'

Eenayah shrugged nonchalantly, glancing at her watch. 'Hmm, okay - hit me with it,' she murmured under her breath.

Elspeth drew her chair closer, looking Eenayah directly in the eyes, maybe to add to the drama.

'There is a myth and maybe this is only Chinese whispers, it is for you to decide. But there is something more to mention about this female line of twins. It is connected to some prophecy that comes from the bible itself. Harriet says it is a pure bloodline, a special bloodline that can only be passed from female to female. The bloodline cannot end, it must continue and it continues through you or your sister, whichever one of you has the twins which indeed are fated to carry the line. It means that your life is in danger until you reach an age when you are no longer fertile. That is your curse. This is what Harriet wanted me to tell you. You must take care, as there are powers that want this bloodline to come to an end.'

Eenayah was by now becoming quite tired of this myth/curse/fairy story scenario, and feeling slightly as though she had stepped back into the Middle Ages and any moment now she would be offered some magical portion and turn into an elf.

'It MUST continue? That's a bit dramatic. What will happen if it doesn't, Aunty Elspeth? Will it be the end of the world?'

Elspeth shrugged. 'I don't know. I am too old to care and it's your bloodline not mine. It's for you to find out'.

Eenayah didn't care to respond. It had been a long day and she wanted to make tracks soon.

'Anyway', continued Elspeth, 'you will soon find out if all this talk is true or not. You girls are pushing forty I believe and you know fertility starts to fall off at your age. However if this myth is true, then one of you needs to give birth to twins for the bloodline to continue. If you are telling me that your husband is firing on blanks after a vasectomathingy- whatever it's called - then only Ruby can have the twins. They need to be born, it's the prophecy. So listen out for a phone call soon to tell you that she is pregnant. Let's just wait and see.'

Eenayah was now feeling quite insulted. 'Aunty, I am still just 38 so I don't consider myself to be hitting the menopause quite yet. Once more, your theory has just failed. Ruby cannot get pregnant. Harry is adopted. Ruby had a burst appendix when she was a child and contracted severe peritonitis afterwards. It destroyed her fallopian tubes and everything had to be removed, so that's put paid to your myth.'

Elspeth smiled with self-satisfaction, believing she had been proven right. 'So you see, it has already happened. One twin either dies or cannot have children and look, the pattern continues.'

Eenayah, had heard enough. 'Thank you for sharing Aunty, but this has been a difficult and tiring day for me. I need to make tracks now. I am sure the world won't end tomorrow. The thing is, Ruby cannot have children and neither can my husband, so it is indeed the end of this particular bloodline I am afraid.'

Elspeth walked her to the door, not sure when she would next see Eenayah, if indeed she ever would see her again. The mood was tense. She suspected that she had overstepped the mark, but she could not resist one last stab. It was a female Lancashire tradition always to have the last word.

'The line will not be allowed to end Eenayah, it isn't time yet,' she said. As though the weather was adding a biblical affect to this unfolding drama, a flash of lightning scored across the sky. With a clap of thunder, the heavens opened and Eenayah dashed to her car before becoming drenched. She considered her great aunt to be a mischief maker who loved nothing more than a good mystery, but none the less she was intrigued. If anyone could dig into the past it was Professor De Vede, her hired expert on all matters family and historical. Maybe she ought to give him a call and assign him another project! Just to check it out – just in case.

CHAPTER 19

Sunday 7th July 2013

Ruby adored her sister's villa just as much, if not more, in the evening than in the bright Florida daylight. After sunset the grounds were illuminated like a Christmas scene, with lights wrapped around the palm trees and subtle lilac uplights buried into the decked pathways. There was nothing discreet about this waterside Santa's grotto, and both Owyn and Harry loved the abundance of light, colour and childlike playful decadence.

Roserie was a much appreciated though temporary child minder, and Ruby had wanted to wrap her up and take her home. It was a much-deserved extravagance to be awarded the time to slow down and rewind from her normally manic working life. Owyn had banned his wife from switching on her mobile or answering emails, which sadly seemed to be an expectation of employees in today's mobile work force. Wi-Fi equated to being at work anywhere and anytime. Sure, she had broken the rule a few times, but aside from brief and urgent exceptions she had abided to her husband's strict rules of complete unbroken relaxation.

Every evening after little Harry was tucked up in bed, the loving couple had got into the daily habit of sharing the hot tub with a chilled glass of Prosecco and idly discussing the events of the day. It was a great treat, and the vacation offered them both some rare and valuable family time together.

Owyn was already mellowing in the whirlpool, and transcendentally lost in his Seal CD by the time Ruby made her entrance. He could immediately tell from the expression on his wife's face that something had happened. Ruby's recent tranquil holiday mood had somehow been disturbed and replaced by a tangible tension. Her lips were pursed tense in a grimace that Owyn had seldom witnessed. She flopped into the Jacuzzi with a big splash, an aggressive air about her as though she had just invaded a small country. The warrior queen's adrenalin was pumping.

'Hey, what's up doll?' asked Owyn, trying to talk with Florida cool, but as a Welshman with a poor American accent, failing badly. Something was obviously wrong and Owyn didn't have any clue as to what it could be. He was a typical 'blokes' bloke' and the more subtle nuances of a female mood swing were something he failed to grasp.

Ruby said nothing for the moment but Owyn noted that she was visibly shaking. After she had knocked back her glass of Prosecco in one, Owyn knew it was time to switch off the whirlpool jets to allow his wife to talk and get whatever it was out of her system. He repeated the question. 'Ruby, what the hell has happened? What's wrong?'

Ruby poured herself a second glass of emergency bubbly, which again was disposed of like cough medicine, with one big throated gulp.

'It's Eenayah. She's been up to all sorts of mischief and crazy stuff back in the UK. I'm furious. I've just come off the phone with her, and I am sorry to say that for the first time ever I just hung up. I couldn't speak with her. I just had to put the phone down before I said something I would regret.'

Owyn wasn't quite sure how to handle this new and dramatic turn of events. This new mean and angry wife person was unfamiliar territory. He decided to try to placate her.

'Ruby, your sister has been really good to us. She has paid for this trip, she has let us live in her house, booked the Disney trip and even paid for your parents, aunt and best friend to come over and join us. Eenayah doesn't do bad things – I mean, she just doesn't do anything to be fair. What could she have possibly have done to get you so angry?'

Owyn was genuinely bemused. In his eyes Eenayah was harmless, in a pale yellow nothing sort of way. As colour palettes go, hers was a wishy-washy vacuum of shades.

Ruby hissed back, 'Well okay, let me start with the least offensive news then. She promised to look after our house and our pets whilst we were over here, but your sister Darcy has been over to ours after work every night this week and the house is dark and empty and bloody deserted. Eenayah isn't there and God only knows what she has done with Barnaby and Bertie.'

Ruby treated her pets more like babies than a mere dog and a cat. To her this was a serious offence, highly emotive, and he wasn't quite sure how to calm the situation down following this revelation. He recognised that to his wife this act of treason would be like someone leaving their own children to fend for themselves in a gutter in Rio de Janeiro. He decided to try to placate her as best he could.

'Rubes, calm it down. You know Eenayah never liked our house. She doesn't do old and gothic and she has always made that 100% crystal clear. Come on, you know she can't handle dark remote places, and Ruby my love, you have to admit that for any woman on her own, our house could be quite menacing. It scares me sometimes when you're away in your posh London hotels. Get a bit of howling wind blowing down from the mountains and it can be a bloody noisy place. Those mountains have a voice and they use it at times. Your sister is a rich overindulged lady my love, she wouldn't have put Barnaby or

Bertie into anywhere rough. You know they will be well looked after, surely?'

Ruby calmed down slightly. 'Yes I know they are fine. Eenayah told me as much, and yes I suspected she wasn't going to stay over the whole time, but I just wished she had talked to me first before just deserting the place. Also I believe I should at least have had a say into where she housed Barnaby and Bertie.'

By now, Ruby's face had softened and she looked to be in less of a rage. However the anger had now been replaced with melancholia, which was confusing to Owyn. Ruby sighed and shrugged.

'You know if she had just picked up the phone and told me, I could have asked Darcy and her latest boyfriend to stay over. Anyway, I've asked Darcy to sort it and she'll be going over to ours tomorrow and bringing the pets home, that's if she can find out where they are. Oh and here's the thing Owyn, more news! Darcy also told me that some guy had been hanging around our house. On at least three occasions, she saw the same chap hanging out on the lane.'

At this point Owyn sat up and paid attention, slightly alarmed.

'But who the heck ever comes to our lane who isn't meant to be there? It's not like we are easy to find.'

Ruby felt victorious that at long last her point had hit home and almost barked out, 'exactly!'

Owyn swung into male protector mode. 'I don't like the thought of some stranger hanging around the lane. I'll have a word with Darcy tomorrow to make sure her boyfriend, whatever his name is, will be sure to stay with her. So,' he continued, treading on eggshells again, 'you said this first bit of news was the lesser evil, in which case what greater sin has pissed you off then? I feel a bit scared to ask, but I know there is something else.'

Ruby filled her glass once more, drinking for all the wrong reasons and looking yet more subdued. The moonlight caught her face and her husband could see the glimmer of a tear escaping from her right eye.

'Oh Owyn,' she wept, 'Eenayah has taken it upon herself to search for our birth mother.'

This newsflash was received in shocked silence. Owyn was stunned, and not for the first time this evening he felt unsure how to handle this situation.

'I don't know what to say Ruby. I am speechless. Why didn't she consult you? Why now of all times when we are so far from home?'

Ruby shrugged. 'It was Mum who told me. I couldn't understand why Eenayah had been acting so odd recently and when I asked Mum, she just coughed out the truth. Of course, it has hit me hard, maybe more so than my sister, because let's face it Owyn, we may have to go through this with Harry one day.'

Owyn put his arms around his wife protectively and held her close. 'If that happens, I will be right by your side to support both you and Harry,' he said. He kissed her forehead. 'So who is your mother then? Has Eenayah managed to find her?'

Ruby didn't mince her words. 'She is dead,' she replied brusquely. 'I don't know anything more at this stage, other than her name was Daisy and she was very young and died just after we were born – oh and guess what, she was a twin as well.'

'So no big reunion Rubes? You know, maybe that's for the best for everyone. I sometimes think the past is best left in the past, sweetie'.

Ruby climbed out of the hot tub and covered herself in a large white fluffy bath towel. Despite the humid Florida evening, she shivered. It was a shiver from the soul rather than anything vaguely temperature related. Sitting cross-legged beside the tub she continued, 'I am told we have a grandmother who is just about alive. To be honest Owyn, I agree with you, I don't really care about my past. What has happened has happened and my present and future are of more concern than some history book. However what has upset me the most is that Eenayah has been doing all of this on her own. It's not so much that she has been secretive about it, as I do understand that she didn't want to ruin our vacation, but it's more to do with her going through with this mission of hers without my help. This can't have been easy for her.'

Owyn held his wife close to his chest and stroked her long brown hair as one would comfort a child. Ruby stood up and paced around the hot tub decking area, stopping for a moment to look up at the star-embroidered sky as though in silent prayer. She still appeared visibly shaken by this latest revelation to blast its way into her life.

'Owyn, you must remember that Eenayah has had mental health issues in the not-so-distant past. She has lost two husbands. So okay, technically she wasn't married to James, but she was only a week away from the altar. Once was a tragedy, but twice - it almost destroyed her. She has made a good recovery, but she is still fragile. I'm far more worried about her than I could ever be angry with her. Although I have noticed that she tells a lot of lies these days and I am less than pleased with all the deception.'

Owyn totally understood the gravity of the situation, but he did not want any emotional traumas to endanger the rest of this much-needed family vacation. He decided to get them both inside, maybe get them both drunk and allay his wife's concerns by whatever means required. He hooked her arm gently to guide her back into the house. Ruby crooked her head to one side so it rested on his shoulder as they walked indoors. He made a mental note to have a confidential chat with her best friend Becky when she joined them for the final week of the holiday after the whole Disney experience. He recalled that Reed had invited her over along with her Italian husband, whose complicated foreign name he couldn't remember, let alone pronounce. He was sure that Becky would be a good source of solace for Ruby.

In the meantime, Owyn tried to be sympathetic as well as moving the situation along, something he seemed to be able to do quite expertly.

'Hey Rubes, your sister is a big girl and she will she be okay I promise you' he said. 'Roserie told me earlier that Reed will be back home soon, either tonight or tomorrow. My advice to you love, is that you need to get that wanderlust sister of yours to pack her cases and get her butt back over to Miami so those two guys can be under the same roof for once. This is Reed's responsibility, not yours. Eenayah is his wife and those two globetrotting married folk need to spend some time together and sort their marriage out. It's not your job love. You already have a job. Harry and I are your job - me more so than Harry, I suspect.' With that he gave her a cheeky nip on the posterior and a seductive wink.

Ruby smiled coyly. She couldn't help but love her uncultured rugby-playing Welsh husband. Owyn always knew just the right things to say and do, and for a guy, his timing was unusually perfect.

'I just need to keep a close eye on her, Owyn' she said. 'She flushed her medication down the loo a few months back, and she thinks she can do without it now. However her marriage doesn't seem to be going too well as far as I can tell. Also Mother tells me that she has been visiting churchyards a lot recently. She seems to be hiding herself away in the past. I'm not a psychologist, but maybe that's something people do when they don't care much for their present. I guess the past is a known thing and to some people it may seem a lot safer than an unknown future. I just need to support her, honey.'

Owyn was sympathetic. 'Look, I do understand your concern Rubes, I really do. However all of this can wait until we get home and if you do or if you don't want to connect with your new-found grandmother, hey that's your choice. Reality check; you can't do anything until you are back in the UK. Right here and now, we have to get on with this vacation and pack our cases for Orlando. We have a sleeping little boy who can't wait to go to Disneyland and our next step on the action plan is to deliver him to Mickey Mouse. It's only for a week honey, and once we get back here to Miami, hopefully all the family will be here and with any luck that should include Mr and Mrs Baratolli. Maybe we can sort everything out together as a family, but next week, not now. Just leave everything to me. I will call Darcy tomorrow and make sure that the moat doors are up and all the ghosts and headless knights in our Welsh castle are safe and secure. Of course, not forgetting that Barnaby and Bertie are being well looked after and behaving themselves. Capisce?'

Ruby beamed, her facial muscles relaxing back into vacation mode as the thought of the next stage of their Florida adventure. Excitement dominated her mood as all the recent negativity evaporated. She kissed her husband cheekily, replying, 'capisce!'

CHAPTER 20

Monday 8ᵗʰ July 2013

Eenayah felt suitably muddled this morning. The conversation yesterday with Ruby had disturbed her in more ways than one. She hadn't knowingly promised Ruby that she would stay over at her shadowy, sprawling part-completed mansion, and was totally flummoxed as to how and why her sister had ever interpreted it to be that way. She was also taken aback by how Ruby had reacted to her unexpected trip into the biological family past. She had expected at least some fireworks to be ignited, or at the very least a good scolding. However Ruby seemed unusually accepting and forgiving of the situation, even showing greater concern about how she had been handling the potential ordeal without her sisterly support.

Eenayah figured that Ruby was simply in holiday mode and ultra-relaxed after a week away from the rigours of employment. She considered her twin to be in a state of delayed shock. Once the reality struck home and all cocktails had been detoxified from her system, she expected a delayed reprimand would be wafting her way. Eager to be seen to be making some amends, Eenayah endured the chaos of checking out of her Manchester hotel suite and reluctantly set out on the long drive back to North Wales and Ruby's stately home.

Once she had negotiated her way out of the busy one-way road system of Manchester with its road works, closed lanes and traffic jams, she was finally on a long, straight, monotonous motorway. Not having to think about traffic lights and roundabouts, Eenayah could now hit cruise control and relax into 'think and reflect' mode.

She revisited what both Darcy and Ruby had told her in her last conversations with them. Some stranger had been hanging around on the lane, near the house. She shuddered at the thought. Ruby's house seemed to lack the high security she had been used to in her reclusive lavish Miami abode.

Of course she had quizzed Darcy in the hope of getting an accurate description of the man, but Owyn's flirty younger sister only viewed men in one of three ways: point 1) was she related to him/them, point 2) was she attracted to him/them and finally point 3) How old were they? If a young adult male, refer to point 2). All Darcy could initially say was that at a distance he appeared to be a good-looking older guy, nobody she recognised and not a family member. Eenayah knew that 'old' to Darcy might not exactly be everyone's definition of old. Most probably anyone who did not frequent a nightclub every weekend in Rhyl could be considered old to Darcy. When pushed for a description of what he wore – for example, did he look like a farmer, a tramp, a multi-millionaire, a burglar or just a guy walking a dog? - all Darcy could really say was, 'I didn't get that close to him, but he was wearing a nice coat. Don't know the brand, something posh… like what country people wear when they go hunting, sort of thing'. It wasn't the most eloquent of descriptions, but it did give Eenayah three possible basic classifications; an elderly man by Darcy's standards, a good-looking man by Darcy's standards, and a posh and maybe even a rich man by Darcy's standards. All of these depictions could easily point to this stranger being Paul Bucklow - ex footballer, ex father-in-law and as much as she hated to contemplate the thought without mentally saying the word 'yuk', a possible ex-lover.

Eenayah drove as though on automatic pilot, deep in thought and hardly taking note of the passing scenery. She considered the possibilities and mumbled to herself out loud, 'Paul is in his sixties, he's a good-looking man for his age and as an ex-footballer, he would be wealthy enough to wear a Holland Cooper shooting coat and the like'. Paul could indeed have been the man on the lane. As she drove, her thoughts started to torment her and she drifted into increasing panic and paranoia. After all, Paul had taken it upon himself to visit her childhood home on the Isle of Man. Although not too far away from North Wales, there was cold bleak sea between the two areas - one didn't exactly take the wrong turn at a junction and just end up on the Isle of Man.

Again, she muttered to herself out loud, 'It is as it bloody is; an island. You have to board a plane or a ferry to get there.' Paul most certainly had made a deliberate trip there. She was totally sure of it and couldn't buy into his explanation of attending a memorial service arranged by his ex-wife, who had every reason to hate him for cheating on him and getting two women pregnant at the same time. As far as reasons for 'getting along with an ex' went, she concluded that Paul bloody Bucklow must be the hated ex of many a woman in the British Isles. Mary had no reason to invite him to some memorial service. She concluded this to be a pathetic feeble lie and a cowardly excuse.

The question now being, was her ex-father-in-law loitering outside her sister's house and if so, why? Eenayah had softened around the edges over her last pampered decade, but was quickly coming to the conclusion that now was the time to revert back to the hard-faced journalist she had once been in her youth, and that meant facing life full on. With an innate tendency to run away from awkward predicaments, actually facing up to a situation was new territory for

Eenayah, but far from home and with neither sister, husband nor faithful maid to back her up, there was little choice in the matter. If Paul was stalking her, she needed to find out why. She had grown tired of avoidance tactics.

For some reason she had saved the satellite navigation unit on her hired car to remember the location of Paul's house. She concluded that this must have been a habit or perhaps a subconscious action, but whatever the reason, her car knew exactly how to find him, even if she didn't. Pulling up on the hard shoulder to set the new satnav waypoint, one of Reed's compositions started to play on a local station as she tuned into the frequency of a nearby radio reception. It was such a weird coincidence. Ruby and Eenayah had always had a sibling in joke about psychic radio. As teenagers they joked (sometimes with all sincerity and seriousness), that if you had a question for the universe, you could just ask it out loud and then the lyrics of next record that came on would answer your question. Psychic radio; not something she had thought about since her teenage years.

She sat in the layby for a moment, closed her eyes and listened to the harmonies, the guitar strum, the lyrics. How privileged she felt at that moment. She wondered how many women had ever had a song written about them, and concluded that the answer was probably very few. Indeed she had remembered Reed writing the song many years ago. It was the week before they were due to be married, and at the time Eenayah had been getting cold feet. She had lost a future husband a week before a wedding once before, and as memories started to flood back about James, an irrational fear of fate repeating itself started to churn up some obscured buried sentiments.

Reed had written the song for her as a reassurance of his love, but in the song he was also asking her to be strong and brave. As she recalled, he was slightly stoned at the time and had just picked up his guitar with no thought or intention of anything very much. Thanks to his musical brilliance, the lyrics and notes flowed out effortlessly. She sat in the layby until the end of the song and relived the moment. If this was psychic radio making a return to the paranormal air waves, then it was telling her to go face her fear – aka Paul.

With that thought and the music still playing in her head, she continued her journey. She needed answers; what had happened the night she stayed over at his cottage and perhaps even more importantly, why he was now stalking her. Stalking was a strong and slightly sinister word to use, but that was exactly how it felt.

Eenayah's satnav had expertly relocated the winding dirt track next to the pub with the identifying large Christmas tree planted at the junction of the car park and driveway up to Paul's cottage. She knew instantly that she was in the right place. Despite the courage crafted by the whole psychic radio event, she now felt butterflies fluttering in the pit of her stomach. The last time her car wheels had met with this surface, they had been speeding in the opposite direction. She gave herself a mental ticking off: 'don't be a wuss Baratolli, as a journalist you took bigger risks than this all the time. Think about the gangland party you gate-crashed and the quick getaway from a 3rd floor window when you were being shot at by a bald drunken mobster. Pull it together girl. This is a nothingness!'

Approaching the familiar cottage, she noted that the black Porsche had been replaced by a silver Mercedes SLX. She hadn't ever really been a car person and rarely understood or cared about the variety of models, but this particular car looked really quite striking as it glinted in the sun. With some apprehension she wrapped on the door with its oversized dragon doorknob, at the same time looking down to her feet so to deflect Paul's anticipated gaze.

What happened next was unexpected. The person who answered the door was a woman, a woman with long razor-sharp straight blond hair and cold clear blue eyes. Her eyes were exquisite, and yet like arctic ice.

Eenayah gasped. She was unable to speak, react or move. It was the woman in red.

It was the woman who spoke first. 'Can I help you madam?' she asked. Eenayah was dumbstruck. She tried to remember her name. Could this be Emmanuelle? She was sure it was the same person she had seen with Reed in the exclusive London restaurant, the place with all the flowers that had looked more like a cottage garden than a place to eat.

Eenayah wondered if she had a French accent. Finally finding her tongue, she asked, 'Erm… is Paul at home?'

How stupid! What had happened to the art of conversation? She sounded like a little girl calling for a friend to come out and play. Was this the best she could do?

The woman replied and Eenayah consciously dissected each syllable as she tried to identify any sign of a foreign accent.

'I am so sorry, I don't know who this Paul is,' replied the woman. It was a short reply, executed with the smarmiest of sickening smiles. She sounded British, but Eenayah was sure she could detect a subtle trace of something else. Eenayah was the mistress of various accents and had often used this ability back in her undercover journalist days. She figured that if she could make herself sound American, then surely a French person could make herself sound British. She reasoned that actors and actresses played with accents all the time. An accent didn't necessarily equate to a place of origin.

'About a week ago I stayed in this house and my former father-in-law Paul Bucklow lived here and his black Porsche was parked in this driveway. Now his car isn't here and he isn't here and I would like to know where he is please? I would also like to know who is living in his house. Who are you?'

She had surprised herself by her own directness. Quietly pleased by her counter attack, she stood firm and awaited a response.

The blonde woman, much to Eenayah's disappointment, remained unruffled and responded with a coolness that matched her emotionless eyes. With yet another nauseating smile, she replied, 'I am so sorry. I don't know anything about the owner of the house. I only moved in here a few days ago. I rented it from a local property agent and I do not know the name of the landlord or the owner. I wish I could be of more help. I am happy to give you the name of the property agent. Perhaps they have a forwarding address for your ex father-in-law. Please do come in for a moment and I will find their business card.'

Game, set and match – with total composure, the aloof blonde woman had won. Eenayah was so annoyed. Her English was perfect, her cool composure was perfect. Hell, *she* was bloody perfect.

Eenayah walked inside the cottage. She couldn't remember too much about Paul's interior design, so she didn't have many details in her memory bank to compare against. She had either been too drunk to notice or had left in too much of a hurry to pay any attention to colour schemes.

The blonde woman, true to her word, handed Eenayah the business card of the property agent, flashing yet another false yet flawless smile. She appeared to be telling the truth. As Eenayah turned to leave, she felt somewhat disappointed that there hadn't been a greater mystery involved. On the surface it seemed to be a legitimate story that Paul had indeed rented out his cottage and the woman was his tenant.

Then just as Eenayah was about to leave, she noticed a teenage girl coyly peeking around the corner of the kitchen door. She was dressed in denim dungarees, ankle socks and a "5SOS" tea shirt. Her flame-red hair was bunched into two girly side plaits, each tied with big green ribbons. She smiled sweetly in Eenayah's direction.

Eenayah walked back to the car trying hard to remember her husband's recent hot musical prodigy, Océane. Eenayah had seen photo-shoots of the young singer in a magazine. The child had been draped in sophisticated gowns, with hair and makeup professionally executed. Add expert lighting with image editing technology, and the child had morphed into a sophisticated woman in her twenties. However, the long and stunning flame-red hair was memorable.

Eenayah's mind turned somersaults. She considered the sweet young girl in the hallway door who looked and dressed like a teenager. Could she be Océane? It was not inconceivable. Pauls' new tenants looked every inch like Reed's new contract signing and her protective mother.

Driving back in the direction of her sister Ruby's house, she tried to make the connection between Paul and Reed's new starlet and her pushy show business mother. How could a connection with Paul be possible? If the woman in red and her talented daughter really had rented Paul's house, this took coincidence to a whole new level of weirdness. She needed to investigate more. She decided to call the property agent and also ask Reed, as surely he was bound to know where his new star was residing. This possibility was too strange to consider and she was already partially dismissing it as a flight of fancy. Of course there could be no possible association. It was an unimaginable coincidence.

As she drove through the Horseshoe Pass, Eenayah noted that the light was just beginning to fade as the sun made its slow descent behind the mountain peaks. She began to feel fearful about driving along the winding road with its deathly drops to the valley below. She felt nervous about driving during daylight, but after nightfall the fear was heightened many times.

Eenayah had been terrified of the dark as long as she could remember. Maybe it was because she suffered from the most petrifying of nightmares and night frights. She would wake up suddenly in a cold sweat, her bed trembling, buzzing noises all around her, and be unable to move a single muscle. She couldn't even blink, and her mouth would freeze open as she attempted a scream. Only the sound of her own heartbeat and breathing acted as a reminder that she was still alive. Often she would feel a heavy presence on her chest, as though she was being sat on by a phantom weight, and occasionally her throat seemed blocked as though she was being strangled. It was an awful and terrifying experience. The doctors had no idea what caused these events. As with most things, they put it down to stress and prescribed yet another pill to dull yet another piece of reality and switch off yet more senses.

Thankfully the night frights didn't last long, although it felt that way at the time. Eventually she would muster the strength to let out an unholy, ear-piercing scream. If she had a bed companion, at least she had the assurance of warm manly arms to hold and comfort her trembling body. However in recent times she had been mostly sleeping alone. In the isolation of a bedroom, she found the darkness menacing. Eenayah usually made a concerted effort to be indoors before sunset – wherever indoors happened to be, and lately that could be any one of many places. Her sister and husband alike had often teased her about this peculiar little custom, nicknaming her 'the vamp'. Whenever she looked at her watch and gave a cursory glance outside the window to check on the light, she knew their jests would begin.

Today Eenayah had set off too late and was running behind time. She had gone through a panic-stricken moment checking out of the hotel when her Mark Silverstein-designed wedding ring had gone astray somewhere in the vicinity of the bedroom suite. She then had to endure Monday Manchester traffic, and her satnav giving her instructions to drive down closed roads as well as directing her the wrong way down one-way streets. She then took a considerable detour to find Paul Bucklow's cottage, which had proven to be a fruitless exercise. Stopping off at a friendly-looking farm shop to stock up on groceries, and then spending more time and money than required, she then hung around for a while to casually sip coffee and people watch.

As the light rapidly started to dwindle, Eenayah reproached herself for taking so much time in getting to her sister's house. She was now on a meandering mountain road as nightfall approached. With a sense of urgency and resolve, she continued to focus on the drive ahead, knowing that once she was off this perilous snake of a road, she only had a ten-minute trek to Ruby's house down in the valley.

Before long, with a massive sense of relief, she spotted the twin turrets of Darwydden Castle Manor towering above the tree line. She followed the zigzag lane down into the woods, the house seemingly pulling her into its peculiar kingdom.

She let out a massive sigh. She had made it off the road in one piece, just as the last crescent of the sun had finally descended behind the mountain range and a dark eerie mist had sunk into the valleys. She concluded that all this driving business was not as much fun as she had originally presumed and maybe she should go back to having a driver chauffeur her around. The thought of entertaining herself with a movie and cocktails in the back of a limo was a temporary pleasant contemplation. The combination of navigating out of hectic city centre traffic and then trying not to drive off a Welsh mountain down into a steep ravine had made this an unpleasant journey. Hiring a driver and returning her rental car was becoming a serious consideration.

Eenayah made a mental note to ask Ruby to do something about the external lighting of Darwydden Castle Manor. The trees on either side of the drive hung dramatically over the road and when caught by the car headlights they looked foreboding and ominous, their branches like tentacles reaching down as if to scoop up any passing vehicle in their wake. She tried to ignore the hungry finger-like twigs reaching out to her and focused on the open gates ahead. She thought, 'If only I had set off just one hour earlier. Just an hour. I cannot believe Ruby has given me a guilt trip and made me feel the need to do this.'

Her own abode back in Miami was illuminated with as many

lights as she could possibly cram into the garden, patio and pool area. Her dislike of the shadows of darkness was more related to the outside world than the inside. None the less, she was relieved to be finally entering the marble floored hallway of her sister's house, her footsteps echoing along the long corridor as she dragged a single overnight case indoors. She did not intend to stay too long, no matter what guilt trip Ruby had inflicted on her. She was here under protest!

Owyn had often described his large garden of many acres as being shaped like a bowl, and when the wind blew down off the mountain, it swirled around the garden as though Mother Nature was stirring up a cup of tea. In autumn this often created a discernible spectacle as the leaves were blown around and around in a circle by the whirlwind. Owyn had a large photo proudly displayed on the mantelpiece of a veritable tornado of brown and orange shrubbery that had been spun into a twister by the unusual way geography played with the air. However in summer all that could be heard was the strange whooshing and whistling noise of a gentle breeze. None the less, the acoustics were most odd and the strange noises unnerving. The house was literally in the middle of nowhere, so add to that the wind and a variety of bird and animal noises and the end result was anything but a peaceful and quiet retreat.

The house was cold and damp. It might have been midsummer, but old houses like this did not have the luxury of modern day insulation. With its high ceilings and ancient stone floors, just a few days without human habitation could chill the heart of the house to the degree where you could see your own breath. Eenayah hated the cold and her immediate action plan was to descend into the Victorian cellar and outwit the complex boiler and entice it to ignite. The boiler had a mind of its own, but Owyn had given her several plumbing and ignition lessons, so she felt suitably trained.

Ascending back up the steep cellar steps into the grand hallway with its imposing alabaster pillars and high coved ceilings, Eenayah recalled a Christmas of many years ago. Baby Harry had just started to walk and as it was his first ever Christmas his parents had gone overboard with the whole festive spirit thing. Eenayah recalled a huge Christmas tree in the hallway, and the grand oak staircase had been draped in holly and ivy. She and Reed had stayed with Owyn and Ruby for two weeks, leaving just after New Year. It was a picture perfect memory of mistletoe and snow. Even though the house was in a valley, it was still a valley in the midst of the Snowdonia mountain range, so inclement weather in winter was more or less the norm. She smiled sadly as she recalled the fun they had all had on Boxing Day, with Reed making a rude snowman with an inappropriately placed carrot. They threw snowballs at each other until they bruised and laughed until it hurt. It was a happy and yet sad memory; back in the days when as a couple, Eenayah and Reed actually made time for each other.

Couples who play together stay together, she thought, recalling that since being away from Miami, she had mostly been either too busy or too tired to call Reed every day. Plus the time difference was a reasonable alibi to add to the pot. She recalled one of Reed's famous sayings, 'if you really want to do something you will find a way to do it, and if you don't, you will find an excuse.' By his definition, she was finding lots of reasons which had all the markings of excuses. The realisation dawned on her that they only seemed to speak because she was the one making all the effort and back in Miami she was mostly bored and would phone him because she had little else to occupy her. Now she was no longer bored and if anything overly occupied, she hadn't found the time to call Reed, and with a piercing stab in her heart she instantaneously understood that Reed had been equally guilty of making zero effort. She hadn't wanted to consider it before and had done all she could to wipe the thought from her head, but free of the anti-depressants clogging up her brain, she was beginning to realise that her marriage was in dire trouble.

Standing in the great hallway stirring up at the memory of what was once a star on a tree, her thoughts drifted into her more recent past. In the last month of being back in the UK, she had been permanently occupied on almost a daily basis. She had done the whole London tourist encounter and partied in Newcastle with lots of middle-aged but still crazy people from her student days. She had spent some wonderfully loving home-from-home time on her parents' farm in the Isle of Man. She had searched for ancestors both living and dead in Manchester, and employed a mysterious detective company to undertake some unusual and yet life-changing work for her. She hadn't come to the UK to find a mother, but by coincidence or fate she had stumbled upon a family she had never known existed.

The Christmas tree memory then took her to the tree that marked out the junction of Paul Bucklow's house and reminded her that she needed to call the property agent to glean some details. Once again, practicalities and a 'to do' list had taken her thoughts away from Reed.

Looking at the hallway as it was right now, it seemed so empty. Eenayah had often thought that a house gets it soul from the people who live there, and even when a house - any house - has been empty for a short period of time, it seems to change and become hollow. Why was that? How was it that when you went away on holiday and then came home, a house seemed so cold, bare and soulless? That was exactly how it felt in the hallway of Ruby's manor house; vacant and barren.

Eenayah resolved to light some fires and bring much-needed warmth to the chilly rooms. She would take a hot bath, put on her PJs and watch some junk TV to blot out any thoughts and override any ghostlike footsteps from the old servants' quarters. She decided that tomorrow she would start to make plans for her return to Miami. She knew that Reed was back home now and she had realised that she had some repair work to do with her relationship if there was still a chance to save it. However, before she could figure out her future, she needed first to bring some closure to her past and tie up some loose ends in the UK. She still had Reed's family history book to finalise with the Professor and some finance she wished to distribute amongst her family before the transatlantic flight home. However all of that was for tomorrow. For tonight's work she had to turn on as many room lights as she could and draw every curtain she could find. She was safe indoors and felt comforted by the security watch Mercy De Vede had insisted she wear. Now… if only she could block out the blackness of the outside world and its hidden bogeymen. She knew they were out there. She had always known they were out there. She could sense them. They were coming closer.

CHAPTER 21

Worn and weary from her travels, Eenayah was dozing in front of a stifling hot fire which stripped the small TV room of all oxygen. Multi-tasking with one eye following a film and the other reading Professors De Vede's draft rendition of Reed's family history, she struggled to fight her yawns. It was mainly the warm air that tired her, because in all fairness the book was quite good. Eenayah hadn't expected to find it remotely interesting, but since her weekend of research and photography by way of a wifely contribution, she had developed a degree of historical fascination with her husband's ancestors. She had just been reading about the Mort's possible connection to the Huguenots (the French Protestants who had fled France during the 16ᵗʰ and 17ᵗʰ century), when her eyelids grew heavy. Lying on her sister's super comfortable duck down settee and with the warm glow of smouldering logs wrapping her up in a cosy heated cocoon, she fell into a deep and much needed slumber.

A few minutes past midnight, she was brusquely awoken by the ringing of a bell. For a minute or so the sound had integrated itself into her dreams, but then came the sudden realisation that the bell outside in the servant's hall was actually ringing. These were miniature Victorian bells distributed around the house and connected by cords. When one of the gentry required a service, the bell would ring in the servant's quarters and would detail the actual room the master or mistress of the house could be located. The ringing of the bells reminded her of the Charles Dickens book and Scrooge being awoken by his ghostly former partner. This did not conjure up a pleasant feeling.

Eenayah had always been spooked by her sister's historic home, without having any logical reason to hate it other than its age and quirky design. Therefore being alone in a very old house and then hearing a servants' bell ring when there was no one around to pull a cord was unnerving, to say the least. Should she walk out into the hall to see from which room the cord had been pulled? What then? Should she go to investigate that room? NO, most certainly not. Not now, not ever. No, no, no!

She concluded that it might be best to just ignore it, because she was not going to follow up on this mysterious ringing.

In a half-asleep state, Eenayah had quite forgotten that Owyn had connected all these bells, plus additional bells, to the outside intercom. It had been a technological feat of which he was quite proud. Darwydden Castle Manor was such a large and rambling building that without his updated bell system, a person could be stood on the doorstep for an eternity and nobody would ever know they were there. Now many of the main living quarters were within earshot of three bells, to denote the three entrances into the manor house – rear entrance, east wing side entrance and the grand front castle entrance.

Eenayah was frozen in fear for a moment or two, until the recollection of Owyn's DIY handiwork finally calmed her spirit. To her relief she realised that someone was at the door – but who?

With one finger gingerly touching the 'call for help' button on her security watch, she removed herself from the cosy cocoon of the TV room and went to see who could be calling at this late hour. She proceeded to the front door with a natural degree of caution, since the bell system had indicated that this was where her unexpected visitor was awaiting. It was past midnight and she was alone in a remote, isolated Welsh valley on a foggy night. The usual security guard (a family pet called Bertie) had been seconded out to the boarding kennels by no other than Eenayah herself. How she wished Bertie was with her at this moment. Maybe his absence was karmic dog revenge. She had no protection and no backup security plan, aside from a mobile phone with poor reception and a security watch to signal distress to someone who might take an hour to get to her.

It had suddenly occurred to her that in the panic of checking out of the Hilton, she had forgotten to call Kerry at MeDeVe to report her intended location for the evening. Looking at her watch, she wondered if a satellite signal would even be able to locate her through the mountainous terrain.

On approaching the substantial oak door (designed specifically to fit the original castle lodge entrance), she observed for the first time that there was no peephole. She hadn't noticed its absence before, but then again with a killer pet dog in the hallway, why would Owyn and Ruby ever consider there to be an issue with security? She had no other choice but to do what people throughout history had been forced to do when the doorbell rung and that was to open the door! It had to be done.

For a second she wished she hadn't. She was frozen to the spot – too shocked to even let out a shriek.

A gothic Halloween 'trick or treat' entity dressed head to toe in black hovered at the doorstep. By accident and yet almost as if to add dramatic effect, a gust of wind happened to catch the person's cloak and blow it vertically as though it had become the wings of a bat and its owner was about to fly off somewhere. Eenayah concluded that she was becoming conditioned to crazy situations, since nothing about her sister's house seemed to surprise or shock her any more. Miami was beginning to feel quite boring in comparison.

As the heavy door creaked open in typical horror-house style, bat woman wafted past Eenayah impatiently and with much urgency.

'Lovely to meet you again Eenayah, but for fuck's sake I need a pee,' she said. 'What took you so bloody long? I have tried every door in this bloody house and I would have pissed my pants if you had left me standing out there any longer. Oh bugger, got to dash!'

She rushed down the corridor towards the WC, and Eenayah let out a huge sigh of relief. With more than one swear word within just a few seconds of a vague yet dramatic introduction, this could only be the infamous Darcy. Yes indeed, this was Owyn's younger sister making her usual theatrical entrance. She was totally unrecognisable from the blonde woman she had met several years back, but then again Eenayah had been warned in advance that Darcy was a chameleon who changed identities with each boyfriend. She quickly surmised that maybe Darcy's latest boyfriend must be into heavy rock, have a ponytail and tattoos and ride a motorbike. A crude initial judgment, but, she concluded, probably accurate.

Darcy soon returned from her urgent toilet visit and composed herself enough to re-introduce herself to her 'famous by marriage' sister-in-law's twin sister.

Always a tad star struck, Darcy could not wait to re-engage with Reed B's wife. With her lovely singsong Welsh accent, Darcy began her feeble attempt at an apology.

'Hell, sorry about that Eenayah. I was stood at the sodding door for ten minutes and I didn't think you were ever going to answer. Ruby has removed the key from under the usual plant pot and now no bugger can bloody get in here. She swans off to Florida and expects the rest of us to keep an eye on the place without a key. Anyway, how are you doing? I am here to keep you company by the way, and whenever you need to bugger off that's okay as I can stay until Owyn gets back. Just got to get the cat and dog back tomorrow though, as Rubes has gone mental about you dumping them like you did. Bit cruel and all that. Anyway, how are you and where's the booze?'

Darcy had spoken without even stopping to draw breath, but it was a welcome and light-hearted introduction. Never had Eenayah been so grateful to have the company of a gothic semi-relative, irrespective of her being rough around the edges. She felt like hugging her new-found friend. Anything had to be better than being alone in her sister's isolated mansion.

Not waiting for a reply, Darcy had already made her way into the kitchen, where she knew chilled wine and beer was readily available. Eenayah followed. Darcy seemed to know her way around her sister's house better than Ruby did, probably because she was there more often than her workaholic sister. If there was anything to be found within the maze of these ancient walls, Darcy would probably know where to look.

Eenayah was curious. 'You have an odd smell about you Darcy, what it is? Not meaning to be offensive, but it isn't a perfume I recognise.'

'Oh that would be sage with a hint of cedar darling' said Darcy, in mock upper-class tones. 'Just been assisting my new beau with some space cleansing. He has been using a smudge stick and the smoke doesn't half stick to one's hair.'

Eenayah had no idea what a smudge stick was and could only guess about space cleansing. She was quickly beginning to get the impression that Darcy was into 'new age' ideas and the like. Even so, Darcy was company and Eenayah had been alone for what seemed like forever. It was getting very late, or very early depending on how one considers 1 am. However, after several hours snoozing by the fire, Eenayah was wide awake and grateful for the companionship. The time was almost irrelevant. Eenayah was keen to talk, and Darcy was more than willing to listen.

Owyn's younger sister could hardly contain her elation at having the wife of a famous music mogul wanting to share the adventures of her last month in the UK. Likewise, Darcy loved to gossip and was keen to blast Eenayah with the intimate details of her latest boyfriend Dylan, who she described as a Wærloga.

'What on earth does that mean?' Eenayah was inquisitive and yet perhaps wishing that she hadn't asked. Darcy took an uncouth slug of beer from the bottle and laughed, 'take your pick, witch, wizard, warlock - I think they all mean the same thing. He is my cute little magic man. I think technically he is a Druid, but whatever the technicalities, you will love him, I know you will.'

Eenayah looked up to the ceiling. Indeed, this was going to be an interesting evening. She already sensed that nothing about Darcy was ever likely to resemble normal. None the less, this crude and foul-mouthed young woman amused her. Reed's PA Arabella pretended to do the whole Goth fashion trip, but with Arabella it was just surface paint and nothing more than superfluous black eye shadow. She got the feeling that with Darcy, and for this moment in time, it was indeed the real deal. What could be more Goth than having a wizard for a boyfriend, a Welsh wizard at that? She couldn't help but like Darcy. There was no pretence about the woman and Eenayah respected that.

'I need more wine Darcy' she said. 'I don't know what the hell you are going to tell me next and I think I need alcohol to deal with your next big revelation.'

They both laughed. It had been quite a while since Eenayah had enjoyed herself as much as this. She wasn't sure what it was about Darcy she liked as they were polar opposites, but she instinctively trusted her. Darcy was hilarious and actually quite lovely, no matter how dark she pretended to be.

Darcy revealed that she was tinkering around the edges of becoming a white witch and was keen to try out her Tarot card skills on Eenayah, who politely refused her offer of a fortune telling session.

'Darcy, I have just spent the last hour telling you all about me finding my birth mother and the awkward situation with my father-in-law who may or may not be stalking me. How can you read my cards, when you already seem to know everything about me?'

Darcy was understandably disappointed, but accepted the polite rebuke. 'Okay dokey Mrs. B, I will wait until you are ready to face your future, but one day I will make a believer of you. All in good time.'

Eenayah smiled at her young friend's attempt to sound wise and profound. 'You so suit this old house Darcy. I'm surprised you haven't moved in with your brother.'

Darcy appreciated what she felt to be a compliment and responded accordingly. 'Trust me, if I didn't work at a call centre that's a tedious forty-minute drive away, I would have taken over the spare wing years ago. You are right, I do love Darwydden Castle Manor. I know parts of this place that even Ruby doesn't know about. Don't get me wrong E, Ruby loves all the mountains, countryside and fresh air stuff, but she is too busy working away in London to spend much time here. It's not her fault. My bro doesn't earn much and she has to work hard to pay for this place, so I guess she just doesn't have the time to uncover its secrets.'

It seemed that Darcy never failed to deliver a mind-blowing line. Whatever she did or said seemed to pull Eenayah in more and more into her strange world. Eenayah knew she was being ever so slightly played, but she was enjoying this game.

She gasped with pretend shock. 'Secrets? The house has secrets and Ruby doesn't even know? Oh you can't keep me dangling on a thread with this one Darcy. I have shared some of my classified data with you.

Come on, cough up. What is it you know?'

Darcy grabbed the large torch she kept tucked away in her bag, took Eenayah by the hand and led her towards the front entrance hall. 'We have run out of chardonnay, my celebrity friend, so a trip to the wine cellar is in order – follow me.'

As they walked down the long straight hall, passing the school room and library, Darcy gave Eenayah a potted history about the house. Darcy was right; she did know far more about her twin's mansion than Ruby would have ever suspected.

'Y' know E – I am so glad my little bro purchased this house. The youngest bits are Victorian, but the oldest areas go back over 900 years, maybe even longer. Nobody really knows its history for sure. It was built by the English to keep us Welsh under control – didn't work with me hey! It was empty for donkeys' years before Ruby and Owyn bought it, and it was in a really bad state. An old lady used to live here and when she died without making a will, it went into probate whilst her family argued about who owned what. Usual legal crap. It stood empty and deteriorating for a long time. My boyfriend grew up in the village around here and he used to play in this place when he was a boy. Most of the villagers know about this house, but they don't talk about it. All very hush hush.'

Eenayah didn't have a clue what Darcy meant by that and had long since given up trying to follow the logic of her random conversation. Reluctantly she followed Darcy down the steep stone steps into the castle casemate. Within the vaulted chamber lay the Kyfinn's family stash of liqueur and copious supplies of wine. Eenayah had assumed that they had reached their destination, as she commandeered the closest bottle of chardonnay within reach. She was a bit shocked when Darcy asked her to put it down, making it quite clear that there was another purpose for their visit deep into the underbelly of the house.

As they approached the very back of the undercroft it became obvious that it had been dug directly into raw earth.

'Is that safe?' asked Eenayah, as she noticed the soil tumbling onto the medieval cobbled cellar floors.

'This is how they dug cellars long ago, Eenayah,' replied Darcy confidently. She led Eenayah towards a large overflow pipe partially covered up by a wood panel and continued, 'Cellars can flood if they are below the water table. Owyn and Ruby are lucky because the castle undercroft was cut directly into the bedrock, but none the less and just in case, this pipe should be able to drain any water into the ground below. It is a bit of ye olde engineering ingenuity. We are guessing that this was built at the same time as the castle, but who knows. Former owners of the mansion have made their own modifications over the years. Dylan and his friends used to climb into this pipe and play down here all the time as kids.'

Eenayah was intrigued 'So what's down there for kids to play in? You mentioned it was just a drainage pipe, where does it drain into?'

Darcy shot her a roguish smile. 'Well if you follow me into here you will soon find out. Don't worry, go in legs first and your feet will find the steps. The pipe is only short. I promise you, it isn't dangerous.'

Yet again, Darcy had delivered a remarkable mystery. The woman and her bizarre revelations seemed to be unstoppable. Although Eenayah was afraid of both the dark and enclosed spaces, she felt unusually brave when she was with Darcy, an unusual young woman who seemed to be afraid of nothing and nobody. Perhaps the wine had also administered a slight anaesthetic effect on her usual phobias.

Feet first, and in a trusting act of unusual valour, Eenayah's feet touched the terra firma of the promised steps. As the rest of her body emerged from the chute and her eyes adjusted to the light, her head slowly rotated as she tried to take on board what she was actually seeing.

'Oh my lord!' was all she could utter. Darcy caught the expression on her face and was quietly delighted that she had delivered a pièce de résistance that few could compete with. Eenayah's breath was taken away.

Darcy held onto Eenayah's hand to guide her down the stone steps onto the ledge below, and then to Eenayah's astonishment she flicked a switch which lit up the immediate surrounding area. A voluminous underground cavern of vast proportions emerged from the dark. Darcy tapped a second switch and the entire cave was illuminated in a mirage of colour, lighting up an underground lake with the clearest turquoise blue. The surrounding granite walls flickered with subtle tones of pink and amethyst, which contrasted majestically against the cool sapphire sides of the lake.

On hearing a faint splashing noise, Eenayah asked Darcy, 'where is the water coming from, I can't see anything?'

Darcy was enjoying these piecemeal moments of revelation. Her finger touched yet another switch and a waterfall of spring water became visible from behind the lake. Red spotlights had been cabled in behind the flow, giving the illusion that the water was blood. Against the palette of the subtle pastel colours, the crimson cascade added a sense of drama and theatre.

'What… how?' was about as much as Eenayah could manage to say.

Darcy felt victorious in her delivery of yet another astonishing exposé. She began to explain, 'Don't tell Ruby, whatever you do. She doesn't know that this place exists.'

Eenayah was indeed still in shock. She had found herself propelled feet first into a fantasy grotto that her own sister wasn't even aware of. It all seemed most improbable.

'My God, Darcy. You certainly know how to put on a show. I have so many questions for you, but the first one is, how and why does my sister not know about any of this? Why the big secret?' Darcy usually spoke first and then thought about it later. Tact was a skill that she didn't normally possess, but on this occasion she paused for thought. She knew she had to pick her words carefully.

'Please don't tell Ruby, whatever you do. This is supposed to be all very hush-hush and secret squirrel stuff. I probably shouldn't have brought you here on reflection, but I couldn't resist. I just love this place.'

Eenayah was beginning to feel she was in the middle of some bizarre, surreal dream. Perhaps she had been Alice in Wonderland and fallen down a rabbit hole. None of this seemed real. She pinched herself to repeat the question which Darcy had unusually skirted around.

'Stop dancing around your handbag D, how and why does my sister not know about any of this?'

The reality suddenly hit Darcy that now the stable door had been unlocked, it was too late to bolt it. She would have to share some details with her inquisitive guest, but she would elect only to tell her what she needed to know to satisfy her curiosity. The cave network was of immense and sacrosanct importance, and Darcy had probably broken some hallowed code of silence by bringing Eenayah here. It dawned on her that Owyn would be furious about his sister sharing something that he had laboured hard to conceal.

Trying to backtrack and lessen the impact of the mystery, Darcy went on to explain. 'Of course my brother knows about these caves. Many of the local people are aware that they exist. They have been here a lot longer than the house, the castle, they could be as old as the mountains. Who knows? Owyn has always felt that one day, this would make the most awe-inspiring of wedding venues. I do believe that this is his ultimate grand plan. However in the meantime Owyn has been working on this caverns in secret for Ruby's 40th surprise party. I mean

- what a surprise. This will blow her away. Shit; I have given the game away haven't I? You will keep it a secret won't you?'

Eenayah was still too stunned to remind Darcy of the fact that Ruby was her twin and maybe it was to be her birthday surprise as well. Darcy had just unknowingly given the game away. Still, she could be forgiven. It was after all a unique venue for <u>both</u> their 40th birthdays.

Noting all the electrical cables running down the sides of the rock face she asked,' has my brother-in-law has done all of this?'

Darcy had yet more disclosures tucked up her sleeve, but she wanted to play down the amount of work that had gone into converting parts of the caves. 'No, he hasn't done all of this Eenayah, although he has put a lot of hours in down here when Ruby has been away in London. Owyn once told me that these cables have been here from at least the mid-70s. Maybe the old women who lived here before stored things down here, who knows? I guess it would make a great chiller. I believe that all Owyn has really done is update some of the junction boxes and add some coloured bulbs. It looks amazing doesn't it?'

Eenayah was still in visible shock as she finally moved from the safety of the ledge and descended down a second set of well-worn steps carved into the granite wall. 'Do you know the history of this place?' she asked.

'Some of it. As I mentioned before, Dylan played throughout all of these caves as a lad.'

'Caves, there are caves as well?' To Eenayah, this was like an earthquake with aftershock after aftershock.

Darcy pointed over to the entrance of a cave which was now becoming more visible as Eenayah's eyes adjusted to the subdued lighting. The mouth of the largest cave had been highlighted with a deep burgundy glow as though it was a porthole to the very gates of hell itself in all its fiery glory.

'You see that hollow over there Eenayah? From that single master cave are around six other tunnels, maybe even more. People have been lost here and never been found, so whatever you do don't ever venture into them alone. Dylan once told me that one of them goes up to what used to be the dungeons of the old castle, the main entrance of which is directly above where we are standing. I am told that another cave leads into a malachite mine deep in the mountain. If you pay attention, you may note that there is an abundance of green stone around the village. Some people wear it as jewellery and some even have a scattering of malachite built into the walls of their cottages. It's a semi-precious stone so it's a bit decadent to use it in a building I suppose, but the villages have all sorts of ancient suspicions. They think it protects them against evil or something. I strongly suspect that this is where it was mined from. More mysteriously, Dylan says another cave leads to a tunnel which goes to the nearby church. The villagers believe it leads to a priest hole – you know, the secret rooms where scared Catholics once hid. There are even stories that outcast Catholics secretly worshipped somewhere down here in a sort of underground cathedral. I think it was very dangerous to be either a Catholic priest or a worshipper back in the mid-1500s. They had these dudes called Pursuivants who were like the secret policemen of Queen Elizabeth the first. If they got nicked saying a prayer they were likely to face confiscation of their lands, torture, imprisonment, execution, beheading in the Tower of London, you name it. Not pleasant.'

Eenayah had taken a new interest in all things historical since being back in the UK and found herself enthralled by all these amazing stories.

'That is fascinating Darcy. Do you know if Ruby's Manor house has any of these priest holes?'

Darcy was quite an authority on her brother's house and was keen to share what she knew, even though she had given away more detail than she had intended. 'Oh my God, yes. Owyn doesn't believe he has even found half of them yet. For instance, a false fireplace in the library leads directly into the attic via a winding flight of steps. I guess a worried priest could rapidly do a runner even if all the manor house exists were guarded. The bricks have even been blackened by fire to make it all look real. Clever buggers they were. The most complex of the priest holes can be found under the slats of the grand stairway. Owyn only discovered this one about a month ago. Two of the steps are linked by a hinge that allows them to be lifted fairly easily. I tell you what, if you have time tomorrow we can do a tour of all the secret hideaways. I just love this place. It has so much mystery.'

Eenayah was beginning to feel as though she had stepped into an Enid Blyton novel. 'Do you know where the other caves go to Darcy?'

'Not a clue I'm afraid. As I told you before, people have been lost in these caves and never been seen again. I believe that even Druids once used this place for worship - but that's just a rumour and nobody really knows for sure. There are all kinds of strange stories around the village. I am guessing that maybe some of these passages are just too dangerous to venture into'.

As the two women ventured back up the stony staircase, Eenayah could only express sincere gratitude towards Darcy. 'Thank you so much for sharing this with me Darcy. I know you have ruined my future 40th birthday surprise but I'm so pleased you have shown me all of this. Who would have ever guessed that there was an underground lake, caves, secret tunnels and maybe even a cathedral beneath Ruby's house? My God woman, you really know how to shock a person. Tonight has been quite magical. This place in enchanting. Thank you - you have over whelmed me. And I promise not to tell my sister. At least one of us will get a big surprise in just over a year's time.'

Eenayah stood looking up at the drainage pipe which had

deposited her into the cavern. 'Please don't tell me I have to climb back up there,' she said.

Darcy laughed in a wickedly girlish way. 'Nah, we'll just use the door this time. I only took you down the pipe because I thought it would be more fun'.

Eenayah grimaced at Darcy as she realised she had been played for entertainment as well as companionship. She spotted other areas of the cavern where inlets had been covered by severe-looking doors. 'Has Owyn been converting some of these into rooms by any chance?'

Darcy shrugged off the question, already realising that she had shown her guest more than she had originally intended. 'Not sure what is behind the doors E. It's probably all connected to his grand plans for this to become some sort of event setting. Have you noticed the acoustics in this place? It would make an amazing venue for a rock concert. Get the pun? Rock! Do you think U2 would be interested?'

Darcy now wanted to leave the caves before Eenayah's curiosity led to yet more questions. Opening a semi-hidden exit around the side of the ledge, they re-entered the casemate via a wine rack that had been cleverly disguised as a door. Walking back towards the vault, Eenayah recovered the same bottle of Chardonnay she had been forced to surrender back at the castle wine cellar. A few goblets, and by 4 am they were both in a deep and happy sleep.

★★★

By ten o'clock that morning, Professor De Vede had been trying to call Eenayah for an hour. He had no chance of waking her from her deep sleep and a fuzzy hangover. She was out for the count, along with her new best friend Darcy, who had also overslept and missed work.

The Professor was perplexed. He had been studying the headstone of Daisy Green, along with that of her great great grandmother, which

Don had located in County Meath in the south of Ireland. There was a strange correlation between the stones, a similarity that should not exist two countries and several generations apart. His research into Eenayah's genealogy had thrown out some strange coincidences and he believed he needed to talk to Eenayah about his findings sooner rather than later.

The Professor was impatient. He had no idea where she was, and for all he knew she was back in the US. He gave his daughter Mercy a call to ask her to locate Eenayah on her security watch. He then decided to call his old friend, the former priest Father Frances. Maybe Frank would be able to decipher the matching hieroglyphics which tied these two remote headstones together.

CHAPTER 22

Thursday 11th July

Frank was elated to open the door and find his former school friend standing patiently on the whitewashed doorstep of his Edwardian mews residence. The two elderly gents gave each other massive hugs.

'Roland, my childhood comrade!' said Frank. 'I am so pleased you could make it. You are two hours late, my friend. I am guessing your flight was delayed. You must be exhausted. Do come in, let me take your bags and raise your caffeine levels.'

They both smiled in recognition of their mutual affection for each other. It was the type of friendship where you could go for years without ever meeting or even communicating, but then pick it up as though you had never been separated.

Frank excitedly walked the Professor down a long narrow hallway into his crisp, white contemporary lounge. It wasn't as he expected. The Professor wasn't entirely sure what it was he had presumed of the former priest's Dublin residence, but it was not this.

Bringing in a pot of tea and oatmeal biscuits and settling the tray on a shiny black marble coffee table, Frank enquired with genial Irish tones, 'So Roland, I am guessing you must have been up since the crack of dawn to catch the first flight over. I am of course delighted you can spend some time with me in my home town, but my friend, it was all a bit of a last minute arrangement. What has brought you over to Ireland with such urgency?'

They had last met three years earlier at a criminology convention in London, and since then Frank had often tried to entice the Professor to visit him, but had been rebuffed with the excuse of too much work. What had changed?

Professor De Vede removed two photographs from his briefcase. 'Frank, these are pictures of two separate headstones. One was taken in a cemetery near Manchester and the headstone is fairly new, less than 40 years old. The other photo was taken by my assistant Don when he was over here doing some genealogy research for me. It was taken in a cemetery not far from here in County Meath – and the stone is closer to 110 years old.'

This caught Frank's attention, and he leaned forward attentively. 'So what has this to do with me Roland? How can I be of any help?'

The Professor then removed two additional photographs from his case. 'When it comes to matters of death, I either call upon the help of a doctor, a funeral director or a priest. You my theological friend, are of course the latter as well as being a doctor, but of course, not the medical kind.'

The Professor passed Frank a magnifying glass and the additional two photographs. He continued to explain. 'I have a client who approached my daughter's company MeDeVe and asked them to locate her birth mother. My client is a twin and both girls had been adopted at birth and knew nothing about the circumstances of their adoption. Tragically my client's birth mother had been little more than a child herself and died shortly after giving birth. These two photographs are a picture of my client's mother's headstone, one taken from the front and the other from the rear. If you look closely you will see an unusual marking at the rear of the headstone, bottom left. I had initially presumed that this must be the stonemason's mark, though it would be an unusual one as they usually use part of their initials to stamp their identity on their work. You know me to be a genealogist Frank, so I get to see a lot of headstones in my line of work. Anyway, my client then became curious about her family tree and asked me to trace her ancestors. I had been working on her husband's family tree and I guess that after finding the family he was born into that maybe she wanted to know more about her own heritage.'

Frank listened in silence. He had no idea where this was leading, but he knew that his friend would not have jumped on a plane with such urgency unless there was a mystery to be solved.

The Professor continued, 'anyway Frank, the investigation into my clients lineage led me in the direction of Ireland, so I sent my research assistant Don over here so we could delve a little deeper. Don came across the headstone of my client's great-great-grandmother and likewise here are two photographs of it front and rear, as before.'

Frank picked up the magnifying glass and scrutinized the mark; it was bottom left as with the other headstone. He looked over to the Professor. 'Well I agree they look identical Roland, but what is your point? You haven't come all the way over to Dublin just to show me these photographs. You could have emailed them. I have been begging you for the last three years to come and visit me, and now you come just to show me squiggles on a tombstone. What aren't you telling me yet?'

The Professor recognised that he was being scolded for three years of avoidance. He emptied his teacup and then stood up to admire the view from Frank's long Georgian sash windows. He was surprised to find that his ageing religious friend lived in such an elegant, up-tempo and fashionable place. Standing four floors high on a pleasant leafy street, the mews house was an interesting mix of old and ultra-new. He hadn't expected an ex-Irish priest to have such commendable taste for interior design. Large modern artwork adorned the whiter-than-white walls and unusual sculptures were irreverently placed with no logical order other than the folly of simply being.

The Professor wasn't sure what to say next. In his own mind he was muddled. He needed someone to pull out and unwrap the tangled spaghetti pieces of this own thoughts. He was also a tad disappointed that Frank seemed cross with him and wasn't really focusing on what he was either trying to tell him or ask him. The Professor himself wasn't even sure what he wanted to do or ask quite yet. He decided to share with him what he had uncovered and then simply ask his for opinion.

The Professor sat back down and tried to figure out his own thoughts.

'Frank, hear me out. These marks are not stonemason's marks, they are hieroglyphics and they must mean something to someone. They weren't carved into these stones by accident. In my world of research I have concluded that true coincidences are far and few. These symbols are sending out a message. They are a communication. Look Frank, as an historian and a genealogist, I have learned to understand how people live as well as how they die. Families who live close to one another tend to adopt similar ways of doing things. The woman this headstone belongs to, Mary Ryan, who was the great-grandmother of Daisy Green. Mary was born in 1878 and died in 1934 in Southern Ireland. Had they been born close to each other in age or in location, I would have assumed this to be some family token that was shared because they knew each other. However these two women have been separated by approximately 230 miles and 41 years in burial time. For them to share the same strange markings on the gravestones when divided by generations and sea must surely mean something. Can you make any sense of what I have just said? I am not sure what I am asking you, but I thought as a priest you may know more than I do about this.'

Frank looked at the markings again, this time paying more heed to the Professor's request. Waving the magnifying glass around each photograph and studying each detail with added precision, he finally reached a conclusion.

'I am not an expert in stonemasonry my friend, but they both seem to be roughly carved and of course worn by time. To me they look like an eagle with a twig. I think the flower within a circle next to it could be an equinox symbol. Roland, where exactly was the cemetery in Ireland that your research assistant found Mary Ryan's gravestone?'

The Professor felt some relief that Frank was at long last taking an interest. Looking at his notes, he responded, 'Don has written 'Oldcastle, County Meath', and of course has mapped out the precise location of the grave.'

Frank was deep in thought. 'If you have time, then we should go to Oldcastle on Saturday. It's just over an hour's drive from here, but I think it may well be a worthwhile journey. There's an ancient tomb near Oldcastle in a place called Schiabhla-Cailliche. I haven't been there in a long time, but locally it's known as Jeremiah's tomb. There is a tombstone there, maybe an end stone, which also displays hieroglyphics. I believe some of these markings are very similar or maybe even the same as those on your photographs. It has been many years since I visited this place so please don't get over excited Roland, in case I am leading you to a dead end. I have but a brief recollection, but I suspect that there are similarities between what you have found on these headstones and what I remember seeing in Jeremiah's tomb.'

The Professor's eyes shone with excitement. 'Can't we go there right now? Please Frank?'

Frank studied his friend's puffy face, noting his bloodshot eyes and the dark circles lining their perimeters. 'You are no longer a spring chicken Roland. I know you are keen and I agree that these markings are most peculiar. It seems likely that these markings must be a message of sorts. However, my ancient friend, you look exhausted and I honestly believe we should talk this over in more detail once you have had some sleep. I'm busy tomorrow, but let's make a day of it on Saturday and maybe we can stay over in a local pub and sample some of the local brew. Let me grab your cases and show you to your room. We can catch up later when you have rested.'

Disappointed, but in agreement, the Professor stood up to be unwillingly led to his room. As he did so, Frank took a second look at the inscription on the headstone:

Daisy Green
Passed away 27th August 1975 aged 15
April Green
Passed away July 6th 1976 aged 16
William Green
Passed away September 1st 1978 aged 44

Trying to do mental calculations and failing, he asked the Professor, 'These two girls, April and Daisy - they seem to be close in age. I am guessing they were sisters?'

The Professor sighed. 'Yes so sad, both so young. They were twins actually. I believe April was disabled; born with cerebral palsy - so very tragic. They didn't have the treatments and medicines back then to deal with such conditions. My client, Daisy Green's daughter, is a twin as well. In fact, from the genealogy I have done on the family so far, they all seem to be twins. It is really most odd. If you have time tomorrow, I would love to show you the chart on my laptop. You know Frank, I have been doing this family tree stuff for over forty years now and never have I come across anything as strange as this before. They must have something in their DNA that just throws out twin girls generation upon generation. Anyway, you're right. I'm exhausted. Please show me where I can rest. The jet lag is starting to hit me.'

Frank smiled. 'Yes my friend - jet lag after a one-hour flight over the Irish Sea. Very funny , old chap.'

As he led his friend back down the narrow hallway, Frank's mind danced in circles. He vaguely remembered something he had read many years ago. A student he had once taught in his capacity as a theology teacher at Dublin University had written a paper about a religious group that followed a line of descent to the possible rebirth of the Messiah; the second coming. He couldn't quite recall the details or remember the name of the sect, but he knew it involved female twins being born generation upon generation in order to carry on some special gene.

Frank's thoughts wandered into another zone. Could it be possible that the hieroglyphics from Jeremiah's tomb were the same as those on the twins' headstones, and could these twins and all those that came before them possibly be linked to this mythical line of descent? It was an astounding thought.

There was a tantalising link between the professor's client, her newly-discovered family history and those strange and prophetic tomb markings.

He wondered if he could trace his ex-student Luke. This indeed was worth the urgency of his friend's visit. This indeed was actually quite exciting.

Frank resolved to do some research as soon as his professor friend was tucked away sound asleep and snoring loudly in bed.

CHAPTER 23

Friday 12th July

Frank had seldom noticed the deeply sunken furrows in his friend's forehead before, but as the Professor sat out in the morning sun drawing on his pipe, his face looked older in the cruel light of day. It reminded Frank of the Rod Stewart song *Maggie May*, and indelicately he started to hum the tune as he approached, not that the Professor would notice or understand the significance.

Placing two mugs of steaming hot coffee on the cast iron garden table he enquired, 'And how are you today Professor De Vede? Better after a good night's sleep I assume.'

'Indeed I have enjoyed a delightful night's rest,' answered the professor. 'Thank you for enquiring, Father Francis.' The two friends chuckled at their identical wit, which would probably have gone amiss on anyone outside their circle. However it wasn't long before the Professor was once again gazing deeply into nothingness, apparently lost in a world of his own.

'Penny for your thoughts' asked Frank, looking puzzled.

'It's my client Frank, the one I told you about yesterday. I worry about her.

'The one with the twin and the weird family tree and the odd tattoos on her ancestor's gravestones?'

'Yes, that's the one.' With that he went quiet as though once again deeply engrossed in thought. Although his daughter Mercy was younger than his client, the Professor viewed Eenayah and Mercy as of a similar age, and in his eyes they were both children. Eenayah seemed to bring out his fatherly protective instinct somehow.

Frank was curious. 'Why are you so worried about her? I mean I don't need to know her personal circumstances as I am aware you have to obey all that client confidentiality stuff and that feisty daughter of yours would castrate you if you broke some bloody stupid data protection rules, but why exactly are you so concerned about a client?'

The Professor took a moment or two to consider his answer, feeling slightly unsure himself.

'I have just come off the phone with her. She has been a bloody bugger to keep track of. My daughter has had to put some sort of sci-fi tracking device on her just to know where she is. Anyway, I asked her if she could question her great aunt about the hieroglyphics to see if she could dig out anything from the family history to explain what they might be. However now she tells me that she is going back home to the States this weekend, so she isn't sure if she'll get the opportunity any time soon – which is a shame. I was hoping her birth family could shine a light on the mystery. It is just a frustration, that's all. I would have thought she would have taken more interest, but her mind seems all over the place.'

'Oh, that is a shame… I guess!' Frank was disappointed with his friend's tepid and vague answer. 'Is that all, or is anything else bothering you?'

'Well not exactly. Tell me Frank, do you believe in instinct?'

'What a question to ask a Catholic priest, my friend. I believe in lots of things I can't see, touch, smell or hear. Believing that something exists without proof that something exists is called faith. Mine is a mysterious world. However, to answer your question, I think instinct is less of a paranormal phenomenon and more of an inbred animalistic survival trait - a sort of natural sixth sense, so yes indeed - I most certainly do believe in instinct, even if mankind has lost some of its primordial abilities.' He looked at his friend. 'Why do you ask?'

'The client I was telling you about, Frank - she is intelligent, beautiful, extremely wealthy, and yet there is a deep sadness about her. She could jump on a private jet or yacht and go anywhere in the world, and yet she comes to the UK to connect with her past. I am not a psychologist, but to me, she is running away from her present - and maybe her future.'

The Professor was silent for a moment as he sipped his hot coffee sucked on his pipe and tried to apply some sort of logic to his random thoughts. He continued, 'I don't know why Frank, but I feel she is in some sort of danger. There is something not quite right about this lady and her situation, but I can't explain what it is. It is like an instinct clawing away at my soul. I can hear its inner voice talking to me, but I can't make out the words. It's quite frustrating.'

Frank's eyes widened. He was also very interested in the Professor's client. He was keen to learn more.

'Let's go inside Roland. You said you had her family tree on your laptop and I would like to learn what you find so strange about it, after all you are the great Professor De Vede, genealogist to the rich and famous.'

Frank put a sturdy arm around the Professor's shoulder, realising that he was a bit unsteady on his feet. He was feeling unusually sympathetic and caring of his old friend, who was now beginning to look very much like an old friend. Linking arms, the two went indoors.

Frank didn't want to look too eager, and nor did he want to play his hand too soon, but he was fascinated by the Professor's anonymous client. Not wanting to give too much away, he said quietly, 'I am beginning to develop a theory about your client Roland, but I need to talk to an ex-student of mine about this - once I know more detail of course. Let's go inside and we can take a look at this family tree of hers.'

The Professor was proud of his work, which was always detailed and evidenced. He opened up his laptop, firing up his ancestry software, and unrolled a poster-sized sheet of paper.

'Much as I love the software and it makes my work so much easier, it just gives you a one-dimensional view of direct lineage. In this case, I'm interested in my client's siblings. Although the software can show me them, it doesn't plot them on the PC screen because simply, there isn't enough room. So I tend to have the family trees I work on specially printed on large rolls. To an old chap like me, it just makes them easier to view.' Frank was enthralled with the level of detail and this new science he was being introduced to and yet none of it made any sense to him.

The Professor continued to explain. 'If you consider all of your ancestors, it gets very crowded. You have two parents, four grandparents, eight great grandparents, sixteen great great grandparents and so on and so forth. With each generation we double up on the amount of direct ancestors we have, and yet if you think about it in terms of world population growth, there were less people alive back in history. You simply cannot continue to get more and more ancestors from a smaller and smaller pool, so what tends to happen Frank is that you get a doubling up. Someone may be your ten times great grandparent on one line and yet an eleven times great grandparent on another line and maybe a cousin thirteen times removed somewhere else. To add to this, small communities tended to marry their neighbours and other parts of society simply intermarried to maintain wealth and status.'

Frank looked suitably fascinated. 'Indeed, I can see this is a complex art and I guess unravelling family relationships must feel like untangling strings of spaghetti sometimes, but how does this reflect upon your clients family tree?'

The Professor pulled out the large magnifying glass he often used when studying the paper version of a family tree, along with a bright yellow highlighter pen.

'In my client's case I am not looking at all these many other family lines, interesting as they may be. I am concerned with just the one line, and that's the direct maternal line and the siblings attached to it. For a genealogist this isn't the usual route to market as we normally have little interest in siblings and of course the paternal line is usually the dominant pattern as regrettably it tends to be more reliable.'

Frank nodded.

The Professor continued, 'If I take her biological mother Daisy Green and run a highlighter pen to Daisy's mother and her mother before her, it blocks out the rest of the ancestral crowd and we can just focus on nothing more than mother to mother to mother - the direct maternal line.'

Frank could see immediately that the yellow highlighted line was long and stretched back many hundreds of years and more. He commented, 'my God Roland, how on earth do you get back so far in time? I am impressed, my friend.'

The Professor was pragmatic. 'In the case of Daisy Green, it has so far been a matter of luck. If her direct maternal lineage had been working class Anglo-Saxon I would have struggled to get beyond the 15th century. You should understand that in the past, genealogy wasn't the entertaining pastime many view it to be today. This was serious stuff. Family trees back then were all about the laws of inheritance, my friend. Power, money, estates and position were passed down from father to son, and usually only the eldest son - hence the phrase 'poor relations'. The family wealth and estates were seldom diluted by sharing them with siblings.'

Frank moved closer to the large paper diagram set out upon his sparkling granite dining room table overlaid with shimmering Swarovski crystal.

'I am presuming from what you have suggested so far that this Daisy Green was descended from a wealthy family, hence why you have been able to dig so far back into the past. However just focusing on the female line must have been a challenge, Roland. How does this work with the ladies of the aristocracy?'

The Professor went into teaching mode, always delighted to be answering questions about his favourite subject.

'It wasn't entirely fair Frank, but if there was no son and heir then the heiress would marry well and in most cases her inheritance would be passed over to her new husband. Hence why sons were favoured. These were unfair and sexist laws, but back in the day there was also a logical reason for their existence and that was about keeping a family hold on the estate. So well done and ten out of ten, you are correct to assume that Daisy Green did come from a wealthy aristocratic family. From my point of view as a genealogist, a wealthy family's ancestry is many times easier to trace because they had a financial incentive to catalogue their lineage. However, if a family was poor and there was little inheritance of note, then quite frankly why bother to record a birth, marriage and death? As you suggested, all of this has been made more challenging because I am looking at a female line of inheritance and often a woman's surname counted for so little that if one digs deep enough into the past, it may not even be recorded in the parish records at all. Fortunately my client came from a Norman line.'

The Professor had won himself an attentive new scholar. Frank asked, 'It's a long time since I did history at school my friend, so can you explain the Norman connection?'

The Professor was delighted to be asked. 'Daisy Green descends from many of the Norman soldiers that fought at the Battle of Hastings in 1066 and those later awarded lands and estates by way of a reward. Lords, ladies, knights and earls are liberally scattered throughout Daisy Green's ancestral line-up. Prior to 1066 I can trace her line back to William the Conqueror and many of the royal houses of Scotland, Ireland, Wales, England, France, Germany and Scandinavia. Ironically it turns out that the poor working class Daisy Green from Daisy Hill in Manchester has quite a pedigree made up of many kings and queens. So that, my dear friend, is how I have been able to reach out so far back in time, and so quickly. If only it was always so simple.'

'So, explain what you have found, dear Roland. This is quite gripping.'

The Professor pointed to the yellow highlighted line. 'In this instance, I have included all the siblings along the female line with their dates of birth. It doesn't jump out at you immediately, but if you pick through the detail re dates of birth, you will note that her ancestors all produced twins. It doesn't become obvious until you note the birth dates, so it could be easily missed if I wasn't looking out for it. Look closer and you will note that there are no twin boys, only girls. Don't you find that most odd Frank?'

Frank knew little about such matters, but he agreed that it did seem unusual.

'Look closer still Frank, and you can see that only those who were twins themselves produced twins, and to make it even more bizarre - on each occasion, only one of any given set of twins produced a twin. I have never seen such a strange pattern before. Yes indeed, twins can run in families, but this is unusual because there are no twin boys, plus none of the singleton births produced twins.'

Frank fell silent. He didn't know what to say. He couldn't help but remember the essay written by his former theological student Luke, who wrote of a hidden prophecy which referred to a line of clones who were born from female twin to female twin. This was starting to ring alarm bells. However he said nothing and let the Professor continue.

The Professor sighed as though exasperated. He struggled to make sense of the pattern he saw emerging.

'It is a most odd configuration and something one could only spot using sophisticated software. Like many other professional genealogists, I would have overlooked the siblings and simply focused on a direct line of inheritance. It is only because my client requested that we look at this particular issue that Don and I went in search of twins. She also informed me that there is some myth in the family relating to these twin births. I believe that is why she wanted me to explore this in detail. From what I can see and as far as I can go back, I have to conclude that this myth seems to be based on fact.'

Frank studied the chart in front of him. He was a logical man and as a former Catholic priest he was well versed in biblical accounts like 'Benjamin begat Bale who had issue who then begat…' and so on.

'Let's slow this down, Roland' he said. 'I need to take in what you are trying to tell me.' He took hold of the professor's magnifying glass.

The Professor excused himself to take a call, leaving Frank to marvel over the chart. When he returned 20 minutes later he found Frank had taken copious notes. Frank was keen to present a new observation to the Professor; something he had so far missed.

'Roland, come over here and see what else I have noted in Daisy Green's family tree. Daisy died in 1975 following childbirth, however her twin April died just a year later and was childless. April was only 16 at the time of death, so sadly both girls were little more than children themselves. I am guessing this is why your client was adopted. If you now move on to her mother Harriet, who was born in 1935, a date of death isn't given, so I presume Harriet is still alive?'

'Well spotted Frank. Indeed my client's grandmother is still alive, and thankfully my client has been able to meet up with her. However

Harriet is in her late seventies and sadly not in good health. I guess that at least she has had the chance to meet her grandmother whilst she is still on this earth and I am happy that the team and I could contribute to that reunion. My assistant Don has done most of the work in bringing that about, so it is his long hours slaving over copious numbers of records that we have to thank.'

'I'm pleased about that Roland, and happy that your client may have found some answers about her adoption, but that isn't the part of the chart I wanted to draw your attention to. If you look at Harriet's twin sister Jayne, it appears that she had only given birth to sons. Just as you mentioned before, the twin daughters only seem to come through one twin; in this case it's Harriet. If you then go back to Harriet's mother, Florrie Keaton, she seems to be the last person in this line born in Ireland before moving over to England. I am guessing that perhaps the economic depression of the 1920s caused many Irish migrants to move over to England around that time, probably to find work, I would suppose. However Florrie left behind a twin sister, Sarah. It looks like Sarah had about five children in total, but none of them were twins, or indeed girls. Sarah and Florrie's mother was Mary Ryan. I believe this was the headstone that Don found near Oldcastle, the one that shared the odd hieroglyphics with Daisy Green -hopefully the burial site we'll find tomorrow. Anyway, this is interesting Roland, because if you take a look at Mary Ryan's twin, named here as Megan, she seems to have died aged two, and so of course was childless. I'm not sure how accurate these records are, and I haven't gone beyond your client's three times great-grandmother Ellen De Lacy, but her twin sister Branna seems to be married, or at least she has a marriage date of 1875. According to these records she lived a good long life, and yet she appears to be childless. What I am seeing so far is a pattern whereby only one of the twins ever seems to have a twin, while the other either dies young, remains childless or only has sons. I am not a geneticist my friend, and it may do no harm to consult one for advice, but all this seems unnatural to me. How can it be possible? According to these records only one of the twins gives birth to the next generation of twins, and they are only ever female.'

Frank shook his head in bafflement. The Professor looked equally bemused. He had already noticed all that Frank had just mentioned.

The Professor concluded, 'in all my many years of producing genealogy reports for clients, I have never seen such a strange pattern emerge. But there is more you should know. I have just taken a call from Don, and he has located the gravestone of Florrie Keaton in a place called Newton Le Willows in England. Florrie is my client's great-grandmother - this stuff gets confusing sometimes. Anyway, I understand that this place is not too far from the Manchester town of Daisy Hill where Daisy Green is now buried. If you recall, Florrie was the twin born in 1905 who moved over from Ireland in the 1920s depression. Don has just sent me a photo of the tombstone he found in Newton - take a look for yourself.'

The Professor held his iPhone up to Frank. It was easy enough to make out the similar squiggles and patterns that made up the hieroglyphics on the headstones of Eenayah's great grandmother Florrie. They were a perfect match for those found on the headstone of Eenayah's birth mother Daisy Green, as well as those found with her great-great grandmother Mary Ryan in County Meath. For the third time the mysterious hieroglyphics were appearing on the headstone of one of Eenayah's direct maternal ancestors.

'This is a real mystery Roland. Without doubt there are patterns emerging within this family that seem strangely cryptic. 1972, 1975 and 1934 over two countries - this cannot be just a coincidence, surely?'

'That's not all Frank. I have yet another item of news for you. Don, who by the way is in County Meath at the moment and will be joining us tomorrow, has managed to locate three other headstones belonging to my client's family. One of these is in the same cemetery as her sister Mary Ryan, and it is the tiny marker for the child Megan who passed away aged two. Don has also located the burial sites for Branna Fitzrichard, who was Ellen De Lacy's twin, and Sarah Redmond, Florrie's twin. They are both in a neighbouring cemetery. Sarah stayed back in Ireland when her twin Florrie moved to England. Sarah was the lady who had five children, but none of them were either twins or girls. Branna was Ellen de Lacy's sister. She died in 1927 aged 80 and despite being married, she was childless. What is interesting about these sibling graves is that neither Megan, Branna nor Sarah's display the odd hieroglyphic markings. The only people we know of so far that do have these strange grave markings seem to be those twins who bore twins – namely Daisy, Mary and Ellen. I don't wish to jump to any conclusions, but this seems more than just a coincidence to me.'

The friends sat in silence for a while. The information seemed hard to digest, and at the same time both suspected they were only just beginning to scratch the surface of what was emerging as a genealogical puzzle.

The Professor gazed through the window, where a delightful summer's day was just beginning. He felt his brain was incapable of consuming any more information. He shut down his PC and rolled up the poster. Then he looked over at Frank, who still looked in deep thought.

'You know Frank, the problem with my job is that it means spending a lot of time sitting in front of a computer or staring at paper records and it doesn't involve much physical exercise. These days my joints have become a bit creaky and I send Don or Simon out to look at cemeteries on my behalf, a necessary component of genealogy I am afraid. Another unfortunate element of doing my job is the constant reminders that life is short and all we really leave behind is some bones and maybe a record of who we were and when we died. My old body could do with a workout'.

'Are you asking me out for a game of golf my friend?'

The Professor smiled knowingly, 'Don has booked himself into a place called Knightsbrooke Hotel and Golf Resort, not far from where we need to be tomorrow. I'm told it has a wonderful 18-hole championship golf course and available rooms. Do you fancy making tracks a day early? We've done as much as we can today and maybe some fresh air will help us unwind and clear our heads.'

Frank needed little persuasion. 'I agree, this all feels quite intensive. If we leave by lunch we could hit the golf course by two, eat some good food, drink some fine wine and then make an early start for tomorrow and catch up on what else Don has found.'

They were in agreement. For now they would put their findings on hold.

★★★

Meanwhile back at Ruby's house, Eenayah had been having fun getting to know her brother in law's younger sister, the formidable yet forever entertaining Darcy Kyfinn. 'Fun' was a word that didn't often appear in the same sentence as her thoughts, but somehow this new childlike friend had lifted Eenayah's spirits. Playing an adult version of 'hide and seek' they had worked their way through all the known priest holes, tunnels and secret chambers within the strange old mansion. They had even discovered a totally new Reformation hiding place hidden just outside one of the turrets. It was a hatch buried into the stone and cleverly disguised within the pointing. Eenayah had enjoyed her time at Ruby's house, thankfully due to the companionship of Darcy. However she was now mindful that her quest back to her British homeland was coming to a close.

Before booking her flights Eenayah had some unfinished business to attend to. The first job was to contact the Professor, whom she found to be taking a short break in Dublin. He tried to engage her in a conversation about headstones and some anomalous markings that had appeared on three sets of slabs. He had caught Eenayah at a bad time, as her head was clouded with a practical list of things to do before she left. Unable to engage in a lengthy conversation, she gave him permission to run with the draft book about Reeds family history and also made a request that it be bound in gold leaf with a ruby heart at its centre. He was instructed to spare no expense, deduct the costs from her account and to have it delivered by courier to her Miami home addressed to Roserie. She knew her faithful maid would keep it hidden until Reeds 50th birthday on New Year's Eve.

She then contacted her financial manager, Jacob. Marriage to Reed had been kind to Eenayah in that he had given her a substantial allowance to run their homes and take care of all their many requirements. By not spending most of the money she had been allocated, she had shrewdly amassed her own personal wealth. Eenayah had always been thrifty with money. Growing up on a farm, she had learned early some important fundamental values. Eenayah had solid Manx principles she had been unable and unwilling to shake, despite her opulent life style in Florida. As she often said to people, 'you can take the girl out of the Isle of Man, but you can't take the Isle of Man out of the girl'.

Jacob was surprised at Eenayah's inventory of requests. He had always referred to her as his most conservative and safest of clients. 'A financial manager's dream' was how he described her. However Eenayah stood firm and would not be shaken in her demands. With some reluctance, he opened a limitless account with the private investigations company MeDeVe Ltd, something he was loathed to do without either quoted or invoiced work. He then transferred a million dollars each into the accounts of Darcy Kyfinn and Eenayah's great Aunt Elspeth's savings account.

The final transaction was immense, and shocked even Jacob. Over the last few days Eenayah had lived within her sister's dream. She recognised that in the past she had lacked diplomacy, tact and sensitivity when mocking the house her sister had been carefully restoring, often at great personal cost. Darcy had opened her eyes to how wonderful Darwydden Castle Manor could be with financial investment. Owyn's sister had shown her a place that was steeped in a tapestry of history. The manor was a story book; a chronicle which began in the underground caverns of the ancient mountains where the Druids worshipped and malachite was mined. The pages moved into the 11th century, with its battlements, dungeons and visions of knights on horseback. The chapters ran on through to the Tudor period, which had given the house its secret hideaways and priest holes. The story finally worked its way through to the pages of a Victorian gentleman's residence, with its servants' quarters and calling bells.

The house needed to be saved; Eenayah recognised that now. The 21st century had yet to leave its mark on the ongoing story. Eenayah clearly understood how due to economics, time and energy restrictions, Ruby and Owyn had struggled to leave their mark in the storybook. No matter how much passion and love they injected into the crumbling walls, they needed money. She was determined to help them. Turning the Manor into a hotel and converting the immense underground cavern into an extraordinary unique wedding venue would release her sister from her daily toil as a Sales Director. She applauded her sister for being a successful, hard-working and driven career woman. However she also understood that Ruby was a mother and a wife who missed her cherub-faced son and wanted nothing more than to swap London for rural Wales.

Eenayah's mind was set in stone and nothing could deter her from what she was about to do. She commanded the transfer of twenty million dollars into her sister Ruby's bank account.

It felt good to give. Eenayah was proud of herself, knowing that she had done the right thing by everybody. The money had been sitting in a bank account gathering dust. It was just a number on a spreadsheet. This way she could change the lives of those she loved and cared about, and add her contribution to the history of a house which deserved to be saved for future generations.

She had one last phone call to make. She detested speaking with the stony-faced, bitchy-voiced Arabella, Reed's personal assistant. However, on occasion needs must. She requested that Arabella locate the local authority nursing home her grandmother was residing in, and arrange for her transfer to the best private facility she could locate within the area and then to contact Jacob, so he could arrange the funds. Eenayah had little in the way of feelings for her grandmother, as she was a stranger she had just met and one with whom she could hardly communicate. None the less, she felt she had to do the right thing for the sake of her biological mother- the tragic Daisy Green. Unknown to Eenayah, Arabella had already met and encountered her grandmother, many years before. Arabella hated the old woman and snarled in compliance when Eenayah issued her with the order.

Having settled her affairs as best she could, Eenayah moved into the grand hallway, where an oversized mirror would not let anyone escape or pass by its often cruel vision of reality. Reluctantly, Eenayah took a long hard look at herself in it. Aware that she was due a reunion with Reed in just a few days' time, she scrutinised her body with a degree of alarm. She had gained weight, her nails were shorter and the rubies that that had been implanted into them were mostly missing. Her hair had grown longer and displayed greying roots, clearly visible against the rest of her auburn-tinted mane. Gone were the designer clothes, now replaced by torn jeans and a tatty Union J hoodie that most likely belonged to Darcy. She resolved to go on an emergency beauty and weight loss mission, and scouted around for her overly scruffy mud stained trainers.

She got into her hired car and set off towards Clogwyn Du'r Arddu. There she tried to run upon the grassy ledge of the eastern buttress, wearing the appropriate apparel for a challenge which incurred as much climbing as running. She didn't know if she would have the time to locate the magical stone of Maen Du'r Arddu, but she would try. As a teenager, she had camped out there with Ruby. Local legend dictated that if two people spent the night there, one would become a great poet while the other would go insane. Eenayah had concluded that with her sister's marketing capability, she was most likely the poet. As for Eenayah, she knew what her fate had been.

Running outside on the panoramic Snowdonia mountainside, inhaling the clear clean air and ingesting the magnificent sight of the greenest of trees against the bluest of skies, Eenayah began to feel rejuvenated. She missed Reed and now she was ready to go back home to Miami. She hoped that she had taught him a lesson, and maybe now he understood that she wasn't some pampered brainless lapdog who would be content with sitting around, waiting patiently for his homecoming. She hoped he would appreciate her more. She had a life, an existence and a family; better still, now she had a new family. Blowing out all the cobwebs, she felt internally clean. She was happy knowing that she had just done the right thing by helping so many people who needed a break in life. She was pleased that she had accumulated the money to offer that financial buffer to those who had taken some hard knocks of late.

As her feet pounded the slippery slate pathway leading up towards the ridge, her thoughts turned to the reunion Arabella had kindly organised back at the Villa. She grew animated just thinking about seeing her parents, Ruby and of course her stepchildren. She wondered what colour Armani's hair would be and what new music group Konnor had attached himself to these days. She smiled as she considered Asher, the eternal heart throb and playboy. She began to speculate on which of the many bored LA housewife cougars would be stalking her handsome stepson at the moment. Asher only needed to wink or smile at a woman and she would be in his arms. She was so proud of them all, as though they were her own. She treated her stepchildren with great tenderness and loved them all equally. Her heart and thoughts began to pound with the excitement of the reunion party Arabella had planned.

She ran past a line of sheep, jumped enthusiastically over a babbling brook and began her ascent over a small crag. Despite the extreme physical exertion, Eenayah couldn't help but marvel at the mystical and barren surroundings she now found herself in. This indeed was the land of dragons and magicians. In Arthurian legend, Bedivere threw Excalibur into a lake somewhere hidden on the slopes of Snowdon. Eenayah looked up to the volcanic rock unfolding above her and wondered where the lake could be. Indeed her entire journey throughout the UK had reconnected her not only with her own hidden past, but with lands steeped in history and intrigue. She was sure she would return home as a new woman and was happy that she had made the effort to retrace her yesteryear. She hoped that free of the shadowy monster of depression, maybe her husband would fall in love with her again.

Suddenly stopping to look back to calculate how far she had run, she thought she saw a shadow slip behind the trees. It was only a momentary glimpse and she couldn't be sure if it was something or nothing. She carried on running, but now she had an unnerving instinct that someone or something was following her. She could feel piercing eyes stabbing into her back.

She tried to turn her head quickly, hoping to catch out whoever was tailing her. Again she thought she saw a shadow stealthily slip out of her line of vision. Was she really being followed?

Her heart began to beat faster, but this time out of a nervous anxiety that shot blasts of adrenalin through her veins. Here she was in a remote mountain location and totally alone. She felt vulnerable. Not wanting to turn back on herself and face whatever it was she believed to be behind her, she headed further up the mountain. She knew that taking the mountain track was a risky decision, but she was too afraid to turn back and face whatever was following her. She knew for sure that something was indeed behind her.

She attempted to comfort herself by saying out loud, 'come on Eenayah, up over the ridge and down the path. It's a straight track from there, down the hill to the Clogwyn Station and all the happy tourists waiting to jump on board Snowdon mountain railway. Lots of people. Keep going, just keep going. Run Eenayah, run!'

As she put all her energy into that final uphill sprint, she felt her ankle turn over with that sharp pain that accompanies a sudden muscle sprain. She tried to control it, but it all happened so fast. She let out a sudden shriek of pain. She didn't want to attract anyone or anything to her dilemma; it was just an instinctual scream as she lost control.

Her hand reached out towards an overhanging tree branch to try to steady herself. It had been raining the night before, and everything was slippery. She cursed herself at having picked a damp, wet day to run through the beautiful Snowdonia countryside. Her feet struggled to keep a grip on the slimy slate as her hand strained to maintain its clutch on the damp bark of the alder tree. She tried hard to maintain her grip, but the branch slowly slipped through her fingers.

She let go and began to tumble. It was as though everything around her had been decelerated into slow motion. She could see the rocky clefts of the ridge fly past her. She felt as if she was being spun around in a washing machine as she continued to roll through the heather and bracken, head below feet. The thorns of a clump of yellow gorse ripped at her flesh. She knew she was falling some distance, and the fear of death gripped her so tightly that she struggled to catch her breath. Mentally she uttered a speedy prayer. She could feel her back hit a jagged rock as she slipped unceremoniously further down the ridge.

Then a cruel, hard blow between her shoulders shook her rib cage. One final crack as her head met with a boulder, and then there was nothing but blackness. It was the last thing she remembered. Eenayah was out cold, lying in a remote isolated place at the bottom of a ridge and far from view from the lonely track high on the hill above her.

* * *

Some time later, a young man, oddly dressed in a velvet burgundy dinner jacket, approached the ridge and crouched down as he saw Eenayah's crumpled form lying pale and motionless in a bed of fluffy white bog cotton. He looked pleased with himself; the floral grave seemed most appropriate. He could tell that she was still alive, but deeply unconscious. Her leg was lying at a peculiar angle to the rest of her body and he concluded that either her pelvis or thigh must be broken. A small stain of clotted blood blemished the boulder which had broken her fall by colliding with her head.

The man looked around to check he was alone. The mountains were deafeningly silent, aside from the eerie sound of a chough soaring above on the breeze and the chirpy songs of redstarts and yellowhammers. He looked at his watch; 3 pm. Within a few hours the mountains would be dark, damp and cold. As the temperature fell, the life would be chilled from his victim. He concluded that she would not make it to daylight.

He looked around again, this time studying the topography of the landscape. The protrusion Eenayah had landed upon was hidden from the upper path. Only if someone took the time and trouble to peer over the ledge would they see the dying sleeping beauty far beneath them. He was content; he had done his job.

Before standing to leave, he shouted down to the unconscious victim, almost by way of a victory chant, 'one down, five to go. Ledanite idiots – you are losing the battle! Farewell Eenayah Baratolli. You will be in the company of King Arthur soon. Be at peace child; the Tylwyth Teg will come to collect you at dawn.'

With that, the mysterious young man left to give his mistress the good news. She had rented a nearby cottage and would be pleased to hear the outcome of today. As he left Eenayah alone to die on the ledge of a mountain, he smirked triumphantly. Another nail in the coffin.

★★★

Zac was sprawled full length along his second-hand sofa in his student loft accommodation. He was alone, drinking beer and watching football on the TV, giving the green turf his full concentration. With the volume hiked up to full notch he had missed the variety of errant alarms buzzing with increasing frequency from his PC.

When he did finally give a cursory glance over to his laptop and noted the flashing lights trying to gain his attention, he was filled with foreboding. In a state of panic he rushed over to his computer screen to log onto the distress signal being automatically generated from Eenayah Baratolli's security watch. Over the last few days there hadn't been much exciting to report back as regards Mrs Baratolli's movements. She had mostly stayed within the confines of her sister's manor house and with boring predictability had done much in the way of nothing. But according to satellite data, she was now far away from home in the middle of nowhere and had been static in the same location for eight hours.

Her vital signs were registering as abnormal, and in particular her temperature had become hypothermic. Zac tried to call Mercy, but she wasn't picking up. He then tried JD. Forever the action man, JD was not too far away and had been staying close by in a local town, as agreed. On hearing the panic in Zac's voice he instantly recognised the danger Eenayah was in.

'Zac, listen to me' he said. 'Call the emergency services. Tell them you are some bloody nutter of a mountain biker who likes to cycle in the dark and give them the co-ordinates of Eenayah's exact location. I am on my way there, but don't wait for me as it could be too late. Say whatever you have to say but make it convincing and get a rescue helicopter out to her now. I'm off to find her. Do as I say.'

CHAPTER 24

Saturday 13th July

The three gentlemen made their way across the cobbled courtyard towards the reception hall of Loughcrew House. As they stood beside the imposing inglenook fireplace, the smoky aroma of previous fires wafted a comforting scent of history in their direction. Don pointed out the formidable stags' heads emerging from a brutal stone wall. He had just started to photograph it enthusiastically when they were interrupted by a shrill 'hello, I am Brigid.' A bonny flaxen-haired girl with a beaming smile bounced her way towards them, bursting with life, energy and happiness.

In a soft Irish lilt, she spoke to the men. 'I'm awaiting the arrival of a Professor De Vede, a Doctor O'Byrne and a Mr Morris. I am assuming I am talking to the correct group; I do hope so or else I may look a mite foolish.' She giggled. Frank held out an assuring hand towards the young girl.

'Indeed, we are your tour group for the morning and please do call us by our Christian names. I am Frank, this old bugger stood next to me is Roland and the chap who arranged this with you is Don. We are all very pleased to meet you and grateful for your time.' Looking around at the grand reception area, he added, 'and I just want add; what a lovely place you have here. Do you live here Brigid?'

Brigid appeared amused at the suggestion. 'Oh gosh no Frank. I just work here, but I have grown up in the area and I hope I can tell you all you need to know about the cairns. As for this house, yes indeed it is magnificent, however it's not quite as old as it looks. It was built around the 1850s and designed by Charles Robert Cockerell, I understand. The interior has been decorated by Emily Naper. Not sure if you have heard of her or not, but as a designer she has great artistic flair.'

Frank concurred, being the only member of the male group who had any understanding of interior design. His two companions merely stood there with blank expressions as the comments floated over their balding heads.

Brigid seemed keen to move on. 'I hope you all have good walking boots with you,' she said. The Professor appeared mortified at the suggestion of doing yet more walking - half a day of golf yesterday had more than strained his calf muscles - but Brigid was in a playful mood and seemed to be enjoying taking the mickey out of her elderly group.

'Hey no worries chaps, I have a 4x4 parked outside. This house sits on 200 acres of parkland and I'm not going to be expecting you to walk around all of that, now am I indeed? At the moment we are within a valley below the Loughcrew Cairns, so we need to be heading up. Everyone set to go?'

The Professor felt an immense sense of relief as he strapped his aching body into the Land Rover, but then he began to wonder if Brigid knew how to drive. She looked too young to be a tour guide.

She continued with her light-hearted approach to what for her guests was actually quite a serious concern. Firing up the ignition, she yelled out, 'Everybody strapped in and ready to go visit the oldest cemetery in the world? It's a shame that you gentlemen aren't here when it's the equinox. You need to come back in March when the light shines through the tombs and illuminates the stones. It's truly awesome'.

Don sniggered to himself. Awesome, really? This was another language.

The Professor asked, 'can you tell us something more about the cairns whilst we travel up to see them please Bridget? We don't have a lot of time and we'd like to learn as much as we can.'

'Yeah sure,' she responded in typical teenage lingo. 'The cairns are on three hills and we are heading for the largest one, known as Cairn T at Cambane East. Although this Land Rover could probably take that hill, I am afraid the driver isn't going to risk it, so you will need to do some walking chaps.'

The gently-sloping peak soon became apparent, looking very obvious in an otherwise green and flat vista. Frank and the Professor became notably excited the closer they drove to the central cairn.

Brigid continued with her tutorial. 'Okay, so here's the deal. Some folks say these burial chambers are considerably older than the pyramids, and like the pyramids they were designed to help the dead go from this world to the next. As megalithic mounds go, they are knocking on a bit and are thought to be aged from between 3200 to 4000 BC, which is pretty mind blowing don't you think? So hey, here is the plan. I am going to park up in the car park we are just approaching. We have a short walk to Cairn T, but I need to warn you that it's fairly steep. Don told me that this is the bump you are interested in. It has a roof and I believe some engravings you want to eyeball. If you want to check out Cambane West later, it is about a two kilometre walk if you are up to it. However there are about 15 cairns in total, so if you want to check them all out, it will take you like a full day, but I would say it's worth the effort. There is also Cairn L, which like the one I am about to show you is roofed and has similar engravings, but it's closed off to the public. If you want to know more, the coffee shop sells some books about the place. Okay, so we are here now. Ready to rock & roll, folks?'

Brigid bounced out of the car as though she really enjoyed her work. Despite the fact that she had visited these ancient hills a multitude of times in her life, she still looked pleased to see them. Quite obviously she was delighted and proud of her national heritage; not something one would normally associate with adolescence.

The Professor groaned yet again, moaning as always about his aching calf muscles. As they made their ascent he grumbled with each movement of his knees, but in anticipation of what lay ahead he heroically continued to walk through the pain. He couldn't wait to see and hear more about the cairn.

Brigid sympathetically slowed down her usual frantic walking speed to keep pace with her older visitors. As they approached the site she stopped to allow them to play catch up and went into more detail.

'The cairn we are about to visit now is sometimes referred to as Jeremiah's tomb,' she said.

'Yes, I have heard of that nickname Brigid,' said Frank. 'It confuses me because as you mentioned, these stones are older than the pyramids and Jeremiah was a lot more recent – circa 600BC. What connection do you think Jeremiah has with this place in Ireland?'

Brigid stopped in her tracks and faced her audience, quietly flattered that such an eminent group consisting of a doctor, a professor and a clever clogs researcher would be interested in her thesis.

'Well Dr O'Byrne, I understand that even the humble cuckoo can commandeer the use of another bird's nest, so just because this old mound existed a long time before Jeremiah doesn't mean to say he didn't make later use of it. I have to say however that this is where we get into the world of legend and fables, and as much as we Irish love a good *scéal* over a pint of Guinness, there are some things you need to take with a pinch of salt.'

314

The Professor concurred. 'That's fine Brigid. History and life are full of things that can't be proven, but we are still interested in the folklore, even if it is just a sweet little story.'

Brigid loved to tell sweet little stories, so she needed no further encouragement. She took a deep breath and then whispered as though telling a classified secret.

'Well, I can only tell you what my father told me. I believe it says in the bible that the Prophet Jeremiah was commanded by God to get the heck out of Jerusalem and go somewhere far away to plant a twig. There are some that think that this is symbolic of doing a runner with some royal daughter who descends from the line of David and King Zedekiah rather than a mere gardening project. Her name was Princess Teia Tephi, which I am told literally translates as 'the Tender Twig'. It gets a bit deep at this point because it all gets connected to Jeremiah hiding in some cave with Teia Tephi along with the Arc of the Covenant. Anyway, so when the coast is clear, off they sail to Tanis in Egypt with the Arc of the Covenant, which maybe they hide there or maybe they don't. Who will ever know? Anyway, so then they all go via Gibraltar to finally end up here in rainy Ireland. He was supposed to have taken God's treasures with him, so make of that what you will. If I am recollecting this correctly, he took the three daughters of King Zedekiah, three handmaidens and another bloke. That detail may not seem significant now, but once you get to see the hieroglyphics you will understand the story they are trying to tell. Fascinating stuff, huh?'

Of course the legend was known to Frank as a teacher of theology, but none the less it was entertaining to hear the casual rendition being uttered from Brigid's young and crimson lips as though she was talking about a plot in a soap opera.

Brigid continued her role as tour guide extraordinaire. She began, 'Here we are at Cairn T. It is about 120ft high and was once covered in white quartz, which must have looked flipping amazing back then. Can you imagine it shining across the landscape at sunrise? Awesome! Anyway, Cairn T has what is referred to as an Irish cruciform layout, which is a posh way of saying that it's some sort of cross. You will see what I mean in a mo. As we walk inside you will note a large central chamber and then other connecting side chambers. It is said that this layout is very similar to the mounds at the Boyne Valley complex and there are loads of inscribed stones throughout. If you want hieroglyphics, you will get hieroglyphics. You have come to the right place chaps, this is like mystic symbolism on steroids. There are theories that these mounds are simply time markers that correspond to the sun's position, a bit like Stonehenge I guess. Who knows? A lot of this history stuff is guesswork.' That comment brought an evil scowl from the less than impressed Professor of history.

Brigid placed a stone at the foot of the entrance, uttering the words, '*Cuiridh mi clach air do chàrn.*' 'It's a tradition,' she explained. 'I am honouring the dead. My father used to bring me up here as a child and he always did this, and he taught me to do it as well. In truth, I think it is actually an old Scottish Gaelic blessing, but we Irish are open to borrowing anything. The tourist like stuff like this.' Yet again she giggled, as though incapable of taking anything seriously.

She then led them to the darkened entrance, allowing her elderly visitors to walk in first.

'Okay, chaps mind your heads. Some of these passages are narrow and have low roofs. Don't want anyone leaving here on a stretcher, worse still in a body bag.' Brigid tittered, amused by her own humour. Sounding more like a teacher supervising a bunch of schoolchildren she asked, 'now has everybody got a torch? Good – use it. I don't want anyone hiring a 'no win no fee' solicitor.'

Much as the men enjoyed Brigid's company, they were all intent to get to the stones and compare markings. Their fervent young tour guide had a charming wit, but their reason for visiting the cairn was deadly serious.

Brigid initially took them to Stone L1, the first to be seen on entering the cairn. She continued to chat as in tour guide mode. 'Okay Don & co, here is the first of the inscribed stones and indeed it is the first stone the rising equinoctial sun illuminates as it enters the passageway from that direction.' She pointed over to the east. They all stopped to take photographs and the Professor studied each of the markings with a large magnifying glass. Don took out the A4 sized photographs from his back pack, and they made comparisons.

Frank commented, 'It's like Neolithic rock art. Very impressive. Lots of circular shapes which look like the sun, but not the same level of detail as we can see on the gravestones. Similar I think, but not the same. Do you both concur?' The others shook their heads, slightly disappointed.

'Can we move on, Brigid?' asked the professor.

Brigid complied, after all she was just the tour guide. 'I am going to take you to the second stone to the left, close to where we entered the tomb. From my conversation with Don, I believe this is what you have all come to see.'

As before out came the magnifying glass, the camera and the oversized photographs of Daisy Green's headstone as well as those of her two forebears. To the group's elation it soon became very clear that the gravestone hieroglyphics bore an amazing resemblance to the cairn stone markings. Eagerly the Professor asked, 'Do you know what any of this means, by any chance Brigid?'

'Well Professor, you can always buy a book at the coffee shop which will tell you a heck of a lot more about this than I could pretend to know, but as far as I am aware it has been interpreted as telling the story of how the Prophet Jeremiah arrived from Jerusalem to Ireland. See this squiggle here? This is supposed to be a boat with five living passengers and three dead ones - see, cos they are lying down. I guess that makes them dead. Now if you look at this other symbol, note that the boat is a bit different, that's because it's Greek. The spiral squiggles means its heading north- can't understand why it means that, it just does. This one is a bit clearer, in that it does actually look like an eagle with a twig in its beak. I think that is all about settling in a new land and the planting the twig thing which I spoke about earlier. There are lots of circular markings relating to astronomy and similar markings on the end stone, which I should take you to look at now. You will love the end stone. Follow, follow - get in line and watch your heads.'

They continued onwards to the farthest opening in the interior of the cairn and through to the final end stone. Frank gasped. One particular marking flew out at him as a 100% match.

'What is that Brigid?' he asked.

She answered without hesitation. 'Oh, the one I always think looks like a leaf. Well actually it is supposed to be a rib cage and it does look like a rib cage, don't you think? Folks around here call this a breast with a right arm. Since I was a child I have been taught that this symbolically represents Jeremiah, the Lord's faithful servant, acting as His right arm. It is the sign of Jeremiah and hence the name of the tomb. This may be a load of old garbage, but I am just telling it to you as it has been told to me.'

They took countless photographs, but even in the subdued light of a darkened tomb it was clear to see that Daisy Green's gravestone and those of her two ancestors bore the symbolic markings which depicted the prophet Jeremiah; the breast and the right arm. They also noted a strong similarity between the eagle with the twig and what they were told represented a partial solar eclipse.

Brigid looked at her watch and was keen to move her group on, although pulling them away from their unusual fascination with the marked stones was proving to be a rare challenge. Her visitors normally had a more general interest in all the various archaeological sites scattered in the area, but Don had made it clear to her that they were here for one reason only; the hieroglyphics in Cairn T.

'Hey guys, lets wander outside now and go and see the Hag's Chair' said Brigid. 'Well, some call it that because they believe all of this was created by a witch flying on a broomstick and dropping stones on the place, but others call it the Judgment Seat. There is still a lot to see, and you might also want to take a peek at Tara's Hill and the Stone of Destiny. Just piles of history to go through in these parts chaps.'

Despite her spirited attempts to lure their interest towards other historical sites in the area, it became clear to Brigid that her team had found what they were looking for and had no further interest in visiting anywhere else.

Don took the lead in steering the team back towards the car. 'Could you do us a favour please Brigid? We oldies have a few creaking bones and aching muscles to deal with, so I don't think any of us are fit enough to climb up any more cairns today. I think I can speak for all of us when I say that we have now seen what we needed to see. It has been a fascinating morning, but could you drive us back to Loughcrew House now please, my dear? I've left my hire car parked next to reception so I am guessing we'll probably make tracks back to the hotel, unless of course there is a nearby pub you could recommend. Fancy a pint of Guinness, gentlemen?' Both Frank and the Professor nodded in eager agreement.

Accommodating as always, the ever-cheerful Brigid replied, 'of course Don, it's your call. We are not short of pubs around this neck of the woods, but if you want a pint with a chaser of the best Irish whiskey then I can recommend The Huntsman – hey it's even got a thatched roof.'

Don continued to push his luck. 'If it's not being too cheeky Brigid, could you just stop at St Marys Cemetery on the way back?

We will only be five minutes – just something I need to show Professor Roland and Frank. Would that be taking you out of your way?'

'I don't mind, honestly. You had me booked out for the whole morning anyway and you guys cut your tour short, or rather your knees did, so I don't mind taking you somewhere else if that helps crack any codes. All sounds most intriguing, I must say. I so love a good mystery.'

As they rode away from Cairn T, still deep in thought and hushed as though contemplating their own thoughts, Frank asked a question which bemused his companions.

'Brigid, you seem to know a great deal about the local folklore. Are any of the stories you are aware of in any way connected to twins, specifically twin girls?'

The Professor shot Frank a bewildered look. He had no idea where his friend was leading with such a question. It wasn't an inquiry that involved either the cairns or the hieroglyphics which had taken them to the ancient site.

'Well sure, Dr O'Byrne. You are in the green land of fables are you not? Not far away from here near Athboy is a place called Tlachtga which is sometimes known as 'Hill of Ward'. I suspect because that's an easier name to pronounce. I guess it's about 10 or so miles from the Hill of Tara. Tlachtga dates from approximately 200 AD I believe and is named after a sorceress who died there giving birth to triplets. Tlachtga was the daughter of the powerful Druid Mug Ruith and I believe she was a twin herself but her sister died, or maybe was even sacrificed. They were into all this pagan stuff back then, I understand. The hill was the location of the Great Fire Festival on the eve of Samhain – that's Halloween to you and me. I even think that's where Halloween originated, long before the Americans stole it and reinvented it with a 'trick or treat' theme. It was never supposed to be about dressing up as a monster, this was about lighting a fire to celebrate the Celtic New Year and honour one's ancestors. A few odd bods still go up there and get up to all sorts on the 31st October. You wouldn't catch me up there on Samhain, but interesting story don't you think?'

Frank was intrigued. 'I have never heard that story before Brigid. Who was this Mug Ruith and what became of his grandchildren?'

Once again Brigid was at her best in Celtic storytelling mode. 'Oh my, oh my, what can I say about Mug Ruith? He was a bit of a legend in these parts. Some say he was only part human, but that's a whole different story. It is told that he was a giant of a man. We Irish love our giants, don't we so? Fionn mac Cumhaill, who built the Giant's Causeway, being an example. However I think Mog was probably just a big bloke as opposed to a giant. It is told that he could grow to a great height if he needed to.'

Brigid had a habit off skiing off-piste from time to time, and Frank had to pull her back to the question. She continued with her colourful yarn, as patiently requested.

'It is told that he was a blind druid or maybe he just had one eye, but whatever the vision impairment, he had awesome supernatural powers, and by that I mean off the scale of normal. His breath could create storms and turn folk into stone. It is said that he wore a bird mask, and flew in a machine that looked like a wheel, and keep in mind that this was thousands of years before we put airplanes in the sky. Must have scared the bloody locals shitless somewhat. It is told that he had an ox-driven chariot which by night glowed, and a star-speckled black shield with a silver rim. Maybe he was an alien and this denoted what constellation he came from? Just a theory, Dr O'Byrne! It also seemed that he had this magic stone which could turn into some poisonous monster when thrown in water. He lived an abnormally long life, saw 19 kings come and go. Wandered around the Holy land for a bit. Got matey with Simon Magus and the apostles.

What else – oh yes, he beheaded John the Baptist – allegedly. It seems this brought upon him and the Irish some sort of a curse – as indeed it would if you put a John the Baptist's head on a plate. Bad political move, hey? All complete bunkum I suppose, but a great story don't you think?'

'What does make me curious is the fate of Mug Ruith's daughter and descendants' said Frank. 'Would you know what became of them?'

Brigid was trying to find her way to the church they had asked to visit and she made several wrong turns as she struggled to combine driving and navigation with storytelling.

'Ah, the beautiful druidess Tlachtga. According to Irish tradition she accompanied her father on his world travels, learning his magical secrets along the way. It is said that she discovered some sacred stones in Italy, although what she ever did with them and why they were sacred, who knows? She was raped by the three sons of her Dad's buddy, Simon Magus. One of you chaps may already know this, but just in case – Simon was a sorcerer who came from a village in biblical Samaria. Everything keeps going back to biblical times, you may note; Ireland does seem to have an ongoing connection. Anyway, I think this Simon sorcerer bloke is mentioned in the bible a few times. You must have heard of him, Dr O'Byrne. The story goes that Tlachtga returned to Ireland where she gave birth to triplets, three boys called Cumma, Doirb and Muach. They were born on the hill that would bear the name of their mother. However there are some tales in Celtic mythology that say prior to the sons, she gave birth to twin daughters, Talitiu and Macha. Like their mother before them, they also had twin births that resulted in their deaths. I mean, even these days multiple births can be dodgy, so back then I guess women just died.'

Frank had of course heard of Simon Magus and Helen of Troy, but right now his specific interest was that of Talitiu and Macha and what became of their descendants. He had no idea if any of these real or fictional characters had the vaguest of connections to his present investigation, but as the hill that was the source of this local fable was so close to Cairn T, he felt he could leave no stone unturned. He was frustrated that his curiosity was still left dangling on a long piece of Celtic string.

Brigid pulled up in the gravel car park of St Mary's Church. She was glad that she had been able to answer many of her visitor's questions, although the constant storytelling had left her mentally exhausted. She applied the handbrake and answered the question that Frank had asked her five miles back. She sensed his irritation; it was within her Goidelic instinct to feel such things.

'Dr O'Byrne, Professor De Vede and Mr Don, we are here now, St Mary's Church, but before you leave the car I have this to add. All I have told you is but local folklore and probably the result of too many whiskeys and a scattering of fertile imaginations; although the part about Halloween beginning on the Hill of Ward does appear to be true. I also understand that the bible does back up some of what I have said about the other stuff. However you asked me about the twin girls, Talitiu and Macha. After their brothers were born they were motherless. They were raised by their grandfather 'Mr Mug' and probably the local women in the area. As a family they were probably both feared and worshipped in these parts. I understand Talitiu became a Druid goddess and was revered, but I know nothing more than that. It is said that their descendants still live around this area of County Meath and maybe even other parts of Ireland. I am guessing that any powers the family may have had are long gone and most likely have been bred out of them through many generations, after all we are talking about something that happened over 2000 years ago. I have certainly not seen any giants or flying wheels of late.

' Their descendants have either kept themselves hidden or maybe don't even realise they are connected to Mug. Maybe they went underground for fear of reprisals – who knows? They just vanished from history. Mug was supposed to have brought a curse on the Irish by doing that thing with John the Baptist's head and maybe that could be good enough reason enough for a family secret. I am so sorry I cannot be of more help, Dr O'Byrne. People in these parts can keep secrets for centuries and then some. I am not sure what you and your lovely friends are looking for but I wish you luck – *Ádh mór.*'

The three men emerged from their tour guide's car none the wiser after their journey through Celtic supernatural history. Mary Ryan's grave was just a short walking distance from the archway leading into the cemetery. Don had already made a visit there and could locate it instantly.

To live in the hearts of those we love is not to die
Mary Ryan 1878 – 1934
A beloved wife and mother
Also Benjamin Ryan 1876 – 1947

It was a simple but loving inscription. Don directed Frank and the Professor around to the back on the headstone, indicating the bottom left-hand corner. Frank knelt down and touched the stone as though asking it a question and hoping a soothing stroke would by some magical clairsentience allow the stone to whisper its secrets.

Frank looked concerned. His two other comrades considered this to be a queer over-reaction to a mere carved slab of cold rock. Frank quoted a passage from the bible, which having a doctorate in theology he was well qualified to do.

'I am not sure if these are the exact words, but in Exodus it says 'Ye have seen what I did unto the Egyptians, and how I bear you on eagle's wings and brought you unto myself'.

The Professor was nonplussed and wasn't sure how to react. Frank continued with his explanation. 'It is the eagle with the twig I see here, the same as I saw on the cairn stones. In biblical history, when God moves his people to safety He does it on the wings of an eagle, hence the eagle with the twig in its mouth. I believe these could be very sacred tymboglyphics. In the literal sense it could mean a passage to safety. The other symbol, the one Brigid described as a leaf, but is actually a chest with an arm, seems to indicate the prophet Jeremiah. I am confused. Why would three headstones, of which two are across the sea in England, all bear the same symbols, which seem to be plagiarised from an ancient cairn? I have a suspicion about this. We can discuss it later over a drink. Let's go now, I have seen all I need to see.'

Frank was in a serious mood. Don and the Professor were both keen to discuss the day's finding openly during the car journey, but Frank surreptitiously pointed towards Brigid and hushed his two companions by a simple glance. No words were required. They took on board the covert nature of whatever was going on, but yet didn't have a clue about. They even made superficial conversation with their young driver about things they didn't understand and for reasons they didn't understand.

Brigid was relieved that the heavy subject of local folklore had been dropped for the time being and she could concentrate on not getting lost down the small country lanes, some little more than narrow farming tracks and with deep potholes to match.

Brigid dropped off the three gents at a pub, with a promise to collect them later. They began to collect their thoughts in a bar – intentionally not the one Brigid had suggested – as they men enjoyed the dark smooth texture of Irish Guinness with a whiskey chaser.

The Professor looked around furtively. 'What the heck was all that secret hush-hush stuff about Frank? Why did you go all weird and guarded on us? I thought young Brigid was a wonderful girl and a very helpful guide. Why did you just shut her down all of a sudden?

What the hell changed after we left St Mary's churchyard?'

Frank leaned forward, talking in a soft voice. 'You have no idea who you can trust. You have no idea what hidden forces you are up against here. Brigid may look and sound like a harmless young filly, but you don't know who and what she knows or who she really is. I suspect very strongly that you have accidentally stumbled across something quite big, Roland. Something bigger than we three ageing musketeers can handle alone. To be honest, I am concerned about your client. I don't know her name, I don't want to know her name. You don't know if you can even trust me. You need to have your wits about you. Don't talk to anybody about what we have found today.'

Don looked down at the stone pub floor in embarrassment. Although he was a close friend of the Professor, he was also on the payroll of his daughter Mercy and MeDeVe Ltd, and as an employee he knew his place.

The Professor just looked confused. It had been a long day. His knees and calf muscles hurt. He hadn't the foggiest idea why his bohemian ultra-modern former priest friend had gone all biblical on him in a dramatic U-turn. He didn't understand the warning or the drama surrounding any of this. He had to confess.

'Frank, I respect you as the scholarly and cultured fellow I know you to be – but Father Francis, what the heck are you actually saying?'

Frank would normally have laughed at this juncture and slapped the Professor on the back for his profanity, but no humour was forthcoming. The mood had changed considerably. He sat silently and waited until Don had to leave to use the toilet facilities.

As Don walked out, Frank apologised. 'I am sorry my friend, but I don't even know if Don can be trusted. He is a paid employee of your daughter's and he can be bought and sold.'

The Professor was baffled by the sudden change in Frank's attitude. He responded, 'Knowing Don's enlarged prostate and his toilet habits intimately as I do, you have several minutes to tell me the shortened version of what the hell is happening and why you have become so bloody paranoid. I know you know something Frank. You have been doing some homework, haven't you? What is it you know that has suddenly scared the bejesus out of you?'

Frank checked his watch. 'Five minutes and counting. Okay, let me try to say as much as I can as quickly as I can. Roland, belief is a very powerful force. I have spent my life preaching it and then teaching it, so of all people I should know how belief can be used for the better or the worse and how it can control and influence beyond sense and logic. Belief is powerful stuff and by saying that I don't intend to be disrespectful of anyone's belief – just stressing that what one believes in can determine who you are and what you do.

'As a lecturer at Dublin University, I did this whole session around cult beliefs. The word cult has been given some bad press as folks associate it with indoctrination and mind-altering techniques. One thinks of the crazy fads of the 60s, when perhaps any left of centre religious group could be called a cult and tarnished with the same marijuana-smoking brush. Anyway, back to what I was quickly trying to impart before Don gets back. A few years ago I asked my students to each do a project on a cult of their choice. One of my students, a chap by the name of Luke, elected to write about the Ledanite group. Very private, secret, guarded and little known about them, but his parents were members, so he had some privileged info he was willing to share for an A+ score. Hey, every man has his price.

'Of course I had heard about Tamar, a powerful woman from the bible. Check out Genesis 38. This cult believed in the reincarnation of Tamar and some very well-hidden prophecy that predicts the recreation of the Masonic line of inheritance which may possibly lead to the second coming of the Messiah. The line of Tamar was to be protected at all costs. The cost of failure was the demise of the goodness of mankind itself. These folks saw themselves as being protectors of some special line of inheritance. From what I recall of the essay, they were a sort of sect whom my student suggested should never be underestimated. I remember that there were those who would fight to protect and maintain the descendants of this line. However as we live in a world of good v evil, there was also those who would do anything to destroy it. I guess for the bad guys their way of thinking could be that if the line was exterminated then the Messiah could not be reborn – or something along those lines.'

The Professor sat in silence and downed his Whiskey chaser in advance of his Guinness – culturally not the norm, but he was in need of a quick alcohol injection. He retorted, 'I respect you a great deal, my knowledgeable biblical friend, but I honestly do not believe I have understood a word you have just said and I have no idea how any of this relates to the markings on headstones which somehow mirror parts of the cairn stones. Plus, how do ancient tomb markings possibly put my client's life in some sort of danger? I admit that it has felt like a long day so far and there is a story to uncover here, but I am more befuddled than ever. This Tamar person and parables from Genesis and weird cults – bugger, it's all too much Frank. This has just flown way over my head along with the fairies. And it's your round.'

Frank understood the situation perfectly. In his enthusiasm to tell as much as he could as quickly as he could he had unintentionally confused the Professor. In the short time he had left before Don returned, he needed to simplify the message he was trying to convey as well as being a bit less scary.

'Roland, I apologise. I blurted all of that out like vomit. I am sorry. It is just that we don't have much time. When you first mentioned to me the history of twins having twins who have twins scenario, it reminded me of the hidden prophecy of Tamar. The student who composed this essay is now a Catholic priest who only lives 50 or so miles away from here and I strongly suggest we visit him soon, tomorrow if possible. I have already had a chat with him over the phone about this and it seems that there is a link with Jeremiah's tomb and the Ledanite prophecies. I would prefer he tell you the story in person rather than it be just me on my own, but if what he says is true then your client could be in mortal danger. If she carries the Line of Tamar, then there are those who would want her dead before she or her twin reproduces and thus maintains the line.

'By the way, I am not sure if the twin daughters of Tlachtga and the whole Halloween hill thing has anything or nothing to do with any of this right now and I don't want to muddy the water. I have heard it in passing that there was an evil line as well as a sacred one, and Tlachtga may represent the line of witches and demons. However, profound as the local legend may be, I suggest we just park that for now.'

The Professor was by now very nearly brain dead. 'Yes indeed Frank. All of this has been way too much for me to take in for the moment and a visit to your former student may be the next best step forward. Don will be back from his toilet trip any time soon and I am guessing or rather hoping, that the next part of the plan is to go back to the hotel and get some welcome sleep. I am not happy about you excluding Don from the conversation however. I do regard him as a highly-respected and valued part of my team. I just don't get where your mistrust comes from.'

Just then Don emerged from the corner of the bar, with refills for Frank and the Professor and had just ordered spring water for himself. The conversation virtually collapsed at that point. The Professor would wait to see what Frank's former student had to say tomorrow.

★★★

Limping back into his hotel room, the Professor noted he had left his mobile phone on the side cabinet and felt instant guilt. His daughter would surely scold him for this. He was always leaving his phone in forgotten places and he knew only too well that his paranoid daughter liked to keep track on his whereabouts via his phone at all times.

Ten missed calls; this was unusual. Nine calls from Mercy or associates and just one from an unknown 01745 number. Mercy had taught him to google unknown numbers before returning the call, just in case it was a spam using a premium rate line. Whilst waiting for his laptop to fire up he checked out his voice messages. The first was from Mercy asking him what he was doing in a hotel in Southern Ireland and why was he not picking up his phone. That was a reprimand he had expected. This was followed by several other messages from both Mercy and Kerry asking him to call back as soon as possible, the note of crisis clearly audible.

The final message was more alarming. 'Hello, I am sorry but I don't know who this phone belongs to. My name is Sister Merandi from the Medical Assessment Unit, Glan Cleed hospital. We have an unidentified patient in the unit and this number was found in her pocket. Can you call me back as soon as you get this message please so we can identify her? 01745 ****** and ask for Sister Merandi. We need to confirm who she is as soon as possible. Thank you.'

The search engine confirmed that indeed this was the number of a hospital in North Wales. The Professor only knew of one person presently in North Wales, and that was Eenayah Baratolli, with whom he had spoken earlier that morning with regard to her husband's book. Less than an hour ago he had assumed that his friend Frank had been overly dramatic in emphasising that perhaps Eenayah and her sister belonged to some mystical genetic line of descent which, because it was attached to some prophecy, put both their lives in danger. However, now it was probable that Eenayah lay sick in a hospital, so perhaps Frank had not been too zealous in his concern.

He knew that his next move was to call Mercy. Since she had been a young girl Mercy had always taken control and always known the right thing to do. She was very much in charge of his life, and he certainly wasn't going to take any further action until he had consulted her.

★★★

Mercy was angry, so the Professor allowed her to reprimand him before she calmed down enough to allow him to talk. 'Father, where the hell have you been?' she asked.

'Playing golf, damaging my knees, walking through an ancient mound, deciphering hieroglyphics, looking at gravestones and drinking too much in the pub with Frank and Don. Just a normal two-day outing for a history teacher.'

Mercy's voice was grave and solemn. 'Something is wrong with Eenayah. The silly girl went out for a run in a terrain more suitable for climbers or fell runners than someone who just jogs on a running machine. It appears she slipped into some gully and knocked herself out. The security watch alarmed Zac last night that her temperature was dropping. We had to send JD out onto the mountain pretending to be some mountain biker who had found her so he could guide the air ambulance in. Not sure they fully bought into the story, seeing as it was about 1 am, but what else could we do? We don't know where she is. In a hospital we presume, but the signal to the watch is being blocked. Zac reckons that hospitals sometimes block signals so they don't mess with the electrical equipment. We are trying to find her as best we can. Everyone here feels very anxious, Dad.'

Of course her father knew exactly where Eenayah was, and relayed the phone message to Mercy. 'That's great. Thank god she had your number tucked away in her pocket. Look, I have to get off now and make some urgent phone calls. Keep your mobile on you and I will call you later.'

The Professor understood her need to rush off, but he made one final request before she hung up. 'Be sure to call me back Mercy. I have uncovered something worrying and it relates to Eenayah, so I need to discuss it with you.'

Within 15 minutes Mercy was back on the phone to him. She had been unable to hold back her curiosity. What was it that her father needed to tell her that couldn't wait? Seldom had he sounded so serious. He explained the events of the last two days, why he was in Ireland and why his friend Frank had introduced the notion that a religious cult might have an interest in Eenayah and possibly Ruby.

Mercy sat and listened in stony silence, making notes as her father relayed the sequence of events. Finally the Professor asked, 'what do I do next, Mercy? I need to call the hospital at some point. Do you believe in any of this biblical prophecy stuff? I am not so sure. This Ledanite sect sounds a bit away with the fairies to me.'

Mercy was pragmatic. 'Father dear, it doesn't matter what I do or don't believe. As a little girl you always taught me that it was people who still had a pulse that I should be more concerned about, not the imaginary shadows of the night. Whether some prophecy is real or just an old wives' tale passed down through the centuries matters not. What is more of a concern is that if people believe in all this prophecy stuff then they may take actions that threaten our client. For all we know, Eenayah's fall may not be the mishap we have so far presumed it to be.'

Her father agreed. He had become extremely concerned, and Mercy concurred with his suspicions.

'Cults worry me. Do you recall the MacDonald case, the young guy we tracked down in Greece recently? The people who kidnapped him didn't need metal bars and chains to imprison him. They just melted his mind by fear and brain washing. Any mention of a cult sends shivers down my spine.'

The Professor sensed the disquiet in his daughters voice. 'Frank seems to believe that everyone is a potential threat because nobody really knows who may or may not be connected to the Ledanite and who may be on which side, good or evil. He was even suspicious of Don and waited until he had gone to the gents' before he would share more details with me. Personally I just thought it was way over the top, but now I am concluding that he may have been right to be cautious.'

Mercy agreed with the prudence displayed by her father's old friend. 'Okay Dad, the deal is this. This may be nothing more than a wild goose chase. Frank may have become disproportionately excited by some random squiggles on a headstone or two and the fact that female twins happens to run in Eenayah's family tree. Dearest Frank could have tied it all together like threads of wool and knit himself a jumper from a few twines of evidence. Or, he may have actually stumbled upon a real hidden prophecy, with a real group of avid believers and a real cult who may wish to either protect Eenayah and her twin, or remove them from the equation by killing them. Having just closed the MacDonald case, which involved a cult who were totally committed to the bullshit they totally believed in, I don't trust this situation. I think we have to assume that Frank has uncovered a real threat until we prove otherwise. As for not trusting anyone, he has a point. With the MacDonald boy, members of the cult groomed him for quite a while. It was very similar to the way a paedophile may groom a young child, by keeping close and growing confidence. The people he presumed to be his best friends were actually orchestrating his capture. They closed a net around him, which is why it was so difficult for any rescuers to break through. As for Don, I think we need to presume he can be trusted because he has worked for us for over ten years now. Having said that, best to keep this on a 'need to know' basis. Does that make sense, Father?'

The Professor understood her point and of course he had known all about the complexity of the MacDonald case, but right at this moment of time he just needed a directive.

'What do I do now Mercy? I am presuming that it is Eenayah lying on a hospital bed in Glan Cleed Hospital and I'll need to return the call and speak to the ward sister some time soon. They have no idea who she is, so I'm guessing she must be unconscious.'

Mercy went into full MeDeVe detective mode. 'So if you are telling me that her ID is totally unknown at this moment of time, and right now she is being cared for' she said, 'then she is as safe now as she will ever be. Out of the whole world population, right now, only you and I can put a name to the unknown woman in the Welsh hospital bed. We could give her any identity we want – and that gives me an idea. IF Eenayah truly is in jeopardy, she won't stay safe for long. People are bound to notice she is missing at some point. She has been something of a wandering gypsy over the last month or so, but eventually her family will wonder where she is. It seems like you were the last person to talk with her father, so you must know more than most. Do you know where she was, who she was with and what she had planned? Same goes for her sister Ruby. You need to tell me everything you know, Father. I am more than aware that you have had a tiring day but please try hard to remember. If you have any details, just spit them out.'

The Professor didn't have to think too long or hard, as his last conversation with Eenayah was still fresh in his mind. 'She told me that her twin sister Ruby has been in Disneyland with her husband and son this week. They are flying back to Miami tomorrow and they'll be spending their final week at Eenayah and Reed's villa. I understand other members of the family will be flying out to Miami and they have some sort of reunion party planned before Ruby flies home the weekend after. Eenayah was very excited about the whole thing.'

Mercy scribbled down notes whilst conversing with her father. 'Well in a way that is good, because I'm sure Reed has an impressive security system around his massive luxury villa. I know the guy well enough to know that privacy and security are his thing. So Ruby will be safe enough there. On the downside, I'm guessing they expect Eenayah to be back in Miami sometime soon to join in with the family party. We can't keep our little gypsy hidden for long. As of late she has been staying at her sister Ruby's house in North Wales. From what she has told me, it is in a remote location in the hills of Snowdonia. To me it sounded really picturesque and secluded, but Eenayah wasn't at all happy living there. It lacked the security of her Miami home and she was a bit concerned that some guy was stalking her. She has been paranoid about this for the last week and mentioned it to me a few times. I believe she managed to persuade Ruby's sister-in -law to stay with her in order to keep her company.' The Professor concurred with Mercy's synopsis adding, I think Owyn's sister is called Darcy, but I may have the name wrong. I had called to ask Eenayah if she wouldn't mind asking more questions of her newly found family, but she brushed me off. I think she was reluctant to go back to Manchester to see her Great Aunt Elspeth. I got the impression that she was missing home and her husband and was busy packing to go back to Miami. I think her flight was booked for Monday. I am not sure which airport she intended to fly out from, but I guess it could be Manchester. That's about as much as I can remember Mercy.'

'Don't fret about it – that's good Dad. Your memory has served you well and you have given me a lot to go on. It sounds like the first person who would notice her missing would be Darcy. We need to throw her off the scent somehow. We already know the address of Ruby's house. It has zero security – it will be a walk in the park for our guys. We need to remove all Eenayah's belongings and leave a note for Darcy indicating that she's wandered off on her travels again. From what I can tell, that's all she has been doing in her life recently so people could easily fall for that line. We don't know how ill she is or what kind of condition she's in, but we need to find out soon. I need to get her a false identity and then arrange for her to be transferred to a private facility as soon as possible. If anyone knows she's been in North Wales, they will know she may be an inpatient in a hospital in North Wales and it won't take long to track her down. I have connections with a high security medical facility in London, so we will work on getting her moved.'

The Professor was overwhelmed by the speed at which his daughter processed her thoughts and turned them into actions. However he had known that her brush with the Greek cult had taught her many lessons which were now being applied, rightly or wrongly, to Eenayah's situation.

Mercy added, 'finally Dad, I need to be you. Thank God you never actually recorded a personal answering message on your phone. The ward sister who contacted you doesn't have a clue who the phone belongs to, so for the time being, your number is my number. I'll get Zac to weave some technical magic and have your number cloned over to my phone and I'll be the one making the call to the hospital, not you. Get it? Don't call them back Father. Eenayah is a similar age to me, so with a wig and some makeup tricks I can look like a sibling. Gee, I've got a lot to do in a short time. I think we need to sort out the new identity for us both first so I can be her legal next of kin. I'll get Simon working on it right away. Oh and I almost forgot, we need to cancel her flight. That's easy enough. Don't want the family becoming suspicious about a 'no show'. Have I forgotten anything? I think I have it all covered.'

The Professor was concerned. 'Slow down Mercy. My goodness child, you are like a whirlwind of mental activity. Do you realise that what you are planning to do is to change someone's identity and basically hold them hostage to a situation they can't agree to because they are not conscious enough to know what's going on? I dread to think how many laws you are about to break. Maybe the stress of the MacDonald case is causing you to over-react.'

Mercy understood. 'Yes I know, and yes I agree. However I would rather take too many precautions and then be proved wrong if we find out later that this is nothing more than Frank's imagination taking a supersonic flight of fancy into the stratosphere. The alternative is to just sit here and do nothing and then discover there's a real cult in existence with a possible intent to do evil, and then suddenly Eenayah and/or Ruby come to some harm and we did nothing to stop it. That would be unforgivable. Eenayah employed you to look into her husband's genealogy and come up with some fancy book about him, which I understand you have done. Then she asked you to look into her own genealogy, which again you have done, and in so doing you've unearthed a mystery. She employed MeDeVe to find her biological family, which we did. Finally she employed me to look after her personal safety, which is exactly what I plan to do, but haven't done such a great job of to date seeing as my client is in hospital right at this moment.

'I know you're concerned Dad, but stop worrying. The false ID is only a temporary measure to get her transferred out of hospital and into a private facility, and for me to do that I need to be her next of kin. It is just a transient little white lie. When she gains consciousness, she will be Eenayah again - I promise you, and then we ship her back to Florida and the security of Reed's domain. By that time, hopefully we will know if there is any truth behind Frank's concerns, and that's your job Father. You need to follow up on this myth of some prophecy and the cult association and keep me informed of your progress.'

The Professor knew he had relinquished all further responsibility for Eenayah to his daughter. Mercy had zoomed in like Superwoman and taken full control. He sighed, 'So what exactly do I need to do now?'

Mercy smiled to herself as she recognised the tone of resignation in her father's voice. He made a similar sound when he gave in to her late mother, which was most of the time.

'Okay Father, just to reconfirm. Do NOT call the hospital; that call will come from me as Eenayah's new next of kin. My team will take care of everything else. I understand that Frank intends to introduce you to the former student who wrote the essay about the cult that follows this twin lineage thing – in which case all you have to do is turn up for that meeting and listen carefully to all he has to say about this alleged hidden prophecy. I've taught you how to record using your mobile phone. Secretly record the conversation so I can listen to it afterwards. No need to take notes. Your job, with Frank's assistance, is to find out as soon as possible about the reality of this situation and if a threat to Eenayah or Ruby is real or imagined. That's all you have to do. Nothing more than that. Is that okay with you? Oh and father - get those knees of yours checked out.'

Of course it was okay. Whatever Mercy said was always okay. Deep down the Professor felt uneasy. He suspected that Frank's mind might be simply weaving a fantasy out of a few fragments of evidence. He was concerned that Mercy's mind had been corrupted through her recent experience with an extreme religious cult, whereby a young man had been placed in severe danger. He was concerned that the toxic combination of Frank's imagination and Mercy's zeal could lead to a cocktail mix with a bitter taste.

He was too tired to ask any more or think any more. He was off to bed. He would deal with this megalithic/biblical/criminal mystery tomorrow.

CHAPTER 25

Mercy and her team had acted with lightning speed, but then again she was now in her professional domain and operating without emotion. Such challenges fell well within the comfort zone of her profession. A quirk of fate had placed someone with her aptitude and experience in the time and place where Eenayah needed help, unconscious, vulnerable and as yet unidentified.

As Eenayah lay in her hospital bed darker forces gathered momentum. A warm front colliding with a cold front out in the Atlantic had agitated the British weather like a cocktail in a Boston shaker. As the storm clouds gathered, the tempest made its way towards North Wales. Mercy De Vede pushed up her mini-umbrella and made a dash across the hospital car park just as a torrent of rain drenched her Gucci shoes, which were now making an ugly, sodden squelch as she dashed across the tarmac. She cradled her handbag in her arms beneath her Thornton Bregazzi waterproof coat, protecting her precious cargo of documentation from the rain. Her father had often joked that her gangster trenchcoat made her look like an archetypal detective, but on days like this in wet Wales Mercy was happy to be well covered.

The back office team at MeDeVe had managed to secure their

unconscious wealthy client with a fake ID and matching NHS number, while Mercy now had documentation to prove her connection to a patient who for now had the identity of Polly Johnson. Mercy had no preconceived idea of how easy or hard it might be to falsify the ID of an unconscious person in an NHS facility, but in comparison with other much tougher assignments, she presumed this to be a walk in the park. She seldom allowed herself to wonder where Zac conjured up the false identities from, but suspected in this case that Polly Johnson must be a living person with a real NHS number, possibly no longer a UK resident. She mentally reminded herself to ask him about it when she got back to Oxford. Right here and now she had a job to do. She would need to use all her thespian skills to convince the staff that she was Polly Johnson's sister.

Making her way down the echoing corridors of the hospital, she mused about the fact that in her vocation she mostly tried to find people, and that actually setting out to deliberately hide someone must be a first. However Mercy had an enviable self-belief. Ultimately this was always the killer weapon that won the battle, every time. She had a zero fail rate. By whatever means, Mercy was convinced she would get Eenayah out of this hospital and into an unspecified place of safety until it could be proven that this cult meant her client no harm.

Mercy also recognised within herself that she had been tarnished by a recent bad experience with a zealous and misguided religious cult, and she accepted the professional critique given, be it by herself to herself. The MacDonald boy had gone missing during a family holiday in Greece. After two years with no sighting and no clues, the police had all but given up on the case. MeDeVe had taken it over on a charity basis. They found that the MacDonald boy had been captured against his will, but then brainwashed by his captors to become part of some bizarre following. So compelling and effective were the techniques applied that the boy had even willingly tied his own legs in chains to his bed every evening. It was a highly disturbing case, and had given Mercy a sharp distaste for any group of people who followed any ideology without question. She had tried not to inflict her prejudice on this situation with Eenayah, but the MacDonald case was still too fresh in her mind and she simply had to act upon her gut instincts. In her professional estimation, she was sure that her intended actions to mask Eenayah's identity were appropriate. Eenayah was in danger; she was sure of it.

From the hospital reception she followed the signs for MAU, although there was some initial confusion, as the directions were written in Welsh as well as English. She was met by a buxom grey-haired nurse with rosy cheeks.

'Can I speak with Sister Merandi please?' she asked.

The nurse responded in singsong Welsh, 'I am so sorry but she is off duty, can I be of help to you my dear?'

'I understand an unknown lady was admitted to the hospital yesterday. I am a relative of hers. Sister Merandi called me because my phone number was found about her person.'

The nurse appeared to be genuinely delighted. 'Oh, thank God! I am so pleased somebody has claimed the lass. Poor little lost soul. She isn't on this ward any more love, but I'll get a student nurse to take you to where she has been moved'.

Mercy was pleased that she had not attracted any suspicion as yet, and in silence she followed the very chatty student nurse to the High Dependency Unit. She remained quiet, to ensure she did not give the game away. She was met by one of the medical consultants, a Dr Forshaw, who had just completed his ward rounds.

'Good day doctor, I understand an unknown lady was admitted to the hospital yesterday,' said Mercy. 'I am her sister Corrine Woods. Sister Merandi from MAU called me because my phone number was found about her person. I am told she has now been transferred to this unit.'

The handsome young doctor seemed genuinely relieved that a name was about to be put to his anonymous patient. Mercy was worried that she had gone slightly over the top with the evidence she had collated for Eenayah's new identity. She often associated making too much effort with a cover-up. She hoped the nice NHS people wouldn't take the same view, or question the authenticity of her documents. She handed over Polly Johnson's passport, driving licence, medical card and NHS number, and Dr Forshaw was impressed.

'Wow, we don't normally get this degree of co-operation, thank you so much Miss?'

'Miss Woods,' she responded politely, 'but please do call me Corrine. It was no trouble really. When I got the phone message from the hospital it so happened that I was over at my sister's house anyway. I know where she stores all her important files, so before I dashed over to North Wales in a mad panic, I just grabbed what I could, anything that I thought might be important in such cases. Have I managed to bring all you needed, doctor?'

She knew she was talking too much, and she knew it was because she was trying to cover up a huge lie. She warned herself to shut up.

Dr Forshaw was cool and calm; he was also red-hot attractive. He picked up the phone and asked for the ward clerk to collect the paperwork scattered on his desk.

'Thank you Corrine' he said. 'We'll just put these onto the computer system and then we can start to talk about your sister. Quick question first; does she have any medical conditions I need to know about? Is she on any regular medications?'

Mercy gabbled out an almost inaudible answer. 'Erm, no and no. She is a fit healthy woman, Doctor Forshaw.' Mercy acted stupefied, hoping this was in keeping with the abnormality of the situation and was acceptable behaviour for a shocked next of kin. However, and loath as she was to admit it, it was actually the cute doctor with the stunning sky blue eyes and blonde floppy hair who had set her pulse raising and tied her tongue up in a knot.

Mercy De Vede seldom had time for any relationships in her life. Her father presumed she was gay, and she had allowed him to think that as it prevented him from asking her any awkward questions. She did have a butch, controlling manner, which came from a lifetime's experience of working in a hard macho environment, but now she felt herself starting to visibly melt. Mercy De Vede was blushing. Whoever would have thought! She was embarrassed by her own embarrassment.

Dr Forshaw continued, 'Well, it's good news that we don't have any additional conditions to consider. I'll take you through to see your sister in a moment Corrine, but before I do let me talk you through what has happened in the last 24 hours, as it's all been very dramatic.'

'Okay, yes please.' It was a brief reply, but the best she could manage.

'Your sister Polly was found in running gear, so we assume she was out jogging or climbing in the mountains. It seems she fell off a ridge and was spotted by someone out on a mountain bike, most unusually and inexplicably riding in the dark. She really is very lucky to have been noticed at all. We presume she must have been lying there for several hours, as she was suffering from fairly severe hypothermia on admission in A&E. I very much doubt she would have survived the night on that ledge had she been there any longer. Running alone in Snowdonia is a brave and stupid thing to do after heavy rainfall.

'Anyway the assumption is that she slipped off the path, fell down onto the ledge and was knocked unconscious. She had to be airlifted by helicopter, so this was quite a dramatic and expensive rescue.'

Mercy had a feeling that Dr Forshaw was almost castigating her for Eenayah's tomfoolery and wasting of public money, and although quietly agreeing with him, she reflected that Eenayah was an adult and responsible for her own actions.

'I will make sure she knows all of this when she recovers, doctor' she replied. 'She will get a fair ticking off, however in the meantime, what is the damage?'

'Your sister has sustained a traumatic brain injury. She hit her head during the fall and she has a small fracture of the skull. It could have been a lot worse. The fortunate thing is that there appears to be no bleeding in the brain and we suspect that she just has severe concussion. The brain has been bounced about in her skull by the impact and although it's too early to say, right now it just looks to be swollen. None the less it is still concerning to us and we need to monitor her to ensure there isn't any further damage or any subsequent bleeding. We are also treating her for a broken leg and it would appear she has a few cracked ribs. We cannot X-Ray her pelvis due to her condition, however her femur is badly bruised and swollen so we are treating it as a fracture.'

Mercy was shocked. 'What condition?'

Dr Forshaw paused and considered his reply, but he concluded that as her next of kin he had to be open and honest with his patient's sister.

'We run a pregnancy test on every woman of child-bearing age before we rush in with CT scans, X-rays or any teratogenic medications. Your sister tested positive. Did she not tell you she was pregnant?' He paused and awaited a reply, but none was forthcoming. Obviously this was new news to his patient's sister. Feeling slightly awkward about the situation he continued, 'It has presented us with quite a challenge as we have had to treat her slightly differently from the way we might have done otherwise. With minor brain injuries like these, things can seem okay to begin with and then suddenly turn for the worse. Ideally we would have preferred to induce a coma and ventilate her, but with her being pregnant we decided not to risk it.'

Mercy had not expected this. The gorgeous Dr Forshaw had thrown her an unexpected curve ball.

'How pregnant is she exactly?' she asked.

The doctor was confused as to why Mercy was more concerned about her sister's pregnancy than the condition of her brain. 'I have booked her in for an ultrasound tomorrow and we will know more after that' he said. 'Obviously we can't move her yet, so it will be a mobile scan and not as accurate as the more expensive equipment in the ante natal department, but it will give us a rough idea. Her uterus isn't palpable yet, so certainly she is in the first trimester. That's why we have had to be cautious with treatment – we want to avoid damaging the foetus or embryo if we can help it. The HCG levels, that is the pregnancy hormone, are fairly high, so it would seem to be a healthy pregnancy but also I suspect in the very early stages. You may need to warn her family that her risk of miscarriage after such a nasty accident has been substantially increased.

'I'm presuming that Polly hadn't told you about her pregnancy. You seem to be quite shaken by this news. Does she have a partner who needs to be informed about this?'

Mercy wasn't sure what to say, as she was busy trying to assimilate several items of information which seemed to be now jeopardising her plans.

'I suspect she wasn't aware herself Dr Forshaw, or she would have told me. Polly and I are very close. I am taken aback however. To my knowledge she doesn't have a partner, so I'm not exactly sure what to think about all of this. I guess we'll have to wait until she has regained consciousness.'

'Can I ask you another question Mercy? Does Polly normally suffer from nightmares or night frights? You see, at the moment she is not in a medically induced coma because of her pregnancy, as I was explaining to you before. We want to avoid anaesthetising her if at all possible. The best we can do for her for the moment is heavily sedate her so she is in a deep sleep rather than being comatose. We want to rest her brain whilst it is so swollen, and keep any external stimulation to a minimum. However she keeps shaking and behaving as if she's having a nightmare. That's the only way I can describe it. We just need to know if this is common for her, or just something that has happened since the accident. It could indicate a degree of brain damage if this is a recent thing.'

Mercy was at a total loss as to what to say. Eenayah was her client, and although she had conversed with her several times about her marital problems, they had never talked about sleep issues.

'I'm not sure, Dr Forshaw,' she replied. 'As a child she had nightmares, as indeed we all do, but I can't vouch for her sleeping patterns as an adult.'

Mercy was beginning to feel as though she had just dived deep into a murky pond and was now sinking fast. She could be jeopardising Eenayah's recovery by pretending to be her sister and guessing her medical history. She needed to get Eenayah into another care facility as promptly as possible.

'On another subject, Dr Forshaw, all my sisters' friends and family live in London. She is a wealthy woman who could afford private treatment. Is it possible for her to be transferred into a private hospital closer to where she lives?' Mercy suspected she knew the answer before she had even paused for a response. Dr Forshaw smiled in a knowing way, also aware that Mercy knew the answer.

'Ms Woods, your sister has been an inpatient here for less than 48 hours. As a doctor, my gut instinct tells me that she isn't too badly damaged and we'll soon have her back in her running shoes. However you need to consider that she has had a bad fall and has broken her legs and ribs, and she'll no doubt wake up with the headache from hell. As the consultant in charge of her care, I can tell you now that there is no way I can allow her to be moved in the immediate future. She does have a skull fracture, and be it minor, there is always the risk of a brain haemorrhage at this early stage. I'm sorry, but her friends and family will just have to travel up from London to see her if that's what they want to do. However for the moment, it may be best to restrict family visits. We need her brain to rest.'

That was the answer Mercy expected. Her thoughts wandered slightly as she gazed deeply into his blue eyes and tried not to feel too self-conscious. Consultant? He looked too young. Or maybe she was the one who looked too old.

Dr Forshaw reached his hand out for Mercy in an unexpected gesture of kindness, 'Come on, let's go and see Polly now. I'm sure you are dying to make sure she is all in one piece and that we have been taking good care of her.'

Mercy was visibly shocked to see Eenayah lying there, drips in her arm, oxygen hissing up her nose, catheter bag hanging from the bed frame and a patient monitor bleeping away on the wall, spitting out her pulse rate in rhythmic beeps. However Mercy was far more concerned by how much Eenayah had physically changed rather than by the space age medical devices surrounding her. Eenayah bore no resemblance to the preened and glamorous woman who had sauntered in like a model into Mercy's Oxford office a little over a month before. Now, with hair bedraggled and unkempt, nails chipped and wearing an NHS standard nightgown, Eenayah looked like a lost little waif and stray as opposed to the multi-millionaire wife of a famous man. And yet her face, devoid of all make-up and with a little extra fat to plump up the skin, looked younger and prettier compared to her previous heavily-manufactured look.

Dr Forshaw noticed the look of woe on Mercy's face and gave her a comforting tap on the shoulder. 'I'm sorry, it must be hard to see your sister like this. However I'm sure she will bounce back quite soon, so try not to worry too much. Just tell her to avoid running on slippery Welsh mountains in future. Stick to shopping on Rodeo Drive, it's safer.'

With that the young consultant with the impeccable bedside manner and princely chiselled face left Mercy to spend time alone with her supposed sister. Turning one last time, he handed her a card. 'Here is the unit number and my direct line. Call me any time with any questions or concerns you may have, Corinne.'

Mercy quickly scanned the card, not knowing if this was standard medical practice or an invitation. 'Tomas Forshaw - hmm nice name, nice doctor,' she murmured.

As soon as Dr Hunk was out of sight, Mercy hastily left the unit, hoping to leave unnoticed. She wished she could have stayed to play the part of distraught sister to maximum impact, but alas she had too much to do. All the plans had to be changed now.

She called her father's phone, wondering if by now he was with the former theological student of Frank's, unravelling hidden biblical mysteries. He didn't pick up. She hoped this was a good sign. He was either busy with Frank, or had misplaced his phone yet again. She often thought her father fitted the caricature of a mad professor to perfection.

She then made an international call to her friend Katia, who by now would just about be waking up in the Atlanta penthouse apartment of her latest boyfriend. She had a reason. Mercy had rapidly come to realise that she had next to no hope of removing Eenayah from the Welsh hospital any time soon, so she had to explain why Eenayah wouldn't be attending the family reunion party Reed's PA had painstakingly planned next weekend back in Miami. This reunion was important to Eenayah, so Mercy had to find a darn good reason for her client's absence. Rightly or wrongly, she was keen to keep Eenayah's internment in hospital under wraps. Maybe she was being overly cautious, but until her father had time to interview Frank's former student about the alleged Ledanite group, she had no idea how at risk Eenayah might be.

Katia picked up the phone, still half asleep. Before she had time to say hello, she heard Mercy's voice at the end of the line.

'Hey girl, do you fancy getting revenge on a certain blast from your past?'

Katia laughed. 'Well hello to you as well. This can only be my old friend Mercy De Vede. Nobody else in the world would start a conversation with such an intriguing proposal as that. Darling, as always you have my full attention.'

Katia's daddy was an obscenely wealthy Russian oligarch, and Katia herself had been a Soviet supermodel back in the 90s. She had hired MeDeVe's services a few times back in her modelling days, mostly concerning a variety of cheating boyfriends. She had learned the hard way that good looks did not always equate to fidelity. Katia and Mercy had become the most unlikely of friends. It was a case of opposites attracting; Mercy as an industrious ball-kicking career woman and Katia an over-indulged playgirl who did little more than turn up at the best parties on the brightest crimson carpets. They were polar opposites. There were those who considered they were having a relationship, and it amused both women to allow those people to think what they liked. They both loved to play with people's minds, which was maybe why they got along so well.

Mercy described the mission in precise detail and Katia soaked up the particulars with delight, paying gleeful attention to the minutiae of her assignment.

'Mercy darling, I was beginning to get supremely bored here in

Atlanta and now you have saved the day. Yes of course I will make the call. Leave it with me. *Do svidaniya*, my friend.'

Mercy was pleased with the outcome of the conversation, half wishing she had asked Katya to tape her confrontation with the 'blast from the past'. Perhaps she would text her later. This would be a testicle-crunching conversation and one she would simply love to eavesdrop on.

Two last calls; one to Steve and JD to check if they had removed all Eenayah's belongings from Ruby's house and had deposited the obligatory 'goodbye and take care of yourself' note for Darcy. Then a call to Kerry to ask her to find a hotel room in the area. It was the weekend, but Kerry, being the wonderful PA she was, would always take a call from her boss, no matter what the day or time. However, on this rare occasion she didn't pick up, and so unusually Mercy had to make her own sleeping arrangements for the next few days. She sat in her parked car and fired up the internet.

***

The hotel was less than her normal five-star standard, but it was warm, the ambience was comfortable, the bed was divine and the staff friendly, and indeed that was all that mattered. Steve and JD would be joining her later on and as usual they would all put the world to rights in the bar.

As she lay on the sumptuous four-poster bed awaiting news of her team's arrival, Mercy couldn't stop thinking about Eenayah's situation. The last month kept replaying in her mind like a needle stuck on a vinyl record. Her actions in hiding her client's true identity could be perceived as bordering upon criminal. Mercy was anxious to hear about the conversation with Frank's former student, the alleged Ledanite expert. In order to protect Eenayah, she needed to know as much about them and their beliefs as she could glean. Backed up by understanding and knowledge, the team had been able to infiltrate the Prásinos cult in Greece, which was how they found the MacDonald boy. Mercy recognised that this was sometimes a slow process requiring much patience, but in Eenayah's case time was a luxury that was lacking. She briefly contemplated how much of a challenge it would be to reverse all her recent actions if it turned out that the cult didn't represent a threat. She dismissed the thought instantly, deciding to take the view that being over-cautious, and if need be hitting reverse gear, was the wisest course of action.

She then reflected upon the shocking news that Dr Forshaw had dumped onto her shoulders. Eenayah was pregnant! Mercy looked at the calendar on her mobile, mentally counting up the weeks. During their various interviews she had been sure that Eenayah had mentioned that Reed had undergone a vasectomy after his first wife had died. She had sensed a poorly-masked sadness in Eenayah's voice, and although she spoke about her stepchildren with adoration, Mercy could pick up on the subtle undertones reflecting Eenayah's despondency about a motherhood she would never personally experience. She wondered who had fathered this pregnancy, if indeed it could not have been Reed. Eenayah hadn't struck her as the kind of woman who would fool around. Mercy and her team of detectives had been trapping unfaithful partners in their snares for over a decade, and her expertise was such that she could smell a cheat a mile away. Eenayah simply didn't have the smell of a cheat. It was a revelation which baffled her.

It had occurred to Mercy that now she had replaced Eenayah Baratolli with Polly Johnson and was pretending to be her sister, she would be Eenayah's only visitor and expected to visit on a daily basis. Should she go back to Oxford and leave Eenayah in hospital alone? Surely the staff would smell a rat?

She had been so carried away in the moment and the rush of

adrenalin that she hadn't anticipated how this new project would affect her other diary commitments. She shrugged her padded shoulders (Mercy had never really let go of the 80s power dressing trend) and stifled a yawn. She contemplated her next actions, which at this point consisted of a snooze, a meal and a team discussion with Steve and JD down in the bar. However, after a 6 am drive up from Oxford, an afternoon snooze most certainly took priority.

***

At approximately the same time on the same Sunday afternoon, but in a different county, Frank and the Professor were making their way south of Dublin to the mountains of County Wicklow. Frank drove whilst the Professor sat back and enjoyed the passing scenery in all its Gaelic greenness. The Professor had already shared with Frank the alarming news that it was highly probable that Eenayah was the young woman lying unconscious in a hospital somewhere in North Wales. Perhaps whatever had happened to Eenayah was little more than an unfortunate coincidence, but none the less the Professor was concerned that there might be something more sinister behind Eenayah's accident. Even though Luke had made it crystal clear that he couldn't spare them much time, the Professor was still as keen as ever to meet him. They didn't know what they were dealing with here and the team were well out of their depth. Luke might be the key to unlocking the strange situation that was unfolding.

'Tell me about this former student of yours, Frank' enquired the Professor. He was curious to learn more about the background to this visit and how and why this person was reputed to be so knowledgeable about an alleged secret society.

Frank was happy to oblige his friend's inquisitiveness. 'Luke is from a very well-respected indigenous Celtic family who have lived in these parts for generations. They are landowners on a massive scale; in fact many of the farmers around this part of Ireland are probably still tenant farmers working on land owned by Luke's family. They are lovely people, a very staunch Catholic clan, and indeed many of Luke's brothers and uncles are priests. I taught him theology when he was at university in Dublin and Luke was amongst my top students. He was expected to either be a priest or a farmer or maybe a director of the family's estate, but in all honestly, I have no idea which won the day. The last time I spoke with him was well over ten years ago, so he could have gone in any direction. I can't wait to find out. I suspect he became a priest.'

The Professor was beginning to understand. 'So Luke is the former student who wrote the essay about the Ledanite?'

'Yes Roland, Luke is indeed that very person. Back then he was my favourite student. Luke always tried to be the very best at everything he did. Such a dedicated and hardworking lad. I recall that his parents were members of the Ledanite following. Sadly they both died in a tragic accident when he was a teenager. Carbon monoxide poisoning whilst on holiday, I believe. They died in their sleep. It must have been heart-breaking for him and his brothers, but what can you say? It was just an accident – a tragic accident.'

The Professor was puzzled. 'I don't yet know what or who these Ledanite are or what they represent, but are you saying that Luke is one of them?'

Frank wasn't entirely sure he knew the answer. ' All I can recall was that Luke grew up understanding what the Ledanite were about and despite them being akin to a secret society, 'shrouded in an enigmatic cloak of mystery' as he once described it in an essay, he is happy to talk it through with us. I'm sure you will like Luke. He was always a relaxed human being and a genuinely nice guy. I suspect he hasn't changed much. The Luke I knew ten years ago certainly wouldn't pay homage to anything that could be referred to as a cult. He just isn't that person, or certainly he wasn't when I last knew him.'

The Professor continued to dig. 'So, does that mean that Luke is a Ledanite and if not, then why not?'

'From my brief conversation with him on the phone Roland, he says not. Luke was always a rebel and the unconventional black sheep of the family. Bless him, he's an angel, but the Luke I once knew wouldn't necessarily walk any path expected of him.'

From Frank's brief description, the Professor was already beginning to both like and admire this Luke person. He sounded interesting and unusual.

As they wound their way through twisting country lanes which were becoming progressively narrower, Frank gave the Professor some homework to help pass the time, leaving him to focus his attention on driving through lanes meant for carthorses rather than cars.

'Roland, open up my glove compartment and read through Genesis 38. Our time with Luke is limited and I would hate to waste his time by having him explain some basics to us which by now we should be familiar with. As you already know, this meeting was arranged at the last minute and he can't spare us a lot of his time.'

The Professor agreed. 'Of course, I keep forgetting it's Sunday today and I guess that's the busiest day of the week for a priest.'

The Professor removed a bible and as per instruction located Genesis 38, reading it out loud.

'And it came to pass at that time that Judah went down from his brethren, and turned in to a certain Adullamite, whose name was Hirah. And Judah saw there a daughter of a certain Canaanite, whose name was Shuah; and he took her, and went in unto he. And she conceived, and bare a son; and he called his name Er. And she conceived again, and bare a son; and she called his name Onan. And she yet again conceived, and bare a son; and called his name Shelah:

and he was at Chezib, when she bare him. And Judah took a wife for Er his firstborn, whose name was Tamar. And Er, Judah's firstborn, was wicked in the sight of the Lord; and the Lord slew him. And Judah said unto Onan, Go in unto thy brother's wife, and marry her, and raise up seed to thy brother. And Onan knew that the seed should not be his; and it came to pass, when he went in unto his brother's wife, that he spilled it on the ground, lest that he should give seed to his brother. And the thing which he did displeased the Lord: wherefore he slew him also.

'Then said Judah to Tamar his daughter in law, Remain a widow at thy father's house, till Shelah my son be grown: for he said, Lest peradventure he die also, as his brethren did. And Tamar went and dwelt in her father's house. And in process of time the daughter of Shuah Judah's wife died; and Judah was comforted, and went up unto his sheepshearers to Timnath, he and his friend Hirah the Adullamite. And it was told Tamar, saying, Behold thy father in law goeth up to Timnath to shear his sheep. And she put her widow's garments off from her, and covered her with a veil, and wrapped herself, and sat in an open place, which is by the way to Timnath; for she saw that Shelah was grown, and she was not given unto him to wife. When Judah saw her, he thought her to be an harlot; because she had covered her face. And he turned unto her by the way, and said, Go to, I pray thee, let me come in unto thee; (for he knew not that she was his daughter in law.) And she said, What wilt thou give me, that thou mayest come in unto me?

'And he said, I will send thee a kid from the flock. And she said, Wilt thou give me a pledge, till thou send it? And he said, What pledge shall I give thee? And she said, Thy signet, and thy bracelets, and thy staff that is in thine hand. And he gave it her, and came in unto her, and she conceived by him. And she arose, and went away, and laid by her veil from her, and put on the garments of her widowhood. And Judah sent the kid by the hand of his friend the Adullamite, to receive his pledge from the woman's hand: but he found her not. Then he asked the men of that place, saying, Where is the harlot, that was openly by the way side? And they said, There was no harlot in this place. And he returned to Judah, and said, I cannot find her; and also the men of the place said, that there was no harlot in this place. And Judah said, Let her take it to her, lest we be shamed: behold, I sent this kid, and thou hast not found her.

And it came to pass about three months after, that it was told Judah, saying, Tamar thy daughter in law hath played the harlot; and also, behold, she is with child by whoredom. And Judah said, Bring her forth, and let her be burnt. When she was brought forth, she sent to her father in law, saying, By the man, whose these are, am I with child: and she said, Discern, I pray thee, whose are these, the signet, and bracelets, and staff. And Judah acknowledged them, and said, She hath been more righteous than I; because that I gave her not to Shelah my son. And he knew her again no more. And it came to pass in the time of her travail that, behold, twins were in her womb. And it came to pass, when she travailed, that the one put out his hand: and the midwife took and bound upon his hand a scarlet thread, saying, This came out first. And it came to pass, as he drew back his hand that, behold, his brother came out: and she said, How hast thou broken forth? this breach be upon thee: therefore his name was called Pharez. And afterward came out his brother that had the scarlet thread upon his hand: and his name was called Zarah.'

The Professor closed the bible with a firm and audible shut, laid it on his lap, and taking a deep intake of air, pronounced to his friend, 'I am confused. What the heck was all that about?'

Frank smiled perceptively. 'My dear friend, I hope Luke will explain more when we meet him, but in short, the woman mentioned in these chapters was called Tamar. What you have just read concerns a story scripted in the bible about how her twin sons were conceived.

One of these sons, Zarah it is alleged, has a connection with Jeremiah's tomb in County Meath and the hieroglyphics we were looking at recently. There are some interesting myths and legends relating to the line of Zarah and his descendants. Maybe you could ask your researcher Don to pick up on what these are exactly. For all we know they may be totally unrelated to the Ledanite, but the hieroglyphics suggest some connection between the line from her son Zarah, the tomb in Ireland and the beliefs of the Ledanite . Should that be the case, then this is an avenue worthy of further exploration, would you not agree?'

The Professor nodded in agreement, paying minute attention to all that Frank was telling him. He loved a mystery, and this story was become more entrenched in mystery by the second.

Frank continued, 'From what I can remember about Luke's essay, as well as having twin boys, Tamar also had twin daughters much later in life, some say as an elderly woman. I recall Luke writing that this was a story from the bible that was hidden, probably deliberately concealed to all but a select few. I believe that pages were literally ripped from the Old Testament to keep the female twins of Tamar concealed; not just throughout the biblical era, but possibly throughout time. There does exist a prophecy surrounding these female twins of Tamar, who would mark the beginning of a line of twins that would continue throughout many generations until Tamar herself was reborn and then the Royal Princes would be reborn. This is all I can recall from what Luke wrote ten years ago. However when you told me about your client and her family tree of female twins you caught my attention. It all sounded very familiar. Then when we made the connection between the strange markings on the gravestones with Jeremiah's tomb it struck a chord. I recalled Luke's essay and wondered if it was possible that your client might be a direct descendent from the lines of Tamar. If she and her sister are Tamar twins, it could place one or both of them in danger. I am aware that I have dragged you all the way over here on what could be a wild goose chase and I am mindful that your health is not as good as it should be dear friend, but I wouldn't be doing this if it wasn't important. There are just too many things that seem to link together and point to a connection.'

The scenery changed as Frank and the Professor drove out of the open terrain with its hills and dales and into the leafy shade of an ancient forest. The light was immediately subdued as the sunken lane became covered with an umbrella of overhanging flora.

'Are you sure we are going in the right direction Frank?' said the Professor. 'I swear these roads are getting narrower and muddier. Charming as a secluded wood might be, I can't see who other than a hermit would live in a place like this. Where is the parish and its population? I see only trees.'

Frank confessed to being equally concerned. He had anticipated that his ex-student would be living in a quintessential Irish village, next door to some 300-year-old church and facing a typical Celtic pub. Frank could see no signs of a church spire, and what had now become little more than a dirt track seemed to be leading them to pretty much nowhere at all.

Frank looked apprehensive. He confessed to his friend, 'well the satnav says I'm in the right place, so I'm hopeful that we are where we are supposed to be. I wouldn't want to be lost around here after nightfall. I may well have a 4x4, but some of these roads are in very bad condition. I hope we get there soon Roland. I confess to having a slight concern that we may be quite lost.' His concern was understated.

It wasn't what either of the two men had expected when a wooden lodge peeped out from the hedgerow at the end of a tapering shadowy lane, smoke from the chimney becoming visible in advance of the hut itself. Frank proclaimed as much to the Professor, 'I can't believe this! We are either lost or Luke is. From what I recall, Luke grew up in a huge manor house within a vast estate and was raised in the lap of Irish luxury. I would be totally dumbfounded if the heir to the manor lived here. This is certainly not what I expected. It seems that even ten years on, Luke remains to be a young man full of surprises.'

They gingerly approached the humble wooden abode and were met at the door by a tall man who must have been at least six feet five inches in height. He had a cheerful and welcoming demeanour and a shaven bald head. His bare crown shone in the few rays of daylight filtering through the trees, giving the illusion of a halo. He was dressed from head to toe in an orange robe.

He held out his hand. 'You must be Professor De Vede. Welcome, I have heard so much about you.' He then went to hug and kiss his former teacher Frank. 'Father Francis, it was been so long. It is wonderful to see you again. I was so happy to hear from you. Please, do come into my simple woodland home.'

Frank was mildly amused, as well as being quite disconcerted. His reaction was an odd mixture of glee and alarm, mingled with a touch of shock. 'What can I say, my dear Luke? The only thing I should have ever expected from you was the unexpected. From your appearance I take in that you are a Buddhist monk and not the Catholic priest I expected to be greeting me.'

Luke grinned like an Irish version of a Cheshire cat and nodded by way of confirmation. 'You know me all too well teacher, and yet not well enough. Please, come and sit on the balcony and let me bring you something to drink. Are you hungry? I have some homemade veggie lasagne with heaps of grilled cheese and I have made far more than I alone could possibly eat.'

Both men were hungry and thirsty after their long journey and welcomed Luke's kind offer of sustenance. The Professor chuckled softly as they made their way out to the balcony. Melodic wind chimes rang softly with the slightest kiss of a breeze, and the aroma of freshly-burnt incense filled the air. Outside, multi-coloured flags fluttered brightly on the branches. It was most unconventional, by Irish norms.

'So Frank, did you ever anticipate that your favourite Catholic student would become a Buddhist monk?' asked the Professor, who obviously considered his friend's reaction a source of amusement. He struggled to contain his laughter, lapping up the moment. Frank just shrugged his shoulders and ignored his friend's sarcasm, still partially mortified by his student's choice of calling. He changed the subject.

'I take it that this is some sort of retreat. The views from this balcony are incredible, stunning. It has a calm aura don't you think? Very lonely though. I couldn't live here. Too isolated for me.'

Luke re-entered the room, steering an old-fashioned trolley. It squeaked as he pushed it onto the decking, carefully balancing a steaming hot casserole pot, plates, tea cups, cutlery and warm homemade crusty bread with a hot yeast perfume.

'I like to cook, that's when I'm not meditating, walking, praying or teaching,' he said. 'There isn't a heck of a lot more to do out here in the forest.'

Luke noted the confusion on Frank's face. 'You are dying to ask me aren't you Father Francis?'

Frank quickly retorted, 'I am not a practising priest these days Luke, so please call me Frank.'

Luke had caught him out, and Frank instantly knew he had fallen into his trap.

'So Frank, it's okay for you to change but not for me? We are both teachers, and in different ways we both teach the same moral lessons. Try not to be too disappointed with me Father, and I will reciprocate.'

Frank did not want to express his disappointment, but silently he had hoped that his top-performing pupil would have climbed the ladders of success and made his way into the Vatican by now. He had to ask, 'so why and how did you become a Buddhist monk?'

Luke handed out tea and then plates to his guests. 'Well I guess, Father – I mean Frank – having lived through the hostilities between Northern and Southern Ireland and watching Catholics and Protestants attempt to kill one another and then having a brother blown up in Afghanistan by a land mine and then having an uncle killed on a ship in the Falklands war – oh, and a cousin who died in the rubble of New York's Twin Towers on his 30th birthday – I just sort of came to the conclusion that religion should be about love and not about war. So I attached myself to a religion I believe to be about peace and humility and here I am – a Buddhist teacher and a recluse who lives a simple life of love and respect for all things on this earth and everything above and beyond. Even the ant that has just climbed onto the Professor's shoe and aims to shortly makes it way up his trouser leg.'

Luke then sat in silence as his sagacious words sank in, knowing his former teacher completely understood. The Professor looked down at the ant, wanting to shake it off his shoe but by now feeling it might be a socially unacceptable and anti-Buddhist thing to do. He felt quite uncomfortable as he allowed it access to his leg.

Luke broke the silence. 'Please tuck in before dinner gets cold. Maybe we can talk whilst we eat. I really must apologise to you both, but I have some guests staying with me tonight for an evening of contemplation and meditation. I'm aware that you have some questions for me and I will endeavour to answer them as best as I can, but as you are aware this meeting with you was quite a last-minute arrangement. You are both very welcome to stay as long as you wish, but my recommendation is that you should not delay your journey back through the forest until nightfall. The lane back to the main road is pitch black after sundown and there are some nasty potholes in the track. We can meet up again or you can call me if you have other questions, but in the meantime maybe we should make a start whilst we eat. Forgive me, I don't mean to hurry you.'

Without verbally sharing their thoughts and yet knowing what each other was thinking, both Frank and the Professor concluded that for a humble Monk, Luke was fairly assertive and forthright. This confused his two guests who perhaps expected a more placid laid back approach. With mouths full of pasta, they each nodded in agreement.

No words were exchanged and yet each had an understanding. Luke began the conversation. 'Fine, so where do you want to start?'

The Professor jumped in first, remembering to hit the record button on his mobile. 'Thank you for agreeing to speak with us Luke, as well as feeding and watering us. We are both very appreciative, however as Frank has no doubt told you I have a client I have been working with who is a twin of a twin and so on and so forth. Frank and I both suspect that she could be a direct descendant from the line of Tamar. My initial concern is for her safety and so my first and most important question is, will she be under any imminent threat from the Ledanite cult?'

Luke almost started to choke as he tried to stifle a laugh which he was certain would be inappropriate, given the seriousness of the question. He took several gulps of water to stop himself choking.

'My dear Professor, the Ledanite are not a cult or a sect or followers of any one belief system, or indeed from any one culture or nation. They are simply a clan. We are a family of people who descend from the Sheolare tribe of Ireland. Many have since migrated to America, Australia and the USA, so now we could be considered a global family, but we have our roots in the Middle East and a lineage which can be traced back thousands of years into biblical scriptures. Boring as this may sound, most of the Ledanite I know of are middle class, middle aged, sweet and intelligent people from a variety of religions who just happen to believe in the words of the Old Testament and in particular words that have been removed from the bible - possibly in error, but possibly for good reason.'

Frank interrupted. 'Luke, would you happen to have a copy of the essay you wrote for me ten years ago when you were a student of mine? I have only a faint memory of what was written. I suspect you have long since disposed of it after all this time, but if you did happen to still have it, that would be wonderful.'

Reckless as his family often considered him to be, Luke was a hoarder who threw nothing away. After his former teacher's phone call, he had located the essay back in his childhood bedroom at the family home. As he held up the grubby sheet of A4 lined paper, he smiled knowingly at his ex-teacher.

'Of course I have kept my essay Frank. You gave me an A star for this work, and I didn't get too many of those back in the day. Would you like me to read it out to you?'

Neither Frank nor the Professor needed to be asked twice. Luke put on his reading glasses and began.

Dated September 20<u>th</u> 1993 – Essay by Luke O'Toole

It is written that there are four lines of Tamar:

The Line of Pharez, tribe of Pharezzites: From Tamar's union with Judah was born her eldest twin son Pharez. There are 10 generations leading up to the birth of King David. From then until Josiah and the Babylonian exile are fourteen generations. From the birth of Jechoniah until the birth of Christ are fourteen generations. Joseph the husband of Mary (mother of Jesus) was a direct descendent of David's royal line and the line of Tamar. The tribe of Pharez were known as the Pharezzites. They lived in Girgashite, inhabiting the south and south-west of Carmel. It is said that Pharez became the King of Persia.

The Line of Zarah, tribe of Zarahites: Also from Tamar's union with

Judah came the birth of the second twin, who should have come first but for the fact that he was a breech who turned. This fact was signified by a red cord which was placed around his wrist when his hand emerged from the womb before his brother. His tribe were called Zarahites. They felt cheated of their birthright, as they argued that it was their ancestor who was awarded the red cord of the firstborn and not his brother Pharez. The descendants of Zarah removed themselves from Israel soon after the exodus. Indeed the Zarah line of the Judah tribe left Egypt hundreds of years before Moses. It is said that some of the children of Zarah went north to Greece. Others went to Troy, near the Dardanelles (named after Zarah's son Darda). They set sail in the ships of Dan (Dan's tribe). Some settled on the island of Zar-Din-ia - Sardinia, as it is now known. After Troy's fall to the Achaeans, it is said that a group of Zarahites under the leadership of Brutus migrated to Britain. Other Zarahites settled down in Ireland, after living for a time in Spain, where they founded the city of Saragossa (the City of Zarah). By the time of King David, circa 1000BC, a princely clan of Zarahites had become established as Ireland's royal family, ruling part of the tribe of Dan; the Tautha de Danann of Irish legend, which had also settled there.

There is a lost passage from Jahwist scriptures which also tells of Tamar having a second set of twins when she was a much older woman. By the time of her second confinement she was living in Ireland along with the Prophet Jeremiah. In the bible, people seemed to live very long lives and chronology can be confusing. It was not told who the father of these female twins was. The hidden prophecy relating to the female twins has been passed down through the generations by word of mouth; the actual bible scrolls telling of this have been long since lost, or indeed destroyed or hidden. Tamar's female twins are as follows:

The line of Sheol, tribe of Sheolare: Sheol was born the youngest female twin of Tamar and it is said that she was born with magical powers so she could protect her sister, who was allegedly Tamar's clone. It is told that with the passage of time some members of the Sheolare tribe misused their powers and practised the dark arts. However this was not true in many cases and the Sheolare tribe mostly adhered to the role of protector of the line of Tamar and have acted as such throughout thousands of years. The descendants of the line could have male as well as female children. This defined them as being different from the line of Leda-mechadash who gave birth mainly to daughters. Sheol had both a mother and a father, although the father was unknown. It was not Judah.

The matriarchal line of the elder twin called Leda-mechadash does not have a tribe because they are too small in numbers and also because this was mainly a female line of decent; males being a rarity. Leda was the eldest of Tamar's twin girls. When she was born a purple cord was wrapped around her wrist to signify that she was from the sacred female lineage and that she was the one child who would carry the bloodline forward into the next generation. This tradition has been maintained when possible, the first born (the clone) being identified with a purple thread around her wrist. Unlike her non identical twin (Sheol), Leda was a pure genetic copy of her mother Tamar. She also gave birth to twin girls of which only the first born would be an exact copy of Leda and of course Tamar before her. And so it went throughout the generations. Each clone of Tamar only giving birth to one set of twins, of which both would be female and only one being a clone. It was a pattern repeated throughout the passing of time. This defined them as being distinct from the line of Sheol.

Occasionally a Tamar twin of the Leda line would give birth to a second clone, and so the number of exact replicas of Tamar once rose to at least 50 to 60 girls worldwide. This unusual and unique population had increased through hundreds of generations. The numbers have since diminished and now there are only six known Tamar clones in existence. The Prophecy stated that at some point Tamar would take possession of one of the cloned twins when the time and conditions were right. The end of the prophecy itself would be marked by the birth of male twins, presumably Pharez and Zarah reincarnated. One would be born to recreate the messianic line of King David and the other to be a peacemaker and ruler of nations. Together as a joint force, they will free mankind from all evil. This is what the prophecy states.

The Sheolare are a tribe with mixed devotees. Some are what could be referred to as the dark forces, jealous of the favouritism shown towards Leda-Mechadash. It is said that those amongst them who have inherited the magical powers awarded to Sheol can conjure demons to assist them with the destruction of the line of Tamar and Leda. The Ledanite are also of the Sheolare tribe, but could be described as followers of the prophecy and protectors of the Leda line. They live their lives devoted towards defending this line until the twin boys can be reborn and the prophecy fulfilled in its entirety. Some of the Ledanite group have also inherited the mystical powers of their ancestor Sheol, and they can enlist the help of angels just as their more menacing cousins can enlist the assistance of demonic forces.

'That's it gents. This is the essay you remembered from ten years back Father F. Is this at all helpful?'

Frank was delighted. 'Yes indeed Luke. The essay is shorter than I remember it to be, but I guess I must have been mostly impressed with the amount of research that went into it to award you the marks I did. So am I correct in surmising that the role of the Ledanite is one of protector for the proven female twin descendants of the line of Tamar via Leda, and that they don't want any of the lines to end because they are sacred and will one day lead to the reincarnation of Tamar and via her twin boys who may or may not be the reincarnation of Pharez and Zarah?'

'Yes, that's about it in a nutshell Frankie. Nice bit of theorizing. As for answering the Professor's question about any danger surrounding this situation, your client, if she is a Tamar twin, is in danger, but more from the occult as opposed to any sort of cult. The Ledanite exist to guard Tamar's twins and to prevent the line from ending until the twin boys are born again. However there are other forces, evil entities, both of this world and not, who would like to see every line end, and it has to be said that they have very nearly succeeded. The dark forces of the Sheolare have created mayhem throughout history. I was told that the witch of Endor was one such woman. She possessed clairvoyant abilities and I am told was also a descendant of Sheol. Others connected with this tribe being Athaliah, who was Queen of Judah and also the Irish Druid known as Mug. It is amazing how many of these unusual and fantastical characters from legends do connect back to Sheol.'

The Professor was immensely interested in the possible connection with the Tomb of Jeremiah and the unusual markings they observed and so asked the question of Luke. He responded, 'It is said that Jeremiah was told by God that he must prepare to set out towards 'that land which he knew not', see Jeremiah 15:14 I believe. Maybe in a vision, he saw the union of the descendants of the two princesses which was to take place a mere 1,600 years after his journey to 'Yon Far Western Isles that hear the Atlantic roar'. Within 12 months of arriving in Sagunto, it is told that the Prophet Jeremiah, along with Princess Tamar, Baruch, and their companions, boarded at Bilbao and then set sail for Ireland. Is that a good enough connection for you Professor?'

The Professor was elated that a connection with the hieroglyphics had finally been made, along with the news that Tamar herself had travelled to Ireland. He jumped in before Frank had any chance to put his point of view across.

'Luke, if this is such a secret, how do you know about all of this? I am aware of the connection of your parents with this group, but could you explain this to me in more detail?'

'The Ledanite followers go back to biblical times. As groups go, this is an organisation well over 3000 years old. It has many followers of many creeds and it is well organised. There is a hierarchy. Some of the clan are active, but most are not. Some may not even be aware of their own Sheolare heritage. Both my parents (bless their souls) were Ledanite, although fairly low to middle ranking. They used to have meetings at our home every now and then. They did try to involve me, but hey, as Frank would tell you, I was a bit of an insurgent back in the day and to the disappointment of my family I've always had a nonconformist streak, as you can see yourself. I don't follow rules and I wasn't ever going to become part of a tiered assemblage. However I was privy to enough meetings to understand the Ledanite thinking, and that's why you are now here in County Wicklow in a log cabin with a Buddhist monk and eating lasagne in the middle of a forest – I presume!'

Luke smiled to himself, finding comedy in the strange irony which had led him to cross paths yet again with his old teacher. He continued to explain.

'Professor, those that are active followers of this prophecy refer to themselves as Ledanite because they support the Leda line. If you cast your mind back to my essay, you will recall me writing that Leda herself did not form a tribe because she and those that followed after her were incapable of giving birth to males. The same was not true of her sister Sheol and therefore all members of the clan descend from Sheol, as indeed do I. They are a structured and organised secret society – but a clan, not a cult. You can't join them as you can a gym. You need to be born into the Sheolare bloodline. For now, I guess I'm the only link you have to this secret as far as you're aware, although you may be linked in other ways you don't know about. The Sheolare who follow this prophecy and strive to protect it as being the sole reason for their existence are the Ledanite. You may relate to them as being the good guys or protectors.'

Frank asked, 'So am I right in thinking, Luke, that you dismissed joining the Ledanite because you didn't want the mission of protector as being the sole reason for your existence?'

'Correct, dearest Frank. I was a selfish little git wasn't I?'

Frank thought back to the Luke he had once known as a student at Dublin University. The year was 1992. A tall handsome boy strode confidently into his class with all the poise and self-assurance of the landed gentry. He had all the material baggage that came with such blessings; the horses, the polo competitions, the girlfriends and of course the sports car. Frank remembered it well - Vertigo.5 Facelift-Spirit in jet black. The young student with his blonde curls and Caribbean tan was not untypical of the students in Father Francis's theology class. However, despite the many advantages that came with Luke's inheritance, he studied hard and was consistently a top-performing scholar.

Luke kept people at a distance emotionally and it was some time before Frank discovered the hidden story of his family tragedy. As time emerged, so did the realisation that this young man carried a lot of weight on his designer-clad shoulders. As the eldest in the family, he had the job of maintaining the dynasty of a large family estate. Few were aware that this carefree student by day was a CEO by night and at lunchtime, and sometimes in between lessons. Of course, once Frank knew this of his young student, his admiration for his courage and work ethic was beyond compare.

However Luke had another side to his yin-yang life. The tattoos on his arm, his Harley-Davidson FXSTC 1340 and his tendency to camp out at rock concerts between taking conference calls with the estate manager gave a glimpse of another side of the young Luke. Frank smiled to himself as the memories drifted back. Luke was anything but a normal Joe Average. Why should he now be surprised that Luke was now a Buddhist monk living in a forest? Why should he also not be shocked by Luke's decision to reject a lifetime of servitude to a 3000-year-old prophecy? The ex-priest was jolted back into the moment as his former student continued with his account.

'The last meeting of the Ledanite I attended I would say I was about 15 years old. I recall some of the discussions, but to be fair I paid little attention. I had already decided by then that I didn't want to be a part of the Tamar protection gang. However I do remember hearing that there were many sets of twins globally who were protected under the Ledanite shield as probable direct descendants. I say probable, because as you know DNA testing is a fairly recent science. The Tamar twins, as a set of people, historically have not been too fertile. I guess that if they were that successful at reproducing themselves the world would be full of Tamar clones and obviously that would be silly and quite worrying for the rest of us.

'However, as I mentioned earlier, every now and then a twin fires off two clones. From what I can recall I think there are about 12 sets of twins, of which I guess six are presumed to be Tamar clones. There could even be less than that now. I think that in the early 1900s there were about 20 sets of twins, so they haven't done too well as regards survival. They seem to be a diminishing breed. If these twins were a species in their own right, as some believe them to be, you may regard them as in danger of extinction.'

Frank was as enthralled as his Professor friend and felt the need to jump in and beat the Prof to the question as soon as Luke paused for breath. They both had so many questions and yet so little time.

'Luke, I think we are jumping ahead of ourselves,' said Frank. 'Can we go back to the beginning? Can you explain what the missing biblical prophecy means, as far as you are aware?'

Luke agreed. 'We don't have a lot of time so yes, that makes more sense. I'll try to keep it simple. I'm sure a bit of internet research can fill in some of the gaps. However, going back far into deep history, much of this begins with a division between two kingdoms in the Holy land. Judah was part of the Sceptre tribe in Israel. This meant that the line of kings was destined to come from Judah. The genetic heritage did prove to be factually correct as the monarchy did indeed come from Judah. King David was a descendant of the first born twin, Pharez, as my essay stated. King David was referred to as having a holy line for good reason. As well as Solomon who is the ancestor to Jesus's father Joseph, few people realise that he also had a son called Nathan, who it is said was the ancestor of the Virgin Mary. King David's other son, Zedekiah, was the ancestor of the kings of Ireland. None of this is classified information. I'm not telling you anything a theological researcher would not be able to tell you and I'm sure that you already know much of this Frank, but how true it is or if it can be proven, who knows?

'However what appears to be factual is that both the Virgin Mary and her husband Joseph did have a common shared ancestor and she was called Tamar, or at least that is the theory. Tamar was therefore an important biblical female and some may debate that there was a good reason that her pure bloodline be protected so she can be reincarnated, should that ever be possible. As a genealogist this should be right up your street, Professor.'

The Professor was almost stunned into silence, and yet he wanted to make the most of his short time with Luke. It was a lot of information to take in. Glancing out from the balcony, he noted the sun was low in the sky and as well advised by the concerned host, they really did need to make tracks before nightfall and before the concealed pothole monsters of the lane played havoc with the car's suspension.

The Professor asked, 'so for clarification, are we are talking here about Jesus having had an earthly body which had a direct genetic connection leading back to one woman, Tamar, and that all the lines of Tamar come from four children, twin boys and twin girls, but only one - that of Leda-Mechadash - was the pure blood of Tamar and held a sacred line of descent into which at some stage Tamar will be reborn. Is that what the prophecy says?'

'Pretty much,', responded Luke.

Both the Professor and Frank fell into a trance-like state, captivated by the emerging story. As a theologian, Frank had heard some of these bible stories before, but the tale about Leda and Sheol and the biblical link to Ireland had been news to him, even as a much-respected lecturer in the subject matter.

Luke continued with his tale. 'I'm trying to trim centuries of history down into a few sentences, and that's quite a challenge. Basically many of Tamar's descendants left Israel after bondage in Egypt. If you study the scriptures you can see evidence of the tribal genealogies as recorded in the Old Testament. You will note that the direct lines of descent from Pharez were documented in detail over a very long period of time. However the record of the descendants of Zarah apparently and mysteriously ended with the third generation and then vanished from the records totally. I guess maybe the reason for this is that they quit the Holy Land.'

The Professor knew nothing about these chronicles and he had become more engrossed with every word. He was fascinated. 'How did female twins enter into this male-dominated equation, and why was their birth hidden and evidence of their existence destroyed? I don't understand how could Tamar could be fertile as an old woman?'

Frank responded before Luke had time to retort. 'God moves in mysterious ways, Roland. Abraham was 100 and his wife Sarah was 90.'

'Frank is correct,' said Luke. 'The bible is full of people who lived an unnaturally long time and gave birth late in life. As for how this could happen, the details are vague, but it seems that a high priest from the Levitical Priesthood granted Tamar a spiritual wish. It was her desire to give birth to twins, but this time around it was to be female twins. She was an old woman at the time of giving birth and many years past childbearing age. For this to happen as it did was probably akin to a miracle, or maybe there are those would say a curse. Tamar could see the kingdoms dividing and witnessed the hostility between her twin sons. She asked to be born again of the same soul and same body so she could right what was wrong in the future. The die was cast and the spell activated. In modern-day terms, Tamar basically cloned herself.

'Why female twins in a male-dominated society, you asked? Well, quite simply a man cannot clone himself, or at least he couldn't do 3000 years ago. We males lack the extra X chromosome. However a woman has all she needs in having both X chromosomes. Perhaps these days and with modern technology one just has to put a mouth swab in a petri dish and watch it grow, but back in history and doing things the old fashioned way, only a woman would have the power to basically give birth to herself. Obviously a man would need a partner and so this gives women a genetic advantage. Of course a clone is an undiluted string of inheritance that is passed down uncontaminated. I know that as I tell you all of this it must seem quite weird and unreal. I recall how baffled I was when I was first told.'

Luke paused to chew on his cold lasagne, surveying the looks on the faces of his stunned audience. He wondered if perhaps he was telling them too much and seemed too much of an authority on the subject. Surely they would realise he had been raised by Ledanite parents. He hoped so.

He continued, 'I am aware how all this must sound to you, but there are lots of people who believe all of this to be true. Tamar was ultimately the carrier of the seed which created King David. That is what the Ledanite followers have believed throughout history. The twin boy Zarah was an ancestor of many of the kings and queens of Scandinavia and France as well as some Cretan, Trojan and Milesian kings. Many a royal family can trace their roots back via Zarah and his mother Tamar. However all three lines of descent are mixed with the lineage of many thousands of other incidental ancestors, aside from the pure bloodline of Leda. This was a long time ago, my friends. Sadly women didn't carry much weight, biblically or otherwise, back in that period. The legacy of her second set of twins was easier to hide because they were female. Sadly girl babies were of lower value and records not often kept. I'm sure you have found that with genealogy, Professor.'

The Professor nodded in agreement. Female lines were a challenge for every such researcher.

Frank was growing increasingly curious. 'So what part of this ancient prophecy can we can relate to our modern day 21st century life, Luke?' he asked. 'I suspect that what my professor friend needs to walk away with in this short time we have with you is how he can best help his client, who appears to have all the signs of being a Tamar twin.'

Luke appeared less confident with his reply to this well-chosen yet awkward question.

'The twins who are the direct descendants of the line of Tamar and Leda-Mechadash are in an odd predicament. In one sense, they need to be hidden and kept secret for their own safety, yet in another sense, they need to be known about to also be protected. Your client may well be one of only six clones surviving, so a lot rests on her modern-day shoulders. I'm sorry, but this is fairly heavyweight stuff. I understand that modern-day Ledanite followers believe that one twin would be conceived by a normal method of fertilisation which would then create enough hormones to stimulate a complete cloned egg to be released by means of asexual reproduction. It's only a theory, but it has been given as the reason why only one of the twins would be a clone and not both. Only the genetic carbon copy of Tamar has the ability to clone. I have heard it told that some believe that this ability to reproduce asexually is a rare chromosomal mutation which may accommodate an immaculate conception. Hence why this rare genetic mutation must be passed along the generations in a pure state. The Ledanite believe that to destroy this lineage would be to destroy the second coming of the Messiah. It is indeed a very serious and controversial belief. Those who totally adhere to this prophecy would dedicate their lives to protecting any Tamar twins, while those with evil intent would do all they could to harm them, or at least prevent them from conceiving. The reduction in their numbers could suggest that the powers of evil may be winning the battle.'

The Professor paced up and down, trying to ingest all he had heard. 'So if I'm hearing you correctly, this prophecy is all about Tamar being physically reborn as a clone throughout thousands of years of history, with an end conclusion that one day Tamar manifests in totality and gives birth to the twin sons who then lead once again to a repeat of King David's holy line. Also, you said that the secrecy of the twins was an odd predicament. I know we are taking up way too much of your time Luke, but what do you mean by that statement?'

Luke was impressed with the Professor's synopsis. 'Without doubt your client will be in need of protection. Professor, I don't know how far you have dug into your client's past, but I'm sure you will find that the line of ancestry will suddenly die on you and you'll reach a point where you will simply be unable to get beyond. Walls will come up and doors will shut in your face. Births, baptisms and deaths may go unrecorded just so the devil's hounds lose the scent of the chase. However the conundrum is that although the twins of Tamar must remain hidden, they must also be followed and protected by the

Ledanite and therefore they also need to be exposed. Discreet signals will be given. There are cyphers, symbols and signs which can only be understood by those who understand.'

With that Luke glanced at his watch and then looked at the forest. The setting sun was throwing a light shower of delicious orange through the clearing of the trees.

'Gentleman, time is running short for us and my students will be with me soon,' he went on. However I can share this with you. Be aware that my parents and the other followers they met with all knew about the tragic Green girls and by now I have surmised that you are aware of them. They died about five years before I was born. I recall meetings when my parents and the others discussed them. Frank, on the phone you mentioned the hieroglyphics you found on the headstones. It was not the family of the deceased who carved these markings. The family knew nothing about any of this other than casual hearsay passed down the generations. The carving was supposed to be discreet and not obvious to those who didn't know where to look. It was a former Ledanite who left the message for future Ledanite, by way of a signal to any forthcoming followers to say 'here lies the body of a child of Leda'. For a twin connected to the Irish line the symbols of Jeremiah's tomb were used. Another county might use other symbols which would mean something personal and specific to them. Perhaps Australian Ledanite use Aborigine symbols, for instance. The markings are nothing more than a message to the future, so that even if paper records are not kept or maybe lost with time, the ones carved in stone can always be found.'

So far the Professor had been totally discreet in protecting the identity of Eenayah, only ever referring to her as his client, even with his most trusted friend Frank. He was also conscious that the entire conversation was being taped for his daughter Mercy and therefore he had to be politically correct or risk a ticking off. As such he was shocked to hear that Luke, who he had only met for the first time a few hours ago, knew the surname of Eenayah's birth mother. He had presumed that her identity was safe, but now he realised that the Ledanite most probably knew all about Ruby and Eenayah, and if the good guys knew of their existence, then so must the bad guys.

The Professor had to reconfirm this with Luke, all the time recording the conversation for his daughter, who had taken it upon herself to adopt the new role of protector.

'Luke, you mentioned the Green girls,' he said. 'Did the Ledanite know all about them as in where they lived, grew up - died?'

'Yes, my parents knew of them. As I mentioned earlier, they died years before I was born, but I heard their names mentioned many times. If my memory serves me right their names were Daisy and April. I understand they were very poor and their situation was incredibly sad and the clone was unusually young in this instance. The children went for adoption and the Ledanite lost sight of them for a while due to the rules and regulations surrounding adoption. The Ledanite are just people like you and me Professor, and need to jump through the same legal hoops. After the age of 18 it is probable the followers would have located them, but so would those who would wish to harm them, or prevent the one who is the clone from reproducing.'

Neither Frank nor the Professor knew what to say next. They had expected some degree of intelligence from Luke, but they hadn't expected anything like the detail he had given them so openly and willingly.

There was a knock on the door and Luke left them for a moment whilst he showed his students into another room. The two ashen faced friends looked at one another in disbelief.

The Professor spoke first, in a soft whisper so as not to be overheard.

'Oh my God Frank, he knew the name of Daisy Green. To me he

has as good as told us that the Ledanite did carve those hieroglyphics on her headstone. As we suspected, my client must surely be a clone candidate. I'm sorry I have not named her in person to you so far Frank, but I was trying to adhere to client confidentiality and data protection rules. My daughter beats me up if I don't comply with official guidelines. However, all of that aside, we seem to have an authentication that my client is a Tamar-Leda twin. I just need to know what to do next as that daughter of mine will expect a full agenda of next steps following this meeting. I honestly think I am getting too old for all this. In all my life I never expected to ever be involved in something as surreal as this.'

Frank agreed and whispered back, 'Same here my friend. What Luke has just disclosed to us almost seems too bizarre to be true, and yet it seems to be true. Quick question before Luke gets back – but what about your client's twin, the sister we haven't really spoken about yet. Could she be the clone?'

The Professor answered whilst they were still alone, and again with the same surreptitious whisper. 'My client and I discussed this in detail when we were trying to locate her birth mother. Her sister had peritonitis as a teenager, which damaged her reproductive organs. She has an adopted son. We need to ask Luke the question before we leave, but if one of the twins is rendered infertile, could they still be the one who is the clone? I do think we need to establish this Frank, as I need to know for sure which twin may be in danger, now that we have established they are highly likely to be Tamar-Leda twins.'

Luke joined the two friends back on the patio, turning on the oil heater now that the dying sun had given way to the chill of dusk. 'I am so sorry my friends. I may be a Buddhist monk earning a meagre living by way of survival, but even I have to find a way to fill my stomach, and my fee-paying students have just arrived. I'm sorry to cut this short, but I'm always on the end of a phone, so please call me with any questions you may have. I am expecting many calls from you, so please do not feel inhibited in any way.'

As they stood up to leave with a degree of reluctance, the Professor felt compelled to get in a few last questions. He believed that Luke still knew much more than he had actually been able to share with them in such a restricted time frame.

'Luke, quickly before we go – just a couple of things. The twins we have been involved with, one of them has been infertile from childhood but has an adopted son and the other presumably could be fertile but is married to a husband who has had a vasectomy. So who is the clone, when neither of them can reproduce?'

Luke guided his friends towards his rudimentary front door and looked down at the primitive stone floor as though in deep thought. 'From what I understand, this is not a biological dilemma as such but more of a spiritual one. My parents' group studied the various lines of Tamar twins in different countries and throughout the centuries, and it has always been obvious who the clone wasn't rather than who the clone was. Typically the non-clone either died in childhood or was infertile, or just gave birth to sons who were not twins or just had singleton births. The clone, from what I can recall, was usually healthy and fertile and the golden rule seemed to be that she could only have twins and these would only be girls. This seems to be the defining rule which gives the game away. With the Green girls, the clone was always considered to be Daisy, as I understand that her sister April had some birth-related brain damage. How old is your client, Professor?'

The Professor pulled out a grubby, well-fingered notebook from his inside pocket and flicked through the pages. '38, soon to be 39, I believe Luke'.

Luke replied as best he could. 'From all the many discussions my parents and their Ledanite group were involved in and certainly the ones I was privy to, I would say 100% that any twin rendered infertile

SHEILA MUGHAL

could not be the clone. This leads to the twin with the partner who has had the snip as being the prime candidate. To coin a phrase from the bible, Genesis 38, Tamar's second husband was said to have 'spilled his seeds on the ground', and this was why she couldn't become pregnant. In modern-day terms, this could equally equate to the 21st century version of wasted male fertility as in with a man who had undergone a vasectomy. However, note that this didn't stop Tamar getting pregnant, as she simply found another father for her children. She was impregnated by her father in law, and that's a bit creepy, but none the less she got around the problem.

'I do know one thing about the psychology of the Ledanite which may be useful to you. There are very few Tamar twins left in the world. The Tamar lines are as precious as the entire world's collection of gold and diamonds put together and multiplied by a billion. The lines will not be allowed to die out - not at any cost. If your client is almost 39, then she is coming towards the end of her fertility. The Ledanite will do whatever it takes to ensure she becomes pregnant soon, and the dark forces will do whatever it takes to prevent such a pregnancy. She probably isn't even aware that she is caught up inside a war zone.'

The Professor concluded that Eenayah must be the clone, and without naming any names he was fairly sure that Luke already knew her identity, although he was being discreet about his knowledge.

'But Luke, what if my client is faithful to her husband?' he asked. 'How then can she become pregnant in order to continue the line?'

Luke found the answer came to him easily. 'By deception, my friend. What happened in the bible will happen again in the future. The past becomes the present. Tamar became pregnant - not by her second husband, but by deception. The same will happen to your client. The Ledanite will not allow yet another line to be extinguished on the mere technicality of a man who has spilled his seeds. If it takes an act of deception, then so be it. Knowing them as I know them, this

380

will be their view. Remember what I have told you, 'The Tamar-Leda line is as precious as the entire world's collection of gold and diamonds put together and multiplied by a billion'.

'So if my client is a clone of Tamar, how much of a threat is she under?' The Professor knew he was becoming an irritation and that Luke had visitors waiting, but he needed to know how to deal with the present situation.

'With Tamar twins, the one who is not the clone will be identified as soon as possible, but sometimes this may not be for many years and sometimes only when their childbearing days are over and all they have produced has been either single pregnancies or sons. The normal twin would never be in any danger, as they do not carry the mutant gene which allows cloning to occur. Once this normal twin has been identified, of course they would not be under threat. Frankly, the other twin would be considered useless. Heartless as this sounds, their only function after conception was to provide the hormonal conditions of pregnancy for the cloned egg to be released. Beyond that, the other twin has no purpose. As for the clone, once identified she would always be in jeopardy until she has either given birth to the next set of twins, and therefore completed her part of the contract, or she is no longer fertile. Professor, as long as your client is able to conceive and pass on the precious DNA of a holy line there are those who will want her harmed. As soon as she hits the menopause, she is no longer of interest to anybody.'

The Professor pushed for a more detailed answer. 'Who would harm her, Luke?'

By now Luke was on the shale pathway outside the lodge and walking the elderly men to their car. He had begun to feel very guilty at having to cut the conversation short, but he had other commitments and was running late for his group meditation session.

'There are always evil people in the world, as you well know

Professor. I am not sure if they are organised into a group as such, but there are individuals of the Sheolare tribe who are able to call upon the power of demons to assist them. Please understand that this is why the Ledanite followers are so important. For centuries they have been fighting the dark forces who are out to destroy this line, and they even have mystical powers of their own that they can utilise, and the odd angel they can evoke. This is a fight between man, beast and seraphs. It is best that you leave your clients' safety to the people who know what they are doing. It will take more than 21st century technology to help your Tamar twin. Trust me, it will take a form of sorcery so powerful that even I cannot imagine it. You can be assured that the Ledanite will have been surveying your client and will have been monitoring them from the second they knew they existed. Usually this would be from childhood, but in this case it was probably a lot later in life due to the adoption process and the confusion that resulted from this. Your twins were lost from the system for quite a number of years, I know that much.'

The Professor asked his final question. 'How can we tell who are the good guys and the bad guys?'

'I am sorry to say you can't,' replied Luke. 'The Ledanite clan are everywhere and could be family, friends or neighbours, but these watchers are there to protect them at all times and will be discreet in their presence. They may even have wrapped themselves up in a guise of friendship, but whatever the façade, they will be close by. The forces of evil will try to trip them up and will become more active should the clone ever become pregnant. All the mighty forces of hell and the underworld would try to prevent a new clone from being born. Their mission is to prevent yet another Tamar clone and the seed of David from being passed onto a new generation. However, be assured that the Ledanite exist to prevent this from happening and are dedicated to protect the line of Tamar. Your twins should be secure soon. From what you have said, it seems they are the end of a line unless the clone conceives.

'One other thing, just by way of a caution. The Tamar-Leda twins only ever have other female twins. It is told that when Tamar reappears on earth in soul as well as the physical body, it marks the rebirth of the male twins, and I suspect that should such a male twin pregnancy ever occur, every demonic force in the universe would be activated to prevent the birth. However, as long as your clone is married to a man who doesn't want any more children and she remains childless into menopause, she is assured of a long healthy life. I hope that helps by way of assurance.'

The Professor let out a long and weary sigh and shook Luke's hand. 'Phew, what can I say? It has been a lot of information to take in, but thank you for being so candid and forthright. Unlike you and Frank, I am not a religious man and I struggle to believe in the whole spiritual good versus evil concept. However I do know that any faith of any creed becomes real as long as there are people who believe in it, and if there are people out there who believe in this story, then my client could be in jeopardy. We have much to discuss on the long road back to Dublin. Thank you for the lasagne, by the way. You really are an excellent cook Luke. Goodbye and God bless.'

Frank took one last look up and down the orange robe of his favoured pupil. 'I was so convinced you would be a Cardinal by now, Luke,' he said. 'I'm gutted! However, whichever way you chose to express your spirituality, you are a good man, and I am sure that whatever you preach, no matter what robe you wear or what religion you profess to be, you will do a grand job. We are all the same really. The best of luck with everything, my dear Luke, we must stay in touch.' With that he gave him a warm, manly embrace that came from the heart.

They proceeded to leave Luke's forest retreat whilst there was still some rays of light squeezing through the thick leafy forest cover.

The Professor still had one more question from the car. 'Apologies Luke, one final final question if I may, but my daughter Mercy would string me up if I didn't ask this. If our client is a clone, is there anything else we need to look out for or be aware of?'

Luke walked over to the open car window. 'Tell your daughter that any threats to your client's safety will increase if she becomes pregnant. That danger increases greatly if the clone shows signs of having similarities to Tamar, and therefore could be not just a physical clone but a spiritual re-embodiment. If such a clone became pregnant with male twins as opposed to females, this would signal the official end of Tamar's line and lead onto the restoration of King David's holy line. Tamar's work will have been completed once this prophecy has been concluded. It hasn't happened in the last 3000 or so years, but it will happen one day. Remember, the clone becomes safe once her twins are born, as generally speaking, she would have no further twins. She is therefore not under any threat after childbirth. If she is pregnant, the Ledanite have nine months by which to guard her.'

'History suggests that each clone only produces a single clone as part of a twin pregnancy. She doesn't seem to shed more than one complete egg other than in rare circumstances. So once she has had her twins, she has done her job and can be left alone to have a long and healthy life. It is best to leave the protection of the clone to the Ledanite. They have centuries of experience and powers that are only known to them. They are the ones best equipped to deal with both the mortals and non-mortals who have a desire to end Tamar's lines. I would warn you not to take on the job of protector, it could become more of a hindrance than an asset.'

Luke waved them goodbye. 'Good luck. I will pray for you all and for the long lives of all the lines of Tamar.'

The two friends travelled back down the forest dirt track in silence, as though muted by all they had heard. Frank was absorbed in picking his way around the variety of potholes, which were harder to view in the reduced light, and the Professor was busy playing with his phone and trying to figure out how to send Mercy a recording of the conversation. He was so pleased that she had suggested recording Luke, as he was sure that it would be a far too complex dialogue for him to repeat accurately.

After ten or so minutes the Professor finally spoke.

'I have to say Frank, that was by far the most bizarre experience I think I have ever encountered. I need to get Wi-Fi so I can email Mercy the recording and get her take on this. We should catch up once she has had a chance to listen to it. You know Frank, I don't believe in all this heeby-jeeby spiritual stuff, but Luke seems convinced that all this is for real and that scares the pants off me.'

Frank didn't answer immediately, but after some thought he asked, 'Roland, I know your client shared a lot of personal information with you and Don when you were collecting information for both her genealogy projects, as well as helping her trace her biological family. Would you say that's true?'

The Professor had no idea where this was leading to, but nodded in agreement.

Frank asked, 'How many times has she been married?'

'Twice, as far as I am aware', replied the Professor.

'Were her husband's brothers by any chance?'

'Oh my God no, of course not. No, most certainly not – where are you leading with this?'

Frank replied, slightly disappointed. 'Hmm, just a shot in the dark. Tamar was also married twice, but her husbands were brothers. Just trying to work out if any parts of your client's life bore similarities to Tamar's, but from what you have told me it seems not. That's a relief, I guess. Beer and bed – let us make tracks my friend. My brain can take no more.'

Having been preoccupied with their interrogation of Luke, both men had failed to notice that no other cars were parked along the shale driveway outside his log cabin. Neither had they seen or heard any sign of his supposed visitors.

As they drove out of the forest and into the clearing, Frank commented, 'Luke told us a great deal, but he knows more than he is saying. I recall that essay being much longer. I would not have awarded an A star for something so brief. He is holding something back.'

CHAPTER 26

Monday 15th July

Reed sat cupping his head in his hands as though his mind was too heavy to rest comfortably on his shoulders. His sister-in-law and her sweet but noisy family had arrived back from their week in Disneyland, full of adrenalin and still in theme park mode. Young Harry was playing at being an aeroplane landing on a runway along the mansion's long cream marble hallway, and Roserie was joining in the fun by pretending to air traffic control.

Reed hadn't been around young children since his own kids were babies, and even then he hadn't exactly been a hands-on father. The hullaballoo of his excited guests disturbed him. He normally worked from his home office on Mondays, but in need of peace and tranquillity, he had opted to work from his Miami studio today. He had hoped to acquire inspiration for some new songs, but his thoughts had been scrambled like cracked eggs.

He looked wistfully at Eenayah's picture, deliberately perched at a slight angle on his desk. He picked it up and gazed upon her exquisite dark Eastern features. It occurred to him that he hadn't seen or spoken with his wife in quite some time. Being honest with his conscience as only one can be, Eenayah had not even entered his thoughts all that often. She was due back home tomorrow and he hadn't given her return much consideration.

He looked at the calendar on his phone. It was June 9th when she had left Miami for her UK pilgrimage. It was now July 15th. It was only three weeks since he had last been with her on the Isle of Man, but that reminiscence now felt like somewhere and something long ago and far away. It had been a magical moment and maybe one he could tap into. He recalled finding Eenayah sitting beneath the old oak tree which had been her teenage confidant as she grew up on the island. That tree knew all her little girlie secrets. Reed had actually serenaded her with his guitar, singing *Fields of Gold*. The unplanned romantic gesture had even taken him by surprise. It had been a beautiful sweet summer's day and there had been the subtle perfume of wild flowers wafting through a light breeze. Looking down into the valley and beyond the yellow fields of Brassica, the village below had been tinted with pink and white rendered cottages and thatched roofs. Eenayah called it a 'memory to put in your pocket for later'.

Reed liked that memory. It was warm and like a romantic fairy tale. Pure escapism. He began to turn the memory into music, strumming on his guitar as the beginnings of a melody started to form a song. Reed was not thinking about Eenayah now. He was simply using the memory for profitable purposes. To some people it may have appeared as cold and calculated, but Reed often reminded them that he made music for money. It was his job; a career. With Machiavellian precision, he would use whatever he needed to use to get whatever he wanted to get.

The phone rang. His receptionist was on the other line. 'I have Alexia Towers on the line for you, Mr Baratolli. Are you free to take the call?'

Reed was annoyed at being disturbed in the midst of a creative moment, but Alexia Towers was his accountant and right at this moment, one of the more important members of his entourage.

He answered the phone. 'Alexia, where the fuck have you been? I've been expecting a call from you for over a bloody week now. Have you managed to hide some of my assets? How is the Vanuatu transfer going on? I'm on a fine time line with this Alexia. As you know, my wife is back in the US tomorrow.'

There was a hushed silence at the other end of the phone as Katya did the best she could to repress a laugh. 'Hello Reed, long time no speak!'

Reed was like a rabbit caught in the headlights. He knew instantly that it wasn't Alexia Towers on the other end of the line, but he didn't have a clue who the impersonator could be. The voice was unfamiliar. Who else knew that Alexia was managing his finances? Had he said too much – given too much away to a stranger? Had Arabella become too close to his banking affairs and betrayed him? Reed was not normally a nervous man, but now the self-assured music mogul was understandably feeling on edge. On the other hand, Katya was cool, demure and irritatingly smug.

She continued, 'Let me jog your memory Reed. How many Russians do you know in Atlanta?'

There was no reply. Reed couldn't think of anyone he knew in Atlanta. Katya was leading the dance.

'Okay, let me jog that idiotic brain of yours some more, Mr B. Think back to Christmas 2012 and Acre's last tour date. You were at the after-party in Manhattan. Admittedly you were drunk, but following me into the ladies' toilets and trying to molest me was slimy and low even for your gutter level standards. I could have had you arrested. You were lucky Reed, I let it go.'

Reed now recognised the American drawl with the slightest hint of Moscow enunciation.

'Katya Beselovaya, Soviet bitch supreme! What the hell do you want after all this time? Has daddy run out of money? Do you need a cheque to buy your silence?'

Katya had expected this reaction. 'Just how many women have you bought off, Mr Baratolli? My God, your chequebook must be hotter than the coals of hell. I suspect your solicitor has made a fortune in gagging orders alone. However, my dear, you must surely realise that I am well out of your league. I have more money in my plastic piggy bank than you can count in your entire offshore portfolio. You know what I'm talking about – all that alleged money you are hiding from your wife. Put your pen and cheque book away, sweetheart. You couldn't afford me anyway.'

Reed was gobsmacked. The blood drained from his face, his skin became ashen and his palms were sweaty. He vaguely knew of Katya as a socialite, a rich Soviet party girl with numerous boyfriends and the occasional girlfriend, but Reed had only met her once or twice. They didn't normally mix in the same circles. Katya hung around with some dodgy people; gangsters, drug barons and affluent contacts from back home in the Arbat-Kropotkinskaya area of Moscow. Reed would never dare entwine himself in the strange underworld Katya frequented.

His mind drifted back to the party she had referred to. He had been tired that night, and lonesome at the bar, he had knocked back too many tequila shots. Katya was a flirt and he had misread the signals. Foolishly he had made the incorrect presumption that she was easy meat. As she walked into the ladies' toilets he had followed her. They were alone and when she walked out of the cubicle he had grabbed her breasts. He recalled that she slapped him and in his drunken state of mind he had mistaken this for rough Russian foreplay. He had chauvinistically assumed that every woman of a certain age was a *Shades of Grey* devotee.

It had been a gigantean error of judgement. As he continued to attempt to kiss her and pull off her underwear, Katya did some sort of martial arts manoeuvre on him which had him rolling around the floor and clasping his groin in agony. The scalding pain had an immediate sobering effect, and once he had realised exactly what he had done, he crawled over to Katya to apologise. She stooped to his level and slapped him across the face. He recalled that it wasn't a soft lady slap, but a powerful whack which left his cheek stinging hours later. He had expected some sort of reprisal afterwards and braced himself for retribution for weeks later.

Reed knew that Katya's father was one of richest men in Russia and that unlike others, she would have no financial requirement to blackmail him for money. Bribery was out of the question, as Katya didn't need anything Reed could possibly offer her. However he did expect some sort of punishment. For months afterwards he lay low and increased the number of security guards who safeguarded his personal bubble.

After three months had passed with no apparent comeback, he had presumed that Katya had forgotten about the incident. However, here she was now; seven months down the line and sitting on the other end of the phone. He had no idea what she wanted, but he knew she wanted something.

'Katya, I am sorry about that night. I was drunk, but that is no excuse. It shouldn't have happened. I apologise, I really do. However, I am confused. Why have you left it so long to make this phone call and why go to the trouble to find out where I am, what number I am on and the name of my accountant? I don't read you as a woman who does something for nothing, so what is it you want?'

Katya was relishing every moment of this phone call. As a teenager she had often imagined herself to be a Soviet spy and frequently used the cold war as a fun excuse to titillate the imaginations of wannabe suitors. Katya concluded that this was fun. Mercy had filled her in on all the details and now she was going to enjoy making this serial cheat and womaniser sweat and have his balls curl back into his pelvic cavity.

'Reed, I know a lot more about you than you realise. I know you have a beautiful faithful wife who you lock away in an ivory tower. To some she must seem overindulged and privileged, but word has it that you have been feeding her a cocktail of tranquilizers and benzodiazepines, to such excess that for years she hasn't even figured out she has been imprisoned, even if it's a very sumptuous penitentiary. Word on the street has it that Rapunzel has finally escaped the tower and you have no idea where she is right now. Is that true Reed?'

Reed didn't know what to say. Everything she said was true. His mind could not compute how Katya could have known all this. She was little more than a vague acquaintance, someone who might be in the same room at the same time occasionally and the type of female who (aside from that humiliating toilet incident) he would evade at all costs.

'How do you know all of this Katya?' he asked. He didn't even bother to deny it.

Katya was smart. 'Oh, well you know – Daddy owns a pharmaceutical manufacturing plant in Siberia, so I can tell you all you want to know about the side effects of selective serotonin reuptake inhibitors, monoamine oxidase inhibitors and tricyclic antidepressants. On the rare occasions your wife has been out and about on social occasions, I have been able to spot the signs.'

Katya was pleased that she had managed to deflect Reed's question. Unknown to him, his former victim had a degree in pharmacology, and if need be she could have described the effect of these medications in detail. It was also true that on social occasions she had noted that Eenayah seemed to have a poor appetite, had dark circles under her eyes, lost her balance from time to time and frequently licked her lips as though her mouth was dry.

Sensing Reed's confusion, Katya continued, 'I also know you travel around the world and are seldom at home. As much and as often as you can get away, you will get away. I bet the alibi you use is hidden within the façade of chasing new talent and making more records. However, you and I both know that behind the veneer of being a music mogul, you are in reality away from home so that you can party with people much younger and more beautiful than you can ever dream of being again, and so you can screw as many women as possible without your lovely wife having a clue about what you get up to.'

Reed was blunt and to the point. 'To begin with Katya, all you have said so far is merely conjecture and the speculation of someone with an insignificant and inexact knowledge of my world. Unless you have a camera perched on my shoulder or have been following me around the globe, you are just supposing that all you have said is probably true. Secondly, who cares if it is true? Why should you worry about the state of my marriage? If this verbal diarrhoea is your way of getting revenge and it makes you feel better, then go for it. Listening to this shit is better than paying for your silence. So please do continue.'

Katya felt as though she had just lost some points. Deuce! Reed was correct in his synopsis. She now had to slice a hard ball down the line to gain an advantage.

'Reed I have not gone to the time and trouble to call you for something as pathetic as revenge. You tried to rape me and I kicked you in the balls, and that must have hurt for a week or so. My retaliation at the time was payback enough. I am calling you for another and more serious reason.'

That did the job. Reed fell silent, and she had his full attention. Katya pulled on the background information Mercy had given her. Reed would not have the faintest idea how Katya would know so much about Eenayah's state of mind.

'Are you remotely aware that one of the reasons your wife went back to her motherland on some soul-searching pilgrimage was to get you to pay her some attention? Yet she has failed, hasn't she? How often have you even given her the minutest of thoughts whilst she has been away? Do you know if she is safe? Do you care? This is a woman who has suffered with mental health issues and is withdrawing from some major medications. Don't you think you have some responsibility to at least check that she is okay?'

Reed was confused. This was a counselling session he had not expected.

'Katya I confess, you have me flummoxed. I am confounded. I didn't have you down as a marriage advisor. In a weird sort of way I feel complimented that you care so much about my relationship with my wife, but I have to be honest – none of this makes any sense to me. You don't even know Eenayah. Why should you care about her? Where are you going with this Katya? Why have you called me? I am a busy man, so please get to the point.'

Katya took a sip of iced water and sucked on a lemon. She hoped that maybe the acidic juice would assist with the tone of the conversation. She checked that the recorder was still activated. Mercy would be chomping at the bit to hear this conversation, especially his initial confession regarding moving assets around to hide them from his wife. Mercy would adore the fact that this was captured on tape.

'Okay Reed, I hear you. We are both busy people, so let me get down to business. Your wife will not be catching a flight back to the US tomorrow. I would like to tell you why that is, but to be honest I don't know and I don't care. I am just the messenger and my message to you is that she won't be coming home, so don't expect her to walk through the door any time soon. I know there is a big party planned next weekend and you will be having all your wife's family over as well as your own children; if you can remember what any of them are called, that is. The party was important to Eenayah and she would have wanted it to go well, so my instruction to you is as follows. You need to come up with some excuse as to why Eenayah won't be at this party. You are going to have to make it a bloody good reason, as under no circumstances do you want to worry anybody to the extent that they panic and catch a flight home. These are the people Eenayah loves. She would want them to have a good time.

'So be a good little boy Reed and be nice to your guests, but use that fertile imagination of yours to excuse Eenayah's absence. You seem to be good at lying, so this should be a simple task for someone like you.'

Katya waited for a response. There was a long silence. Reed didn't know what to say and his hands were shaking. He had not expected this. Katya seemed to have some intimate knowledge about his wife. It was well known in celebrity society that Ms Beselovaya had some dubious associations. The thought crossed his mind – had Eenayah been kidnapped? Would the next phone call allude to a ransom? He didn't know what to think.

Eventually he responded. He sounded nervous and his voice was trembling.

'How do you know my wife? How do you know about this big reunion party? How do you know she isn't coming home and why isn't she coming home? What has happened to her? Is she okay? You have me feeling very worried. Where is Eenayah? What the fuck is going on?'

Katya didn't know if the emotion in his voice was sincere or fabricated, but she strongly suspected that Reed was more concerned about the effects Eenayah's absence would have on his own plans, rather than having a sincere concern about his wife's whereabouts and wellbeing. She couldn't wait to deal him with the final blow. She had one final bit of information stored up her sleeve that would pull the world from under his feet, and she could hardly wait to deliver the final punch to his stomach.

'Cut the crap about caring Reed. You and I both know that you don't love your wife, so stop bloody pretending. Bigamy - that's illegal isn't it?'

Reed's nervousness was now beginning to turn into anger. 'What kind of bullshit are you talking, Katya?'

'Let me see what kind of bullshit I can conjure up. How about you going through all the pretence of a family reunion, and then the second you pack your wife's family back to where they came from, you ask your loyal wife for a divorce? I strongly suspect that must be why you hired a world famous asset concealer, sorry I meant to say accountant. Freudian slip, I do apologise. What was her name again? Oh yes, Alexia Towers. How cunning, how cold, how calculated. I am shocked, Reed. I knew you were a slimeball, but this is a new low level even for the likes of you.'

Reed was by now trembling from a rush of adrenalin which was giving him a flight or fight response, and he wasn't quite sure at this point which to do.

'You seem to believe you know a lot about my life Katya. Hell, I know I grabbed your tits at a party and it was an inappropriate, ill-timed, badly judged and bloody stupid drunken move on my part, but I never thought you would go to this level just to punish me. As revenge goes, I can tell you are enjoying every second of this. Have you had a surveillance team on me or something? This is well over the top. You must be crazy, either that or bored. Have you really nothing better to do than try to ruin my life?'

Reed had read Katya correctly. She was enjoying every second of the conversation, and she didn't mind her voice giving her gratification away.

'I don't want to ruin your life Reed. I don't care about you enough to lose sleep over your happiness or otherwise. Nor have I had a surveillance team on you. Even I am not that crazy. I told you before

– I am just the messenger. Hey don't go shooting the messenger – isn't that the saying? However Mr Baratolli, what you should realise is that the 25-year-old bimbo you have just got engaged to has a big mouth and has been flashing her ring around town. Don't forget Reed – a rich socialite knows a lot of people. I have an extensive social circle, and I am more than aware of what Amanda has been telling anybody and everybody who cares to listen. Also don't forget that her father is a politician, a US Senator even. He isn't going to want his little girl getting tangled up with a married man now, is he? Don't you think that if anyone was going to put your life under a microscope it would be your fiancée's daddy? But oh no – I forgot about the 'B' word didn't I. Bigamy; that's a horrid word, Reed. Oh, I get it now! That is why you were going to ask Eenayah for a divorce when she got back to Miami. Poor you – I mean now that Eenayah won't be coming home, you can't ask her for a divorce. That must really piss you off Reed. And as for Amanda Primetta, she is going to be really furious with you. How are you going to marry a girl young enough to be your daughter if you can't divorce Eenayah? Still – look on the bright side, it gives Alexia Towers more time to hide more of your pathetic assets and if all else fails, Amanda walks away with the mega bling of a 15-carat emerald cut diamond. Not a bad day's work for a 25-year-old.'

The reality of the situation hit Reed in the stomach, just as Katya had predicted. 'What do you want from me Katya?' he replied. 'I smell some sort of blackmail in the wind.'

'Oh me? Want something from you!' Katya could not stifle her laugh. The mere suggestion of her ever wanting anything from Reed Baratolli (aside from hearing him squirm – which she had now attained) was unthinkable.

'Personally, I don't want anything from you Reed. There isn't anything in the world you could possibly give me. I have already given you your instructions. Find a way to tell your house guest and various party goers that your wife will not be joining them. Make the excuse a good one, but under no circumstances alarm them. Ensure they all have a jolly good time.'

'That's it?' Reed was confused. 'That's it, that's all you want me to do? Ensure my guests have a jolly good time. No other threats or demands?'

Katya was happy with the way the conversation had gone. Listening to Reed Baratolli wriggle and sweat his way through an unpleasant tête-à-tête had been a most satisfactory way to pass the morning. She hoped Mercy would be pleased with her.

'Yes, that's it - BUT handle this well Reed. If one single friend or relative jumps on a plane to come and find Eenayah prior to the party, I will see that as a failure. The gossip magazines will love this story, as will Amanda's daddy, so be sure to do a good job. Got to go now. My manicurist is on her way and I have my talons to sharpen for my next quarry. Cheerio Reed. Remember my orders.'

With that she put the phone down. Then she curled up on her white leather settee in fits of laughter. 'My God Katya, you are good at this shit!' she chuckled to herself. With that she went to her computer to download the recording to a file share site where Mercy could retrieve it later. She couldn't help but walk with an exaggerated swagger as she made her way across the room, still giggling like a schoolgirl as she sauntered towards her laptop.

***

Meanwhile Mercy had spent most of Sunday night and Monday morning listening repeatedly to her father's recording. Trying to make sense of the many deep revelations imparted by the Buddhist monk had given her a migraine. There was only so much information she could take in at any one time, yet she knew that every single word was of colossal importance to her client. Headache or not, she had to inwardly digest as much as she could.

The veiled warning that not only would the Ledanite followers do anything in their power to protect the line, but the opposition forces would equally do anything to destroy it, left her with a chill. In addition it seemed that not knowing who were the bad guys or the good guys would be a major challenge. Mercy was beginning to realise that this situation was far more complex than the MacDonald case. With regard to Eenayah, the friend or foe could have spent a lifetime getting close to their target. Mercy was starting to feel as though she was in way over her head, and the final caution, that maybe the lives of those meddling in this situation could also be in danger, resonated in her thoughts. Humans with 'other world' powers evoking angels or demons was indeed unknown and untrodden terrain for an atheist sceptic ex-policewoman such as Mercy.

It was therefore with light relief that she listened to Katya's recording. Although Katya hadn't followed the script exactly and the part at the end about giving the story to a gossip tabloid had been a last-minute addition generated by her vindictive imagination, it was none the less hilarious. She reminded herself to call Katya later to thank her, but for now she had a more important call to make.

'Hey father, just to say well done re your meeting with Father Luke, or Monk Luke, whatever he calls himself. You asked some good questions. It was very deep, a lot for me to take in, but well done anyway. Lots to think about, Paps.'

The Professor sounded tired and let a yawn escape as he replied, 'Thanks Mercy. I wish we could have had more time with him, but we got as much as we could in the short time available. I'm glad I followed your advice about not taking notes but recording the conversation instead. Was much easier. I am having a nice time here in Dublin with Frank. We have a lot of catching up to do. Am I okay to stay here a bit longer? With it being the summer holidays there are no classes going on at the university, so there isn't any real hurry for me to get home. Mercy, have you any issues with that? How is Eenayah by the way?'

Mercy didn't really know how to even begin updating her father on all the events of the last couple of days. So much had happened in such a short time. She decided to condense the information.

'Yes father, the unidentified patient in the hospital was Eenayah. The silly woman had gone running up a mountain in the rain and they guess she slipped and was knocked out. The bad news is that she has a broken leg and ribs and is unconscious with a swollen brain.' Mercy heard her father gasp in horror. 'I'm assured that it's not as bad as it sounds. There is no bleeding inside the brain itself, although she has a minor skull fracture. I'm told she will make a full recovery. For now they are just sedating her so she keeps still and pain free, or something like that.'

The Professor was shocked. 'Well it sounds bad enough to me, but I guess you're right, it could have been worse.'

'Father, it does get worse. Brace yourself for this; Eenayah is pregnant. It has created an issue with the way they have been able to treat her medically. I can't believe it. I listened to your recording again and again, and Luke says that if she gets pregnant the threat to her life will be much greater. I'm not sure how we can protect her any more. For all I know she is in a hospital bed because she is pregnant. What if she didn't fall? What if she was pushed? My team had been hired to protect her, but now I feel we have let her down.'

'How did she get pregnant?' stuttered the Professor. No, don't answer that. What I meant to say is that you told me her husband can't have any more kids. So who is the daddy? How pregnant is she?'

'Father, you know more about Eenayah than I do. I have no idea who the father could be. I went to visit her this afternoon and the consultant in charge of her care had a chat with me about her condition. She had an ultrasound this morning, and it's early days. There isn't even a heartbeat yet, so he tells me she must be less than six weeks, probably just five weeks, I suppose. It seems she has become pregnant since being here in the UK, but I don't understand how. Aside from a blowout weekend with an ex-boyfriend and student friends in Newcastle, she has just been doing boring history things and reconnecting with her birth mother's family. Sorry father, didn't mean to insult history. You know what I'm saying.'

The Professor didn't feel affronted. His tomboy daughter was a hardnosed CEO who lived life in the present and played around with futuristic gadgets. His world was in the past and he understood that Mercy failed to embrace the charm of days gone by, just as he didn't identify with her hi-tech space-age crime-busting methods.

'They want to transfer her to a brain rehabilitation unit soon,' Mercy went on. 'I just feel that the net is closing in on me, Dad. She could wake up at any moment and blurt out her real name. I gave her a false name and pretended I was her sister. It could all be blown apart at any moment if she wakes up and tells people who she really is. I honestly don't know what to do and I can't stay here in North Wales forever. I have other clients and other business. I need to get back to Oxford. I have a company to run. Shit! Father, what do I do?'

This was a rare moment, as Mercy was normally so self-assured. Her father did not usually have to bolster her confidence, but this was different.

'Mercy, you are a professional and you have a team of people around you, don't forget that. Delegate anything you can't deal with. It may be a good thing if they transfer Eenayah elsewhere and then you can replace yourself with Lilly as the false sister. In retrospect, you should have requisitioned Lilly to do this job from day one. The problem with you Mercy is that you are a control freak.'

'Thanks Dad. Don't hold back, hey.'

'To be honest, part of me believes you have acted with too much haste. I have been concerned that the MacDonald case may have affected your judgement. Not everything on the edge of our understanding represents a threat. However, by way of reassurance Mercy, I believe you did the right thing. As you know, I am not into religion or biblical prophecies, but there was something about Luke's words which gave me goose bumps. He came across as an intelligent guy with a sensible bald head on his shoulders, yet he believed all he told us with total conviction. Don't beat yourself up about it girl. You've hidden Eenayah away from the world, so for the moment she is safe. You had to move fast and you did the best you could for her in the spur of the moment, especially now we know she is pregnant. What about her husband though. Surely he must be worried about her?'

For a moment Mercy remembered Katya's conversation, and her voice lightened as she recalled the comedy of their exchange. 'Father, don't worry about Reed. I have taken care of him. He will do as he is told, besides I don't think he is overly concerned about his wife's welfare. He has just become engaged to another woman, so what else can I say?'

The Professor knew not to probe further. Whenever his daughter cut the sentence short it was her way of saying 'shut up, I won't tell you anything more'.

'Okay Mercy. I will let you go now. I can hear Frank calling me and I can smell something good cooking in the kitchen. Just promise me that you will take care of yourself. I feel nervous for all of us. Part of me can hardly believe what we have uncovered so far. I don't know what we have got ourselves involved in here, but it feels as though it could be something significant, maybe apocalyptic. You are good at protecting other people, but Mercy, now I need you to protect yourself. Please promise me that you will take care. We may have just opened Pandora's Box and uncovered a can of pythons.'

Mercy was exhausted both mentally and physically, which was unusual for such a high-octane woman. She was worried, but she did not want to worry her father. If anything, she needed to release them both from this case, but she didn't know how. Rarely had Mercy wanted to bail out, but her bobby's instinct was telling her to run.

'Goodnight Father. Try not to worry about me. Remember, I am an ex-policewoman, martial arts expert, weaver of dreams and so on. I'm a big girl, I'll be fine. You go and enjoy yourself with Frank.'

She had a strange thought as she hung up. Looking at her reflection, she spoke out loud. 'Life is a strange thing. You don't always know when it may be the last time you see someone or know the last words you may say to the ones you love. What if your last words were something really stupid like, 'have you seen my socks' or something equally trivial?'

It was an odd thing to consider, but then Eenayah's situation and the whole prophecy thing had been unnerving her. She needed a drink.

CHAPTER 27

Wednesday 17th July

Storm clouds had started to gather over the Miami skyline. They were darker, heavier and more sinister than any clouds Reed had ever seen before. Anarchic forks of electricity were fired downwards, sideways and upwards, adding a tumultuous illumination to the horizon. A tropical storm was fast approaching. Reed could feel the change in the air - not that any of his guests noticed the slight drop in temperature.

Ruby, Owyn and Harry were happily playing at sharks in his swimming pool. Roserie, the ever attentive maid, was busying herself preparing lunch for all the guests. She was in her element when they had a large group of people to entertain. More often than not, Reed's mansion was an empty and silent vacuum, void of all fun. Roserie hated those hollow moments, even though for her it meant less work.

His mother-in-law Ellie, father-in law-Chris and the majority of his wife's family and friends had been in Florida since Monday. Eenayah's parents were lying by the pool drinking in the sight of their grandson as he screamed, giggled and splashed down the water slides. Eenayah's Aunt Ginny was absorbed in some risqué book that she had purchased from the airport and to everyone's bemusement hadn't been able to put down since. It was obviously something entertaining, as every now and then, much to everyone's distraction, she would burst into spontaneous laughter. The deliciously dazzling Armani had just turned up with her new boyfriend in tow and was being giggly and gregarious in some exaggerated attempt to impress him. Asher and Konnor were having a game of tennis on the courts at the rear of the house and in their ultra-competitiveness were swearing at each other in loud testosterone-loaded bellows.

Asher was a younger version of his father, with deep emerald eyes and mocha brown kiss curls which clung to his sweaty tanned forehead. His thick tresses framed his face like a Renaissance painting. He was quite the playboy; affluent, beguiling and almost too pretty for a lad. Charm oozed from his pores.

Konnor was simply Konnor; warm, loving and with a forever smile radiating from his face. Reed tried not to look at him and see the eyes of Bert Montana staring back. He took some comfort from the fact that his youngest son was the image of his first wife Julia and tried not to consider who Konnor's father might be. He had raised the boy as his own and ironically out of all his children he felt the greatest connection with Konnor, even though a DNA test had confirmed Julia's infidelity. Konnor was the court jester who kept everyone entertained and Reed loved the fact that his surfer-dude youngest son with the feral blonde locks had such mature social skills. Eenayah adored him, and just for a moment Reed felt genuine sorrow that she wouldn't be around to laugh at his jokes and wrap him up in her arms.

Becky was Ruby's childhood friend, over in Florida with her Italian hotelier husband Amedeo. They were playing a card game of Snap and being a tad too gung-ho for what should have been tame entertainment. Music blasted out from Becky's iPod speakers, the base beat vibrating around the poolside area. It was about as raucous and loud as the volume control would allow.

Indeed Reed's home was a cocktail of energy, laughter and ear splitting noise. Yet Reed was perturbed. He sat in silence, amongst the crowd and yet apart from it.

Everyone had expected Eenayah to drive up in a taxi at any moment, and Reed didn't have a clue how on earth he was going to burst their bubble and tell them she wasn't going to be joining them. He wanted to just walk out and go somewhere far away; leave all these family and friends alone to just get along with their superficial merriment. However he clearly remembered Katya's threat about taking her story to some gossip magazine, so he thought he had better make at least some effort to deal with the situation in a sensitive way.

As Ruby climbed out of the pool he saw his moment.

'Ruby, can I have a word with you in private? I have something I need to talk with you about.'

Ruby was slightly taken aback. Since being in Florida, Reed had hardly exchanged a word with her. She had never had the closest of relationships with her brother-in-law, but she could tell from his expression that something was bothering him.

'Sure,' she said. She wrapped herself up in a massive white bath towel and followed him down to the moorings. Reed led her to a secluded patio next to the water. It was partially hidden behind the overgrown yellow Allamanda bushes, creating a concealed place few of the guests would have known about. It was a lovely and private part of the garden; a place where Eenayah often went for uninterrupted yoga and meditation.

Ruby sensed the gravity of the situation. 'What's up Reed? Its Eenayah isn't it? I have been having a bad feeling about my sister for the past few days and she isn't answering her phone. Is she okay?'

Katya's warning was ringing in Reed's ears. He didn't want to spook Ruby into dashing off home and he had to box clever with this cringingly awkward situation. He made an effort to explain, and in a false display of caring, gently held his sister-in-law's hand so as to comfort her.

'To begin with, Eenayah is fine. She is healthy and well, so please don't worry yourself on that score. However there is a problem between us. This is difficult for me to say Ruby, so please hear me out.'

Ruby's dark eyes welled up as though she knew what Reed was about to say before he could say it. She braced herself for what was to come next.

'I suspect it won't surprise you to learn that our marriage has hit rocky ground and it has been difficult for some time. We have jointly decided that we need a complete break from each other to work out how our future is going to look. Eenayah doesn't want to ruin this reunion gathering for anyone and she deeply wants you all to enjoy yourself, but neither does she want to be the party pooper and right now, she isn't in the best of moods for a party.'

'Are you trying to tell me Eenayah won't be coming?' Ruby didn't know if she should be shocked, sad or annoyed. She was aware that the situation between them was less than perfect, but hearing it for the first time from Reed's lips was mortifying.

'She is upset and she wants to be left alone, Ruby. I suspect she may have met someone else back in the UK. Who knows? All I know is that she doesn't want to be here and she just wants to be left alone to work things out in her own head.'

Ruby's disappointment now turned to anger. 'The selfish cow! I knew I shouldn't have left her alone to go wandering around Britain and re-connecting with the past. She really has lost the plot this time. Do you know what she has been doing, Reed? Visiting graves of former lovers and our biological mother, and God only knows what or who else. Every time I have spoken with her recently she has just been to some cemetery or the other and she delights in telling me about what type of flowers she has purchased for which skeleton. I was actually beginning to think she might have had another mental breakdown. It would have been better if she had just stayed in Miami and kept popping her bloody pills.'

Reed was relieved, in a gutless, spineless way. At least Ruby was angry with her twin and not with him. He felt exonerated, and pleased that he had handled the situation so well. He tried not to smirk. However Ruby was far from happy, and stomped around the normally peaceful Zen area with the ferocious might of a wild beast.

'But Reed, I can't believe she would be unfaithful to you. I am pissed off with her if she has been shagging around. I mean she did go on a bit of a blow-out weekend in Newcastle, but I would still struggle to believe she would cheat on you. Maybe having time out back home has made her consider her future. I know you have been a good husband to her Reed, and materialistically you have given her anything any woman would ever want, but I do know she was lonely.'

The tranquillity of the serene Zen area must have begun to work its magic on Ruby, as she finally calmed down and thought about things carefully. She sat down cross-legged on the grass, touching the ground as though trying to communicate with her missing sister through the earth.

She let out a deep, soulful sigh. 'If I'm honest Reed, I don't think Eenayah has ever really been happy. Losing James as she did was awful. It was such a tragic accident. Poor lad! His death was a massive blow and none of us thought she would ever recover from losing him. But then she met Greg and found happiness again. Okay, so he was James' half-brother and that caused a bit of a family scandal at the time. Truth was though, nobody really cared about that. We were all so happy that Eenayah was happy. When you love someone, that's all you ever want for them - happiness.'

A single tear escaped from her eyes and slowly meandered down her cheek. Reed played the sympathetic cuckolded husband to perfection, offering her a silk handkerchief and seeming to put on a brave face. She continued, 'Then Greg died and Eenayah blamed herself. I'm sure you know the story Reed. I think what made it worse for Eenayah was that with Greg it was preventable. If she had been at home he would have been treated. With James, it was just an accident – a spot of oil on the road on a tight corner. Nobody could have averted James' death and in some bizarre way that helped her to deal with it. I am sorry Reed, I shouldn't be talking about Eenayah's past loves. I think in my own mind I am just trying to work her out. I mean, you rescued her. You were her salvation. It this makes it any easier for you I don't think it was all your fault. You were away a lot, but I guess with your line of work that was unavoidable. You can't be to blame for my sister being so needy. Anyway, how are you? I mean how are you coping?'

Reed was pleased with the way this was going. Ruby was being sympathetic towards him, which was a better reaction than he had expected or could have hoped for.

'It is a struggle Ruby. Right now I am confused, but if Eenayah needs her space to work things out then I think we should all respect her wishes. Please, I want you all to stay and enjoy your holiday in my home, but I hope you will understand that I need time away to be reflective and consider my options. I will be flying out to LA some time tomorrow. This whole situation is massively embarrassing for me. Can you help me out please and delicately explain what has happened to all the others, as respectfully and as sensitively as you can?'

Ruby put a comforting arm around Reed's shoulder. 'Yes of course I will. I'm so sorry Reed. Eenayah has done this before. I don't mean she has been unfaithful. What I mean is that on occasions in the past she has just flipped and gone off and done silly things. Running away seems to be her coping mechanism. I hope you two can work it out, but don't worry about the others. I will be tactful and make sure that everyone has a great time. I'll deal with my sister once I get home.'

Reed was immensely proud of himself. He had deflected the task of telling everyone about Eenayah's absence onto Ruby's shoulders, and she had taken the responsibility on board with ease. It hadn't been as difficult as he had assumed it would be.

'Thank you for your support Ruby. I am off to pack my cases now. I just need to get away from here, too many memories and too many people having too much fun whilst my heart is breaking. Roserie will look after everyone in the meantime. Thank you for understanding. This means a lot to me.'

He walked off, trying hard to disguise the smile which was quickly enveloping his face. He took a back pathway over to the main house so to avoid his gleeful guests. Tonight he had dealt splendidly with an uncomfortable situation, but tomorrow he had to brace himself for the next challenge over in LA. He started to wonder why on God's earth he had ever hooked up with a senator's daughter with Mafia connections, Amanda Primetta. This was possibly going to be the more difficult conversation. No wife physically present equated to no imminent divorce proceedings, meaning no marriage any time soon - so why be engaged? How the hell was he going to worm himself out of this one without ending up in concrete boots?

Ruby followed soon after. What a silly bitch her sister was. She had probably hooked up with Jonathan Cook from her Newcastle student days. 'Wait until I get home!' she muttered under her breath.

For Reed, it was job done. He had escaped with minimal damage. Or so he believed.

CHAPTER 28

Thursday 18th July

Reed stepped out of his rain forest-inspired jungle shower and sauntered over to an 8ft high mirror to comb his mane of curls. For a man of his age he was proud that he hadn't yet developed a bald patch and was conceitedly pleased that his hair helped him retain his youthful looks.

Mid-comb he caught a red image in his mirror. It was but a blur and dissipated before he could focus clearly, but he knew that something was there. The scarlet mirage was floating outside on his tiered balcony, but the contours were smudged by the fine lace curtains which blew gently in the breeze. The vision moved slightly, and he grew concerned as to what it could possibly be.

Rushing over to the enormous sliding doors which separated his bedroom from the outside world, he found himself looking at the back view of a woman. She was dressed in designer red leather shorts, a loose white see-through silk blouse and thigh-high demonic red leather boots. Her long platinum hair fell below her waist and was laser straight. It could only be one person. She swivelled around on Reed's wicker chair to face him.

Reed could not hide his astonishment. 'Emmanuelle Poulain, who the hell let you in here?'

Emmanuelle grinned. 'You have just answered your own question, Reed. Hell let me in here.'

'Very funny, nice play on words,' responded Reed. 'Seriously though, I didn't know you were on the guest list for this weekend's shindig. Have you brought Océane with you?'

'I am not here for your party Reed, and neither am I here to discuss the musical career of Océane. I have far more pressing business matters to discuss with you.'

Emmanuelle stood up and paraded up and down the balcony. From where she stood she had a panoramic view of the wealthiest area of Miami, with its prestigious line-up of gleaming white boats moored up to the passage of water leading out to the Caribbean. Her fingers ran along the pure gold face of King Canute, embedded in the marble balustrade. It was a lavish piece of art especially commissioned by Reed, and faced out to sea as though to hold back its almighty forces. His eyes were made from tiny shreds of emeralds. King C had not come cheap.

Emmanuelle turned to face Reed, inhaling deeply. 'I so love the air after a storm Reed. It gives a fresh crisp energy to the place don't you think. Did you see the lightning last night? Truly breathtaking.'

Reed was not in a mood for a woman with a forked tongue. He hadn't quite recovered from the insult of Katya's phone call.

'Yes I did watch the storm Emmanuelle, and for a tiny moment I think I saw your broomstick bobbing around over the clouds.'

Emmanuelle laughed with menacing disregard as she took in all the splendour and decadence of Reed's surroundings. 'You know, we gave you all of this Reed, and it was a trade-off. You had one simple job to do, and you failed.'

Reed was less than amused. 'How dare you! I earned all of this,

Emmanuelle. I was and I still am a talented musician. I bought all of this with blood, sweat and tears.'

Emmanuelle was less than impressed by his answer. 'Indeed Reed, you were a talented young musician. Every street in the world is littered with the busking melodies of musicians equally as talented as you deem yourself to be, yet never get anywhere or become anything because unlike you, they were not in the right place at the right time. Your destiny was never to have been this great, and you would have ended up teaching music in the New York Juilliard Music Conservatory. Yes, you had earned yourself some success with your band DLV, but you would have squandered away all your money before you hit 40. You would have been happy – but no, you would not have had any of this without our help. We put you in that right place at the right time; never forget that.'

She strolled back over to the luxurious cast of King Canute and added, 'No way would you have been able to afford this guy here. I just love him. He was the Viking King of Denmark, you know. Legend says he can turn back the tides. I doubt you could turn back any tides, Reed. You are too far out at sea to paddle back to any shore. Expensive little statue wasn't he? Do you know he was an ancestor of your wife? Talking of which, where is she? Isn't she supposed to be here for the party on Saturday?'

Reed had a bad feeling in the pit of his stomach. He had known Emmanuelle for many years and in his former dealings with her she had always been fun, flirty and friendly. He hadn't yet seen this vitriolic side to her nature. Her present mood was most certainly darker and she had a cold sinister glint in her eyes. But he did not know what else to say other than to be truthful.

'I don't know where she is. She isn't coming to the party. I don't know why. I am sorry. I can't tell you anything more than that, because I don't know anything more than that.'

Emmanuelle was less than impressed and shot him a glare that could kill. She raised her hands up and looking up at the ceiling, then spun around slowly in a circle. 'We gave you all of this. All of this fame and fortune, and in return you had just one simple job to do and that was to take care of your wife. Reed, you complete idiot, was it really so hard for you to make your wife happy? If she had been content in her relationship with you, she might have stayed locked up in this magnificent mansion out of harm's way. But no, you let her go roaming off back to Britain on her own, because in her own innocent pathetic little way she was trying to prove she was worthy of your love and attention.'

Reed held his head down like a scolded schoolboy. He knew Emmanuelle was right.

'You know Reed, you humans flummox me, especially the male gender. I mean, could you have not kept it in your pants for just a little while longer? We told you from the start that Eenayah would lose her fertility by her 39th birthday. Once she reached that magical age your contract would be released. Historically, all the clones have limited fertility and that usually works in our favour. You bloody stupid fool, all of this would have been yours to keep, because you would have accomplished what you were targeted to complete. All you had to do was stay married to her as long as it took to prevent her from getting pregnant and then we all get to be happy bad immortals. You have your millions in the bank and as for us, we succeed in closing down this particular line of Tamar-Lada. You are an idiot. We are not pleased.'

Reed pleaded with her. 'Cut me some slack Emmanuelle. I have spent years married to a woman I don't love just so I could obey the terms and conditions of our agreement. My God, I had my first wife killed in a supposed car accident just so I could be free to marry Eenayah. I have put my soul on the line here. Yes, for now I don't know where she is, so I guess you could say I have lost her, but she will be

39 next month. It's only a few weeks away, so how can you say I have failed? Eenayah is just some sad crazy person on a childish adventure. She will turn up again.'

'Losing someone like Eenayah was not part of the plan Reed. After her 39th birthday she would be barren and free, you were both free. You should have stopped her from leaving. Oh and by the way, as for your first wife, Julia cheated on you for most of your marriage. You would have disposed of her eventually, contract or no contract. We could already see that in your future, so don't give me this pathetic story about the sacrifice you had to make by tampering with the car brakes. Look into your heart Reed and tell me that you wouldn't have done it anyway.'

Despite having just come out of the shower into an air-conditioned room, Reed was sweating profusely. He was uncomfortable with the conversation, and the malevolent Emmanuelle was the last creature he was prepared to have a fight with.

Emmanuelle looked at her wrist and the broken purple cord that hovered above her hand, constantly defying gravity and never once seeming to slip. 'I have worn this bracelet for over 3000 years Reed. It is a reminder of my task, which is to break the line of Tamar as denoted by the royal purple line. I have done quite well to date and extinguished many of the Tamar-Leda direct descendants over the centuries. Only a few of them remain, of which your wife Eenayah is one. I entrusted you to keep her here in this mansion, sedated and content. You failed!'

Emmanuelle used another tone when she was angry. Her cold blue eyes turned blood red and her aura became menacing. Her patience was running thin.

'This isn't just about you, Reed. Don't you understand that I have failed as well and I also will have a price to pay for my mistakes? What about the men Eenayah was in love with before you came along, the two brothers I had to dispose of so she could be free to marry you? James and Greg, both so young. Don't you think I also have blood on my hands?'

Reed finally broke his silence. 'I had assumed that their deaths were both tragic accidents, wrong time, wrong place.'

Emmanuelle shot him a look of contempt. 'When will you mortals ever learn that there is no such thing as coincidence? Whether it be the holy will of the Divine or the conjuring mayhem of Beelzebub, everything and everyone is connected to a plan. How do you think the drops of oil just happened to be on the corner when James took it too fast? Who do you suppose conjured up that last-minute story for Eenayah, the one that had to be submitted before a critical deadline? The very story that kept her away from home while Greg lay alone in a coma? Listen to me Reed, if you are going to play in our world you need to understand the rules. For everything that happens to you, and I mean everything, you have to ask which side is pulling the strings and why.'

'There is no need to panic, Emmanuelle. I can still find her. I got a strange phone call from some woman in Atlanta to tell me she wouldn't be catching her flight back and instructing me to make up some excuse to cover for her absence. It was an odd conversation and not at all what I expected. She obviously knew something more than she was telling me. Before I go to LA I'll go to Atlanta and try to find her. I'll get Arabella to organise it for me.'

'What is this woman of Atlanta's name?

'Katya Beselovaya.'

'I know that name. If I'm not mistaken, she is the party-going daughter of a Soviet oligarch.'

'Yes, you are correct as always Emmanuelle. That is the very lady - if anyone could ever describe Katya as a lady in the true meaning of the word.'

'I am concerned, Reed. Your dull and boring wife would never associate herself with such a person. The animalistic demon in me can smell the interference of a 3rd party. How else would brimstone and milk ever have a connection? One turns the other sour and the other cools the very stones of hell. They don't fit together. Someone – and I don't know who – has put these two opposites together. I will find out who this is, they too will feel my wrath. As for you, do whatever it takes, but find your wife. This is not a request, it's a command.'

Emmanuelle looked as though she had become weary of Reed, and picked her handbag up to leave. She turned to face him before walking out of his bedroom door in a blaze of crimson.

'There is a stronger power controlling this, Reed. A force greater than mine, and one you should also fear, one that I certainly fear. Look at your tattoo. It's starting to fade. Eenayah could already be pregnant. My purple cord is starting to claw into my skin like a bracelet of thorns. Throughout all the many centuries I have worn it, this has never happened before. You only had one month left to keep her here and away from any situation where this could happen. You are a failure Reed, and unless we can find her and destroy any possible pregnancy, we are both under threat. Do I make myself perfectly clear?'

Reed was visibly shaken. 'How could Eenayah be pregnant? She isn't the type of woman to mess around.'

Emmanuelle opened her palms upwards to indicate that she knew nothing more. 'The Ledanite may have got to her first I guess. Isn't that the risk you take when you let your wife loose to wander around in her past life? They'll stop at nothing, in the same way that we would stop at nothing. What is it you say? "*Faciam quodlibet quod necesse est*". You always knew this was a risk. You could have been a better husband. I won't defend your behaviour or the part you have played in all of this. I have no loyalty to you. You are the one who sold your soul to the spoils of success, and now you're the one who will need to make the effort to recover it. This is your problem. I bid you farewell, Mr Reed Baratolli.'

As Emmanuelle walked down the wide, sweeping staircase with a gush of arctic wind tailing behind her, she passed by Ruby, who was rushing upstairs to get changed. Ruby recognised the platinum blond woman in her red shorts and boots, but couldn't quite work out where she had seen her before. It sent an uneasy shiver down her spine as they momentarily shared the same marble step.

Emmanuelle felt Ruby's eyes on her back and turned to give her a glacial stare as she left the house. Her look seemed to penetrate Ruby's soul and stabbed right into her heart. It made Ruby gasp, and she clutched at her chest.

As Emmanuelle left the house, Ruby looked up in the direction of Reed's room. He was standing motionless on the top of the galleried landing, watching the woman leave. His face looked ashen. The thought crossed Ruby's mind that maybe the woman was something to do with Reed's marital problems or connected in some way with Eenayah's absence. However she quickly dismissed the thought, and went off to jump into a steaming hot shower and wash away the chill of the encounter.

***

Reed looked at his mobile and the numerous missed calls from Arabella. He was sure that all she wanted to discuss with him was the party she had arranged. He was in no mood for her, or the party at the weekend. He was beginning to regret ever having agreed to it; the timing could not have been worse. However he could only ignore his PA for so long, and eventually he would need to check in and find out what was so important. It often occurred to him that she was the one in control, rather than the other way around. The tail wagging the dog.

Arabella sounded relieved that he had finally returned her many calls and voice messages, but a croaky frog in her throat also gave away her concern.

'Reed, thank God you have finally got back to me. Miami Police Department have been on the phone. They're on their way round to see you. I wanted to give you as much warning as I could, but you wouldn't pick up. I'm guessing they will be with you any moment now. Sorry boss.'

Reed was surprised. He was a law-abiding citizen who didn't speed, in fact he mostly had a driver who took him to places and his only vice was watching crap daytime TV shows in the back of a limo.

'Did they tell you what it's about?'

'I did ask them, but they weren't going to disclose anything. Hope it's nothing to serious. Give me a call if you want me to bail you out or if you need your solicitor - only joking. I'm sure it will be something trivial.'

'Arabella, before you hang up can you cancel my flight to LA? I may have to go to Atlanta first, so just hold fire on any travel arrangements for the moment.'

'Sure thing Reed. Good luck with the police situation.'

Reed couldn't quite believe what was happening to him. In a warped way he considered his life to be that of a normal man approaching his half-century. He spent the majority of his time in a recording studio and the rest with his new girlfriend, Amanda. All in all he considered his earthly existence to be mainly dull, but the bubble of middle-aged domestic normality had to be popped somewhere along the line, he guessed, and it might as well happen sooner rather than later. Even today, perhaps.

First came the strange cryptic phone call from Katya, which came flying out of the blue like a flying saucer and was totally unexpected. Next the menacing visit from Emmanuelle with her veiled threats of eternal damnation. What next?

Just five minutes later, Roserie knocked timidly on his office door. 'Sorry to disturb you sir, but the police are here to see you,' she said. Two police officers walked into Reed's office. One of them looked like a rookie and the other appeared to be a wily old guy, long in the tooth and nearing retirement.

The younger officer looked star-struck as he eyed up the palatial surroundings. No doubt being in the presence of a well-known music mogul was slightly overwhelming. The older guy had probably seen it all before, having worked over 30 years in Miami, and it seemed nothing could faze him. They showed Reed their ID and got the legal and social niceties out of the way first.

Reed was polite and courteous and asked them to sit, and Roserie went to fetch everyone glasses of chilled water. It was all very dignified and Reed felt under no threat as he was certain he hadn't committed any crime aside from being a bastard to women and callous in his business dealings.

The younger policeman got out his notebook as the older officer began to question Reed. 'Sir, we have been asked to do a personal house call on behalf of a police department in another state, but before I go into any further details can you please tell me how you know Katya Beselovaya and what your relationship is with her?'

Reed had not expected this question. He wasn't sure quite what he expected from a police visit, but it sure as hell wasn't this. He hesitated for a second. His normal impulse was to lie, but his inner sensible voice told him that he couldn't totally hoodwink a law enforcement officer. He knew that Katya lived a strange life, one that often touched the underbelly of the criminal fraternity. He presumed she must have become tangled up in something illegal. He needed to say something soon, but it couldn't be an out-and-out lie or maybe he would also come under suspicion of whatever it was that the crazy Russian woman had become involved in. He had to think quickly.

'I do know of Katya Beselovaya, officer, but only vaguely,' he said. 'She has occasionally attended the same parties as me, but we don't mix in the same circles so that isn't a frequent occurrence. I have no relationship with her at all, she is just someone I happen to know.'

The older officer jumped quickly to the point. 'Okay, that's fine Mr Baratolli. I just needed to check first. Unfortunately, I regret to tell you that Miss Beselovaya was found dead in her boyfriend's apartment two days ago. I'm sorry, this isn't the sort of news we like to break over the telephone. I just wanted to check how close you were to the lady before I broke the news.'

This day was getting queerer and queerer by the moment. Reed felt a genuine sadness. Although he hadn't liked Katya, she had been too young to die.

'I'm shocked,' he said. 'I feel so sorry for her father. She was the apple of his eye. Sergei will be distraught. Can you tell me how it happened, officer? Was it an accident?'

The older officer obliged with an answer as best he could, quickly followed by a question. 'According to the Atlanta Police Department, it would appear to be a heroin overdose. Of course, until they get the toxicology back it is still being treated as suspicious. Pending an established cause of death, anyone who had any recent contact with the deceased will be questioned. Mr Baratolli, according to her phone records it seems you were one of the last people she spoke to.'

Reed's cool composure was broken. The reality hit him that by default he could have become implicated with something that might turn out to be murder. He couldn't tell them the truth. He had to think swiftly and create a clever but realistic response.

'I do know Katya used cocaine and she often hung around with some dodgy drug dealers, but I didn't think she would be stupid enough to OD on Heroin,' he said.

'Mr Baratolli, it seems you were one of the last people she spoke to. I need to ask you what the phone call was about and if there was anything in her voice or anything she told you that might indicate suicidal thoughts.'

Reed would need to tell them something soon. 'This is a bit embarrassing,' he replied. 'I was at a party last Christmas. You will have heard of Acre, the rap artist. He is signed up to my record label. Anyway, it was the last date of his global tour in New York and we were having a wrap up celebration. Katya was there as a guest of Acre. I had not been formally introduced to her before, but of course I had heard of her. Everybody knew about Katya. Her life wasn't exactly mundane and she was often the centre of some infamy. I flirted with her a little and she took it the wrong way and she came onto me. I'm a married man officer and it wasn't going to go anywhere. She was a bit pissed off about being rejected, at least for about ten minutes before she hit on someone else. I'm guessing you know about her reputation. Anyway, I suppose she heard through the grapevine that my marriage had been on a shaky footing recently. I don't suppose you get to keep that many secrets once you find fame. I had been away on a global talent scouting tour for many weeks and at the same time my wife flew off to the UK on some personal crusade and then omitted to come home. She is still there. To put it bluntly, she rang to find out if she could have a second bite of the apple. I wasn't interested. It was a brief conversation and that was the end of that. I said no. I'm sorry about what happened to her though – quite tragic for one so young.'

The young officer scribbled away as fast as he could. The older man turned towards his colleague and raised an eyebrow, then turned back to Reed.

'You're a famous man Mr Baratolli, and you have a PA gatekeeper who guards your privacy with her life. Trust me, it was hard enough for us to get through her defences to find you. If Katya Beselovaya was just someone you had only met the once and was a vague association from the past, how did she get your personal number?'

Reed was quick to respond, as he could actually tell the truth on this occasion. 'Katya was as I said a casual association, a woman who was at the same party as me and nothing more than that. She did not have my personal number. She rang my office and spoke to my receptionist and pretended to be someone else. I was expecting a very important call from my accountant, Alexia Towers, and Katya pretended to be Alexia so I would take the call. That is exactly how the call happened and my receptionist would be a witness to that.'

For once, he had given an honest answer, so it was spoken with force and confidence. The officers had all they needed for the moment. They elected not to share with him the fact that Katya had indeed recorded the conversation and it had been found on her hard drive and been shared with a detective agency in the United Kingdom. They had no idea why Katya had done this and what her business was with MeDeVe Ltd, but the tape did disclose threats bordering on blackmail and that could make Reed Baratolli a prime suspect should foul play be suspected. It also revealed Reed as a confident fibber and fabricator of the truth. It had been clear from the tapes that it was he who had attempted to sexually molest Katya and not the other way around, as he had suggested.

The older officer bit his lip. It would have been easy to confront him with the contents of the recording, but the time wasn't right quite yet. Best to keep it back.

'Thank you, Mr Baratolli,' said the older officer. 'We won't take any more of your time. If we need to speak with your receptionist for confirmation of your account, we will get in touch. At the moment this isn't being treated as a homicide, but we need to cover all bases just in case the post mortem proves otherwise. Oh by the way – just in case you haven't heard – if I was you I wouldn't be hanging around too long awaiting a call from Alexia Towers. I'm surprised you don't know about this already, but she has been arrested on suspected embezzlement of her clients' funds. If I were you Mr Baratolli, I would start checking what's left in your bank account. If you suspect you are a victim of fraud, please get in touch. Take care, sir.'

The colour drained from Reed's face. He knew full well that he had asked Alexia to hide money, and only she knew where it was. What more shit could today bring?

The two officers drove out through the electric gates and back down the tree-lined avenues of the rich and famous of Florida. The younger officer remarked, 'You thought he was lying about that phone call. I can read you like a book Dave.'

'Sure he was lying,' replied the older man. 'What he didn't know is that Katya recorded the call and the Atlanta police shared it with me before we made our visit here today. It seems Reed tried to rape Katya at that showbiz Christmas party he referred to. It wasn't her that hit on him, but the other way around. Katya was out to blackmail him, but not for money. She did require other favours and from the sound of it she had him bent over a barrel. She threatened to go to the press if he didn't obey her. So I hope for his sake that she did accidentally kill herself, because if it did turn out to be a homicide, I am guessing that Reed Baratolli would be a prime suspect. My gut feeling tells me that there is something more to this story. He is hiding something – I am sure of it. We better keep an eye on him just in case.'

***

Emmanuelle was parked in her lipstick red Ferrari in the layby opposite Reed's grand mansion. Just as the police vehicle drove out, she pressed the shutter of her camera. Success! She had managed to get a photograph of the police leaving his property. She considered that the police visit might be of interest to the tabloid-reading public.

Tapping her long red fingernails on the steering wheel she

considered the dilemma that both Reed and Alexia were in. Such mere mortals made her job so much easier. Without human greed and lust, a demon's job would be a difficult one.

She fired up the Ferrari and roared off into the distance. The die had been cast, the plan set. Reed's fall from grace was now only a matter of waiting. She cast her eyes downwards towards the opaline face of her Patek Philippe watch. The hands of time were in motion.

CHAPTER 29

Friday 19th July

Part of Kerry's job was managing Mercy's email and sorting her Outlook into files by case number. It was a weekly IT housekeeping job which she scheduled for Friday afternoon. Looking at the name of a recent incoming email triggered a recollection. She had seen the name Katya Beselovaya somewhere before, but she couldn't remember exactly where. It was a strange email: 'Did as you told me. Listen to the bastard wriggle'. She should call Mercy; she wasn't sure where to file this particular message.

Kerry went to make some coffee and engage in idle conversation with Simon about everybody's plans for the weekend. By way of a casual aside, she asked her young colleague, 'Do you know who Katya Beselovaya is, Simes? I don't know what case the email belongs to and I need to clean up Mercy's inbox. Name sounds familiar, but I can't quite place who she is.'

Simon could not believe that Kerry had not fully understood who Katya was, hadn't caught up with yesterday's news and had overlooked the significance of the email. Excitedly he ran off to find Thursday's newspaper and then returned to waft it triumphantly under Kerry's nose.

'Read this,' he said. The headline said, 'Russian Heiress found dead in boyfriend's Atlanta apartment'.

Kerry was shocked. 'Oh bugger! It says here that Katya was found dead on Tuesday and the date on her email to Mercy was just the day before. I think Mercy needs to know about this. She needs to get back here in case the police need to speak with her. I hope she won't be implicated in any way.'

'I agree, you need to get my aunt on the phone right away,' replied Simon. 'She needs to be back in Oxford to deal with any fallout that may follow on from this. Do it now, Kerry.'

★★★

Even prior to Kerry's call, Mercy had already come to the decision that she couldn't hang around North Wales much longer. She had other clients to attend to, and the MacDonald case was coming to final closure and needed some attention. She was off to visit Eenayah for the final time before she was transferred elsewhere for longer term rehabilitation. Mercy felt assured that she had hidden her client's identity well enough to afford her some protection in the interim. On the plus side she might even get a final glimpse of the lovely doctor Tomas.

In truth, she hadn't known how to react to the news about Katya and for the time being she was trying to push it to the back of her mind. It wasn't that she wasn't upset, but Mercy had acquired the skill of parking her feelings and moving them aside until she was in the right circumstances and frame of mind to give her emotions free reign. They hadn't been the closest of friends, but she knew Katya well enough to know she wasn't a heroin addict. There was something about the overdose story that didn't ring true. She suspected that the police would have already commandeered Katya's computer and would have been filtering through her hard drive with microscopic detail. After all, Katya belonged to the world of the super-rich and had dubious felonious connections. It was a no-brainer - the police were bound to instigate a detailed investigation.

Mercy fully understood that the wording on Katya's email to her could be interpreted as incriminating. She hadn't instructed Katya to blackmail Reed; Katya had included this threat as a spontaneous final knife in the back. Most probably she had been caught up in the moment. However, in the email she had written that she had 'done what Mercy had asked her to do'. Mercy knew that attack was often the best form of defence, so rather than wait for the police to knock on her door, she would approach them first. The police were probably the least of her worries. Katya was connected to some unscrupulous people and if any of them believed she had died following Mercy's instructions, well… it made her own safety a concern. However in the meantime she had a chapter to close, and this meant leaving Eenayah in a safe situation with people she could trust.

Tomas Forshaw welcomed Mercy, or Corinne as he knew her, into his office. Mercy imagined he had virtually no idea how superhuman he was in looks and personality. Always friendly, caring, compassionate, yet with the chiselled features, dimples and 'come to bed' eyes that were totally wasted on someone who didn't recognise their sexual pulling power. However, on this occasion Tomas wore a serious face.

'Corrine, I'm glad you could make it before you head back home to Oxford,' he began. 'I appreciate you have a full time job and can't stay here to sister-sit all the time, but before you leave we do need to discuss Polly's prognosis and plan for recovery.'

Mercy was taken aback by his candour. 'Sure, go ahead,' she said.

'Let's start with the good news. It has been a week since Polly's fall and since then she hasn't shown any signs of cerebral haemorrhage, and by that I mean bleeding into the brain. That is positive news. It is unlikely that any bleeding would happen at this stage, so everything seems to be settling down. The concern however is that she still has some swelling of the brain. Again this is subsiding, but I do worry that a degree of brain damage may have occurred. The pregnancy does give us a moral dilemma, as there are treatments we are withholding because of her condition. She is in early first trimester so unfortunately that is the most risky stage in embryonic development. However, until she regains full consciousness, we won't know if there's any lasting damage.'

Mercy was naturally alarmed. She felt protective of her client, whom she saw as a vulnerable visitor far from home, but was equally concerned that she was somehow messing up the diagnosis, by feigning a medical history of which she knew nothing.

'Can you explain what you mean by that statement Tomas, er I mean Dr Forshaw?'

Dr Forshaw was fairly skilled at taking complex conditions and explaining them to his patients' relatives in a way that was simplistic and yet not derogatory or demeaning to their intelligence. 'Corrine, can you recall ever falling asleep lying on your hand, cutting off your circulation and then waking up with a ghastly painful 'pins and needles' sensation, basically because the blood was cut off to your hand?'

'Yes, of course.'

'Well can you imagine not waking up and yet still having your circulation cut off to your hand for hours, days, weeks even? What do you think would happen to your hand?'

'Well, I suspect I would damage it, possibly even lose it.' Tomas had made his point with great clarity.

'Correct. Exactly. You see the thing is Corinne, when the brain has been swollen for as long as it has been in your sister's case, the pressure may have occluded some of the blood flow to some parts of the brain, and as with the analogy with the hand, some brain tissue may have died.'

'Do you think this may have happened to Polly?'

'We don't know for sure, but Polly doesn't even recognise her name and that is a significant sign - something we need to be concerned about. There could be a degree of amnesia. She is very confused about what has happened, where she is, who she is, all alarming signs I am afraid to say.'

Mercy felt a stinging sense of guilt. This was the moment she had always feared. Giving Eenayah the false identity of Polly Johnson had only ever been designed to be a short-term solution to an emergency situation, with the hope that Eenayah would have been out of hospital before now. It was possible that she was being incorrectly treated as someone with brain damage, because of Mercy's deception.

'Has she shown any other signs of brain damage? Does she call herself by any name other than Polly?' Mercy crossed her fingers behind her back and held her breath.

'Well, she is still not totally conscious as yet. We are still sedating her to control the pain. We cannot be totally sure if she has any lasting brain damage, but there are other worrying signs. She is very agitated and restless, sometimes aggressive. She also seems to have some strange speech tendencies. She rambles away in pigeon English and then occasionally falls into some language that doesn't seem to be recognisable as English at all; Hebrew or Yiddish maybe - it's hard to tell. I had a Jewish girlfriend once and I vaguely recognise some of her Gran's words in Polly's vocabulary. It sounds Middle Eastern, but truth is that none of us in the unit can recognise it and we are a multi-cultural melting pot of all races in this place. However, believe it or not, this language transference is less uncommon that you might think in such situations. I have come across brain damage affecting language skills before now, sometimes with the patient talking in a tongue which was thought to be unknown to them. It's an odd phenomenon. However, the bottom line is, she will certainly need a period of rehabilitation in a specialist centre. Be prepared to be patient with our patient. This is a long-haul flight.'

Mercy thanked Tomas for his advice and concern and walked over to Eenayah's private side-room to say her goodbyes. She felt a strong sense of responsibility for this woman. A woman who she knew so little about, yet someone who seemed to bring out a motherly instinct in her. It was a nurturing and protective impulse which she didn't even know she possessed. Eenayah was simply a client. It was a professional relationship. Yet there was something about this fragile china doll which made the hard-nosed Mercy De Vede actually care, and Mercy cared for very few people.

Eenayah had changed so much from the spoiled little rich wife Mercy had first encountered many weeks ago in Oxford. She had even altered from the unconscious woman she had seen lying helpless in a hospital bed just seven days ago. Mercy didn't know if the change was a good or a bad thing and presumed that maybe the hormones of pregnancy along with the trauma of her accident had altered her physical appearance, and yet - she noted a distinct transformation in the way she looked. Eenayah was somehow morphing into something or someone different. Mercy couldn't work out exactly how or why and it made no logical sense, but she just felt it.

Mercy got up to leave, but just then Eenayah opened her eyes wide and grabbed her arm. The clasp of her hand on Mercy's slender wrist was brutal. It felt as though Eenayah was dangling over the edge of a cliff and clinging on for dear life. It was as dramatic and unnerving as it was sudden. Maybe it should have been reassuring, a demonstration of Eenayah's mental recovery, but it wasn't. It was as disturbing as a scene from a black and white horror movie.

Eenayah didn't say anything; she just looked up at Mercy with lugubrious eyes. It was a deep penetrating stare, and slightly fearful. Her voice was raspy and weak. She tried to speak, but her words were difficult to understand; it sounded like 'hylp myr byt'. It made no sense. Mercy instinctively felt Eenayah was asking for help, but the speech was too muddled to make any discernible logic.

The patient with the dual identities then closed her eyes as suddenly as she had opened them and seemed to fall into an instant, profound sleep. It was an uncomfortable experience. Mercy was more than pleased to exit the unit, although part of her was worrying about who and what she had left behind. She just hoped against hope that she had covered this poor woman's tracks enough to keep her safe for a meantime as yet to be defined.

Leaving the hospital deep in thought, she knew she needed the hand of expert spiritual guidance, and the only person able to help her make sense of any of this was Luke, the unexpected Buddhist monk informant. Unfortunately Luke didn't trust anybody in the world, and the only people he would speak to about the Ledanite following and their alleged opposing forces were Frank and her absent father, Professor Roland de Vede. Both gents were most likely in some Dublin bar or on a golf course.

Mercy had welcomed her father's input into this case. Up until now this incongruous project had really been her father's special assignment. She had often thought what an odd pair of aging reprobates they must seem. However, what her father had achieved with his genealogy research, plus the various other explorations he had undertaken in Ireland with his priest friend Frank, were commendable. From what she could ascertain, Luke seemed to be the only source available to them who had any insight into the world of the Ledanite and the enigmatic hidden prophecy surrounding the reincarnation of Tamar. Yet Mercy was becoming increasingly uneasy about her father's involvement. She smelled something sinister and had an uneasy feeling rumbling around her gut.

There was something about the way Eenayah had changed in the past week that perplexed her. She couldn't quite put her finger on it, but she knew something had altered within her client drastically; not just physically, but at some deeper level.

Mercy shared everything with her father, who was her best friend and confidante as well as her Dad. Since her mother had passed away the two had become much closer. But she worried about him constantly. She recognised that he was getting past his sell-by date and his body was tired and creaky. With increasing age he was also becoming more forgetful and clumsy. She constantly checked up on his location using a mobile app, but often he would forget his phone. She had even considered getting him tagged, but it was considered an infringement of his so-called civil liberty.

Mercy wondered if Katya's death was a mere coincidence or something more sinister. The news had felt like a punch in the stomach. She had suppressed her reaction for the time being, but she knew that a few glasses of red wine later the shock would hit her like a thunderbolt. For now, her friend's death was unthinkable, so she elected not to think about it.

She then remembered the warnings given by Luke, the friendly Buddhist priest. He had suggested that their interference could be seen as meddling, and perhaps the guardianship of Eenayah should be left to the Ledanite followers. She needed to talk with her father so he could ask Luke more questions.

It was getting late and the temptation to go back to the hotel for respite was strong, but she really needed to be back in Oxford sooner rather than later. There was a requirement to call the police about Katya and then again the MacDonald case was at a critical stage of completion. Time to pack her suitcase. Life never stood still - not even for a moment.

***

Mercy suffered from night blindness. The glare of headlights in her eyes from approaching cars on dark country lanes was a constant irritation. She was tired, hungry, emotionally exhausted and yet was driven by a need to get home. Her home was her only true solace from a world that often seemed loud and inconsiderate.

She monitored the miles and the ETA given on her Satnav. On long journeys she often entertained herself by 'racing against the Satnav's estimated time of arrival'. It was a source of trivial amusement and it passed the time. She made a phone call from her hands free to her father. She told him all about Katya and her tragic death and then about Eenayah and her strange condition, especially regarding her speech difficulties. 'I need you to go back to Luke and tell him about the change in Eenayah's demeanour and also inform him about the details surrounding Katya's death. We need to know if any of this is in any way connected or just a coincidence. I don't know if we can trust Luke, but neither do we have any options. He is our only link to this odd biblical world that has trespassed into our 21st century lives.' Her father tried to reassure her with the elderly voice of reason. 'Mercy, stop panicking. As the nice Doctor explained to you, Eenayah may have a degree of minor brain damage. As for Katya, even you once told me long ago that this was a woman who hung out with drug barons. For her to die of a drug overdose is not beyond the realms of possibilities. You simply have to stop worrying. Your imagination has gone into overdrive, but yes of course; I will ask Luke.'

Mercy wasn't happy, but she was certainly happier. At least she had got her main points across and pushed the fact that another conversation with Luke was an absolute requirement. Luke was their link to the inner intelligence surrounding the Ledanite, and also to what she now referred to as 'the anti-Ledanite brigade'. She hadn't known what else to call them, and she needed to give them a name for her wall of post-it notes. She had concluded that there were two distinct factions, even she didn't know which were the good guys and which the bad guys. It seemed to her that either side would do whatever it took to get whatever they wanted. The bad guys seemed to do bad things for bad reasons, while the good guys seemed to do bad things for good reasons. Whatever the motivation, they were both equally capable of concocting some bad shit.

Her mind was whirling around in circles, like being caught in a rip tide. Time to close down her brain. The last week had been mentally wearing and physically demanding. She just wanted to be home and in her own cosy bed.

Mercy sat back in the lush leather seat of her Mercedes and flicked on the audio system to listen to some easy driving music. She would attempt to enjoy the drive home and stay alert at the same time.

A summer mist descended as the temperature fell. The fog was not static. As though it had a life of its own, it moved around, twisting and curling as it played childish games in the headlights. Mercy's car was the only one on the road. The winding country lane was dark, silent and ghostly. Mercy sank back into the driving seat as U2's *Unforgettable Fire* permeated the car with its enigmatic guitar breaks and mysterious lyrics. She had no idea what the song actually meant, but knew it had hidden meaning and poignancy. She sang along, knowing each and every line. *Ice, your only rivers run cold. These city lights, they shine as silver and gold. Dug from the night, your eyes as black as coal. Walk on by, walk on through. Walk till you run and don't look back. For here I am.* Magical, transcendental and fittingly perfect. Mercy hadn't heard that song in such a long time, but it could still lull her into a trance-like state. Not such a great idea on a meandering Welsh road when the driver suffered from night blindness and was over-tired.

She lost herself in the moment. The world outside was silent, dark and eerie. The menacing branches of the trees seemed to clap as her car rushed by. She became cocooned inside the safety of the music, and that was a mistake. She closed her eyes only fleetingly, but when she opened them she was sure that the approaching car was careering towards her on her side of the road. It was an illusion; a trick of the light, but she was convinced it was real and that she was on a collision course. She veered to the left. It was an unnecessary correction. A slight pull on the steering wheel was all it took.

There came a smashing noise as she collided with the tree; the vibration of the impact through the metal of the car; the pulsation that ran along her spine; and the disorientation of being flipped upside down as her car hit the ditch and overturned. Then the pop of the airbags as they exploded and the clouds of smoke within the car. The confusion, the searing pain across her shoulder blades; then the blackness. The music played on, but Mercy could not hear it.

CHAPTER 30

Saturday 20th July

The Professor was unusually fidgety. He had just received a call from the hospital to say that his beloved daughter had been involved in a car crash. The message was that she had been very lucky and had sustained only a fractured collar bone. None the less, the Professor was uneasy. Too many accidents seemed to be happening within too short a time. Eenayah, Katya and now his own daughter.

Frank tried to calm him down. 'Stop worrying Roland,' he told his friend. 'Simon will pick her up and drive her back to Oxford as soon as she has the thumbs up for discharge. She will be fine.'

'You don't understand Frank. Mercy is one of the safest drivers I know. She even has an advanced driving qualification from her days in the force. She could chase a wanted criminal around a skating rink if she needed to. She has never had an accident in her life.'

Frank did his best to reassure his friend. 'These things happen to everyone, Roland. Mercy has been under a lot of pressure recently. From what you have told me, the MacDonald case has been a bit of a bugger. Her friend Katya dying just a few days ago must have been an awful shock, and what can I say about Eenayah? Remember, I used to be a priest. I am used to dealing with all things hidden, whether they're human emotions or spiritual forces. In comparison both you and your daughter are less than one step removed from being atheist. Your involvement with some secret biblical prophecy from 3000 years ago must seem like a weird alien world to you. Of course Mercy must be confused and exhausted. Think about it Roland. It was just an accident. Don't read anything more into it.'

The Professor wasn't convinced. Against his better judgement and Frank's opposition, he put in a call in to Luke. Luke had just finished his morning meditation and completed a simple brunch of oatmeal. He just happened to be available for a call and was sitting on the floor cross-legged. He listened patiently as the agitated Professor went into great detail. Hardly pausing for breath, he described Eenayah's admission into hospital, Katya's death and Mercy's accident. Speaking quickly, he tried to squeeze in as much information as was possible. He was forever wary that Luke could get a knock on his lodge door any second and that would be the end of the conversation. For a monk, he seemed to have an unexpectedly crammed diary.

The Professor had broken MeDeVe's golden code of a 'need to know basis only', even referring to Eenayah by name. He knew Mercy would not have approved of that degree of disclosure, but right now he didn't care. He was in a state of panic. Rightly or wrongly, Frank and Luke felt like the only people he could trust right now. The Professor was on high alert and was beginning to get spooked by recent events.

Luke was calm and composed. He listened to the tense, rapid voice of the Professor in a state of perfect tranquillity, perhaps in the Zen way that maybe only a Mahayana Buddhist could master. He proceeded to pacify the Professor as best he could, but he also felt duty bound to tell the truth.

'Professor, from all you have described to me it seems that Eenayah may be turning. Frank will know more about this than I do, so you should consult with him. Catholic priests are familiar with exorcisms. The Catholic Church deems that lost spirits can occupy another person's body – take possession, if you wish to call it that. If the Prophecy is beginning to fulfil its destiny, then maybe Eenayah has begun the process of becoming possessed with Tamar. Should this be the case, the person you know as Eenayah is in grave danger. There is a chance she may not survive being taken over by a spirit as strong and as powerful as Tamar, especially if her body has been weakened.'

The Professor did not expect this answer, but then again he never expected anything normal to be uttered from Luke's mouth.

'What about the news that Eenayah is pregnant?'

'Again Professor, as I told you when we last met – this puts her under great threat and she may be best placed with those better qualified to look after her spiritually as well as physically. I do not believe that this is your job, and it certainly isn't Mercy's job. You are not equipped for this special task.'

The Professor was exasperated by this reply. He was in need of Luke's advice, not his opinions. 'What about Katya's sudden death, so shortly after speaking with Mercy? Then just a few days later Mercy finds herself upside down in a ditch, and trust me when I say that my daughter is a skilled driver. Could these events just be coincidental?'

The eternally serene monk made an attempt at diplomacy, but he knew there was a real danger around this situation and he had to warn the Professor.

'I will let you into a secret, Professor. The Ledanite, along with their opponents, are just people. They are flesh and blood like you and me. If they want information, they have to dig around in phonebooks, search the internet and ask questions – just as we do. Yes indeed, there are some of them who believe they have powers beyond us normal folk, but in general they are brothers, sister, aunts and uncles. Just regular people. However, they do have spirit guides who are not of this earth. I am not sure how best to describe them to you Professor, so I will use language you will understand.'

The Professor was hanging onto his every word. 'Go on Luke, please.'

Luke took a sip of cold water. 'Okay, let us talk about the opponents to the Ledanite followers. Indeed there are people who walk amongst us who would want to see all the lines of Tamar end and for the world to become a place of wickedness and immorality for eternity. Their guide would be akin to a demon. That is the best way I can describe such a powerful evil spirit guide. Technically I suspect this spirit may not be a demon as such, but be aware that they would have the appearance of a normal person. A person who would have the powers to play games with someone's mind and distract them enough to have a car swerve off the road. Maybe they could put a person into a temporary state of insanity where they inject themselves with heroin. The demon will be potent and could easily manipulate situations, should there be a justifiable reason for doing so. Even they are answerable for their actions.'

The Professor gulped. The hairs on his arms stood on end and a chill shot down his spine. He was becoming increasingly perturbed that they had tripped into something that was catastrophically out of their experience. More than ever he now believed that Mercy and her entire team should back off, get out and move on.

'What about the good guys Luke? What of their spirit guide?'

'The Ledanite followers are not as goody two shoes as you think they are, Professor.' It wasn't the answer the Professor had hoped to hear.

Luke continued. 'Yes the Ledanite collective would also have an assigned spirit guide who I can best describe as an angel. Don't expect this person to have big wings and a halo. They also would have the appearance of an ordinary person. The guide will have been assigned to watch over Eenayah from way back in time and most likely would be somebody who could be around her a great deal in a normal capacity. Like the demon, they have similar powers. Good and bad are probably equally matched. The universe likes to play fair. Nearly all ethereal combats have hindrances and recompenses on both sides of the battle line.'

The Professor was confused. 'So what did you mean when you said the Ledanite were not as goody two shoes as I believe them to be?' He was slightly surprised at the kindergarten terminology used to describe this elusive clan of devotees.

'Professor De Vede, think of this angel to be akin to an over-protective mother watching over a child. However loving and as caring a mother might be, if anyone threatened the life of her child, she could turn into a lioness willing and able to claw any would-be assailant to death. The same rule applies here. Should there be any threat to Eenayah and the line of Tamar-Leda, then the threat will be dealt with as required and the outcome may not be pleasant. If for example it was deemed that there was good reason to throw your daughter a warning shot, then an angel could cause a car to swerve off a road every bit as much as a demon could. This is a battle for the future of the mankind, not a game of chess.'

The Professor understood with crystal clarity. He didn't like what he had been told. The threat now appeared to be from both the Ledanite, who fought to preserve a sacred line of lineage that had its roots in a hidden prophecy from the days of the Old Testament, and the opposition forces. Luke was taking the role of honest broker and simply delivering the truth as he had understood it, having himself grown up within a Ledanite family.

'So basically Luke, we are under threat from both sides?'

'Sorry Professor, but yes, I suspect that is correct. You need to vacate this project. You don't know who to trust and either side may see you and your daughter as an irritating obstacle to be removed. I am sorry to be the messenger of doom. You are a good friend of Frank O'Byrne, an ex-teacher of mine who I admire and respect. I don't want to see any of you harmed as innocent bystanders. There is nothing more you can do to help Eenayah and if anything your involvement could be more treacherous for her.'

The Professor thanked Luke for his time and hung up. He was greatly troubled. He needed to contact his grandson Simon to ensure he drove safely when collecting Mercy from the hospital. On second thoughts, he would get someone else from the team to make the journey up to Wales to recover his daughter, rather than put his grandson at risk. He needed to tell Frank all that Luke had shared with him. They had become involved with something that was beyond their capability to control. He was justifiably worried.

Luke stared at the phone, perplexed. He had a momentous decision to make. Luke had often wondered if his own parent's tragic death from a faulty heater and carbon monoxide poisoning had been less of a coincidence and more the act of a demon. He was no longer part of the Ledanite movement, having shunned it as a teenager. However he still had connections. He didn't want to become involved, and the Professor had entrusted him with confidential information, but he felt compelled to do something. Once a Ledanite always a Ledanite. It was hard to remove himself from something he had been conditioned to. He picked up the phone.

He spoke just five words. 'I know where Eenayah is.'

★★★

By music industry standards, the party was fairly tame. With a select guest list of less than 50 people, it felt more of an intimate dinner

442

gathering than what Reed would deem a party. He was indeed a reluctant host to an event he hadn't planned. Without the ferocity and determination of his PA Arabella, none of this would have happened at all. Minus any notable 'A' listers or the usual sex, drugs and rock & roll expectations, this was about as boring a Saturday evening as he could imagine. All that were present were the people he loved and treasured the most in the entire world. A minor party, by his standards.

He sat back, slightly in the shadows and out of view. He watched as his parents laughed and joked with his three children. His father chased Asher around the pool table, having just lost a game to his grandson. Konnor danced a silly dance with his grandmother, only stopping to play air guitar to the Guns and Roses song *Sweet Child of Mine*. Ruby and Armani were actively participating in the Karaoke and working their way through just about all of the Abba hits. The air was filled with joy and laughter. Maybe just a little rock & roll, but certainly no sex & drugs.

Just for an instant, Reed appreciated the scene unfolding in front of him for what it was; a treasured prize moment, a memory for his pocket. An unusual hint of nostalgia permeated his mind. He drank in the picture of his parents having fun with his children and for a minute or so, he just watched. His parents were growing old. This might not be a sight he would ever see again, and deep down he knew it. He understood that one day his parents would be gone and he would look back at the memory of this moment and ache to be back here. By then it would be too late. He understood the situation fully. So, unusually for Reed, he just sat back and observed.

The sound system blasted out Konnor's selection of records. Heavy bass ghetto rap was not exactly Reed's choice of music, but his youngest son had bagged the DJ's medley before any of the other guests could have a look in. However, in some act of mutiny the DJ played a song that brought his olive-skinned wife to mind: '*But I can see you, your brown skin shinin' in the sun. You got your hair combed back and your sunglasses on'*. He thought about Eenayah, his patient, tolerant, faithful, beautiful, exotic-looking wife. She would have loved this party and would have been the perfect hostess. Maybe for the first time ever, he felt guilt. The guilt was layered with shame, regret and deep remorse. He did love Eenayah, but was not 'in love' with her as such. His relationship with a wife he had been duty bound to marry did not compare with the carefree, youthful exuberance of being with Amanda. The lustful romantic honeymoon days of his marriage were long gone, but he did miss Eenayah. Right now, right here, he wished she was by his side. She would have loved everything about this magical evening. He hoped she was safe, wherever she was in the world right now. However, he feared the worst. He clearly understood the forces attacking her and dared not consider what peril she might be in. Poor sweet Eenayah! She always blamed herself for everything and yet she was born into a world where nothing was ever really her fault, and where coincidence would seldom exist alongside reality.

She could never understand how someone like Reed could have picked her in preference to a line-up of women who were far younger, richer, prettier, better connected and carried far less emotional baggage from the past. The gossip columns of the time had made a big deal about this and Reed knew that resilient as Eenayah pretended to be, deep down the comments were deeply wounding. She thought it was her fault that her husband did not love her as much as he could have done, but in truth detachment was the only way he could deal with what he knew about his wife's possible fate. It was the first time he had ever really thought about his family and his wife in such depth. It was easier for Reed to remain manically busy in order to drown out the noise of his own conscience.

He slumped into a corner, trying to disappear into the angle of the wall so he wouldn't be seen. He had no intention of joining in with the festivities. Reed was content to just observe and get smashed. Indeed he intended to get very drunk. Find the sand and dig the hole; he had lost the will to be conscious. He would call Konnor and get him to ask the DJ to put the mindless music back on so he didn't have to carry on thinking and be carried down a sentimental road he didn't want to tread. Reed looked into the bottom of the bottle and sang, *'Those days are gone forever - I should just let them go.'*

★★★

 Perhaps it wasn't the ideal moment for his trusted friend and PR manager to make his approach, but Magnus rarely got an audience with Reed these days. So although he conceded that the timing could have been better, he overrode this by the urgency of the situation.

Magnus sauntered over casually with a half-drunk bottle of beer hanging loosely from his hand. He had a wide Californian smile on his face and hugged his friend with a warmth only appropriate from a long-standing acquaintance. 'You mind me joining you in your corner Reed? What's with the hiding stuff?'

Magnus was a Canadian of Norwegian decent living in the apple pie town of Julian, San Diego. Not exactly logistically ideal for a man with his job, but Magnus loved his lakeside farm retreat and he was only a helicopter ride away from LA and the lion's share of his clientele base. He lived with his civil partner Crispen and enjoyed what he considered to be a perfect life, aside from having to safeguard the hype around a portfolio of clients who seemed hell bent to get into all sorts of murky trouble, which he then had to fix. Celebs, celebs! He had grown tired of precocious adolescent divas and licentious balding old men, but they paid him a handsome fee to keep their public veneers squeaky clean. High fees meant more horses and the serene pleasure of Sunday afternoons riding through the mountain pine forest of his home town.

Magnus sank down next to Reed on the porch without making eye contact. He took a gulp of beer, sucked on a cigar and began his subtle warmup to a far more sobering conversation.

'Nice party you got going on here, Reed. A bit on the twee and cutesy side for you, but still good to see your wives' folks having such a good time. You got some good-looking kids. They have grown so much since I last saw them. Time flies, huh?'

Reed was not in the mood for a moral lecture and he knew that with Magnus that was all it was ever going to be. 'Stop with the small talk, Maggie' he replied. This was Reed's pet name for his PR manager; he knew how much he hated it. 'I know Arabella put you on the guest list, but we both know you weren't really expected to turn up. There are no networking opportunities in this for you, so why are you here?'

'OK, so why isn't your wife here?' retorted Magnus. 'These are her family I take it? I can sure as hell spot her twin.'

Magnus was not an employee of Reed's Great Record Company Ltd; he knew better than to have someone as a boss whom he might also need to control. Instead he had his own company and sub-contracted his media and PR management skills out to Reed and the artists on his label. As a hired associate he felt this gave him the freedom to speak more openly and honestly with his client, who was also occasionally his friend.

'You are very touchy tonight Reed. On a bit of a knife's edge if I may say so.'

'Well Maggie, as you just mentioned, Eenayah isn't here and I am missing her.'

Magnus nearly choked on his beer after hearing Reed's declaration of love, but pulled himself back to a discreet silence. Many years of experience had forged a tight lip

'Reed, I consider myself to be a buddy as well as your PR advisor, and I need to have an honest man-to-man chat with you, my friend.'

Reed had known this was coming. The stark proclamation wasn't exactly a total shock. Reed had expected some sort of dressing down from the moment Magnus had invaded his dark corner. Magnus was a chap whose job it was to know everything going on everywhere, and he was bound to have heard some gossip surrounding recent events.

'Yeah, shoot pal, let's get this over with,' was Reed's carefree inebriated response.

Magnus pulled out a rolled-up magazine from his inside pocket. Ironically it was the same publication Eenayah had worked for when she initially met Reed. Magnus flipped over to page 4 and a photo of the police driving away from Reed's house. Reed sounded like a teenager caught sneaking home late at night as he justified the incident. 'Mate, what can I say? It wasn't anything to do with me. It's a long story, but honestly I am innocent.'

Magnus tutted, sounding in his turn like the parent who had caught the sneaking teenager. 'Of all the stars I have represented over the years, you were the only one to shun notoriety and publicity. For many of my lesser known clientele I have had to search for valid reasons to get them into the tabloids just to keep the publicity mill turning – lest they forget and all that! However for you my friend, I have searched every which way to keep you out of the public eye at your own request. You have the award for being the most private famous person I know. So, dear chap, what the hell were you doing playing Russian roulette with Katya Beselovaya?'

Reed went quiet. What could he say? How could he explain to anyone why Katya Beselovaya had called him immediately prior to departing this life?

Magnus seemed genuinely concerned. He continued with his lecture.

'That woman has always been bad news. When I read that you had been interviewed in relation to her sudden death, bloody hell

Reed! I could have imagined anyone of hundreds of guys being linked to Katya B. But you, really? How?'

Reed was cherishing a bottle of vodka in an ice bucket and was drinking it straight with little more than ice and a twist of lime. He was quickly becoming very drunk. Slurring his words he uttered, 'In vino veritas. I will tell you it the way it was, Mags. I hit on her, okay? I made a fuckin' huge mistake. I only met the bitch once. She called me to blackmail me and it wasn't even real blackmail. All she rang to tell me was that this pissin' party had to go ahead without Eenayah and I had to keep the bloody guests happy. What sort of lame blackmail is that anyway? I have nothing to do with her death, I can promise you. More to the point; how the hell did someone photograph the police leaving my house, and how did someone know what the interview was about anyway?'

Magnus was philosophical. 'The paparazzi! Those guys get everywhere. You know that.' Reed was less than philosophical. 'Yeah I do, but I don't buy the fact that they connected Katya's drug-fuelled demise with a police visit to my house. It's as though the editor has had some sort of inside informer. How else would they know?'

Reed half suspected Emmanuelle, but dared not mention her name. He was under strict instructions to keep her ID out of any possible scandals, and he fully understood the consequences of disobeying her orders. A chill went down his spine as he thought about her and her wicked threats.

Reed flicked to page 9 of the magazine and pushed it under Reed's slumping face.

'I am employed to protect your reputation, and in the last ten years it has been an easy job because you have either been a goody two shoes or else you have been a bad boy who never got caught. As far as popular perception has been concerned, you are very well regarded as the nice guy of the music world. So please explain to me in simple language why the hell you proposed to a senator's daughter when you were still married?'

Reed crouched over, his head in his hands. His brow was covered with bubbles of perspiration which reflected the DJ's disco lights. He was not happy.

'I didn't know what I was doing. I was a bloody fool, Mags. I just got carried away in the moment and she blew her mouth out to everyone she knew. Don't get me wrong, I was going to ask her for a divorce when Eenayah got back to the States anyway. In fact I was going to do it immediately after this stupid party, but I guess I could have steered one boat out of the bay before I docked the next one into the same moorings. I was an idiot, I admit that. Ego stultus.'

Magnus couldn't help but like and admire Reed. He considered his client to have an almost childlike vulnerability, and nobody could deny his genius. However Reed was becoming a major publicity problem to him very rapidly.

'Hey man, I am going to hit you with this straight,' he said. 'You need to dump the new girl, Amanda whatever. She is too young, too well connected to the US political scene and she blabbers way too much. That's three toos too many! Then you need to keep your head down and be a good boy. The Great label is a platform for a lot of country and western singers, as you know only too well my friend. The bible belt of America idolises many of the artists you have on your label. The last thing you need right now is a ton of established C&W stars leaving you because they don't want to be associated with you or Great Records. Do you get my drift?'

Reed just nodded, as a schoolboy would after a scolding from his master. Magnus shook her head in disappointment. He wafted the magazine in front of Reed yet again. 'Page 4 and page 9, Reed. One a suspicious death and the other a bigamous engagement. One the daughter of an oligarch and the other the daughter of a senator. You don't do things by halves, my friend. It is fortunate that this publication doesn't go out until tomorrow. Let's hope your guests have too much of a hangover to read.'

Magnus stood up to leave, as Reed looked set for a night of drinking himself into a lonesome oblivion. 'Reed, let me get you some water and ask someone to escort you to your room. With all these lovely people here, this isn't the right setting for you to become inebriated. Don't make a fool of yourself buddy, keep that for the privacy of your bedroom. Just one last word from me before I go, and this is a warning. For you to have just one article associating you with the death of a dubious Soviet woman is worrying. For you to then have a second article in the same publication associating you with a senator's daughter half your age when you are still married, is concerning. Should any ambitious pimple-faced journalist dig up anything else about you anytime soon, you could be finished my friend. Look at all of this -everything you have worked so hard to achieve. It could all be gone. The public are fickle, love you one minute and dump you the next. I am pissed off with the journalistic liberty taken with story 1 and 2 and I will be putting in a complaint about this, but if there is a story 3 or 4 looming in the wings, it could be the end of you my friend. Stay good and keep it zipped, huh, and I don't just mean your mouth.'

Reed threw back a shot of vodka in one and looked concerned, as well an inebriated man could look concerned. 'Mags, I'm not going anywhere and I won't be doing anything to anyone anytime soon. I will lay low, I promise you pal.'

'That's good to know my friend because making the news on two pages of this jugular-ripping and celebrity-devouring tabloid is bad enough, I mean, pity the poor sod who makes the front page headlines. Let's see, who would that be… ah yes, Alexia Towers. The accountant from the pits of hell is making serious news at the moment. Let me

THE LINES OF TAMAR

read what it says so far; larceny, embezzlement, theft, lies and deception. Tut tut! Alexia has been a very bad girl. Oh and look, it lists all the famous people who she has represented and hidden money for on their behalf in offshore accounts that cannot be traced and may not even exist. More like money stolen and hidden under her mattress, by the sound of it. Hey Reed, some of these stars are your clients and signed up to your record label. Seems like a lot of musicians want to avoid paying tax, I mean who can blame them? Singing has to be a hard job. Oh my god Reed, you are named as well! Now bugger me, what have you to say about that buddy?'

Reed snatched the paper from Magnus's hands. He knew Alexia had been arrested, but not that this was now public news. He skimmed the words. It seemed he wasn't the only person Alexia had conned, although he suspected that in dollar terms he could have been the biggest victim.

Magnus felt some sympathy for his client, who now seemed to be a man who had reached his pinnacle early in life but was now sinking fast.

'How much did she take you for Reed?'

'Almost half my fortune. I mean, I still have a lot left, but I guess that's not the point. Hopefully I can make it up somewhere else. Perhaps I just have to put that early retirement on hold. What do you think?'

It was at moments like this, when Magnus was forced to hold a mirror in front of a client's face, that he was relieved that he was not an employee. People might be tempted to shoot the messenger. If Reed had been his boss, he understood clearly that he could be sacked for what he was about to say. Fortunately, Reed was a paying client and that made it easier for Magnus to be brutally honest.

'Reed, as your PR agent I have to tell you things the way they are,' he said. Yet again he thrust the paper in front of Reed's nose. 'How do you think these three articles, in just the one publication, will be perceived? Let's just see it from the reader's point of view, shall we? You have associations with the daughter of a Russian oligarch, a woman who has just been found dead and has strong ties with the criminal underworld. By your own admission you were one of the last people she spoke to. Flick a few pages over and it now seems you are engaged to a US senator's daughter who is half your age, plus, you are still a married man. That doesn't quite make you a bigamist, but none the less the female readers will be less than impressed. Flick back to the front and the key story and you are now on a list of several rich people suspected of hiding money and who have fallen victim to the incredibly cute looking bandit with a degree in accountancy. I mean Reed, how have you managed so many cock ups? Be honest. If you were an up-and-coming young musician right now and wanted a label to sign to, do you honestly think you would choose Great records when the CEO has all this shit flying around in his private life?'

It wasn't what Reed wanted to hear, but he knew Magnus was right.

'Look, I'm sorry Reed. This is a lovely family reunion party and I have no right to come here and talk shop. I honestly didn't want to ruin this night for you. However it is my professional duty to warn you that the shit will hit the fan tomorrow once this news hits the streets. I expect a considerable number of musicians will be giving me a call and asking how they can claw their way out of their contractual obligations with you, or at least how they can avoid association with you until things calm down. So don't get too drunk tonight, Reed. You can expect your phone to be red hot tomorrow. If I was you, I would grab an early night whilst you still can. Oh and one last parting shot; find your wife. She isn't here for a reason, a fucking big gargantuan reason. I don't know what you are hiding from me, but I smell revelation number four working its way into the tabloids.'

Magnus felt awful leaving Reed as he did. Had he been too stern? He mulled that thought over in his mind. However the guy was in trouble, and he suspected that Reed had no idea just how much trouble.

Reed took his agent's advice and pulled himself to his feet. Perhaps it was for the best that he retired whilst he could still walk. As he swayed back and forth and held onto the villa's walls for dear life, he thought back to his meeting with Emmanuelle. He recalled her words: 'We put you in the right place at the right time, never forget that.' It had been a poorly-concealed threat. He knew what she was saying: that what could be given could equally be taken away. It was a worry. Reed had already lost part of his fortune through Alexia, and now, with all this bad press, his record label was at risk. He hoped against hope that Magnus would be able to squash the publication in time, but deep down he knew that it was already too late.

CHAPTER 31

Sunday 21st July

Mercy had endured the most uncomfortable two days of her life, aside from being shot in the thigh on a drugs raid in 1998. Her arm was in a sling and her back was braced with bandages in an attempt to stabilise her broken collarbone. It was useless. She had to sleep propped up with four or five pillows, and she couldn't move without excruciating pain. Everyone kept telling her how lucky she was, but at this moment of time she felt far from lucky. Why do people say that? An accident is anything but an auspicious event.

She wasn't sure how she would make the long car journey home even with powerful analgesics, but none the less she was assured that a professional driver was on his way to collect her. She had been told originally that her nephew Simon would be picking her up, so Mercy was confused as to why the plan had been changed at the last minute, but she was beyond caring. She just wanted to get back to Oxford.

She was in dreadful pain, so the considerate nurse found a private room for her in the discharge lounge whilst she awaited her driver. After a lukewarm cup of tea (in a hospital feeding beaker, since it was her right arm that had been incapacitated), life seemed better. Add to that a digestive biscuit, a morphine injection and co-codamol for the journey home; the world seemed to be a slightly better place. But it still hurt!

Dr Tomas Forshaw peered over at Mercy from a distance as she was wheeled into a side room. He had begun to take a shine to her. He felt sorely disappointed to have been deceived by someone he had grown to like. He approached her as she sat in the transfer lounge awaiting her driver.

'Can I have a brief word please, Ms Mercy De Vede?' he said. Mercy had her back turned to the doctor, but on hearing her name she gingerly rotated her bruised and battered body to face whoever was addressing her. She was saddened to find Tomas. Her cover was now splattered all over the disinfected ward floor.

'So who exactly are or were Corrine Woods and Polly Johnson?' asked Tomas.

Mercy answered truthfully. 'I'm sorry Tomas, I don't know who they are, but there was a good reason for me doing what I did. How did you find out my name?'

Tomas handed Mercy her driving licence. 'You were found upside down in a ditch Mercy, so the police did a DVLA search on your registration plate, and oh, this was in your pocket. Who was or is Polly Johnson by the way? I would like to know the name of the patient I thought I was treating.'

Mercy sensed she was in trouble in more ways than one. In life there was a time for subterfuge and a time for honesty, and now was the time to start telling the truth. Tomas had made her feel like a worm hiding under a stone. He was a lovely, dedicated doctor who made sick people better and did all that was required of his noble profession as best he could. In contrast Mercy felt that she was a conniving, devious detective who did anything required of her scheming profession as best she could.

'Tomas, your patient's name is Eenayah Baratolli, the wife of the famous Reed B. She is my client. I run a detective company and I was paid to protect her. I masked her identity because I believed her life to be endangered by people, things and situations that I cannot even begin to describe to you. Tomas, I am so sorry I was devious, but in my line of work we sometimes need to do bad things for good reasons.'

Two smartly-suited men walked in behind Tomas as she was finishing her sentence. They had overheard the conversation.

'Is this the Miss De Vede you referred to, Dr Forshaw?' asked one of them. Tomas nodded his head as though he had just taken 30 pieces of silver to betray a friend. He turned to Mercy and apologised. His head hung low and his cheeks shone red. He bent down and kissed her cheek, whispering 'sorry.' Regaining his professional posture he continued to explain.

'Mercy, we transferred Polly, or rather Eenayah, to a brain rehabilitation unit last evening. To cut a long story short, we have been informed by the unit that the ambulance never turned up in Golborne where it had been destined for. We suspect the drivers may have been bogus. There seems to be no other explanation. Obviously you turn up with a false ID and we start to smell a rat. I am sorry, but I had to inform the police about you. I had no choice in the matter. You lied. We have a missing patient with a false identity and you seem to be the person holding the key to who she is.'

The police officers stepped forward. 'Detective Sergeant Allwyn-Jones and DC Bevan, madam,' said one of them. 'We apologise about the need to interview you in these circumstances and we appreciate that you are in a lot of pain. However there is a sense that this may be a complicated case and we need to know your side of the story as soon as possible.'

Mercy didn't know what to say or how to react. In these circumstances perhaps many people would go into defensive mode and think only about themselves and their own sorry situation, but Mercy wasn't most people. Her first reaction was an intense concern about Eenayah. Any emotions secondary to that focused on the fact that she had let her down - badly. In her rush to get back to Oxford, she had left her alone. She had made the dreadful professional mistake of trusting other people to ensure her client's safety. It was partially her fault because she hadn't shared with these other people the fact that Eenayah could be in danger. Why would any of these wonderful clinical staff ever consider that a patient would be abducted in the journey between the hospital and a separate specialist unit 50 or 60 miles away?

Mercy hadn't put anyone on heightened alert, so of course the medical staff had trusted the situation. Maybe the ambulance team weren't bogus. Perhaps they had been flagged down and kidnapped themselves. Shit - who knew? Mercy was in intense pain and slightly fearful of her own safety. Had her accident been an accident? Luke's words, recorded and sent over to her from her father, resonated fatefully in her mind. A million thoughts flew through her head in a mass stampede of confusion. She knew she had to co-operate with the police, but how could she tell them that Eenayah was implicated in some religious prophecy which had begun to untwine itself in an almost supernatural way? These were policemen, after all. She knew how their minds worked. She had been one of them once. They would think the story ridiculous. How could she walk the line between credibility and honesty? It was a tough call, but she knew one thing, and that was that she wanted Eenayah found every bit as much as they did. She would co-operate fully.

She held out a shaking left hand and tried to compose herself, despite the pain and shock. 'I'm pleased to meet you both, but I am sorry it is in this situation. Of course I will co-operate with you fully, but this will be a long and strange story. My name is Mercy De Vede and I am the CEO and founder of a private investigations company called MeDeVe Ltd. We are the same company that recently found and returned the MacDonald boy who was held captive in Greece. I am also an ex CID police officer, formerly with Thames Valley Police. You can search my former employment records. I will help you as best I can.'

Tomas was impressed at this declaration of Mercy's background and let out a 'wow' under his breath. He murmured it just a tad too loud and shuffled around on his feet in embarrassment as everyone turned to look at him. DS Allwyn-Jones scowled at the inappropriate verbal gesture of the handsome young doctor.

'Thank you for everything Dr Forshaw, but do you mind if we have a chat with Ms De Vede in private please?'

Tomas was finding all this intensely interesting, but he reluctantly left to get on with his ward round. As he closed the door, DS Allwyn-Jones continued.

'Ms De Vede, yes indeed we have heard of your reputation and all the admirable work your team have accomplished with the MacDonald case. However I do need to warn you that the Atlanta Police team also want to interview you with regard to the death of Katya Beselovaya, the Russian socialite. As soon as we did a name check on your registration plates, it flagged up an Interpol message.'

Mercy looked up to the heavens and sighed. She had known that this was coming and had wanted to get to the police before they had got to her. She had a risky job in a dangerous world. As a police officer she came under the protective umbrella of a mightier public body and the safeguard of being part of a team. More so, a government team. As an independent, she also worked with a team, but as Chief Executive of MDV Ltd she wore the cap of ultimate responsibility and had no other safety net to catch her fall. She was in command, and there was nobody else to blame but herself if anything went wrong. She hadn't considered the weight of her position prior to today.

Mercy sensed that she was now swimming around in crap up to her neck. The only factual explanation she could offer these bobbies was a story so bizarre and extraordinary that it beggared belief.

The police officers recognised who Mercy was by her name and reputation. From a professional standing they admired and respected her. Any police officer who had been round the block a few times had heard of MeDeVe, as occasionally even the police contracted cul-de-sac jobs out to them. However, right now all the officers could see before them was a fragile human being with two black eyes, shoulders braced and her right arm resting in a sling to take the pressure off her shattered shoulder. With a pasty face and dark sunken eyes, they could tell she was in immense pain. She also looked visibly shattered about the abduction of her client Eenayah. They both felt compassion towards her.

'Mercy, this is what we are going to do,' said DS Allwyn-Jones. 'We won't interview you for too long right now as we can see you're not physically up to it. However we do need to take as many details as we can regarding the missing patient. If we can get that done today it means we can start the ball rolling at our end. We also need to inform her family in the States, and that means we need to organise some collaboration with the police on the other side of the pond. Do you mind me talking frankly?'

Mercy knew what the DS was going to say before he opened his mouth. She had done his job once upon a time and she knew what she would say to someone like her. 'Yeah - go for it detective,' she said.

'Mercy, you used to be one of us and in many ways you still are. We do recognise and sympathise with how you must be feeling right now. However the fact is that you are closely associated with a missing person who happens to be married to a very wealthy music mogul and a recently-deceased person who is the daughter of some Soviet bigwig. Even I have heard the names of Eenayah Baratolli and Katya Beselovaya and as my wife would tell you, I don't know anybody famous. I haven't time to watch the news or read papers. All I ever seem to do is work, watch rugby, drink beer, take a piss and go to sleep. So if I have heard of someone it must mean they are either very important, very wealthy or very famous. Do you get what I am saying?'

Mercy understood completely where the officer was coming from. She already knew that the publicity around this was going to go viral. The exposure around the MacDonald case would seem small fry compared to the media hype that would connect these two unlikely females. Eenayah and Katya; an implausible association tied together by Mercy. At some point she would have to risk her professional standing by telling the truth, and the truth was off the planet of possibilities. The words flew around inside her mind: 'Protecting the clone of a woman born over 3000 years ago'. Even she had to laugh at the obscure thought. She would be sectioned! The world would consider her as totally bonkers. Her company was finished. She couldn't think of any lie good enough to cover her back, and the reality was too whacky to be believed. There was nowhere to run. It was over.

The DS had been quite compassionate up until now, but he was mindful that this was a complex case and his body language became unyielding as he drummed the severity of the situation home to roost.

'I am sure you have already considered this, but if there should be any inferred connection between you and the death of Katya Beselovaya it could place your life at risk. From what I have been told by colleagues, the woman had many criminal associations. I also understand that her father Sergei would not be averse to seeking vengeance if his daughter's death turned out to be anything other than accidental. One of the last things she did was send you a file and an email that implies you got her to blackmail Reed Baratolli. You must understand how bad this looks for you. I don't know much about Reed B, but the missing person is his wife, and that means this news is going to go global. This case is much bigger than I think any of us originally realised. Brace yourself, Mercy; I think you are in for a rocky ride.'

The DS turned to face DC Bevan, his face contorted by internal angst. He felt sorry for Mercy, but she was in deep trouble. 'Dave, can you organise a driver to escort Ms De Vede's driver back to Oxford? After what happened to the missing patient in transit, I don't think we can risk anything happening to Ms De Vede at this early stage of our enquiries.' DC Dave Bevan rushed off to make some calls, leaving DS Allwyn-Jones to begin the interview process.

'We'll keep this fairly brief and to the point this morning Mercy, but I'll need to arrange a follow up visit to you when you are back in Oxford,' he said. Mercy appreciated the officer's congenial demeanour and empathy. Her head hurt, her shoulder throbbed and every joint in her body felt sore. She just wanted to go home, but she fully recognised that this was indeed global news and she had a large part to play as this peculiar story began to unfold, most likely under the judgemental glare of the public spotlight.

If the helpful Buddhist monk had been correct with his doom and gloom warnings, then the secretive Ledanite society would not be pleased with the full details of their well-guarded prophecy being aired on a public stage. It slowly began to dawn on Mercy that they might want to shut her up every bit as much as some Russian hired contract killer. Boy, was she in trouble!

Mercy gave the detective the briefest of details, mainly relating to Eenayah's identity.

'Here is the number of my assistant, Kerry,' she said. 'Of course it is Sunday and she won't be in the office, but as long as she picks up the phone to you she should be able to access all the information we have on file regarding Eenayah Baratolli and any contact details we have for her. I know we have her sister Ruby's address, which as far as

I am aware was the last place she stayed before she went out on her tragic mountain run. I am also aware that Ruby and her family have been in Florida on vacation and are due back any day now. I suspect she may even be in the air as we speak, so it's probably worth doing a search on flights coming into Manchester. We also have Reed's contact details, so it may be worth asking Kerry to email these over to you as well. I take it that you have recovered her hire car, wherever it was she left it. The area where she fell is some distance from Ruby's house, so she must have got herself over to the mountain range somehow. Maybe worth doing some forensics on the car to check if anybody else was in there with her.'

Mercy couldn't help but give the young DC instructions. She had once been in the position of his superior and old habits die hard.

Her eyes started to close as the analgesia kicked in. She exaggerated a yawn in order to stress that she couldn't carry on with the meeting any longer. She was keen to keep any cross-examination brief and to the point. She urgently needed to speak with her father to agree an exit strategy, and hoped that giving the officers her PA's details would suffice for the time being.

'I do apologise, Detective Sergeant,' she said. 'The nurse gave me a morphine injection to help me cope with the drive back to Oxford and it's just starting to take effect. Would it be okay if we deferred this interview until tomorrow? I am sure Kerry can give you what information you require for the time being.'

Thankfully DS Allwyn-Jones could see that Mercy wasn't in any fit state to continue, and interviewing someone whilst they were under the influence of drugs probably wasn't legally submissible evidence anyway. Of course Mercy was aware of that and played upon the timing of her morphine injection.

'That's fine. DC Bevan has just informed me that your driver and our escort are both sitting outside waiting to take you home. So I agree

– best you try and get some sleep and we will pick this up tomorrow. I'll give Kerry a call now. Thank you for your co-operation so far. I hope you start to feel better soon.'

With a sensation of floating above her own body due to the morphine, Mercy carefully slid inside the rear seat of the limo. She tried to keep her mind alert enough to consider the reality of the situation she had become entangled in. There were serious decisions to be made. Should she walk the path of righteousness and tell the police the truth and nothing but the truth, knowing that this would throw out sparks which might endanger her professional reputation, and perhaps have other, more potent repercussions? Or should she make a false statement, knowing full well that this could be seen as an obstruction of justice, and should any of this go to trial even be construed as perjury?

While she still had some of her wits about her, she called Kerry to warn her about a possible call from the police. 'Only give him the basics Kerry - nothing more,' she said. 'Just an address and contact details. Got it?'

'Affirmative - I understand, Mercy.'

She then tried her father's mobile phone. As usual, the Professor didn't pick up. She left a long, detailed message explaining how Eenayah had apparently gone missing somewhere along the route between the hospital and the specialist brain injury unit at Golborne, some 60 miles away. She was sure the police would be sifting through CCTV images along the expected journey route and would have some clear answers very soon. Almost childlike, she asked her father for help. She needed to consult with him before the police visited her tomorrow. Possibly for the first time ever in her entire life she was afraid. Mercy De Vede didn't know what to do.

★★★

The mood in the O'Byrne household was light and jovial. It had been a peaceful Sunday, with Nat King Cole and the like providing background mood music. Frank had endeavoured to calm his friend down as best he could and had succeeded admirably. Frank and the Professor played cards and laughed hysterically as they each tried their hardest to cheat each other out of winning. The Professor knew his time with Frank was nearing an end and he wanted to store up as many happy memories from his Dublin visit as was possible.

Frank went to make them both a hot toddy when he noticed the Professor's mobile flashing away in the corner of the kitchen. 'Hey Roland, you have missed calls from that possessive daughter of yours again,' he said. 'She may have her arm in a sling, but she can still use a handset, eh?'

The Professor looked at his watch and panicked when he saw the time. 'Where has the day gone? I had better give her a call. She is getting out of hospital today. I have sent a driver to go and collect her as I didn't want to trust young Simon with the job. I had better check that she's okay. Just give me a moment Frank, and no bloody peeking at my hand while I am out.'

The Professor returned with an uneasy look on his face. 'Brandy, hot milk, nutmeg and honey – this will put hairs on your chest Roland. Get that down you. You okay pal? You look troubled.'

Indeed the Professor was troubled. 'I tried to call Mercy back but she isn't picking up. However I did listen to the message she left me. It seems Eenayah has been taken. You need to listen to this message, Frank. It's quite disturbing.'

Both men sat in silence as Mercy explained what had happened and described the ensuing police interview scenario. Frank felt he had to comfort his old friend and add sense, logic and reason.

'Roland, we should give Luke a call,' he said. 'There is a part of me which wonders if he can be trusted, but at the end of the day he is the only person we know close enough to the Ledanite followers to have a handle on the situation. He may know something. I would be surprised if he doesn't.'

The Professor knocked his hot toddy back in one. 'Oh shit Frank! I think I told Luke where Eenayah was. This could all be my fault. It never dawned on me that he could still be connected to them. He sold himself to me as a Buddhist monk so well that I just fell for the fact that he didn't want any association with some secret society who worship the threads of a hidden biblical prophecy. It didn't seem to be his thing any more. I am so sorry. I hope Luke hasn't betrayed us. I am also sorry to you Frank. I hid Eenayah's identity from you because that was Mercy's instructions and then I go and blow it and tell a monk. I apologise Frank, it wasn't that I didn't trust you. I just do what my daughter tells me to do - mostly!'

Frank tried to offer solace to his anxious friend. 'Don't beat yourself up about it Roland. You did right to exclude me. Also, if the Ledanite are as numerous, powerful and well-connected as they are supposed to be, then they would have found her soon anyway. It may even be a good thing if they do have her, as at least they will know how to keep her safe. We just have to hope she is with the good guys rather than the bad guys.'

'It's not just Eenayah's welfare that concerns me Frank. I have never heard Mercy sound so scared. She was a policewoman herself once, she would hate to lie to them. However the truth just sounds too ridiculous to be plausible to normal folks. She doesn't know what to do. She feels trapped.'

Frank gave it some deep thought and concluded, 'You know, she can be honest with the police to a point as long as she omits the biblical prophecy part. At the end of the day, we don't even know if any of this is actually true or not. After the MacDonald case I recall you telling me that it was only a person's belief that makes anything seem real. Faith and belief can make the biggest pile of nothingness grow wings. This whole Tamar bloodline story may be nothing more than folklore passed down through the ages, but there are people out there who believe it and that's all it takes I guess.'

The Professor looked embarrassed as he recalled that he had forgotten to share with his friend some vital new evidence. He squirmed, feeling the embodiment of the archetypal absent-minded professor.

'I'm sorry Frank, but I do believe this prophecy is for real. There is something I have forgotten to tell you. I can't believe it slipped my mind. It was so important. I think I am getting dementia.'

'Hey it's okay Roland. At our age, memory is not what it used to be. What is it you need to tell me?'

The Professor went to remove a piece of paper from his wallet and put on his reading glasses. 'You see this? It's a DNA test. I offer all my clients genealogical testing. In a female's case we specifically looks at mitochondrial DNA, because of course a woman doesn't have a Y chromosome. For Eenayah we did an mtFullSequence, which is highest level mtDNA test for HVR1 and HVR2.'

'This means nothing to me at all Professor, other than you acquired some of Eenayah's DNA, which sounds like it was an excellent idea for mapping genealogical geographic origins.'

'We can take this back 16 generations Frank. If you look at Eenayah's results you will note that most of her ancestry originates in the Middle East, with virtually nil European input. Do you not find it remarkable that over 16 generations of moving around Europe she displays so little European DNA?'

Frank was impressed by the results. He responded, 'well I guess that does add some weight to Eenayah's possible connection to Tamar. All we have had to go by so far is a suggestive family tree and some hieroglyphics, so yes, very useful Roland, but hardly what I would call conclusive.'

'I haven't told you everything,' responded a very guilty looking Professor. 'I am afraid I was a bit naughty and I sent Lilly to visit Eenayah's biological grandmother in the nursing home. She swabbed her inside cheek. Take a look at these results. We compared them to Eenayah's.'

Frank studied the sheets of information. 'But they are the same. These are just Eenayah's results replicated.'

'I don't think you understand Frank. These DNA profiles are from both Eenayah and her natural grandmother. They are identical. It has been confirmed. Eenayah is an exact clone of her grandmother. This is hard evidence. I should have told you sooner, but I only got the results back late last night and for some reason it just slipped my mind. I was so busy worrying about Mercy after her accident…'

Frank had to take a seat. He kept looking at the reports again and again, trying to find a flaw or a variance, but there was none to be seen. He asked, 'Aside from artificial cloning in a test tube as with Dolly the sheep or the natural cloning of identical twins, do you know if there any other instances of a mother giving birth to her clone?'

The Professor shook his head, 'nothing that I know of, Frank. I only know that this mysterious prophecy describes Tamar reproducing herself physically throughout the generations until such a time as she reincarnates her own soul into one of the clones. Eenayah is of Middle Eastern origin. It fits.'

Frank had to agree. 'The evidence seems too compelling. Through your brilliance as a genealogist, you have uncovered a long line of twins. We have seen the hieroglyphic markings that signal the resting place of each clone and now we have the DNA evidence. The prophecy must be true, and if it is true then everything else is true. I think we could be in jeopardy and so could Mercy. I believe we may know too much.'

Frank went to the kitchen and brought back the entire bottle of brandy. 'Screw the milk and the honey my friend, I think we are need some of this in its purest form. Okay – let's not panic. First things first, Mercy asked for advice on how to handle the police. We all know that they have only let her off the hook for now because she is drugged up on morphine. I can bet they will be in Oxford by first light tomorrow to get more details.'

'I know Frank, and I am here in Dublin and I don't know what to advise her to do. She normally calls the shots. This is a weird role reversal.'

Frank tried to think as clearly as he could, given the immediate crisis. 'Look, I don't think you should be too disturbed by the police, Roland. At the end of the day Mercy hasn't committed any crime other than trying to protect a young lady who asked for protection should it be required. Cash changed hands. It was a commercial transaction and Mercy was doing what she was employed to do. In good faith she believed that protecting Eenayah's identity was the right thing to do and indeed time has proven this to be a correct assumption. Who can argue against that?'

'Maybe you are right, Frank. As long as she keeps the prophecy out of the story she tells the police, she can say she was simply doing a job that she was paid to do and act dumb. I don't know how she can explain the Katya tape though. Shall I give her another ring?'

'Yes, try to call her Roland and yes, tell her that she must NOT mention the prophecy to the police at all. A vast secret organisation on a scale of which we know nothing has been protecting this story consistently for over 3000 years, and the last thing they would want is for this to be headline news on the front page of a tabloid. I am not sure we could vouch for her safety if she let that big cat out of the bag.'

Both men became increasingly concerned as time went on and Mercy wasn't answering her phone. She was tied to her phone via a wireless umbilical cord and always picked up, no matter what. They made the presumption that she must be in a morphine-induced sleep, but none the less the lack of communication was burning a hole in her father's head. His imagination was running wild. Nobody from the office was picking up their phones either, so he was unable to get the driver's number.

'I know it's Sunday evening Frank, but we are a 24/7 service and I would expect at least one person to answer their bloody mobile. I need to get a flight back home tonight.'

Frank understood. 'I'm coming with you Roland,' he said. He picked up a bible and said a silent prayer. It wasn't something he had done in a long time. He had once lost someone very dear to him. It hadn't shattered his faith - nothing could do that - but it had taken him away from the priesthood and into the realms of teaching.

The two friends instantly went to pack. The situation had suddenly become worryingly urgent and in light of the DNA results, more sinister. They had no idea what they would find when they left the tarmac of the runway.

★★★

The driver swerved to a sudden halt in the nearest layby, almost doing an emergency stop and burning rubber. The police escort following him also had to brake suddenly to veer into the layby. The officer was about to give the driver a major ticking off having nearly come off his motorbike, but the look of concern on the drivers face as he swung open the door and rushed to the rear passenger seat told him that something was greatly amiss. By the time the police escort caught up to him, the driver was checking Mercy's pulse, which was thready and faint. Her face was a sickly blue.

'Can you get some blue lights mate?' said the driver. 'I thought she was just asleep, but then I noticed her colour. This lady really isn't well.'

The police officer agreed; it was plainly obvious that Mercy was unconscious. 'Stay with her, pal,' he said. 'I'll call for an ambulance. Do you know this area? Do you know where the nearest A&E is?'

'Straight over the roundabout and left at the next junction. Under ten minutes away.'

The policeman was concerned that an ambulance might arrive too late for Mercy. She seemed to be slipping away. The police driver recognised the severity of the situation. 'Screw that, we can do it under five. Follow me - let's get her there now.'

CHAPTER 32

Tuesday 23rd July

Reed had been expecting the news to break about Eenayah for well over 24 hours now. He had already received a call from the British police and he was well aware that Ruby had been detained when she landed at Manchester airport yesterday. Any retrieval plans he had hatched to find his missing wife had been scuppered before he had even had the chance to issue Arabella with the command of 'fetch'.

By now his recent guest would understand that during the three weeks she had been on the vacation of a lifetime, her twin sister had gone missing. Ruby must surely be in shock. She would have no idea what any of this was about. The police also seemed to have no real idea. Everybody seemed to be clueless, and those who could unravel the mystery were either silent or had been silenced.

The police had interviewed Reed earlier in the day, and although the unusual events had seemed to be connected, they couldn't find the piece of string that tied everything together. It appeared to Reed that knowledge of the prophecy was akin to a death sentence, so he was playing dumb; and he wasn't the only one. The Professor had also been interviewed when back on English soil, and like Reed he had feigned ignorance. It seemed that nobody had been willing to lift the lid on a prophecy that had been hidden in the mists of time. The police were stumped, and unless a ransom was about to peek its head out of Pandora's box some time soon, Reed would remain as the more obvious suspect. After all, he was the only person with a motive.

Reed empathised with his sister-in-law. Although they hadn't always seen eye to eye, they had jelled during the short time she had stayed at Reed's house and he was genuinely sorry that she had to go home from a lovely family holiday and face such a huge family dilemma. He knew that as twins they were very close. Eenayah had often said, 'You don't get to share a uterus with someone and not be close'. He had really wanted to call Ruby and offer some comfort, but Reed didn't do sympathy very well and was afraid that anything he said might come over as a false emotion. So he thought it better to keep his distance, something he was fairly good at. That and the fact that he was considered the prime suspect at the moment. In fact, the only suspect. He was innocent and he knew that all the police had to go on was little more than a hunch, but recent events had not shown Reed in the best of lights. However, he had the assurance that he was indeed innocent of any crime and he knew that no matter how deep they dug, they would find no skeletons under his patio.

Reed had expected the call from Magnus. He knew he was going to get a major ticking off and then perhaps a long lecture about the commercial fallout which would ensue. Magnus had warned him to keep out of the news, unusual for a PR agent who normally courted publicity. Reed had avoided the conversation all morning, but when Magnus suddenly appeared at his door he knew there was nothing left to hide behind aside from his face. He braced himself for an uncomfortable dialogue.

Magnus began with an unexpectedly sarcastic approach. 'So, Mr Baratolli, how does it feel to be a potential bigamist with a girl half your age? What about the money you tried to keep hidden from your wife? It must really suck to have it stolen by the accountant you employed to hide it. Oh and talking about your wife, where is she by the way? Rumour has it that she was abducted from a Welsh hospital and nobody can find her. Let's hope she is in safer hands than the Soviet socialite who died after last talking to you. I have to hand it to you Reed, you have been a delightful client and a pleasure to work with over the last ten years, but boy oh boy- when you fall, you do it from a great height and you do it so dramatically. Honestly, I couldn't make this up if I tried. Do you think you have a case of temporary insanity or are you just making up for lost time in the province of boringdom?'

Magnus had such an eloquent way of stringing words together. If he had wanted Reed to feel guilt-ridden, shamefaced and embarrassed then he had succeeded. Reed hung his head low, looking like a man whose world had come to an end. 'Point taken Magnus., what's the damage?' Reed felt it better to keep the discussion as short and as concise as possible. No point prolonging the agony.

'Hot coal, my friend. You are the sizzling scrap of anthracite that nobody wants to touch. Aside from the heavy metal rock bands who seem to like this new dangerous side to you and a few rap artists who feel you have gained some sort of delinquent street cred, the majority of the middle of the road mainstream artists do not want to be associated with you. People are contacting solicitors and trying to pull out of their contracts. I am sorry Reed, it has all been a bit too much too soon. Great Records is in trouble. I can't wrap it up in nice paper with bows and fancy ribbons and make it look any better. You are in a truly crap situation. When shit floats up, turd rains down. I am sorry pal, you need a good umbrella. '

Magnus was not gloating as much as Reed had anticipated. He gave him a friendly slap on his upper arm and looked as though he was genuinely sorry about the situation 'Hey, I'll do what I can to salvage what I can, and I'll try to persuade artists to stay with the label, but prepare yourself for casualties. This isn't going to be an easy ride for anyone. Brace yourself for the fallout.' He left.

Reed didn't know what to make of the brief meeting. He had expected a long lecture from Magnus. This short, succinct conversation felt worse on so many levels. Reed remembered being told that often the first sign of an impending divorce wasn't actually when couples started to argue more than usual; it was in fact quite the opposite - deathly silence. The death knell being when folk lose so much interest in one another that they couldn't even put the energy into arguing any more. That was how it had felt between Eenayah and Reed. They had just floated apart, and communication had dried up. This was how it now felt between Magnus and Reed. Magnus could not even be bothered to deliver his usual sermon. Reed felt his friend and PR agent had given up on him.

Reed walked up to his bedroom, dragging his feet as though his legs had become heavier. As he walked up the grand curved staircase, he took a moment to observe the palatial surroundings. His home was regal, opulent and lavish. He had taken it for granted. On the rare occasions he had been at home, he dashed up this same staircase and hardly paid attention to his grand surroundings. Suddenly - and perhaps now that he felt under threat of losing it all - he paid attention. Too little too late. He wondered why that was. Why do you have to be at the point of losing something to fully appreciate it?

He sat at his wife's dressing table, looking down at the .40 calibre pistol which had been taped to the back of her mirror, just in case. It was already loaded, just in case. Reed then spent quite a long time just looking at it. The temptation was flirting with him. It would be quick, painless and an easy way out. As far as he could see, he had lost everything anyway and there was little point left in living.

He picked up the pistol and held it to his ear. He was within seconds of pulling the trigger when a soft, warm hand folded itself around his hand and gently moved the pistol away from his head.

He looked up. It was Roserie. She almost seem to glow. Her face was soft, smiling and comforting.

'Roserie, I locked my bedroom door. In God's name how did you get in here?'

'You have answered your own question Reed. In God's name I got in here.'

Roserie was his maid, his cook and his cleaner. During the last week she had performed the role of Harry's childminder and playmate to perfection. She had been Eenayah's friend and guardian ever since they had lived in Miami. She was the perfect mistress of ceremonies at all his many parties and ensured that his home was run to flawless perfection. Yet she had always kept a professional distance, as an employee rather than a friend. However, she now looked quite different. Her aura was iridescent. She quite literally took Reed's breath away. He felt warm and comforted in her presence. He had never noticed it before, but now he knew who and what Roserie was. He had been told that both sides of this particular war would have a spirit guide. He now believed Roserie to be Eenayah's spirit guide. Of course now it made sense. Eenayah had been safe when she was with Roserie. Once she had flown out of the country, that protection would have been compromised.

Reed totally understood, and yet knew nothing.

'Why did you save me?' he asked.

'Because without you knowing it, and I presume this was unintentional on your part, you saved humanity, dear Reed.'

'No, I failed both sides. I failed Emmanuelle and all that she required of me. I failed my wife and all that she required of me.' Unusually and perhaps for the first time since primary school, tears started to make their way down Reed's cheek.

Roserie placed her hand on his forehead and comforted him as a mother would a child. 'You only failed Satan; you have never failed God. God forgives you and still loves you. Always remember this Reed, the main difference between good and bad is exoneration.'

Roserie gently wiped the tears from his eyes and placed a soft kiss on his forehead. 'Emmanuelle will not be pleased with you. You have lost Eenayah. You should have kept her prisoner in this gilded cage until her 39th birthday, but you failed. You let her go. Now she is pregnant and the lines of Tamar have fulfilled their destiny for the greater good of mankind. Emmanuelle will be angry, but I will whisper in your ears and I will tell you what to say. Do not be afraid - I will be beside you.'

'But Roserie, I have lost everything.'

'No, you have not lost your soul or your life, just these material trinkets that mean nothing. Yes you have some forgiveness which you need to earn, but I will show you how. Just trust me.'

It was a surreal moment. Reed's life had become so complicated that the unusual wasn't exactly unexpected. However to discover who Roserie really was had come as an unexpected surprise.

'Roserie, one last thing - is Eenayah okay? Is she safe?'

Roserie paused, unsure of what to say, but decided on honesty.

'You must not worry about Eenayah. Yes she is safe and being well looked after. Her twin boys, although tiny and less than the size of a fingernail, will also be safe. Eenayah will not be alive long. You are not to worry about that Reed. I know this sounds dramatic, but she will be going to a far better place. It is God's will. It is her time. She is turning, and her spirit hovers over her body as Tamar begins to take control. It has always been her destiny, and that is something that could not be wrestled with. You could not have changed it even if you had tried. You will not see your wife again. I am sorry Reed, but I do know that she will soon be at peace. The sacrifice she will make will be for a better world.'

Reed fell to the ground and covered his face with his hands as though he could cover up his thoughts with his fingers. The realisation that his wife was in the process of dying created a massive emotional rush which hit him in the pit of his stomach. He looked up at a photograph of Eenayah on her dressing table. She looked beautiful, tanned, happy, relaxed. He remembered their last time together under the big oak tree in the Isle of Man, a happy moment when he had serenaded her with his guitar and sung *Fields of Gold*. She had told him to put the memory in his pocket and keep for later. He guessed that right here and right now was the later Eenayah referred to.

He put his hand in his empty pocket and pulled it out, looking at his empty palm. It confused Roserie, but she guessed he was going through his own personal moment. The sadness was soon replaced by an overriding sense of guilt, knowing that he had never treated Eenayah with the love and respect she had deserved. He realised that the one thing we humans have so little of is time. Time; always running out, more cannot be bought and there is never enough. The most cherished thing anyone could ask of someone else is their time, and giving them that time was the most precious of gifts. No amount of money, diamonds or fast cars, could be a greater gift than time itself. Reed never gave Eenayah enough of his time and now the time had gone. He would never see her again.

Raising his tear-stained face to look for Roserie, he noted that she had disappeared. At some point whilst he had been lost in the moment, she had vanished.

Roserie had been his faithful maid for many years; the cook, cleaner and the childminder. In all these years of service Reed had never guessed her true identity. Playing back the scene in his mind he found himself in shock. Here he was; a sinner amongst men, saved by an angel. He could not compute why he had just been rescued. He knew there had to be a reason; there was always a reason. Just because he hadn't figured it out it didn't mean it didn't exist. There had to be a plan; a purpose why both good and evil had been fighting for his soul. He wondered what to expect next.

He had no choice but to sit it out and wait for what was to unravel before him.

***

An inclement weather system had gathered above the Miami sky and a clap of thunder bellowed from the darkening heavens. Reed had learned to understand the significance of the sudden change in temperature. The wind blew open a door on his balcony and the delicate cream chiffon curtains blew up into the air like ivory ghosts. Behind the semi-transparent material, all he could see was a sea of red. He sat and waited, determined not to be the one to move first.

Emmanuelle ambled slowly into his bedroom like a slinking jaguar stalking its prey. She was wearing a cowled cloak made out of the lushest deep scarlet velvet. Her straight platinum hair fell to her waist and she was wearing a pagan headdress and a pentacle in the centre of her forehead. She looked dramatic and exquisite. Reed's breath was quite taken away by her beauty, but he knew not to be fooled. Beneath the extravagant facade was a foul and ugly heart. Emmanuelle made a beeline for the pistol, which she picked up and caressed like a baby. 'Poor sad little Reed. Has your life become so awful that you really considered using this?' Emmanuelle sniggered. She had a knack of making him feel insignificant in her presence. 'You knew I would come back to see you, and you know why I am here now. I did warn you that you would be punished for losing the one and only thing you were instructed to protect. I take it that you are starting to feel how all you have been given is now melting away?'

She pulled the flimsy curtains aside and brought his attention to the intense rain lashing against the window. She taunted him, knowing full well that she was playing with his raw emotions.

'Pitter patter pitter patter. See how it all runs down the drain and bleeds into the sewers below. Water, so very valuable as it falls from the sky and yet all flowing into a gutter. How does it feel to have it all and then watch as it all starts to disappear?'

Reed hated Emmanuelle with every pore in his body. More so, he was intensely angry with himself for ever being taken in by her false splendour and empty promises of owning all he could survey. She had stood beside him on the Hollywood hills and pointed to the smoggy vista below proclaiming, 'all this I will give you', and he had fallen for it hook, line and sinker. What a fool he had been. He had no further patience for her games. 'Get to the point Emmanuelle. What do you want?'

'We are impatient today, aren't we? What I want is something I doubt you can give me. I want you to find Eenayah, but to be honest, I doubt your ability.'

Reed was becoming increasingly incensed, but he was trying to remain calm. 'Why would you need me to do that? After all, I am just a mere inconsequential human. You are the one with all the supernatural powers. Don't you have some sort of all-seeing eye floating around your sixth chakra? You tell me where Eenayah is and I'll go and bring her home.'

Emmanuelle's expression changed. She was not pleased with Reed's comment. 'If it was that easy Reed, I would go and bring her back myself. Unfortunately she has been veiled, so I cannot see her.'

'What does that mean? Veiled? How and by what or by whom?'

Emmanuelle moved away from the balcony and looked Reed directly in the eyes with an intimidating stare which sent a chill down his spine. 'She has a powerful human around her. Someone who understands the order of the Magi. It is a male. I can see him. I do not know who this mágos is. There are two others with him who have formed a chain around her. It blocks my vision. I fear she is turning. There are celestial signs in the heavens that suggest Tamar is returning, and with her she brings the royal line of David, a pure line protected for centuries by a succession of women who carry the code. A line that both you and I and all the armies of Hell failed to destroy, and this means that we are both doomed Reed. You for sure. I may get another chance to break the second line of succession, but you, my friend, are ash.'

Reed's reaction was unexpected. Maybe it was because Roserie was somewhere in the background giving him comfort and courage, but suddenly he did not feel afraid of Emmanuelle and her idle threats. Roserie's soft voice was whispering in his ear, guiding him through what he should say.

He retorted, 'Who knows? Maybe you are doomed Emmanuelle, or maybe you will just be reallocated another demonic contract. Let's face it, how else can you be punished? You have already fallen as low as any spirit can fall. However, don't tar me with the same brush as yourself, because I still have a chance of salvation. You see, your master is not my master. I can be redeemed. You cannot, because it was you, ironically, who caused all of this to happen.'

Emmanuelle laughed. It was an arrogant, wicked laugh, but with a tinge of nervousness. 'How have I caused this to happen, you stupid moron?' she snapped.

'You didn't stop to think. You failed to understand the prophecy. You didn't do your homework. For Tamar to be reborn into one of the many twins carrying her DNA throughout history, just one of the clones had to show signs of following in her footsteps – living a similar life, walking a similar path to her.'

He had caught Emmanuelle's attention. She was listening intently. 'Eenayah only had two true loves in her life and one of them wasn't me. I wish I could put my hand on my heart and say that my wife did truly love me, but that was not the case. When I met her, she was heartbroken - a shattered woman. She just needed someone to pick her up and look after her and I just happened to be that person. She had lost the two men in her life that she had really cared for and truly loved. They were brothers. They both died young and Emmanuelle, you killed them. In so doing, almost by accident you allowed Eenayah to follow Tamar's destiny. Tamar also loved two brothers, who also died young. Emmanuelle, it was your intervention which allowed Eenayah to follow Tamar's path.'

Emmanuelle was furious, realising that Reed was speaking the truth. She spun around, throwing her cloak into the air, the whites of her eyes now matching its colour.

'That is not quite the case Reed. I will own up to what happened to James. Yes I did put the oil on the corner, but it was his choice to drive too fast and oversteer around the bend. James was partially responsible for his own death. As for Greg, he just picked up meningitis and died. It was all natural. You cannot blame me for that.'

'You are correct Emmanuelle, you cannot be blamed for Greg contracting meningitis. However, if Eenayah had been at home at the time she would have got him to hospital and he would have been treated and he would have survived. You concocted a whole series of events in her life and some major news story she had to cover back in the days when she was a journalist. But for all those obstacles you put in her way, she would have been with Greg when he became ill. You stopped him from being treated, so you killed him by default.'

Emmanuelle became unusually silent. She dared not admit it, but she knew that she had been the silent assassin and Reed was speaking the truth.

Reed continued his attack. 'And what is more, I happen to know that that you have done some homework recently with regard to this prophecy thing. The reason I know this is because you then went on to monitor Paul Bucklow, in other words James and Greg's father. If Eenayah was going to follow Tamar's life story, then this meant her becoming pregnant with her father-in-law in an act of deceit, just as stated in Genesis 38. Did you or did you not rent Paul's cottage? I know you did because I had a phone call from my wife to ask why you were there. I presume you must have been concerned about Eenayah going anywhere near Paul, as this would be the final part of the prophecy realised. You have been quietly monitoring them both. Is this not true?'

Emmanuelle was shocked. 'How could you possibly know all of this?'

Of course Reed didn't know it. It was Roserie whispering in his ear, telling him exactly what to say.

She retorted, 'Hey, but when you found out that Julia was cheating on you, you were more than happy for me to help you arrange the car accident that killed her and her lover boy - what was he called? Bert Montana, that's it. What a jerk! That affair broke your pathetic little heart, didn't it?'

Emmanuelle had touched a raw nerve. 'Yes I was hurt, but I was wrong to get in league with you. Revenge didn't make me any happier. Hey Emmanuelle, I am not saying that I am going to get a free pass into heaven any time soon. I have done a lot of bad things to a lot of people for all the wrong reasons. I have a lot to do to work my way up the ladder of clemency, but you know what - I am going to give it a try.'

Emmanuelle was puzzled. 'I don't understand you Reed. I thought I would come here to find you a shattered little shipwreck. How are you so composed and strong? It makes no sense. Have you a guardian spirit helping you? Is it Eenayah's guardian? I bet it is! I can sense a presence in the room. There is a manifestation around us. Who is it, Reed?'

'Nobody you would know, Emmanuelle. Time for you to go now. I believe you and I have no further business to discuss.'

Emmanuelle flew down the grand staircase in a rage, her red cloak flying up behind her like satanic wings. Roserie was there at the door to show her out. As Emmanuelle wafted through the open space, she paused for a moment to look at Roserie. She wondered if this could be the spirit guide, but then she looked her up and down and noted her simplistic maids outfit. 'Too plain and too ugly, it can't be you,' were the first and last words she uttered to Roserie.

Roserie closed the door. 'Adiós, estúpido demonio,' she murmured. Emmanuelle heard, and paused outside the closed door. Could it be… She reached for the door handle, and sparks flew off the doorknob and burned her hand. As she cradled her red raw palm, she stood back and saw the entire house encapsulated in a faint blue light.

'Yes, it is the maid,' she mused. 'She is protecting Reed now. Hmm, she is powerful.'

Emmanuelle knew that this had been her last encounter with Reed. From now on she would not be allowed to go anywhere near him; he was under the protection of the spirit guide. She didn't understand it. How could the good guys protect someone so bad and corrupt? As she walked away she considered their strange, godly attitude. It was a mind-set that felt alien to her.

'Forgiveness - pile of shit. Who bothers with that?' she snorted. She looked back at the house one last time and uttered, *'Porro tu animam tuam liberasti Ut destitutae sunt tantae divitiae'*. Then the lady in red simply vanished into the stormy Miami air.

Emmanuelle and Océane were never to be seen or heard of again. Their sudden disappearance became the talk of the music industry for a short while, and was to become yet another nail in Reed's coffin as he became prime suspect once again. Yet more missing people had been added to his criminal portfolio, their disappearance part of the plot in Reed's fall from grace. Soon Emmanuelle and Océane would be forgotten; such is the transient nature of an industry which targets the young who grow old and then forget.

CHAPTER 33

Monday 26th August

Everybody expected Ruby to fall apart. Nobody would have blamed her if she had crashed to the ground in grief. Yet she stood firm. At first, maybe it was the shock. Being met at the airport by the police and pulled aside after going through passport control was a devastating experience.

To begin with, she didn't quite believe that Eenayah was missing. She had told the police that her twin had a history of running away from situations she couldn't deal with. Despite her being an in-patient with concussion and minor brain damage, Ruby still hoped this was one big elaborate hoax on Eenayah's part. Perhaps she had staged the whole thing just to avoid facing up to an existence and marriage which was far from ideal? However, as the hours turned into days, the days into weeks and now the weeks into a month, the reality began to dawn that her sister wasn't just missing, she had been kidnapped and worse still, nobody could think of any valid reason as to why.

The police had interviewed many people and followed several lines of enquiry, but each time they had hit a stone wall. Eenayah's Facebook and Twitter accounts seemed to be lacking any useful personal information, and descriptions of her activities were sparse and vague. The police concluded that her kidnap had been planned. Neither the ambulance men nor the nurse escorting her during the transfer process were legitimate members of staff and the actual ambulance itself was found abandoned close to the hospital. It had seemed to be a professional crime. There were no fingerprints or any other clues. There was no useful CCTV footage and basically the police had drawn a blank. As for a motive, this was a mystery. Eenayah was the wife of a wealthy man, so blackmail could be the incentive. However nobody had attempted to demand a ransom, so as time went on, this seemed to be more and more unlikely.

Reed was possibly the main suspect. It had now become public knowledge that he was about to ask his wife for a divorce. Yet his attempt to hide his assets did not point to a man who was planning to kill his wife. Why bother to hide his money if he had murder on his mind? More to the point, all Reed's movements could be fully accounted for. And there was no body, so no evidence of murder. Eenayah Baratolli had simply been lost in transit.

Ruby was also a suspect, so the police had been cagey about how much information they shared with her. Eenayah had made a large deposit of several millions into Ruby and Owyn's joint bank account the morning of her accident. The transfer was made electronically from Ruby's ISP address. Although Ruby was away in Florida as her sister's dilemma started to unfold, the amount of money was so large and the timing so coincidental that Ruby was bound to be under investigation, unlikely as her participation in her sister's abduction may have appeared. The police were not making any assumptions of innocence.

It had been Katya Beselovaya who had made the call to Reed to inform him that Eenayah wouldn't be attending the family reunion, which ironically had been planned for the day Eenayah was abducted; July 20th. The conversation had been recorded and sent to Mercy De

Vede. The timing seemed beyond happenstance. The police were bamboozled about the relationship triangle that linked these three unusual woman: Katya Beselovaya, Russian heiress, dead; Eenayah Baratolli, music mogul's wife, missing and Mercy De Vede, CEO, dead from a morphine overdose, deemed to have been deliberate.

The investigating officers could not put the jigsaw puzzle together. None of the pieces seemed to fit.

Mercy had been the person responsible for masking Eenayah's true identity whilst she was in hospital, yet with what possible motive? Ruby could not work it out. It was an extreme step to take. Why had Mercy assumed Eenayah was in danger? Mercy knew something, but what? None of the files kept on the case stated anything more elaborate than basic demographics and details of her quest for her birth mother and the genealogical work she had commissioned for her husband. MeDeVe was about to be dissolved as a company and the soon to be ex-employees either knew nothing or said nothing. Mercy seemed to be the one person holding many of the clues, but due to a tragic pharmaceutical incident she was no longer around to tell her side of the story. The nurse who gave Mercy the injection was never traced and the overdose was considered to have been deliberate. It made no sense to anybody. It was an elaborate, well-planned kidnap which had been executed to perfection, and yet nobody knew how or why.

Where was Eenayah Baratolli?

***

Ruby had been unable to concentrate since being back at work. It was to be expected, and all her colleagues were sympathetic, treading delicately whilst around her. She would sit for hours in her sky-high office, staring out to nowhere and wondering where her twin could be. Spreadsheets and financial forecasts were the least of her priorities and uncompleted work started to pile up in an increasing blur of unopened emails. It soon became clear to her line manager that she was unable to carry on, so Ruby had been offered a sabbatical from work. It was a kind and sympathetic consideration and Ruby was relieved to have some time to focus on this awful situation. She emptied her drawers, packed her laptop bag with the few personal items scattered around the office, closed the door and walked.

On arriving back from Florida she learned that Eenayah had given her a considerable sum of money to complete the renovation of their large and rickety Welsh mansion house. Maybe it had been a prophetic gesture on Eenayah's part, but none the less if need be it procured Ruby some precious time away from work.

Many people had expected Ruby to have an almost magical telepathic sensitivity linking her to her twin. There was some truth in this supposition. As a child, she could feel if her twin was hurt or sad or in danger. Now there was nothing, and she couldn't understand why. It was like trying to read a blank sheet of paper. Ruby was shocked by how little she could perceive about her sister. Was she dead, was she alive? She didn't even know that. She had many long, late night conversations with her distraught parents about it and all she could say was, 'It just feels like something or someone is blocking me. I know that sounds weird, but that's the only way I can describe it. It is like a curtain has been drawn around her and I cannot sense anything.'

Ruby couldn't just sit there and do nothing. Following the death of her Gran many years back, she had learned that keeping busy with everyday practical things was the best way to channel grief, so Ruby, being Ruby, took matters into her own hands. The police seemed to be doing the best they could, but not getting anywhere fast. Even if they did know something more than they were saying, they were being guarded in what they communicated. Ruby decided that the only way she could cope with this harrowing situation was to keep her mind busy. She sat down at her laptop and wrote down what recollections she had of recent conversations with Eenayah. She intended to track down all the people Eenayah had spoken to and visited during her pilgrimage to the UK. Much as she tried to focus, her mind kept wandering down the bumpy road of regret. If only she hadn't been away in Florida whilst Eenayah was in the UK. If only she had been with her whilst she tried to untangle her past. If only she hadn't been swimming with dolphins, whilst Eenayah was drowning in her mind. If only!

26th August; it was their birthday today. Of course Ruby had no idea just how important this day was and that it was the birthday when Eenayah had been prophesied to lose her fertility. It had been written in the hidden parables that all those female clones carrying the line of Tamar would only be fertile until the age of 'two score less one', which in modern terms equated to 39. It was the day by which Eenayah would have been safe from both the Ledanite ambitions and the dark forces that opposed them. It was a momentous day, the day that the line of Tamar would have ended for the Layne twins. After this day some other twin girls somewhere else in the world would have had to carry the mantle of Tamar's line. Eenayah would have been safe from this day forth, but Ruby knew none of this. To Ruby, this was a summer Bank Holiday Monday like any other boring Bank Holiday. Ruby was blissfully ignorant of the prophecy that had meddled in her life and that of her twin since birth.

She couldn't just spend the day at home watching the sheep in the field eat grass. Trying to hold back what were now becoming tears of grief, she kissed goodbye to Harry and Owyn. Harry had drawn her a birthday card from a piece of yellow cardboard he found in the drawer. It was a cute crayoned image of flowers with a rainbow and two ladies holding hands. Harry still saw his mummy as being one of two people. The image struck a nerve. Ruby hadn't actually cried over her sister to date, but her eyes started to sparkle with the tears she was holding back. Reality was starting to dawn on her. The longer Eenayah was missing and the more hopeless she felt, the sooner she knew that tears were on the horizon.

She recalled the name of the company Eenayah had allegedly been engaged with regarding the genealogy project she was involved in, alongside the search for their biological family. Ruby had searched for the company address of MeDeVe Ltd and set off to Oxford to locate their offices. Maybe a wild goose chase, but for her own sanity she needed to keep her mind active. Ruby was a practical person and being pro-active was her way of dealing with a crisis. She had made a plan: Oxford first and then Manchester to meet her new family, and Newcastle upon Tyne to pursue the trail with Jonathan Cook. She would follow in her sister's footsteps in the hope that Eenayah had left clues in her wake.

★★★

52 Carrington Lock, Oxford- it was a slightly awkward place to find, but none the less aesthetically delightful. As she went to knock on the office door of MeDeVe Ltd, the door began to open on its own. She hadn't expected that, and stood back slightly to meet whoever was on the other side - but there was nobody.

She entered cautiously. The office was totally empty and the sound of her footsteps echoed around the void. It had that moist coldness that old buildings retain when they haven't been heated for a while, and Ruby could see her breath steam up. The reception, probably once a place of heightened activity, was now eerily quiet. You could hear a pin drop, such was the stillness.

'Hey, you're early - do come in.' Ruby nearly jumped out of her skin as she turned to find a most attractive, flamboyant young man standing behind her. He seemed to have anticipated her visit.

'What do you think?' he continued, apparently believing Ruby was someone else. 'Personally I don't think this space suits an office at all. I know I can get good money by way of a commercial rent, but I feel more inclined to convert this into three large apartments. I mean, have you seen the view from the windows? I was thinking of having a four-bedroomed apartment on each of the three floors. Take a look around and let me know what you think. Oh, and there are cellars as well and I was thinking, ideal garage space.'

Whoever this young chap was expecting, it certainly didn't seem to be Ruby. He rushed off to answer his mobile before she could introduce herself and correct him. 'Sorry darling, awaiting a call from Japan. Just take a look around and I will be with you shorts.' Off he flew in a whirlwind of activity. Ruby presumed he must be the property owner. She would take him up on his offer whilst he was busy on the line to Japan.

The office looked as though it had been totally abandoned. She could see where computers had rested for years, where furniture had left indentations on the floor and where network cables had been torn hastily from the wall. Ruby paused outside the Professor's study. She read the name plate on the door: 'Professor Roland De Vede'. The name sounded familiar. Where had she heard that name before?

The Professor's study looked out of kilter compared to the rest of the neat white office space. She gazed out from his window onto the spires of Oxford's antiquated architecture. She understood what the young man meant about the great views. She continued to look around for clues, and noted some of the Professor's old books just bagged up in black bin bags, as though wiped from their shelves without thought. She ran her finger along the dust on his desk; clearly nobody had sat at this table for weeks.

She was quite unaware of the man standing quietly in the doorway. 'You are correct, Ms Hawthorne. The last residents left in something of a hurry.' For the second time in a row, the dashing young landlord had appeared unexpectedly behind her and startled her. 'Oh my God, you made me jump,' she said. 'Look I am sorry, we haven't been introduced. I think you may think I am somebody I am not.'

The landlord appeared to be confused. 'Oh, so you are not Lesley Hawthorne the architect? That is disappointing.'

Ruby laughed, 'No I am not your architect. I wish I was. It was a career choice I would have loved to have made. I have however been renovating a very old listed manor house in Wales for the last few years, so if you want any pointers on how to convert this lovely old building into apartments, I would be happy to give you some. Sorry I haven't introduced myself; Ruby Kyfinn.'

'Ruby Kyfinn indeed. Well I am sorry you aren't my architect. I bet Lesley Hawthorne isn't anywhere near as attractive as you are. Tobiah Zemel, pleased to meet you. I own this building and you are here – why exactly?'

Tobiah was like a blast of fresh air. He was full of energy and wit, with a wicked twinkle in his engaging dark brown eyes. Ruby couldn't help but like him. He was rather ostentatious, with shoulder-length dark curls and an oversized pointed collar. He didn't really look as though he belonged to the 21st century and Ruby could imagine that in the past his type would have been referred to as a bit of a cad or a rake. Old-fashioned terms suited Tobiah. He made Ruby smile and she hadn't done that since she was in Miami.

'Mr Zemel, I apologise,' she replied. 'I didn't mean to just walk in, but the door was unlocked. I am here to find MeDeVe Ltd, so I am a bit shocked to find this place deserted. I was hoping I could talk to someone here about my sister. She had some business with these guys before she….' Her voice trailed off as she started to become emotional, unable to hold back the tears a second longer.

With his bright red Lamborghini Veneno roadster parked just outside the entrance, Ruby soon understood that Tobiah Zemel was probably a very successful and well-heeled property investor, who was most likely extremely busy and would have little time for her or her problems. He probably had a plane waiting to jet him off to Japan once he had met with his architect, and it was unlikely that he had anything interesting to tell her about MeDeVe which would help her in her search. She felt embarrassed that she had let go of some private emotions in front of a total stranger who had better things to do with his time than talk to a weepy woman.

'I am very sorry Mr Zemel,' she said. 'This is all very difficult for me. I think I had better leave. Your real architect will probably be here any moment now and I had better let you get on with your business.'

She hadn't expected someone like Tobiah Zemel to have a caring and attentive side to his nature, but she had misjudged him. He pulled out a solid gold Breguet pocket watch from inside his velvet trimmed Edwardian morning coat. He really was quite a dashing young fellow, but almost from another century.

'Ms Ruby Kyfinn, I don't believe you are going anywhere in your state,' he said. 'I have made a mistake of the time and my architect isn't due for another hour, so don't concern yourself with her. Maybe I can be of some assistance to you.'

He took Ruby by the hand and guided her towards the window seat in the bay of the Professor's office. He was quite assured and commanding.

'In my line of work I spend a lot of time in cold buildings with neither kettle nor electricity, so I always pack a flask and a picnic. Let me fetch my hamper. I always make enough to share just in case a beautiful young woman walks into my world. Please stay here and you can tell me all about your sister and perhaps I can help you. Oh and one other thing, please call me Tobiah. Whenever you say Mr Zemel I expect my father to be standing behind me.'

Ruby instantly felt at ease. Despite his philandering, she didn't feel that Tobiah was hitting on her. He was simply being a perfect gentleman with impeccable manners. She simply had to smile.

Tobiah walked in with a wicker Harrods's hamper and a tartan picnic blanket. He handed the blanket to Ruby. 'I just thought you looked cold,' he explained. As he opened up the hamper she couldn't help but laugh. 'My goodness, I suspect nothing you do in life comes cheap.'

Ruby felt as if she had just stepped into a period costume drama. None of this felt real. Tobiah handed Ruby a small container of white truffle risotto with smoked salmon and then pulled out a black flask and poured her a hot steaming cup of Jamaican blue coffee.

'My goodness, I just bet you eat like this every day don't you? Gee it's my birthday today and I don't usually celebrate with such luxuries.'

Tobiah rummaged around in the picnic hamper and located a bottle of Champagne Cuvee Blanc de Noirs Maxim's De Paris. 'Happy birthday,' he said. 'I suspect we are both driving, so it's only one drink each, but please take the bottle with you for your onward journey. Now, how can I help you?'

Ruby's face had been relaxed and calm, but now that she had been reminded about Eenayah her forehead creased tightly. 'My sister has gone missing' she said. 'You have probably read about her in the papers. She is Eenayah Baratolli wife of the musician and record producer Reed B.'

Tobiah had suspected as much. 'Yes, I have read about your sister. I am so sorry Ruby. It all sounded very sudden and very mysterious.'

Ruby tried not to be emotional as she explained the situation. 'Eenayah had hired MeDeVe for a variety of reasons and I was hoping they would be able to fill me in on some details. I know the police have already interviewed the employees, but they are not sharing that much with me so I am on a mission to find out what I can for myself. I must say, I am shocked to find they are no longer here. Do you know what happened? You're the landlord so I'm guessing somebody must have served you notice.'

Tobiah was sympathetic. He could see that Ruby was hurting inside, but was putting on a brave face.

'MeDeVe had a five year-contract with me. They took over the whole building and as you can see it's fair sized. I simply presumed they were a fruitful and thriving company. They have been my tenants for a good three years now and very satisfactory tenants at that. Always paid their rent on time and rarely moaned about anything much. About two weeks ago I got this urgent call from Kerry - she is the girl who worked on the front desk and seemed to be an office manager. She rang to tell me they had moved out. They had another two years left on the contract, but they had paid the whole amount. I drove down here immediately, but by the time I got here the place was vacant. Well - aside from this bag full of the Professor's books and his antique grandfather clock. I was told a shipping company would be collecting the clock later. It looks to me like they have left in a hurry.'

'Did Kerry give you any indication why they were leaving? I'm sure you must have asked them for some sort of explanation.'

'Yes indeed, of course I asked. The Professor co-owned MeDeVe with his daughter Mercy. He adored his daughter, totally idolised her. I'm not sure how true this is, but I was told that she was on her way back to Oxford following an accident and had been given an injection of morphine to control the pain for the journey back home. I believe she was found dead in the back of the car. I was told she had been given an overdose. Not sure if this was accidental or deliberate. Maybe you need to ask the police about it. All I know from what Kerry told me was that this was a terrible shock for everybody. I understand her father was beside himself with grief. He was very close to his daughter. They were virtually inseparable. Kerry told me that everyone had been given six months' redundancy pay and the company was being wound up.'

Ruby felt a sense of hopelessness. This was not the news she had hoped for.

'That's awful Tobiah! No, the police did not tell me about this. Maybe they will at some stage, but for now they just aren't updating me about anything. Would you happen to know where the Professor has gone to?'

Tobiah downed his glass of champagne and shrugged his shoulders. 'All I know for sure is that some of the personal items have been shipped to Spain. I'm sure the Professor once told me told me he had a son who lived over there. It's a big place so you may struggle to locate him, but I can bet that's where he has moved to. I wouldn't blame him if that was the case. He was quite a frail old bird and probably long overdue for retirement. Such a pleasant chap. I feel so sorry for his loss.'

Ruby gazed out of the windows and sighed. Grasping at straws she asked, 'Would you happen to have Kerry's number or anyone else's contact details from MeDeVe?'

Tobiah stood to his feet and gave her an unexpected hug. It was warm and sincere.

'I don't think I have Ruby, but I do promise I will go through my files and let you know if I find anything. Please give me your mobile number, just in case. I wish I could have been more helpful. Do you have far to go when you leave here?'

'Manchester. I am off to meet my grandmother along with a newly-discovered elderly aunt. Life is strange isn't it? You lose someone and gain someone. One goes as the other comes.'

Ruby stood up to leave, and Tobiah went to help her to her feet from the low window seat. Ruby glanced out of the window and remarked, 'I think this is your architect arriving, and you're right, I am better looking.' She giggled slightly.

Tobiah was shocked, until he also caught sight of Leslie Hawthorne, who was quite clearly a middle-aged balding man. 'Nice one Ruby. You had me going there for a second. Let me show you to the door. Don't forget your champagne and have a glass for me when you get to Manchester. Oh and if you want the Professor's bag of books, please do take them. I was instructed to just throw them into the skip – but who knows, maybe there will be some clues hidden in the pages.'

'Thank you, that is a nice gesture. I will take them if you don't mind. I am happy to consider anything that will help direct me towards where my sister is.' She paused for a second as though a thought had just entered her mind. 'Gosh, you know Tobiah – I have just remembered where I have come across Professor De Vede before. October 2009. He was the replacement keynote speaker at a criminology convention. How weird is that, I even asked him a question.'

Tobiah smiled knowingly. 'My dearest Ruby, Albert Einstein once said that coincidence is God's way of remaining anonymous. I was also at that convention and I do believe I recall you asking your question. I had wondered why your face looked familiar. Stranger still, it was supposed to be my father delivering that speech – Sir William Zemel. The Professor was his replacement when he broke his hip. Small world isn't it?'

'Will your father know the Professor?' asked Ruby. 'If so, will he know where he is?'

'If he does, I am afraid he cannot tell us. He passed away over a year ago. I am so sorry Ruby. I will call you if I find anything out at all.'

With that he reached for her hand and kissed it. A gesture from a time long past. A much appreciated gesture.

At that point Leslie arrived and Ruby made tracks with her bag of books flung over her left shoulder and the bottle of half-drunk champagne in her right hand. She considered that the journey to Oxford had been worthwhile, even though sadly she hadn't learned as much as she had hoped. More doors had opened and then closed in her face as soon as she had found them. It was like being in a rotating doorway; as soon as she thought she was in, she was out. At least she had the pleasurable companionship of the adorable Tobiah. What a coincidence that they had both briefly met at the criminology conference four years earlier. She considered how odd life was.

As she walked out of the door, the phone rang. Whilst the architect was messing around in his briefcase for various measuring devices, Tobiah took the call, moving discreetly out of earshot. He listened in silence for several minutes before responding.

'Well yes, we could observe her - but in my opinion she hasn't a clue where her sister is so I think we would be wasting our time.' He listened to a response before adding, 'well hopefully she believed what I told her. The last thing we need is her interfering with our own search. I tried to put her off the scent and I am sure she will give up fairly soon. She looks like a beaten woman to me.' Again he listened intently before finally responding, 'No, I've been through this building with a fine tooth comb and there is nothing here. Aside from some old books they have cleared the place out. Anyway, the architect has just arrived and the real property owner will not be too far behind him, so I had better go now. Don't want anyone calling the police. Will catch up with you later. Bye for now Emmanuelle.'

Leslie Hawthorne was confused. He wandered around the building, calling out for the debonair young gent who had just greeted him. At that point, the real landlord walked in.

'Mr Hawthorne I presume, who on earth let you into the building?'

CHAPTER 34

Saturday 21ˢᵗ December

Ruby was out walking her pet dog Bertie, if the term walking was appropriate for what seemed to be more like an extreme physical sport. With feet mashing their way through the thick snow, it was a trial for both dog and woman. Bertie's four little legs struggled to rise above the white powdery drift and keep pace with his owner's strides.

The snow absorbed nearly all sound, and the valley was totally still and silent, aside from a vague droning noise somewhere in the background. She paused to listen.

The scene around her was tinted toothpaste white, with a church-like hush. Just the faintest trace of a hum suffused the iced air, like distant angels singing. It had always been rumoured that the area was haunted by the ghosts of former Druids who once worshipped in the local hills. However Ruby concluded this to be nonsense and supposed that Chris, her hard of hearing father, had probably left the TV volume turned up.

The cotton wool-coated trees against the backdrop of ice-covered slopes made Ruby's garden look like a scene from a Christmas card. She found herself joyfully singing the lyrics, *'Above thy deep and dreamless sleep, the silent stars go by'* as her chilled fingers struggled to fit the key into the frozen keyhole of her front door. It was a big long key for a big long door. In the hallway, a huge Christmas tree welcomed her home as its pine vapour suffused the entrance gallery.

Her mind drifted to memories of her childhood back in the Isle of Man; many happy festive memories. It was an evocative time of year. Ruby found herself thinking about Eenayah with ever-increasing frequency, especially as the festive season made its jolly presence known. Her father and mother were staying with her for the Christmas holidays. They had tried to make out that Ruby was doing them a favour and they were in need of her support, but everyone knew it was actually the other way around. They had not wanted to add any further stress to the situation, but inevitably they were worried about both daughters.

Ruby had everyone concerned. She had travelled the length and breadth of the UK following in her sister's footsteps and hunting for a clue - any clue. She eventually came home none the wiser, broken and despondent. Her heart and soul were both in tatters.

Her father had lit the fire; she could smell that smoky bituminous aroma as soon as she opened the door. She called out everybody's names 'Mum, Dad, Owyn, Harry darling?' Silence. Nobody responded, except Barnaby the ginger cat, who pushed himself against her legs, making his familiar purring sound in a bid for some attention.

A note was magnetically pinned against the fridge door. It read, 'we have all gone out to the shop for some last-minute provisions. Dinner is in the oven - be home soon. PS happy Yuletide.'

Ruby pulled off her wet and heavy boots. She felt lost in the house on her own. It was only 3.30pm, but already the night had begun to draw in and the white glistening snow was quickly becoming shrouded by the descending shadows of darkness. The 5pm rule had not yet come into effect, but sod it she thought, somewhere in the world it was five o'clock. She always thought of Eenayah when she thought those words. Sometimes she missed her sister so badly that it physically hurt.

She poured herself a generous helping of red wine and raising her glass to her sister, she said the words, 'here is to you Eenayah, and here is to five o'clock somewhere. I wish I knew where you are. I wish you could show me.'

She felt so disappointed in herself. She had set off in high hopes that she could outwit the police and their investigations, uncovering more than they had. The sad reality was that this just hadn't happened. The very people who might have been able to answer the questions had either died or disappeared. It felt more like a conspiracy theory as time went on.

She had learned that her twin had been more than generous with her money during her time in the UK. Aside from the millions she had donated to her, she was also financing their biological grandmother's private health care, upgraded considerably from the government-funded care that had been sustaining her to date. Her Great Aunt Elspeth had a new roof and boiler to crow about, and a healthy top-up to her minimal state pension. Jonathan, Eenayah's long-time friend from Newcastle, also had £500,000 injected into his bank account. It was crazy. It was as though Eenayah didn't care about money any more, or had some fatalistic premonition of the fate awaiting her. The police had entertained the thought of suicide, given the amount Enayah had given away the day before she went missing.

Ruby then thought about Reed and felt genuinely sorry for him. With his music label on its knees, his reputation in tatters and part of his wealth embezzled from him, the last thing he needed was a wife who had given the rest of their money away to all and sundry. How time and a throw of the dice could quickly change everything. Reed had been publicly demolished in the tabloids and his career shattered.

Ruby then considered the other unexpected news the police had delivered to her, that whilst in hospital Eenayah was found to be in the early stages of pregnancy. She hadn't believed it to begin with. Reed couldn't father any more children and Eenayah simply wasn't the unfaithful type. She would have been too frightened of her own shadow to dive into the murky depths of an affair. It wasn't like the twin sister who she knew as well as she knew herself. The only person she could consider to be a candidate was Jonathan Cook, Eenayah's old friend from their student days back in Newcastle. She had quietly interrogated Jonathan whilst his wife wasn't around. He adored Eenayah and had always put her on a pedestal of womanly perfection; he was horrified by the suggestion that on a drunken night he had seduced her. The appalled look of dismay at the mere suggestion convinced Ruby that Jonathan wasn't the father. She knew of no other man her sister could have been involved with. Yet another mystery of many mysteries surrounding her sister's abduction.

Given the fact that it was still only 4.30pm, she knew she would hit her limit of units per day early doors, but none the less Ruby simply needed that second glass of Barolo whilst she was quietly alone with her thoughts. She considered the visit to her biological family. This had not been her quest, her mission or her desire. As far as Ruby was concerned her parents were Chris and Ellie and her family home was on a farm back on the Isle of Man. She had never shown any interest in her past, her background, her genealogy or any of the historical links her twin had been chasing whilst in the UK. She failed to understand why yesteryear had become such a driving compulsion for Eenayah. None the less, Ruby had been to visit her Great Aunt Elspeth and her biological grandmother out of duty. She was of course pleased that she had been given the unexpected chance to meet her biological granny. She had noted the vivid resemblance between Eenayah and her gran, who was frail and in an advanced stage of dementia. She had liked

Great Aunt Elspeth a great deal and was pleased that Eenayah had given her some financial comfort for her later years. However, aside from random mumblings about twins being born to twins, which Ruby didn't find remotely interesting, there were no clues to be found on her visit to the two old ladies. If only Ruby had paid more attention and listened closer, she would have heard a story within a story which might have pointed her in the right direction. However, Ruby had no time for such things and although she pretended to listen to all her Great Aunt had to say, she didn't hear a word.

Her quest to follow in her sister's footsteps had brought her no further to the truth. Five months on and her sister was still missing. No ransom had been demanded. There was nothing but thin air to go by.

As she sat at the kitchen table, head in hand and in deep thought, she became aware of a scent. It was a familiar concoction of myrrh, frankincense, amber, jasmine, geranium, and ylang-ylang. What else was in the mix? She inhaled deeply and picked up a dizzy fusion of cardamom, basil, myrtle, sandalwood and musk. Ruby had always possessed a good nose for fragrances. What was this? Where was it coming from? It was lovely, but why was it here? It then hit her like a lightning bolt. Baccarat's Les Larmes Sacrées de Thebes! The Sacred Tears of Thebes, Eenayah's favourite perfume. Ostentatiously expensive and beyond the means of a mere normal woman. But how?

Initially, it was just a voice: 'Ruby, Ruby - it is me, it's Eenayah!' Ruby searched around the room, scanning each area in detail as though with x-ray vision. She saw nothing. Then the glass from which she had been drinking started to move slowly around the table. She was transfixed watching it. She looked under the table. It wasn't on a slope. She touched the table top for signs of liquid which might cause the glass to slide. The table was dry.

The voice came again, 'Ruby, look up - it is me, it is your sister Eenayah.'

In slow motion, Ruby raised her head away from the glass which had been transfixing her. A glimmering, ethereal light hovered in the corner of the kitchen. It was like a swirling miasma, pure and unsullied. It almost seemed to glow. As it came slowly closer, features appeared within the mist of the growing orb. Before long, she could clearly see her twin sister's features. Ruby gasped and then started to weep. 'Eenayah is this you? Oh my sweet sister, pray tell me that you are not dead.' She needn't have asked the question. She knew exactly who this was. She instinctively felt no fear. The voice was weak and slightly distant, yet calm and full of love.

The vision spoke in a soft whisper. 'Ruby; I don't have long left with this life. I have been struggling to cling onto this world for many weeks now. It has been difficult. I am being pushed out of my body by a much greater and more powerful force. I don't want to go, but my body is failing me, so tonight I must leave. They have weakened the veil around me for a short time. Just long enough for me to come to you and for me to say goodbye. I am here to stop you from searching for me. Get on with your own life now. I will always love you Ruby, but you need to stop looking for me.'

The light around her started to fade, and as it did, so did the perfume. Ruby felt desperate. She didn't want the soul of her sister to disappear into the dark, cold night. Ruby pleaded will all her heart.

'Eenayah, I do not know and cannot tell if exhaustion is making me hallucinate or not, but if this is truly you please just tell me where you are?'

'Beneath your feet sister, I am beneath your feet. I will always be close to you.'

'I don't know what that means Eenayah, please come back to me – please!' The light was drawing away from her and the final words were spoken. 'I am beneath your feet Ruby. You don't have to look far. I will always love you. Pray for my children.' With that the spectre simply evaporated. The perfume had gone.

Ruby had no idea what these words meant. She was confused and troubled. It had been many months since her sister had last been seen. As time passed the likelihood of anyone finding Eenayah alive and well had seemed to be waning. This final spiritual visitation, if indeed that was what it was, did not sound like good news. It was beginning to seem like a final ending. Could it be true that her sister would die tonight as foretold?

Ruby lit a white candle. She didn't know quite why as she wasn't a religious person, but it was an instinctive reaction. Maybe some pagan throwback from long ago when cavemen sat around a fire and chanted in acclamation of their ancestors. If what she had just experienced was indeed a truth, then she would sit outside in the snow, look up to the heavens and say a prayer for her sister's soul. She knew it seemed peculiar, but somehow it just seemed the right thing to do. She held the flickering candle and with tears in her eyes, walked outside into the frozen night.

A meteor sped across the clear, dark sky as she walked outside into the chilled December air. From out of the firmament blasted a fireball containing every colour of the rainbow. Never before had she seen such a thing. Somehow in her heart of hearts she knew it meant Eenayah had gone. She looked at her watch – 5pm. Somewhere in the world it was always five o'clock, and now that time and place was here and now. It was a significant time; something that meant something meaningful to both twins. Although she was not a spiritual person, she fell to her knees and said the Lord's Prayer and then crouched down in the snow. Her heart was utterly broken.

***

In every way the room looked as though it belonged to a modern high-tech medical facility. It contained devices for measuring vital signs, had a cardiac monitor installed on the wall and the room even contained a foetal monitor and an ultrasound scan. No expense had been spared in equipping the space with as much technology as was required, and more.

Eenayah lay on the bed in a trance. Occasionally she would speak, although seldom coherently, and periodically Tamar would mumble away in her native language. Mostly there was silence in the room. As time went on, the person they recognised to be Eenayah was beginning to fade. Three men stood at the foot of the bed holding hands in a ceremonial gesture, something they had done on a monthly basis since the group had been caring for Eenayah.

Dylan was the Druid member of the group and ultimately the most powerful, a master warlock who held the magic key to protecting Eenayah and sealing off her location to those who would try to find her. He had evoked a powerful veil to shroud her so none outside could sense her whereabouts. He was dressed from head to toe in a long dark gown, his face almost hidden by his caped hood. To his left was the Buddhist priest Luke, wearing a bright orange robe and with his eyes closed as though in a deeply transcendental meditative state. On the right side of Dylan was the priest from the local church, St Oswald's. He held a bible in his left hand and a thurible in his right hand. He swung it back and forth as the smoky incense escaped into the surrounding chambers. He quietly muttered a prayer beneath his breath, looking sombre and concerned.

Darcy stood in quiet observance in the corner of the room, next to her brother Owyn. The mood in the room was intense and solemn. Darcy nudged her brother and whispered, 'Can we go into the kitchen please? I am in desperate need of a coffee and a chat.' The two siblings tiptoed out, leaving the three men alone to conclude some ritualistic process.

They quietly descended down the stone steps which had been carved into the rock face. The caverns were voluminous and the slightest noise made an echo which bounced off the granite walls. Opening a large oak door, they entered into a second room which had been chiselled into a kitchen worthy of any modern showhouse.

Owyn had done an admirable job in converting the caverns under his house into a habitable dwelling with three bedrooms, a lounge, a bathroom, a kitchen and of course a hospital room/operating theatre. It had cost a huge amount of money, but the Ledanite followers had funded the full conversion. The underground caves with their myriad tunnels and secret entrances had proven to be an ideal place to hide Eenayah. Once the twins were born, the light of goodness had won and the dark forces could do no harm - at least for the time being. With the foretold rebirth and reincarnation of Zarah and Pharez, the gospel could be rewritten, the line of Tamar concluded and the prophecy recognised and closed. But until the twin boys had been born, everything was still at risk. The twins were not due until March 25th and with many weeks yet to go, nothing was certain. Nothing was safe.

The protectors recognised that the dark forces were on the hunt for Eenayah, which was why Dylan with his powerful sorcery shielded her inside a potent veil which none but he could release. It necessitated the power of three; holy men from differing religions were required to put the protection spell into place. The veil needed to be charged at regular intervals. The secret caverns became a frequent meeting place for the Ledanite. It was indeed a fitting purpose for the ancient caves, which prior to this had been a sacred meeting place for the Druids many centuries before. Both from a practical point of view as well and a spiritual perspective, the caverns served an ideal purpose. This had all been part of a carefully-considered master plan. The vast house and its hidden underground grottos were the very reason that Owyn had persuaded Ruby to purchase the rickety old mansion in the first place, although Ruby didn't even know what existed beneath her feet. What may have appeared to be a coincidence was actually a well-thought-out strategy that had been in put into action ever since the Ledanite had located the missing Layne twins and understood that either Ruby or Eenayah were possible carriers of the line. Nothing had been left to chance.

Darcy ambled over to the pot of filtered coffee, which seemed to always be full and ready for immediate consumption. Pouring herself and her brother a large mug she quizzed Owyn. 'What exactly are they doing with Eenayah? What is going on? I sense it is something serious. It looks very intense down there.'

Her brother looked sad as he responded, 'Yes, it's about as serious as anything could get. We had hoped we could save Eenayah. If only we could have kept her going until the twins had been born. We really had hoped that we could eventually perform an exorcism and push Tamar out and return Eenayah back to her body. The 21st century is no place for a woman from biblical times. Tamar simply could not exist in our era. How could a woman born 1700 years BC, give or take a few hundred years, ever have adjusted to 2013? It would never have worked. However, saving Eenayah doesn't seem possible now. Eenayah's energy is becoming weak and her brain isn't functioning as it should.'

'Are you telling me Eenayah is dying?'

'Yes Darcy. Her body is still alive, but Tamar owns it now. Eenayah's spirit has nowhere to go, it just drifts above the remains which once belonged to her. That's why Dylan and the group are reverting the veil.'

Darcy was surprised. 'But why are they removing the veil? Isn't that dangerous? Won't the dark forces be able to see her with the veil missing? I don't get it.'

Owyn wasn't part of the inner sanctum of the Ledanite and

neither was he too sure himself of the hows and whys, but did as best as he could to explain. 'The veil may shelter Eenayah against anything coming into her, but it also works the other way around and it prevents anything from getting out. Eenayah's soul is misplaced and is just hovering in a miserable limbo above her body. It cannot escape the veil, it cannot go anywhere. She is neither dead nor alive. We need to let her die and we need to release her so she can move on. In order to do that, we need to pull the veil down for a short period. Yes Darcy, it is a risk. The dark forces may finally get a vision of her and of us. It is a vision that they have been desperately trying to find. This is exactly why we have about 600 Ledanite spread out in a mystic circle in the surrounding hills and caverns, each praying or chanting a spell of protection according to their religion. Some call to Aradia, some to Diancecht, some to Druantia and some to God.'

Darcy was deeply saddened. 'I really liked Eenayah. I mean, I didn't know her all that well, but we spent some time together in the house and I will never forget the night when we both got totally plastered and went in search of secret hideaways, we had such fun. I really bonded with her. I think it was probably the first time I ever heard her laugh. So sad! Is there anything I can do Owyn?'

Owyn touched his young sister's cheek in a gesture of affection and gratitude. Like her, he had been saddened by Eenayah's demise. As children they had been raised by Ledanite parents and as soon as the missing Layne twins had been located following botched-up adoption papers, Owyn had been directed to find a way into Ruby's life. He was a decent bloke at heart, a normal Welsh guy with simple needs and even simpler emotions. However he didn't have a heart of steel and there had been many a time when he had to question his own moral yardstick. He had also sold himself out for a belief.

'Yes, there is actually something you can do Darcy. We are expecting Fabien to fly in from Paris. He is the obstetrician who will be delivering the twins by C-section. We asked him to come and check her over. We are not sure what will happen to the pregnancy when Eenayah passes, so we just want to make sure the body will be fine and the switch goes to plan. Can you greet him and guide him here? Fabien has been here before but he always gets lost.'

Darcy had met Fabien many times before. Just like her older brother, Darcy was a simple soul who made one-dimensional judgements of folk. To her, Fabien was the cute French doctor, and that was about as deep as it went in her uncomplicated mind. However she also knew that Fabien had also been born into a Ledanite family, and as with her brother, he had been commanded to get close to Eenayah from the moment she had been identified as a Tamar clone. Darcy was aware that by default Fabien had also become close to her husband Reed, but unusually that association had been more of an accident than by design. Children born into a Ledanite family cultivated many of their friendships and associations by instruction from a higher level and deliberate intent. The followers existed in a world of pre-calculated, carefully drawn out plans. Ledanite children were project managed from youth and rarely did they have the luxury of coincidence. Fabien's acquaintance with Reed had been an unusual unplanned alliance, but the Ledanite seniors had allowed it to continue because it was convenient. It had long been suspected that Reed was aligned with the darker forces, so Fabien served a useful purpose in monitoring the opposition's activity. Had Fabien been instructed to drop the friendship, despite any warm feeling he might have for his friend Reed, it would have been executed within a split second. A far greater humanitarian fate overshadowed any personal desires.

For a moment Darcy had drifted into a world of her own as she contemplated the strange life Ledanite children were raised into. She had been more of a rebel and less of a devout follower than Owyn, but none the less happy to assist with the birth process of the long-awaited twin boys. This birth, when it finally occurred, would be the epitome of the existence and belief of every Ledanite the world over. The delivery by caesarean section had been scheduled to occur on the high feast of Ostara. March 20th 2014, the spring equinox, the day when daylight and darkness are equal and the beginning of the season of rebirth. This was a victory of good against evil and all that they had strived for in many a millennium. It was so very nearly here – the big moment that the Ledanite had fought to protect and that the dark forces had fought to prevent. The Prophecy would finally be realised.

The magnitude of the situation suddenly caught up with her and she had to take a few deep breaths and steady herself against the slippery, dripping cave wall. She lost her footing and almost went flying over the precipice of the chiselled stairs.

Owyn was unsympathetic to her near fall and instead grew exasperated. 'Darcy, move! Go and bring Fabien. We need him here NOW.'

'Sure Owyn, the atmosphere in here is depressing so it will be good to just do something – anything. I feel like I am at a wake. What time and what entrance will he be coming into?'

Owyn looked at his watch. 'It's 3pm now and he is due here in 30 minutes, so you better get going. He's coming in via the cottage next to the post office, Margaret Lear's house. He will probably be there now, sat having a cup of tea with Maggie. Don't dawdle!'

'Bloody hell Owyn! That's the long way around. It's at least a 20-minute walk. Why did he pick the long route?'

Owyn started to laugh at his sister's question. 'We are talking about Fabien here, the guy who is terrified of heights and water. Do you honestly think he would come via the church tunnel and climb over the extremely steep giant's wall, or enter via the hill caves and jump around on stepping stones as he manoeuvres his way through the underground lake, pretty as it is? The cottage route is long, but it's dry and on level ground and besides, he likes Maggie's home-made scones. Now stop loitering and go and get him.'

Darcy did as she was told, as every good Ledanite always did. She knew her way around the network of tunnels with her eyes shut, which was useful since most of them were in pitch blackness. Owyn had only modernised the caves directly below the house. For practical reasons it was easier to run water pipes and electricity cables down to the chambers below the cellar. The further from the house one wandered, the more untouched it was by human hand.

She could hear the faint sound of chanting in the distance. It seemed to come at her from every angle. It was an eerie spine-chilling chant that resonated around the myriad of underground passageways and caverns. Despite being a Ledanite by birth herself, the haunting melody still unnerved her.

As she descended deeper into the cave system, she came to the tunnel which was directly below the old castle dungeons. The floor was level and padded down with rushes and herbs which must have been laid there hundreds of years ago. With around 600 guests arriving discreetly and secretly in the darkness of the evening beforehand, Owyn had lit the multitude of tunnels which fed into the many hidden entrances. As such the smell of tallow lay heavy in the stale air.

Rush lights were impaled on vertical spikes driven into the stone walls. In places deemed to be dangerous underfoot, larger flares hung from iron rings in the granite. Much of the lighting system was centuries old, and it was only as you approached the caverns below the house that electricity and modern lighting came into play. For now, Darcy would have to contend with medieval illumination.

Climbing the final set of steps, she arrived at Maggie Lear's house. Gathering her strength, she pushed open the solid trap door into Maggie's cellar. The old woman had clearly been expecting someone and the cellar was lit up so she could find her way up to the kitchen and the door which was disguised as a pantry. Just as was foretold, Fabien was already there. He was smiling and laughing as he drank tea and consumed lemon drizzle cake. On noting the sombre look on Darcy's face, he knew immediately that all was not well.

'You need to come quickly Fabien,' said Darcy.

Without so much of a hello or goodbye, Fabien grabbed his bags and sprung to his feet. He sensed the urgency of the situation. He asked, 'Darcy maybe we should just drive to the house, it would be quicker. I have a hire car outside.' Darcy shook her head and responded, 'not a good idea Fabien. Ruby and her parents are at the house and you would be the last person she would expect to pull up in her driveway. We have to keep this secret. Have you a coat? The tunnels are cold.'

Fabien buttoned up his coat and gave Maggie two kisses on each cheek, and they descended the steps into the maze of an underground tunnel system.

★★★

Fabien put the ultrasound machine on Eenayah's swollen and blossoming tummy. The twins were fine, but Eenayah certainly wasn't.

Fabien turned to face the small crowd of people gathered in the converted cave room. He announced, 'The babies each have a strong regular heartbeat, but Eenayah isn't in a good condition. There isn't much of a reaction in her eyes and her neurological signs are not good. I honestly believe that if we don't let Eenayah go soon, her body will die and so will the twins. It is too early to deliver them safely at this stage. You now need to surrender her body fully to Tamar, who will be strong enough to heal this damage.'

Darcy started to cry a little. 'Is there no other way Fabien? Is there nothing we can do to save her?'

His response was cold and direct. 'Sorry - no.'

Dylan, the Druid Magus, stepped forward and threw both hands into the air, thus completely removing the veil, which had been partially weakened just an hour earlier. Everybody gasped as a thin, straight funnel of the purest light came down from above and pierced Eenayah through the heart. They could just about make out the image of two hands within the light, both reaching out to Eenayah's soul. The beam disappeared. It all happened quickly and was over and done with within a minute. There was little time to grieve as Dylan quickly moved in and activated his magic to replace the veil before the body could be seen by the dark forces.

Eenayah's expression changed instantly. Still deeply asleep but now with a contented smile on her face, the pregnant woman lying in the bed in front of them was now Tamar. A woman who last drew breath thousands of years ago. She had returned, and Eenayah was no more. Time of death recorded as 5pm. It is always 5 o'clock somewhere in the world. This was Eenayah's last 5 o'clock in this world.

★★★

Emmanuelle, Tobiah and Arabella were puzzled. They knew the veil had been lifted. They could see it and feel it immediately. They could see a location close to Ruby, and yet Ruby genuinely didn't know where her sister was. It made no sense. It was a worrying sign. Eenayah must have been hidden from her sister Ruby. That was the only conclusion they could reach.

They knew that those protecting Eenayah would have only have lifted the veil for one reason and for one reason only; and that was to release Eenayah's spirit. Should this be the case, they both realised that Tamar was back, and this would make their job so much more of a challenge. The forces of darkness were losing this battle. Tamar was a mighty and powerful soul, and it seemed that now she could be back on earth.

Preventing the birth of the next generation would be harder now that the awesome might and power of Tamar nurtured them in her womb.

The broken purple bracelets on their skinny satanic wrists fell to the ground. It was a sign. The game was over

CHAPTER 35

Saturday 5ᵗʰ April

Time had passed by and the golden promise of spring had chased away the grey dull days of winter. It was lambing season in the Welsh hills. Ruby leant over the picket fence as she watched the playful baby lambs jump over the clumps of daffodils as they amused themselves with their sheep siblings. Most of the lambs were twins, and watching the charming blobs of wool frolic in the April sunshine reminded her of her own twin. Not once had she ever been forgotten.

The police had recently informed her that Eenayah has been confirmed as missing, presumed dead. The case had been left open, but search activity had been downgraded. Ruby had been expecting this decision. With no ransom ever emerging, it seemed that there was no logical reason why her sister had been kidnapped. It remained a mystery.

Reed had been implicated, but then with no evidence against him he had been cleared of any involvement. With his business in collapse and personal empire in freefall, he had disappeared from public life. Nobody knew where he was, and Ruby didn't care to find out. As more facts were revealed about his sordid personal activities, he was not someone Ruby wished to meet with or talk to ever again.

The one and only person who had been in active contact with Eenayah was some woman called Mercy De Vede, a person Ruby had never met. Sadly she was no longer around to tell her side of the story. She was sure that this Mercy person had known something. There had to be a reason why she had changed her sister's identity as she lay semiconscious in a hospital bed, but now nobody would know what that reason was. From what her friend Becky had told her in her capacity as an ex-police sergeant, it was probable that Ms De Vede's father had either been put on some sort of witness protection scheme or had conjured up his own disappearing act. The Professor had vanished. Ruby was sure that there were people out there who knew what had happened to Eenayah and why, but nobody was for talking.

She remained philosophical. In her heart of hearts she knew her sister was dead. She might never know why or how, only that she would never see her again. Not in this life.

***

It was spring, a time of hope and new life. The scene before Ruby's eyes displayed a story of optimism for the future. The extreme emerald green of the grass was dashed with speckles of yellow flowers and moving white balls of fluff. The azure blue of the sky accentuated the gentle contours of the Snowdonia mountain range. A mellow breeze pushed the scent of 'Flowering Currant' in her direction. It was a distinctive bouquet that evoked memories of her childhood and growing up on the Isle of Man with her sister. It was the comforting smell of nostalgia.

Close by, a babbling brook could be heard. Its trickling droplets of water were hitting and then tumbling over the granite boulders in perfect harmony with the landscape.

Ruby had turned a corner. She was content. She had always joked with her sister that she had been the one living in paradise, with her multi-million-dollar Miami mansion and every luxury that money could buy. In all of that time, during all those many Monday 5pm conversations; Ruby had failed to see that actually it was she who lived in paradise. Eenayah had been little more than a prisoner in a beautiful ivory tower, while on the other hand Ruby had freedom and more importantly, love.

The noise from inside of the house disrupted her thoughts. It was such a rambling old place and it suited company. The more people walked through its doors, the more it seemed to come to life. The house had been fully renovated thanks to Eenayah's financial legacy, and now it almost seemed to breathe. Ruby would soon be among a crowd of enthusiastic guests, but just for a moment she wanted to savour a few extra minutes on her own, alone with her thoughts.

She looked over towards the mansion's ivy-clad walls. No longer did they seem angry and menacing, tainted with the blood of former battles. Eenayah had always hated this house, but Ruby was sure that her sister would have been so proud with the way they had spent the money she had gifted them. Its former history and whatever barbaric acts had been committed in the castle grounds had now been swept away by a new aura which immersed it in harmony. The house was at peace. If bricks could smile, then the house would be smiling.

Ruby made tracks to go inside, but not before collecting the champagne breakfast cocktail with which the waiter on duty outside the drawbridge tantalised her. She had never tasted a drink like this before. Made with pomegranate liqueur and amaretto mixed with coconut cream and topped off with a liberal splash of grenadine with a lime twist, it was divine. It had been the creation of Becky's brother in law and chef supreme Nico, and he had jokingly named it after the mansion, 'The Darwydden Ghost'. Ruby could hardly believe the good fortune that someone like Nico, who had trained at Via della

Camilluccia and worked through his apprentice at a three-star Michelin restaurant in Rome, could possibly want to relocate to the remote hills and dales of North Wales, and yet here he was, now an employee of Ruby and Owyn and Darwydden Castle Manor Hotel.

Her best friend Becky had cast an enormous influence over Nico's nepotistic decision to join them at the newly-founded hotel, being married to his handsome brother Amedeo obviously being a major factor. Ruby had been so grateful for the support of Becky and Amedeo since her twin sister's disappearance. Not only had they acted as an emotional buffer, they had given her practical advice on a day-to-day basis. They were her salvation. Ruby fully understood that without their friendship and support that she would have most probably crumbled. There had been many a day when she had teetered close to the edge, but whenever that happened her best friend would pull her to her feet again, as only a true friend could. As a buddy since their schooldays, Becky had realised that since giving up work to search for Eenayah, and having hit a million dead ends and brick walls, Ruby would need something to keep her mind occupied. Going above and beyond what a normal friend would have done, she had offered the assistance of her hotelier husband, in a gesture which went above and beyond humility and compassion. With one of the most competent hotel managers in the UK running her business and one of the finest chefs in Europe in charge of the restaurant, in one of the most unusual quirky historical buildings that one could imagine, sitting within one of the most visual panoramic localities to be found anywhere in Britain, Ruby and Owyn were onto a winner.

***

It was the day of the grand opening and people had started to arrive. Becky rushed out to find where Ruby had gone walkabout. The press wanted to take a photograph of the celebrated owners and could only locate Owyn. Lilly, the main photographer (ex-paparazzi), was exceptionally skilled at her job and was delighted by all the many unusual facades and veneers the manor presented her with. Between the historical setting of the house and the views from the gardens, it was a photographer's dream come true. Becky had understood that this was a big day for Ruby and perhaps after all she had been through in the last few months, maybe she had needed some time out on her own. Running through the maze and the various structured garden areas, she was relieved to locate her friend in the courtyard clutching her champagne flute as though it was a lifeline.

'You had me worried Ruby. Lilly wants to take some shots of you and Owyn together and we have all been searching everywhere for you,' she said.

Ruby was appreciative of her friend's concern and cast an eye up and down her silhouette to admire her outfit. 'I have just been watching the sheep beyond the paddock. There was no need to worry Becky. I am with the plot. By the way girl, you look hot. I can't believe that you gave birth just over two weeks ago. You really do look fab.'

Becky looked down at her stomach, appreciative of her friend's comments. 'Bit of a tum still, but nothing I can't deal with. The midwife says that after six weeks I can start to exercise again. I'm not going to rush into it though.'

'Do you like your bedroom, and what about the nursery? We converted the old servant's quarters into an apartment for you and your family so you can have your privacy. Is it okay for you Becky?'

How could it not be okay? Of course, Becky was delighted. She had given up the grime of inner city London to live in a picture postcard home with her handsome husband Amedeo and their new children. Having her best friend around was simply icing on an already perfect cake.

Becky guided her friend towards a group of people gathering in the grand hall as Owyn was about to make some sort of speech.

'It's wonderful, Ruby. We are going to love living with you and Owyn and Harry. The boys can all grow up together and I get to spend lots of time with my best friend. What's not to like?'

Ruby looked around. 'Talking about boys, where are Angelo and Alessandro? They are so unbelievably cute. Who would have ever thought you would have had twins? I'm so pleased that the IVF finally paid off.'

For a moment Becky was lost in her own thoughts. Ruby had been more than aware how she and Amedeo had struggled to have children and how after five failed attempts at IVF they had virtually given up.

'I think the vacation with you and your family in Florida may have de-stressed us and I'm sure that's why the final attempt succeeded, but anyway they are here now and that is all that matters,' said Becky.

'So, where are my little godsons then?'

Becky pointed over to Roserie, who was pushing the twin pram in the corner of the courtyard and lovingly guarding the babies. 'We all really bonded with Roserie when we were out in Miami together, and we felt so sorry for her after Eenayah disappeared,' said Becky. 'Amedeo and I thought she would make the perfect nanny.'

Ruby nodded approval. 'Good decision, Becky. I must go over and say hello to her. I'm so glad Roserie will be living here as well. Harry so adores her.'

Becky pulled her back. 'I'm here on a mission Ruby, and that is to get you on that stage with Owyn so Lilly can take her shots, or whatever it is she does with her lens. You can say hello to Roserie and go cuddle the boys later, but for now, you have an opening day to host so let's get this party started.'

★★★

It was now Owyn's turn to stand aside and watch as Ruby played the part of the perfect hostess.

Leading a discerning crowd out into the long hallway, Owyn could hear her carefully explaining how the deserted east wing had been transformed into a 30-bedroomed hotel and how the medieval great hall had been adapted into a function room with a marriage licence application actively being progressed. He could hear her audience gasp at the enormous gothic chandeliers swinging from sturdy oak beams. It was a room worthy of any feudal banquet.

Darcy slipped discreetly to her brother Owyn's side. In a whisper she asked, 'Does any of this ever make you feel guilty?'

'Why should I feel guilty? I have done my job and done it well.'

'You know why you should feel guilty. I don't need to spell it out to you. Ruby has to live through the pain and agony of never knowing what became of her sister, and yet half the people in this house right here, right now are your Ledanite guests and all know exactly what happened to her. Do you ever feel like putting her out of her misery and telling her the truth?'

'The truth would kill her Darcy! What should I tell her? That at the age of 18 our parents told me who it was I had to marry and I had no choice in the matter? They are Ledanite followers and their part in this grand plan was to stay close to Eenayah's twin, so I had to do what I was told to do. As it happened, I took one look at Ruby and I fell in love. But how would that sound to her now? She would think I have just used her, and in part she would be right.'

'I get your point Owyn, but I still feel for her. Can you not just drop her a few clues?'

Owyn often wondered about his sister Darcy's IQ. He could not understand why she could not understand.

'How would she react to the fact that all along I knew that Eenayah had been hidden in the caves below our house?' he said. 'Until recently she didn't even know about the caves. Get real, Darcy! It would destroy our marriage. Do you want me to confess that we stole her sister? I love Ruby and I adore my son Harry, so the answer is no. She must never never know that any of this had been pre-planned.'

Darcy was and yet wasn't a Ledanite. This wasn't a belief system that anyone just could walk into and enlist in, as with a gym membership. You needed to be born into the Ledanite and be descended from the Tamar bloodline, as indeed both Darcy and Owyn had been. However, you still had the free will not to engage with them if that was your desire. Nothing was ever forced. Her parents had tried to involve her in the organisation, but Darcy hadn't been prepared to be controlled by some prophecy that for all she knew, was total bunkum. Yes, she had assisted her brother because she loved him and part of her was attracted to the mystique of the paranormal, but she often didn't agree with the methods they used to infiltrate situations. She would willingly guide members through the many caverns and tunnels when they came for meetings or worship, but aside from that Darcy preferred to keep her distance. Since she had been a small girl she had felt slightly afraid of them, with their rituals and covered faces.

She confronted her brother. 'What you have done is no different from what Reed Baratolli did. He married Eenayah because he was told to, and most probably he was financially rewarded for it. You married Ruby because you were told to. It seems to me that the only difference between the good guys and the bad guys in this arrangement was that the good guys did it for free.'

'You have a point, dear sister. At the end of the day two opposing forces wanted two different results and we were both willing to go to any lengths to win the battle. I am just a minion and I count for very little, but I played my part. I am done now. I can enjoy my life with my wife and child and our extended family and friends and enjoy this magnificent building.'

Darcy wasn't convinced and no amount of persuasion would cultivate her approval. 'I just find it sickening that Eenayah's twin boys will be raised here as Becky's children and Ruby will never know that they are her nephews. I find it disturbing that what some people think to be coincidence is simply part of a calculated and well-executed strategy. I find it worrying that people sometimes die, go missing, have accidents, and fall off mountains, and I for one cannot work out if it is the dark forces to blame or the Ledanite way of shutting someone up so all their secrets remain hidden. To me, the whole thing seems to be a twisted moral malfunction.'

Owyn wasn't the type to get angry, but his sister's condemnation of something he followed and believed in deeply was giving him a great deal of angst.

'Darcy, get off your high horse. Many a religion has done many a bad thing for what it considered to be many a good reason.'

People were starting to look over in their direction, aware that brother and sister were having a heated debate. Owyn tried to shut her down by walking away, but Darcy made after him. She continued with her verbal assault. 'I am not a fool, brother. I can see that half the people here aren't actually potential guests, publicity agents and networking opportunities for the new hotel. This whole charade is only pretending to be an opening day, isn't it?'

Owyn continued to walk in the direction of the family kitchen, keen to move away from the eavesdropping crowds fraternising in the east wing of the manor. Darcy followed her brother into the kitchen.

'Why are Fabien and Louisa here? What about the three wise men? What possible interest do Father Michael, Luke and Dylan have in the hotel business? Even that slime ball womaniser Paul Bucklow is nibbling away on some waffle creation in the corner. I remember him well, he was Eenayah's father-in-law. He must be delighted to meet his sons for the first time. What are you covering up Owyn? And don't tell me it's nothing. I know that isn't true. You have some sort of secret ceremony planned for tonight, don't you? Let me do some maths. Yes that figures, this is a *celebratione sexdecim dierum* isn't it?'

Owyn was growing annoyed by his sister's constant stream of questioning. 'Darcy, you have chosen not to join the sacred order, so you are not entitled to know, but since you ask, yes. Tonight we have a ceremony for the twins, call it a baptism if you like. At the same time we will have a burial service for Eenayah. It is fitting to say goodbye to one life as we welcome new life.

Darcy suspected as much. It seemed too much of a coincidence that so many familiar faces had been gathered in one place at the same time. She even wondered if Becky might also have been selected at an early age to befriend Ruby. Maybe she had always been destined to become the surrogate mother of the twins. Darcy despaired. In the world of the Ledanite and the prophecy they adhered to, one could never be totally sure that anything was an accident, that any friend was genuine, that any meeting was just a fluke. Darcy was a free spirit and she hated manipulation. She wanted control of her own destiny, and wasn't sure that would ever be possible with people who presumed control was all theirs to take. In her book, ownership of another was incarceration, no matter how nicely it might be framed in a pretty picture.

It had not escaped her attention that Owyn had always been subservient and respectful in the presence of Ruby, forever the attentive husband and perfect father. However with her, his only sister, he could be quite cruel and forceful. She had often teased him with the names of Dr. Jekyll and Mr. Hyde.

Trying to change the subject, she asked, 'What will become of the caverns now they are no longer needed?'

Owyn looked at her with contempt, as though he had expected her to know. 'We will do what we had always planned to do with them. They will be decked out for Ruby's surprise 40th party in four months' time. If you're referring to the makeshift hospital, then of course that will be disbanded after tonight. The equipment will be removed piecemeal and given to charity. The cave rooms already converted will be transformed into bridal suites and the entire cave system will be turned into one giant cathedral fit for any wedding. Can you imagine the acoustics down there once we pipe in music, Darcy? I intend to have lights reflected on the cave wall in any pattern the bride and groom desire. If they want snow, we will superimpose snow on the cave walls. If they want a beach, we will overlay the caves with a beach scene. I've been working on the computer programme to do this for years. We will have the most unusual wedding venue in Europe. That is the plan.'

Darcy had not processed the financial aspect of this massive project before, but now suddenly things were beginning to make sense. Indeed, Eenayah's gift to her sister had made a massive contribution to the restoration of a crumbling manor house, although Owyn had been converting the caverns long before the cash injection from his sister in law had hit their bank account.

The question was simple and direct. 'Who funded the cave conversion, Owyn?'

His response was equally blunt. 'The Ledanite following, of course. How do you think we came up with the deposit to buy this place? Ruby was on a good wage – but enough to afford a place like this? Come on sister, get real. Is that what you believed?'

'So all of this was premeditated?'

'Your gullibility surprises me sometimes. Have you not already realised that in our world everything follows a plan? Yes, I was assisted in buying this house. The Ledanite knew of the underground system and knew it to be perfect. The Druids used these tunnels and caves long before we did. This has always been a place of secret worship.'

Darcy began to mentally take back the words she had uttered just five minutes earlier. She played it back in her mind. It seemed the only difference between the good guys and the bad guys in this arrangement was that the good guys did it for free. The truth hit her like a thunderbolt. He had been planning this for years. Owyn hadn't done any of this for free; he would gain financially. He had ended up with a wonderful manor house, a magnificent hotel and then a wedding venue which might be the most unusual place in the world to get married. For the last few years he had been writing a computer programme which would cause light to dance on and off the cave walls and project holographic images to make these gargantuan underground grottos turn into anything anyone wanted them to be. Owyn had indeed gained from Eenayah's demise, and there was no way she could wrap this up in fancy paper with pink bows and make it seem to be anything otherwise. He was no better than Reed.

Darcy stomped off, leaving Owyn alone in the kitchen, and made her way back to the great hall and the exquisite buffet. She observed Ruby as she flitted in between the many visitors, making small talk along the way. She looked very happy. Darcy hadn't actually seen her sister-in-law smile since the day Eenayah had been declared missing. For a moment she felt intense pity for Ruby and her total ignorance of the events about to unfold, quite literally, beneath her feet.

Darcy had already guessed that tonight, most likely at midnight, the body of Ruby's missing twin sister would be wrapped in a purple silk shroud and lowered into a deep chasm under the depths of the mountain. Her final resting place would be within a sacred Druid abyss and her body would go undiscovered for centuries, maybe even forever. All traces of her existence would have been wiped away. She would have served her purpose. Tamar had been unable to exist in Eenayah's body for long after the twins had been born. A blood clot caused a pulmonary embolism - that was the official line.

Angelo and Alessandro would be anointed, as was the tradition, and the bracelet cords of sacred royal lineage would be entwined around their wrists. Each of the lines of Tamar had worn their own colour. Of Tamar's former twin sons, Pharez wore a blue cord and and Zarah a red cord. Of her twin daughters, Sheol wore a yellow cord and Leda-Mechadash a purple one. The clone of Tamar was born through the line of the purple cord and Leda, the broken purple bracelet being a symbol to enable demons and their human cohorts to recognise each other. Breaking the cord was an objective, so it was symbolically denoted by a break in the cord.

On this occasion the Ledanite had won. The lines of Tamar had not been broken. It had remained intact for many generations until it was concluded with the birth of Angelo and Alessandro, united by a powerful green and white cord, symbolic of the new generation. Little wonder that this was such a grand and special celebration. Darcy understood that Ruby was a victim of a cover-up. In her ignorance she was completely unaware that she was hosting both a funeral and a baptism. Her heart went out to Ruby, who was oblivious to the part she had played in some strange game of which she knew nothing. She guessed that in all probability, at about 11pm, Ruby's drink would be spiked and she would be carried up to bed whilst the rest of the guests prepared for the forthcoming rituals. She knew such herbal drugs were frequently used by the Ledanite. Her parents had taught her as a child about the plants in the forest that could be administered safely or fatally as required.

Darcy conceded that all in all, Ruby would be fine. The hotel would no doubt be prosperous. With Ruby's ability to play with forecasts on spreadsheets and her undeniable flair for sales and marketing, she was bound to make this venture successful. Owyn would create some technologically supreme website to promote the hotel, and with an experienced hotelier and talented chef, how could the hotel fail? Ruby would have her best friend living with her, and most likely she would persuade her mother and father to retire from the Isle of Man, and join them in their colossal mansion. Perhaps stage two would include their own food produce, utilising the experience and farming skills of her parents. The mansion certainly had the land to accommodate. It would be like one big happy family. As for the boys, they had an actual angel of sorts as a nanny and would have a lifetime of supernatural protection. They had their role to play and no doubt some plan had been created for their future, but for the time being a charmed childhood in an idyllic Welsh retreat was to be their providence.

Darcy found it all too twee; sugar sweet with a bitter after taste. People had lost their lives as part of this plan and she knew not which side had taken whom. She didn't know if she would be next. After all she had just openly condemned her brother. How could she ever trust someone who had married a person just because they were told to? Anybody who obeyed without question or without thought to the moral consequences could be capable of doing anything, and that made them a hazard. A man with no fear must surely be the most feared. Darcy was an insider on the outside, and perhaps that made her a threat – an incongruent piece of string. Nobody likes a loose end. She had heard what had happened to Mercy and Katya.

She had made her decision. She would stay for the hotel's alleged open day party sham and tomorrow she would leave, forever. She had been offered a job in New York and that was exactly where she was heading. Away from her native Wales and away from the influence of the Ledanite followers.

Eenayah had once run away to a new life in New York. Two 'news' in the same sentence had sounded good enough for her. She was off to do the same. New life, New York.

CHAPTER 36

Wednesday 31ˢᵗ December 2014

Over a year had passed since the tragic death of the ill-fated Eenayah Baratolli, and although she had never been forgotten, people had moved on, as people do and as people should.

Darwydden Castle Manor was about to host its first New Year's Eve party, which had been booked to full capacity. Ruby's parents had moved over to Wales and the mansion was now at last one big happy family home. Everyone did their part when it came to running the hotel and indeed, business was booming. The eerie turrets which had once emerged like tall monsters from the shadows of the forest now had flashing Christmas lights wound around them and the ominous dark tree-lined driveway sparkled like a multi-coloured winter wonderland. The once eerie silence of the ghostlike valley, had been broken with the melody of Scottish bagpipes playing *Flowers of the Forest*. Darwydden Castle Manor, like a butterfly breaking out of its stagnating chrysalis, was now a very different place.

★★★

In New York, the blizzard had created an icy snow-blasted spectacle. As temperatures fell many degrees below zero, the Arctic chill was not favourable to the homeless and dispossessed.

One of those who found himself adrift on a cold New York sidewalk was a young man who, having just turned 18, was barely out of boyhood. Micah was lost and lonely in a strange city which to him seemed huge and unfamiliar. His eyes were blackened from thumps he could not dodge and his face covered with a patchwork quilt of old yellow and purple bruises. His back bore the scars of broken beer bottles smashed upon his shoulders and his veins were already displaying the tell-tale puncture marks of escapism.

On a regular basis and at increasingly frequent intervals, his drunken stepfather would attempt to kick the life out of him, and occasionally he had almost succeeded.

Today, New Year's Eve, Micah could finally take no more. He had come to the end of his resilience. He had no more fight left and now he had also given up trying to defend himself. He ran out of the house, not looking back and not really looking forward; especially not looking forward.

Jumping onto the first train out of Connecticut to anywhere, and with only the clothes on his back and a few dollars spare, he found himself on the streets of New York. He hadn't eaten in two days and with a thin body and no fat supplies to deplete, he had little energy to walk. Growing colder and weaker, Micah curled up on the hard frosty side-walk and closed his eyes to die.

Just at that moment, a man called Big Kirk or more usually BK, tripped over Micah's sleeping body, presuming it to be a discarded old coat. He stared down at him for a moment, then gave him a slap to test his reaction. Micah reluctantly opened his eyes to see a giant of a man peering down on him.

BK was concerned. 'Lad, you'll die if you stay here. You're new at this aren't you? I don't think you belong on the street. Get to your feet and come with me.'

BK had been a tramp and a beggar on the streets of New York for the past twenty or so years. It was a hard life and not one most people would have been able to survive. However he was an old hand at street living. In many ways, he enjoyed the freedom. He had once been a successful businessman with his own company, but then the stress caused him to have a nervous breakdown and as his mental state had deteriorated, his marriage had crumbled. He had gambled to pass the time and make money, but then drank to forget when he backed the losing horse. The downward spiral had brought him onto the streets, and on the streets he had found a new family. Where others had walked over him, his new-found comrades walked with him. He found friends in the tramps and beggars who didn't judge him and the homeless community that went unnoticed to busy New Yorkers. In BK's itinerant life, everyone looked out for everyone else, and BK was very much a part of that unseen village.

BK pulled out a rolled cigarette made from discarded butt ends, lit it and placed it between Micah's cold lips. He didn't bother to ask him if he smoked. The boy appreciated the gesture as he inhaled deeply on the warm roll-up, his only source of heat. The tramp then gave him his bottle of beer so he could take a swig. BK was obviously intelligent and well spoken. 'I shouldn't be giving you alcohol when you have hypothermia lad, but if you're going to die on New Year's Eve, you may as well die a little bit happy.'

BK was still a big, strong man, and could easily pull the boy to his feet. He noticed the bruises on his face and could see from his cherubic soft cheeks that the boy was quite young. His nails were manicured and clean, and his eyes innocent yet deeply troubled. BK knew this wasn't some hardened little street urchin. Like a lamb to the slaughter, he realised the boy had no chance of survival left alone in New York's bitterly cold wilderness.

'Come on, I'm going to take you somewhere you will be safe. It has a funny old address, View of the Stars. Not sure who came up with the name, but it's a good place to be. It isn't much of a walk. Link my arms. What's your name lad?'

'My name is Micah, and thank you for helping me sir.' The boy was well spoken and polite. BK was glad he had stumbled upon him.

'Well Micah, my name is Kirk but please call me BK. Until I know you're out of harm's way, I'm gonna be your best friend, so stick with me.'

For all he knew, BK could have been a mass murderer leading him towards a violent death, but Micah had little choice but to trust this tall stranger and hope he was as kindly as his voice sounded.

He led the boy into an encampment area which was filled with many tents and lit with a multitude of open fires. The place was bright and loud, alive with the sound of music and chatter. It almost had the atmosphere of a medieval courtyard with jesters, minstrels, tents and smoking coals. Surprisingly, this was not a place of despair and desperation, but of happiness.

Micah grew hungry as he smelled the comforting aroma of the soup kitchen in the centre of the encampment. Bright and cheerful servers with smiling faces joked with the hungry queue of waiting diners. Broth, stew and mugs of coffee were handed to anyone who asked for them, as many times as was asked. Behind was the largest of the tents, where the homeless could at least have a bed for the night. It was basic and the sleeping facilities were little more than a floor strewn with straw and covered with blankets, but the blankets were clean and it was safe and a shelter from the harsh East Coast winds that could chill a man to his very bones. 'Stay here Micah,' said BK. 'I'll bring you something hot to eat and save a space for you to sleep for the night. They're good people here. Don't worry.'

Micah collapsed onto a haystack, which was one up from the cold concrete ground he had been squatting on earlier. As he awaited the much-needed hot soup, he listened to a man playing a guitar and sat mesmerised by the music. The haunting tones were pitch perfect. Micah recognised that the man was a highly-skilled musician with a well-trained and accomplished voice; Micah was a musician himself. The player had attracted a large crowd around him, who all seemed to be as enthralled by his songs as Micah was.

BK returned with a steaming cup of broiling chicken soup and a loaf of bread. 'Who is that man?' said Micah. 'He's good, I mean really good. I've never heard anyone play as well as that before and I play the guitar myself so I should know.'

'That guy? Gee, nobody really knows his name. He owns this place. You know land in New York doesn't come cheap, even crap wasteland like this, but somehow he bought it and got the Mayor's permission to run it and everything. He put the whole thing together about a year ago and made it into a registered charity. He's here every night handing out food, making sure clean blankets are available and serenading everyone with his music. Even tonight, on New Year's Eve when he could be at a smart party, he's here entertaining hungry people with dirty faces. He never turns anyone away and he doesn't judge. He's a saint. However I've heard other stories about him which say quite the opposite.'

Micah was hungry to the point of starving, so he could not gulp the soup down quick enough, yet despite uncontrollable hiccups he was curious to know more. He asked, 'Whoever he is, he's an amazing musician, but tell me more BK. What are these other stories?'

BK sat down beside Micah and warmed his hands on his coffee cup, letting the nearby fire turn his cheeks pink. Then he went into full-on story-telling mode.

'Well, I've heard it told that he was once a very rich man, a multi-millionaire. People say he did a lot of bad things. Some say he killed his wife, some say he sold his soul to the devil. Anyway, something happened and he lost his business. I think he was in the music business, so maybe that's why he is so good with that guitar. Anyway, some shit went down. Not sure what, but I heard he lost most of what he had. With what bucks he had left, he upped sticks, came to New York and spent his savings on all this. The guys on the street reckon he is trying to buy his soul back. Who knows? All I know is that he is a good guy right now and without him a lot of people would be hurting tonight.'

Micah was younger than the normal clientele of the camp and was more in touch with the music scene than his middle-aged and elderly bedfellows. He recognised the riches to rags story immediately. 'Bloody hell BK, I think that could be Reed B. The beard threw me a bit, but the talent gave him away. Yeah - he was massively famous and mega wealthy. I read all about him in the papers. His wife disappeared and he was the number one suspect, but nobody could pin anything on him. He was implicated with all sorts of dodgy stuff, Soviet spies and drug cartels and so on. I heard his record label collapsed because lots of musicians pulled their contracts and then he just kind of disappeared. Wow! If that really is Reed B that would be amazing. I am gonna go and say hi to him.'

'Well', muttered BK, 'that was a quick recovery. Typical teenager, brief mention of a famous person and he's off.'

Micah approached the musician and quizzed him, but he was having none of it and denied his identity. He had invested considerable time and money making his escape from Miami and he now felt at home with his humble new life. He enjoyed the appreciation of the needy folks who did truly value his help and he was happy to be back in the city where he was born. Reverting back to his former name of Anthony Mort, the former Reed Baratolli was all but dead to him. This was his life now. To get the boy off his case, he handed him his guitar. Micah had mentioned he could play and Reed, ever the talent scout, couldn't resist the opportunity to listen to another musician.

Micah was gifted with an impressive natural ability. Alone in his bedroom back in Hartford, Connecticut, he had taught himself to play guitar to drown out the sounds of his mother and stepfather fighting. For him, music was not just a release but a salvation.

Once upon a time, the Reed of old would have listened to him and seen only dollar signs float in front of his eyes. For him, notes had a differing meaning. The new Reed listened to Micah and saw only the chords playing in his head and heard only the beautiful harmonies created by the musician's fingers. The irony was not lost on him. All these years of being around music, yet he had never really listened to it, hearing only the cha-ching of money rather than the actual song. He considered all those lost years spent listening to the wrong things. Reed applauded Micah when he had finished his set. 'You keep the guitar, it's yours,' he said. 'If you intend to make a life on the streets then you need to find a way of making some money, and busking is not a bad start. I was a busker myself, but hey, that was many years ago, before...' Reed stopped himself before he could add the words, 'before I became famous.'

Reed left the boy with his newly-inherited audience and went to find an isolated fire to warm himself by. He hadn't been reminded of his past in a long time, and it felt strange and sad to have his memory jogged. He didn't miss the past in the slightest, although he often wondered about Eenayah. He did still miss his wife. Still, what had gone had gone. He had lost the comfort, the glamour and the many false friends who had quickly abandoned him when his life hit a downward spiral, including his new fiancée Amanda, but what he had gained felt so much better - it was real. He looked around the encampment he had created and felt intense pride. This was his life now.

As he pondered, a small, gentle hand touched his shoulder. He turned to find the familiar face of Roserie, his former housekeeper, cook, cleaner, child-minder and general saver of souls. The dark-haired Spanish woman who had kept the home fires burning for a decade of loyal service. Seeing such a friendly face after a year in the camp with complete strangers warmed him more than any camp fire could. As he stood to hug her, she patted his back as a mother would a baby and whispered, 'Happy birthday Reed. I have a present for you here. Eenayah meant to give this to you for your 50th birthday last year, but as we both know, she wasn't around to deliver it in person and you had done a disappearing act. Still, better late than never.'

Reed looked down at the perfectly-wrapped box, decorated with ornate silver ribbons. It felt strange to consider that the last person to open the box had been Eenayah. He gently undid the lid to find a book covered in pure gold leaf. In the centre of the front cover was an illustration of a heart with a genuine ruby embedded in its centre. This blood-red stone had always been Eenayah's favourite gem, mainly because it reminded her of her beloved twin. The book was entitled, 'Anthony Reed Baratolli Mort - past and present' and beneath the title it read 'Happy 50th birthday to a remarkable man, from your loving wife Eenayah'.

Reed flicked through the pages with glistening eyes. Few things had made him cry since his fall from grace, but this loving gesture from his missing wife stirred long-buried emotions. He could see that Eenayah had gone to an enormous amount of trouble with the creation of this exquisite gift. It included photographs of his childhood, the places where his parents were born and illustrations of his ancestry. She had even researched the lives of his forebears and included these stories within the gilt-framed hardback. Some of the photographs had been taken by Eenayah herself during her UK pilgrimage. Reed guessed that maybe these were the last photographs she had ever taken.

It was a strange thought. He deliberated on the fact that one never really knows about the 'last times'. The last time you ever put your shoes on, get out of bed, make love, brush your teeth. It was New Year's Eve, and the moment and the beer were getting to him.

The book finished him off emotionally. As gifts go, it was a one off; unique in every way and delivered from beyond the grave. It was an amazing gift, and it immediately sent a cold shiver of pure guilt down his spine. He wasn't sure if that was Roserie's intention, but if it was, it had worked.

Reed felt a mixture of sentiments. Sorrow, delight, nostalgia - they were all there - but shame was the overwhelming feeling he had when he considered the care and attention with which this present had been created.

'Thank you for bringing this to me, Roserie,' he said. 'I had thought that with all this good work at the camp I might have purchased myself some salvation, but to think back on what I was doing behind Eenayah's back whilst she was putting this wonderful book together for me, well… it makes me feel like the scum of the earth. I don't know if I will ever deserve forgiveness.'

Roserie tried to reassure him. 'I didn't bring you this gift for you to feel bad about the past, Reed. I brought it to you because it belongs to you. This book means nothing to anybody else aside from its owner, which of course is you. Only you can be responsible for your past, command your present and of course shape a future which is yet to be written. This book is important - it was for this that she went to the UK in the first place and as we both know, it was a journey from which she never returned. So, keep this book safe, Reed. Treasure it. Eenayah paid a high price to have this written, more than just money.

Those words resounded in Reed's ears. He had long suspected that Eenayah was dead. It had been 17 months since she went missing from a hospital bed and as time went on, any hope of finding her alive had disappeared. However Roserie seemed to know more than most, after all she wasn't just a maid. It was a question he had to ask.

'Whatever happened to Eenayah? I understand she was pregnant.'

'Eenayah wasn't kidnapped, she was rescued by the Ledanite. You know better than most that the dark forces would have killed her and her unborn children if they had found her first. So she had to be taken and then hidden. I'm sorry Reed, but Eenayah's soul departed on the 21st December last year. Her body was kept alive with the spirit of Tamar until the boys were born, but the body had endured more damage than I believe anybody realised at the time. Her twin boys were born in March this year. They have been placed with a good family, their identities have been hidden and hopefully they will live a normal life. Tamar could never realistically dwell in Eenayah's body for long. Too much damage had been endured and besides, there was no place in our world for someone belonging to another time. About a week after the boys were born, a blood clot became lodged in the lungs and she died. It was very sad, but it was the right outcome.'

Reed didn't say so in as many words, but he suspected that Roserie might assume the role of nanny for the boys at some future stage, as well as that of spiritual guide and protector. He recalled how good she had been with his nephew Harry back in Miami. It would be a perfect role for her.

He hung his head low as his thoughts returned to Eenayah. Although he had married his second wife by way of a contractual obligation, he did have feelings for her and he was deeply saddened to hear about her death. Reed needed to know more. There were so many unanswered questions.

He handed Roserie a mug of eggnog and wished her a happy New Year. Aside from beer, eggnog was about as strong a drink as he allowed inside the camp.

Despite the drink and the general merriment of the evening, his face was strained and serious.

'Do you mind if I ask you more questions please, Roserie?'

'Of course, that's partly why I'm here. Old year ends and new one begins. For your own sake you need closure. You cannot step forward into the future whilst you still have one foot in the past. You have so much still to accomplish in life, but it cannot happen until you forgive yourself and allow yourself to move on. So darling Reed, please ask as many questions as you like, but know just this. I don't mean this to sound like I am some sort of Cinderella and my carriage will turn into a pumpkin at the stroke of twelve, but in truth I cannot stay beyond midnight. We have contracts in our world as you have in yours. My contract was to assist both you and Eenayah find your true destiny, and I had just ten years to do that. Eenayah completed her destiny and you are almost there, but not quite. However, the ten-year target runs out on the last second of 2014 and as you can see, that is a mere 13 minutes away. So ask away Reed, but ask quickly.'

Reed had set up a large widescreen TV at the centre of the camp. Many of his vagrant guests were gathered around the TV watching live footage from Times Square and the final count-down to 2015. The others were still circled around Micah, who, rejuvenated by chicken soup, was now singing and playing away to his heart's content and had attracted a large appreciative fan base. As Reed noted the time on the plasma screen, he realised he didn't have much time left with Roserie.

'Maybe I have no right to ask this of you given my own morals at the time, but who is the father to Eenayah's sons? I mean - I doubt it could have been me. We had a lovely romantic time together in the Isle of Man, but I cannot father children.'

Roserie looked at him scornfully. 'Considering your many affairs Reed, yes, you probably don't have any right to ask. However since one of the reasons for me coming here is about closure, I will answer your question with honesty. Eenayah's fertility was coming to an end and with it, so was her contribution to the line of Tamar. Tamar twins typically are not the most fertile of people. Eenayah was not the only twin in the world to carry the direct line of descent, but the clones have been decreasing in number for a long time now, so each of those that remain are vitally important to the Tamar prophecy. Your favourite phrase was always, *Faciam quodlibet quod necesse est* – do whatever it takes.'

Roserie paused for a few moments. She was reluctant to share the next piece of information with Reed, but given that he was entitled to honest answers, she was obliged to tell him the truth.

'You see Reed, the Ledanite followers were also prepared to do whatever it took. She conceived while she was in an induced sleep. As per Tamar's fate in the book of Genesis, this was by an act of deceit, except in this case it wasn't the female doing the deceiving. As with the bible story, it was with the seed of her father-in-law. I know that to you that this must sound deplorable, but to follow the prophecy to the letter, the father of the two brothers she loved had to sire her children. This wasn't something the Ledanite were proud of nor would boast about, but given her age it was a necessity. Time was running out. Also she had shown signs of having lived a similar life path to Tamar. There was a good chance that she would be the one clone among hundreds that had been born in well over three thousand years who could possibly be a host to Tamar's reincarnation. Should this be the case, then rather than the usual twin girls, she would be the one to have the twin boys who would mark the generation of a new legacy. Because of this, they weren't going to take any chances. They did what needed to be done. Their judgement was correct. She did turn as was predicted. Tamar was reincarnated and the twin boys, this time unified as one, will become great rulers of kingdoms and the heads of other sacred lines. It continues.'

It wasn't the answer Reed had expected. He had been sure

Eenayah's friend from her student days, Jonathan, was the father and he found some strange comfort in believing that Eenayah had been as unfaithful to him as he had been to her. The knowledge that this was not the case and in essence, Eenayah was pure and had been technically raped, punctured an even greater hole of guilt in his heart. He sighed a deep sigh of remorse.

'Phew! Bloody hell Roserie. I didn't expect you to tell me this. Now I feel even worse. I mean, what kind of people are these Ledanite? They sound crazy to me. Folks go on about how the dark evil forces are naughty because they break the rules, and now you tell me that the so-called 'good guys' break the rules every bit as much, as long as it can be justified. They drugged and raped my wife, and I don't care what nice terminology you wrap it up in. It happened without her permission. Then she ended up dying and for all know, she was killed. The police told me that she just fell off the edge of a mountain whilst out running and now I don't know if that was an accident or all part of some plan. I am appalled, quite frankly. I don't know where the curtain lies between good or bad any more. I am really confused.'

Roserie looked on sympathetically. It was an understandable reaction. She wasn't one to judge, but she did feel that given the fact that Reed had been about to hit his wife with a divorce and defraud her from the true settlement amount that would have been due to her that Reed had no place standing on the moral high ground.

'Sounds like the cat calling the kettle black. I am only here to answer your questions and uncomfortable as the answers may be, I can only tell you the facts. I am not a Ledanite, so I neither condone nor commend them. Personally I am neither good nor bad. I know you like to think of me as an angel and if it helps for you humans to see me as such then I am happy to don a halo and big wings. However, in truth I am more of a spiritual guide who whispers to you in thoughts that you believe to be your own. I was contracted to help both you and Eenayah find your true paths of destiny. I was alive once Reed, a very long time ago, and I made more than my share of mistakes. My deliverance is to now help others for as long as it takes for me to find salvation, and as eternity is my time keeper, that could be a long time away. As for the Ledanite, they do what they do for reasons they feel able to justify. There are cultures, politicians and religions that justify bad deeds all the time. Maybe even wars were created because someone somewhere believed killing people was justified if it was for a good reason. Be they right or wrong, ultimately they have to answer to a greater power, as indeed do you, Mr. Mort. Sleep with your conscience Reed, and then wake up and throw your stones from your glass house if you are able.'

Reed felt as though he had just had just been on the receiving end of a ticking off from a schoolteacher. He diverted his attention to the book Eenayah had prepared for him. He opened the front cover and read the credits. The genealogy has been researched by Professor Roland De Vede. He knew that name. On her journeys and subsequent phone calls to Reed, Eenayah had mentioned the Professor several times, alongside that of his daughter Mercy. He recalled that Mercy had died from some sort of morphine incident. It was well reported in the tabloids and Reed himself had been interviewed by the police in relation to her demise, as well being questioned about Mercy's connection to Katya. For reasons that mystified him, he had become tied up in the deaths of two women he had hardly known, but his pleas of innocence and ignorance were mostly shunned.

'What happened to Professor De Vede after his daughter's death?' he asked. 'It must have nearly killed the old chap. Eenayah told me how much he adored her.'

Roserie of course knew the true story and was obliged to reveal what she could in the short time she had left with Reed. Her mission was the deliverance of truth in all its ugliness.

'Mercy De Vede didn't die. She was the victim of a deliberate morphine overdose, which reacted with some other medication she had taken. However they were able to give her an antidote just in time. It was deemed safer for her to pretend she was dead and get out of the country. Don't forget that Mercy was very well connected in the police force. Maybe it was like a witness protection programme. She and the Professor shut up shop, changed identities and flew off into the sunset. She is living a new life now. Mercy, her father and her nephew Simon are very happy, I believe.'

Reed was only just beginning to understand the complexity of everything that had happened in the run-up to his wife's disappearance. The police had interrogated him and there was little he could tell them because in truth, he knew nothing. Only now was he beginning to comprehend that both sides of this particular battle, were equally to blame for a succession of cover ups and in some cases this had involved sinister acts. He did not know which side had done what.

'I am happy to hear that,' he said. 'I know Eenayah really respected her and Mercy only did what she did to try and protect Eenayah.'

Roserie's eyes suddenly focused on the young man called Micah. His guitar playing and singing had attracted quite an audience, both from the homeless community and passers-by who were curious about the impromptu concert. A stunning young woman with short black hair, held out a red gloved hand towards Micah by way of a handshake. Roserie could hear the conversation psychically, and she was concerned.

'Are you not worried Reed? The woman is a demon and is promising him all the things that were once promised to you. Can you not stop this?'

Reed shrugged his shoulders and tried to be philosophical. 'Roserie, you are so sweet but out here on the cold streets with a hungry belly, this is the reality of a hard life. There are demons on this camp all the time. Having been around Emmanuelle and Arabella for so long, I can recognise them instantly. It is amazing how easily they give themselves away. I have come to the conclusion that it doesn't matter if you're rich and want to become richer, or poor and just want to be less poor, as long as you have ambition and a goal then you can be corrupted. It seems that as long as you will do whatever it takes, you are Satan's prey. The dice has been thrown. These stupid low-ranking demons come here because they believe that these poor and desperate people are easy pickings. What they don't understand is that most of them have no hope, no ambition and no goal, and so are beyond corruption.'

Roserie remained concerned. 'I know you don't need to and it's none of your business, but the young boy over there is the one person on this camp who does have hope and ambition. You will try to rescue him, won't you Reed? The demon won't leave him alone.'

Reed sighed. 'Only because you asked me, Roserie. I wouldn't do this for anyone else.'

'Thank you Reed.' Roserie looked up to the clear black sky and took a long breath of the icy New York air. She looked at Reed with deep affection. They had been on opposite sides, but a good Samaritan always likes a sinner to rescue.

'Reed, It's almost midnight and I believe it is tradition for you to play and sing Auld Lang Syne to your audience soon. It's a lovely song, and I told Robbie Burns as much when he first sang it to me, but I don't want to get in the way of your festivities. I came here for three reasons. Of course I'm here to give you birthday greetings and to deliver a present to you, one I hope you will read and treasure. I also came to assure you that you are doing a wonderful job with the charity you have created, and you're well on the path to forgiveness. Last but not least, I also came to offer you closure. Have you any final questions before I leave? If it helps you to move on, ask me what you need to ask me and I am duty bound to answer you truthfully.'

Reed thought deep and hard. He knew he might never see Roserie again; another of those other 'last times' moments.

'What about Ruby? I became quite close to her in the end and I've often wondered if she ever recovered from the loss of her twin.'

'Ruby is fine. Eenayah came to her just as she passed over and Ruby knows she has gone. They had an opportunity to say goodbye. She stopped searching for her sister after that visitation. With the money Eenayah gave to her, she no longer has to work and can focus on being a mother to her son Harry and simply being the home-maker she always wanted to be. Ruby has found happiness and a new career direction, but one that keeps her in the home she loves. The manor house is a successful hotel.'

'Roserie, do you know where Eenayah is buried? If I ever go back to the UK, I would like to place some flowers on her grave.'

'Your flowers could never reach her. She is in a hallowed place, very deep inside the mountains where nobody will ever find her. The body is just a discarded shell, but it served its purpose well. The spirit of Eenayah is free and at peace. I have spoken with her and she has told me to pass along the message that she does not blame you for anything. When she met you her heart was torn apart by the loss of two brothers whom she loved, one after the other. Her mind was in a dark, lonely place and you rescued her. Even though your union may have been designed for another purpose, it is because of you she had a wonderful and privileged life and she says you must not have any regrets. She does not need your flowers. She is already in a garden and surrounded by more scented petals than you could ever imagine.'

Despite Roserie's comforting words, Reed did have many regrets, and his treatment of Eenayah was one that weighed heavily on his conscience.

'Why James and Greg Bucklow? Why their father? Why their family? I met Paul once - good footballer once upon a time, but nothing that special in my opinion and a bit of a creep.'

'Maybe not special to you Reed, but they did share a historical lineage. Tamar had a descendant named Tamar Tephi, known in Irish legend as 'the daughter of a Pharaoh.' She married Eochaidh, King of Ireland, who was known as the Prince of the Scarlet Thread. They united Tamar's divided children. The Bucklow family are direct descendants of Tamar Tephi and Eochaidh. Quite simply Paul Bucklow is from the descendants of Shem and that in itself made his involvement with Eenayah – as well as that of his sons – a destiny that could not be avoided. He completed the missing genetic jigsaw puzzle. I understand that all I have told you may make no sense, so just understand that Paul Bucklow's lineage was connected to that of Eenayah's, and that is why the Bucklow family were chosen. There are few coincidences in a world designed by an almighty power. Reed, our time together is coming to a close. If you need to ask me anything else, you need to make it quick.'

Reed looked over to the clock on the TV, which was counting down to the New Year. He needed to make this last question count.

'Roserie, earlier on you told me that your job was to help both Eenayah and me find our destinies. From all you have told me so far, it seems that everything that has happened to Eenayah throughout her entire life, was leading to that point in time when she was to become pregnant with twin boys by a man who was a descendant of Shem, and therefore, whether I like the guy or not, it was his destiny also. I now understand that the prophecy of the line of Tamar was Eenayah's birth right and always has been. I can see that now, but what about me? Was I meant to be running a camp for homeless people and dishing out soup no matter what the weather? Don't I get a guardian angel looking over my shoulder? Sometimes I could sure do with one.'

These were the exact questions Roserie was hoping Reed would ask. She couldn't put words into his mouth and neither could she steer him in the direction she wanted him to go, but she was pleased he had asked about his own fate.

'You are destined to become what is in your heart, Reed. If you live it and breathe it and the passion for it fills your every pore, then whatever or whoever it is that you love, it is meant to be. Maybe it was not meant to be yours - disappointment and rejection are part of life and these things make us stronger - but it was certainly meant to be that you make the best possible effort to try and get what your heart desires. So with regard to this camp and you dishing out soup, if you leave your warm bed every morning to rush to get here and are then loath to go home, the answer is simple - you belong here. Your passion is your destiny. However if you are just doing this because some low-life demon threatened to take everything away from you and then told you there is a corner of hell with your name on it, know that you cannot buy your way into heaven. You can deceive others, but you can never deceive yourself. Forgiveness comes when in your heart of hearts you feel genuine remorse. You didn't have to go to this extreme to buy back your soul.'

'But I love it here Roserie, and I do genuinely enjoy helping these poor cold souls.'

Roserie looked around the encampment to drink up the atmosphere. Reed had done a wonderful job; there was no disputing that. This wasn't a miserable place for desperados to come to, a last chance saloon. Reed had made it into a safe refuge, full of joy, music, noise, companionship and fun. He wasn't just feeding the stomachs of some lost and homeless drifters, he was feeding their hearts and souls as well. Somehow he had understood that hope is the one thing most destitute people lose first, but put a song in their hearts and the healing process begins. Hope was the defining boundary between surviving and living. He had intuitively realised this and tapped into the healing power of music and laughter.

Despite his fine achievement with the camp, Roserie also knew that there would only ever be one true passion running through Reed's veins.

'During the whole time we have been talking Reed, not once did I see you cast your eyes towards any of these cold hungry people to check on how they were,' she said. 'I'm not saying you don't care about your guests, as clearly you do, but there is one person here you care about more than anyone else. The young man Micah. You can't take your eyes off him. You're transfixed with the way his fingers move up and down the frets of his guitar and how his hands strum a beat on the soundboard to the rhythm of his voice. You can't take music out of your soul Reed, it's your passion and therefore your destiny. It's a shame you sold yourself short to the demon Emmanuelle, because in truth you would have succeeded without going over to the dark side. Disregard all the lies she told you about being spent out at 40; you were too gifted for this to be your fate. It would be so sad if you now avoided music because you feared walking the same path and stumbling into the same potholes. However, this time I can promise you that you are wiser and you have learned your lessons. Help Micah if you can. He is your destiny, along with this wonderful camp of yours. If you don't get him, that minor low life demon flirting with him over there will. To Micah, she is a very beautiful woman, but he hasn't seen her first thing in the morning without her make-up on. Demons don't have a great morning look - you know that. Only you can save that boy.'

Reed had sung a duet with the devil. It had been a close call, and he resolved never to venture into the music industry again. He had run away, changed his name and tried to live another life, but deep down he missed the world of music with a burning ache. He knew Roserie was speaking the truth. The clock was ticking.

'Reed, you also asked me – be it in a roundabout way, if you have a guardian angel, and indeed you do,' said Roserie. 'He is a man who actually perished in a wildfire in his home town of Julian in July 2013. Not that those around him know he's dead, as his body was never found. He is like me now. He looks, acts, sleeps, eats and drinks as a living person does. However, like me he has contracts to fulfil. You are now his. He will help you with Micah. As soon as I am gone, he will be with you. Make him welcome, my old friend, and well done on all your great work. By the way, prepare the camp for the end of January, the snow will be heavier than usual.'

Reed turned to reply to her, but just as in the fairy story, midnight had struck and Roserie had vanished.

As requested, he went to retrieve Micah from the clutches of the woman with the red gloves.

'Do you know how to play Auld Lang Syne, Micah?' he asked. The boy, still star-struck by the presence of Reed B, simply nodded. 'Then come on, join me on stage. Let's sing it together and maybe we can both put our pasts behind us and start afresh.'

Over the New York skyline, fireworks illuminated the skyscraper horizon and every person on Reed's camp sang loudly and was happy. Most of them owned little else but the shirts on their backs, but because of Reed they had music, and that music lifted their spirits. As Reed and Micah played and sang in unison, the lyrics seemed to hit a deeper meaning. The two men caught each other's gazes as they both sang from a deeper place of unspoken pain and with their own personal interpretation, '*should auld acquaintance be forgot, and never brought to mind*'.

The angel Magnus looked on and smiled. He had much work to do.

***

An elderly gentlemen among the audience was absorbing the lively atmosphere and noting the beaming smiles on a hundred grimy faces.

He had heard about the work Mr Mort had accomplished with the vagrants of New York, and word was beginning to spread outside America. The man had been considering starting something similar in his own country, so during a holiday in New York to visit family, he had seized the opportunity to go to the site. He was indeed inspired and motivated by what he was seeing.

As he went to leave, a lovely woman with a warm, caring face followed him out. She didn't look like a beggar and if anything she smelled of rose petals. It was a soft, delicate aroma. Her face was familiar, although he had never met her.

She moved closer to him and whispered in his ear, 'What do I call you these days? Is it Father Francis or Mr Frank O'Byrne? Teacher or priest? To many they are one and the same.'

Frank was stunned. How did she known him? Few people aside from very close friends and family members had been aware that he was once a Catholic priest.

'How on earth do you know me?' he asked. 'Oh, and I'm Frank by the way.'

Roserie took his hand and walked out with him. 'Dearest Frank, do you recall all the many sleepless nights you had when you were deciding whether to leave the priesthood or not? Do you recall all the many prayers you uttered, asking for guidance on which direction to take? Well, maybe sometimes you heard my voice whisper to you or maybe you saw my face in a dream. Does any of this sound familiar?'

He knew not how, but it did. Frank stepped back to take a long look at Roserie's face. She did have the appearance of someone he recognised from many years ago, and her soft Spanish tones did sound like a voice he had heard before. Studying her unusual features, he began to believe that maybe he had seen her in a dream, implausible as that seemed, even to a former priest.

She continued, 'if I was to say what I am about to say to anyone else other than a man of faith, they would not believe me and might even think I was some madwoman. However, as you are a man of faith, I can be open with you. My name is Roserie and I am the spirit guide who has been helping to steer Eenayah and Reed towards their destinies. You may not have understood it at the time, but your friend the Professor, his daughter Mercy and of course you Frank, all had a role to play. You may not have realised I was there, but in the background I was directing you all. I even made Eenayah's eyes notice and then photograph the well-hidden hieroglyphics on Daisy Green's tombstone. I was the one who brought you and the Professor together at the convention so you could swap contact details. I knew he would need you one day. So thank you for supporting me. You were all part of my team.'

It wasn't often in life that Frank O'Byrne was stopped in his tracks, but this was one of those occasions. There wasn't a cell in his body that didn't believe Roserie was telling anything other than the truth. It was impossible for her to know what she knew without indeed being the spirit guide she claimed to be. He was paralysed; stuck to the spot and unable to move.

His gaze was transfixed by her face. She didn't look like an apparition; she wasn't glowing or transparent. She just looked like an ordinary woman, and yet Frank knew he was in the presence of a seraph. He instinctively fell to his knees in awe.

Roserie was shocked and looked around to see if anyone else had clocked his spontaneous gesture of veneration. 'Frank, get up. I am supposed to walk amongst you in secret and you are blowing my cover.'

Frank stumbled to his feet, still in wonder at the presence standing before him. 'I am humble before you Roserie, but why have you come to see me?'

'Frank, have you any idea who created this camp site?'

'I have read about him in the church papers. I only know him to be a Mr Mort.'

Roserie held Frank's hand as she continued to explain, partly to prevent him dropping to his knees again.

'Indeed, that is correct. He has reverted to his birth name of Mort. However you may have once known him as Reed Baratolli, the husband of Eenayah.'

Frank was justifiably shocked. 'No way. I wondered what had become of him. After all the furore and bad publicity, he just seemed to disappear. I'm shocked and yet full of admiration for what he has achieved. Reed B – who would have thought?'

'Indeed, I am proud of him as well. At the time you were not aware of this Frank, but he did bat for the other side. Reed was in league with the dark forces and was part of a conspiracy to end the lines of Tamar. For me to rescue him from the mouths of demons and for him to go from that level of depravity to all of this…'

Roserie raised her arms and turned through 360 degrees to gesture that she was referring to the entire camp site. 'To create all of this is amazing. Reed is my greatest achievement to date. We almost lost him, but the sheep has returned to its shepherd. But hey ho Frankie, that is all history now. Reed is the old project and now I need to move onto my new project.'

'Which is what, if you don't mind me asking?'

'You, Frank. You are my next project. You still have much to achieve. You may not believe me, but you haven't realised your true destiny as yet, so you may expect to see a lot of me from now on.'

Frank shook his head in disbelief and joy. Deliverance was the word that flew into his head. Frank hadn't admitted it to anyone, but he had recently given up on himself. He had caught his reflection in the mirror and saw himself as old and useless. Therefore Roserie's words were music to an elderly man's ears. He had a purpose, and he had realised that a useful purpose is what everyone needs out of life,

'Whatever became of Eenayah and her pregnancy?' he asked. 'As far as I am aware she was never found. What will become of Reed? Does he know about Eenayah? '

Roserie took a liking to her new project. He was a colourful and interesting human. 'All in good time Frank. Your brother and sister-in-law are worried about you as you promised to be back before midnight, so, my lovely friend, you really do need to make tracks and give them a call before they dial 911 and send a search party out for you. The story of Eenayah is long and complicated and when we next meet I will explain all, but just know that what happened to her was meant to be. Two opposing forces pre-ordained her destiny. However, I can share with you some glimpses into the future if you like.'

Frank glanced at his watch, realising he was running late. However, he was too inquisitive to reject Roserie's offer.

'Yes, Eenayah did have twin boys and their legacy will continue to be played out silently and in secret over the next hundred years or so. Her sons belong to an unusual genealogical line from a lost species of humans who once had the ability to reproduce themselves by cloning, plus we are told they held other powers. Some even say they were originally not of this earth. There are few of them left now, but what is left and what will come to pass will remain protected, hidden and shrouded in mystique. It remains a sacred line, protected by some who are often referred to as the Ledanite. The continuity of their heritage ultimately required the sacrifice of a brave young woman, but be assured that Eenayah's death was not in vain. Within your lifetime Frank, nothing more will be heard of Eenayah's twin boys. They have been safely concealed from those forces that tried for many centuries to prevent their birth. History may indeed be in the process of replaying itself, and those wheels may have been put into motion many years previously, but mankind will not know about any of this for a very long time to come. The seeds have been sown, but the fruits are yet to be harvested and the threat to prevent their line from going forward continues.'

Frank was slightly bamboozled by Roserie's puzzling prediction, but decided to try to untangle the strings of divine knots at a later date. He pointed over to Reed and Micah, who were still on stage and engaged in an intense jamming session.

'What about Reed Baratolli, or Mr Mort as I understand he is now called?' Although Frank knew of Reed, he had never actually met him in person. Roserie glanced over with pride as she watched her former disciple do what he did best; inspire, mentor, but most of all just make music.

'Reed will gain fame yet again. It was always his fate to become famous and so no matter how far he tries to run from it, it will always catch up with him in the end. However the second time around it won't be for his music and nor will it be in the name of Reed B, but through his real birth name of Anthony Reed Baratolli Mort. He will be recognised for his compassion and humanity to the homeless people of New York. One day, many years from now; there will be a statue in Central Park in his honour. I could even point to the spot where it will stand, but we don't have time right now. Another day maybe.'

'What of the young man on the stage with him? I noticed the bruising on his face. He is such a talented young musician. It seems such a shame that one so young has ended up in such a place as this.'

Roserie took mock offence. 'Hey Frank, ease off with the criticism. BK accidentally tripping up on the boy and bringing him here was all my doing you know. The tragic reality is that Micah would have frozen to death by 5.21am precisely, today, 1st January 2015. That would have been his fate if he hadn't been brought here. But, since you ask, Micah will do just fine. Reed, along with his designated spirit guide of Magnus, will support him, but very much in the background. He will keep the demons and the temptations of rock & roll well away from his door, and the boy will have a happy and successful life. As for the tramp that found the boy, BK, you wouldn't think he had a Master's degree in Business Administration from Harvard, would you? No worry – he will get the chance to use it again once Reed puts him in charge of the View of the Stars charity franchise.'

Frank was fascinated. He sorely didn't want to leave and could have chatted with Roserie for hours, but alas he knew that wasn't a practical option.

He had to ask. 'A long time ago an older priest once told me that there was a seraph called the Angel of Destiny. At the time I argued against this and debated the principle of free will, but now I am beginning to think this may be you, Roserie. Is it true? Is this who you are?'

Roserie smiled. 'Have you heard of Alfred Nobel, the founder of the Nobel prize?'

'Of course.'

'Before you go, here is a short story for you. Back in 1888 he picked up a French newspaper and read the headline 'The merchant of death is dead'. Horror of horrors, he was reading his own obituary. It was a heck of a shock, although personally I thought I had played a really neat trick on him. The thing is, Frank, it was actually his brother who had died. Alfred wasn't due to die for another eight years; 1896, if my memory serves me right. The point being that the article perturbed him and he became concerned about how he would be remembered. Following that experience, he changed his will and then went on to create the Nobel Prize so that people who had achieved great things would continue to be recognised long after they are dead and buried. Just think Frank, if that journalist hadn't have made that mistake and Alfred hadn't purchased the paper that day and then read that headline, no Nobel Prize. Don't you just love coincidence? I was so proud of that coincidence. It took a lot of planning.'

'Wow Roserie, that was you? You did that?'

'Just saying! Don't mean to brag. Anyway Frank, my work is done here now and I must leave and you must catch the next subway back to your family and make a very apologetic phone call. Time waits for no man. Or angel.'

Roserie turned, walked away and simply faded. The first stages of the prophecy had been completed and her work was done. For now.

★★★

Just beyond the encampment and bordering on its parameters was a hill. It was a large mound made of metal; steel, tin, aluminium, with fragments of leather, cloth and fibre glass. Crushed cars were mounted one upon the other, piled high. Sitting on top of this metallic elevation were three exasperated demons, See No Good, Hear No Good and Speak No Good. Like three fiendish monkeys, they sat cross-legged observing the camp as the New Year merriment continued well into 2015.

Arabella shivered in the icy air and whinged at her mistress. 'I cannot believe you have brought me here to sit on top of this dumb ass scrapheap.'

Emmanuelle was displeased and flashed the inferior demon with her icy stare. 'Fail again Arabella, and we are all on the scrap heap. However there is hope for us, look at your bracelets.'

Tobiah raised his hand to note that the purple band he had worn for millennia had been replaced by a fresh green broken cord, defying gravity and hovering slightly above his wrist. Arabella did the same and noted hers was pure white.

'What does this mean Emmanuelle?'

'New Year, new generation, new challenge. We have been given a second chance. The new project is to be the extermination of whichever lines replaced those of Tamar, the line of the male twins.'

Emmanuelle perused the encampment. She pointed over to one of the serving girls handing out non-alcoholic mulled wine to her thirsty dirty-faced clientele. 'Tobiah, my command to you is to get close to that girl. Her name is Darcy. She is ex-Ledanite and she has tired of their ways. She is corruptible. Those fallen from their faith, no matter what that faith that may be, can fall into our arms as babes into the mouths of wolves. Catch her as she falls, Tobiah. Only humans distinguish between faiths. For demons such as us we care not of denomination; they are all fodder to be devoured and she awaits your plate.'

'What of my quest?' asked Arabella feeling slightly left out in the cold as well as being unheeded by her mistress.

Emmanuelle responded with her usual commanding tone. 'For you Arabella, I give the young singer Micah. Lesser demons have tried to entrap him tonight, but they do not have our powers. We can exterminate these minor beasts with just a blinking of an eye. Ignore these ravenous underdogs and their attempted feeding frenzy. I deplore them. Reed and his angel Magnus will try to protect Micah, but I sense his desire for fame and fortune will be too great and his greed will become the currency he will trade with. It is a two-sided coin, which suits our purpose well. All is not lost, my young fiends, just simply reinvented. Now be off with you and set about your work. We cannot fail again. There are new generations to ensnare. The new lines of Angelo and Alessandro need to be cut out and discarded from the future.'

***

Thursday 1st January 2015

Emmanuelle stood up and sneered at Reed with such animal menace that it was like a growl from the very hounds of hell. Even in the bitterly cold New York night, Reed felt his heart freeze over and crack like ice on a pond. He had sensed her in the distance and looked over in the direction of the salvage yard. He smiled at her. It wasn't a smile of victory, but one of understanding. Reed had learned the painful but valuable lesson that recognising one's enemy was in itself salvation. Emmanuelle had paved a road that seemed to shimmer with fool's gold. It was not a road he would ever walk upon again and this most intoxicating of She-Devils knew this to be the case. His soul had been lost and then regained.

It had been an evening of spectacular fireworks, and the pungent smell of gunpowder lingered in the air. At 1.30am everyone considered the New Year's Eve display to have been concluded. However there was yet one last performance that awaited the unsuspecting crowd.

The vagrant audience gasped as a deafening blast pulsed through the air and the most awesome of rockets flew into the night sky. It was cherry red with platinum blond sparks which ignited with a sizzle. Following in its wake was a long crimson trail which looked like sacrificial droplets of blood. Reed knew it wasn't a firework. He blew her a kiss goodbye, more in a gesture of good riddance than to wish her well. Yet he knew this wasn't the end. A mutant and mystical gene code, carried on through millennia of hosts, had repeatedly recreated itself in its purest form. Humankind would not totally understand its purpose until all had been made clear, perhaps thousands of years hence. Until then, we would remain blindly ignorant of its power. All Reed knew for sure was that the battle between good and evil was not destined to end any time soon. Within the laws of infinity, there was no end.

THE END

'If the doors of perception were cleansed everything would appear to man as it is; Infinite. For man has closed himself up, till he sees all things thro' narrow chinks of his cavern.'
William Blake

ND - #0048 - 270225 - C0 - 203/127/31 - PB - 9781861513229 - Matt Lamination